I0320982

Minty

Christina Banach is a former head teacher who lives in Scotland with her husband and their two rescue dogs. She loves walking; delicious food and wine; evenings at the theatre; exploring new places; surfing the Net; listening to music; and anything that makes her laugh. Plus she has a penchant for shoes and handbags. A voracious reader, she particularly enjoys children's fiction (all those years buying for school libraries) - which led her to writing. Christina is hard at work on her next novel.

MINTY

CHRISTINA BANACH

Published by Three Hares Publishing 2014

First published in Great Britain in 2014
www.threeharespublishing.com

Three Hares Publishing Ltd Reg. No 8531198
Registered address: Suite 201, Berkshire House,
39-51 High Street,
Ascot, Berkshire, SL5 7HY

ISBN-13: 978-1-910153-02-4

To my husband and best friend, Edward,
for his unfailing love and support.
And in memory of my wonderful dad, Roy Heywood

Chapter One

Sorry. That's all it takes – just one word and she's off on one.

"Dad," Jess says, stretching out his name. "You're not sorry at all." She furrows her brow. "This *always* happens."

Then she does this toddler thing of shoving out her bottom lip until, geez, she looks so bloomin' daft that I need to stuff a hand over my mouth to squash the snigger that's threatening to burst out.

But my sis must have the hearing of a bat because she wheels round to me and says, "I don't know why you're laughing, Minty, you were looking forward to it as much as me."

There's more than a spark of annoyance in her eyes. Crikey, she *has* got the hump.

Before I get the chance to think of something to calm her down, Dad butts in. "Girls, I really am sorry. I hate having to do this to you but…that phone call…" He glances at the mobile in his hand. "There's a problem with the network this morning and I might have to go in if they can't fix it."

Jess plucks at the fringes on her stripy scarf. "Why can't someone else do it? Why's it always you?"

He pulls on an ear, screws up his nose. "It's not as simple as that. Look, I know you're disappointed but it just can't be helped. I'll make it up to you, though. Promise. I'll take you to Edinburgh next Saturday. Then you can look at all the Roman artefacts you want."

I smile back at him cos, well, it's not as if he planned for the computers to act up or anything, is it?

Jess tugs off her scarf, bundles it into an untidy ball and throws it on the kitchen table. "I bet you don't. I bet there'll be another problem at work and you'll call off...again." She pulls out a chair and plonks herself down, elbows on the table, and rests her chin on her fists. "And anyway, I don't see why you can't just let us go to Edinburgh on our own, like normal parents would."

I sit down beside her. "Don't be a diva, J," I whisper into her ear. "It's no big deal. What's another seven days?"

Mum breezes into the kitchen in a cloud of her latest perfume. "All ready for the off?" she says, her voice slicing through the strained atmosphere in the room. Then she checks out our faces and her smile falters. "All right," she says, "What's up?"

Not giving Jess a chance to tell it her way, I say, "Change of plan. We're going next week instead."

Mum frowns. "Why?"

"It's OK though." I elbow J in the arm. "Isn't it?" I add, under my breath.

Jess doesn't say anything, although the tight set of her mouth seems to relax a bit.

Dad holds up his phone, smiles sheepishly. "Work called. Bit of a crisis, I'm afraid. They reckon they should have it sorted by lunchtime but I need to stay in Fife in case I have to pop in."

Mum tuts. "Oh, Geoff, no. What about our outing?"

"Sorry, Mary, it can't be helped."

I fidget with the garnet on my pinkie ring. Catch the look that passes between my parents, one that I can't quite read. Then Mum claps her hands and her face brightens with a grin that's about as genuine as an Essex girl's boobs. "Oh well, never mind." She glances at Dad and turns to us. "Why don't we make it a girls' day out instead? The museum, a long girlie lunch, maybe a little shopping – we'll have lots of fun."

"I don't want to go anywhere now," Jess says. She bends down and rubs at the scuffed toe on one of her Uggs.

"Jess," I hiss. "Quit acting like a five-year-old. Get a grip."

She straightens up and stares at me. "Count me out."

"Why're you being like this?" I say, pushing the leather bracelets up my left wrist.

"You go if you want to. I'm staying here."

"I want you to come."

"Why? Are we Siamese twins now?" she snaps. "We're not joined at the hip – even if we are twins."

"Stop being an eedjit. We do everything together—"

"Well maybe that's the problem," she says in an undertone. "Maybe I just want a break from the Jess and Minty show. Maybe for once in my fourteen years I want to do something on my own. Or have something that just belongs to me." She glares at me. Her cheeks are flushed. "Me. Jess."

"And what's that meant to mean?" I say, feeling the heat rise in my own face.

I glance across at Mum and Dad, wondering if they're listening, but they're having a murmured 'conversation' of their own.

Jess lets out a sigh, and slicks her silky locks into a makeshift updo. Then, looking out from under her thick brown lashes, she says, "Sorry. Forget I said it. I'm just being a grump." A look of apology flits across her face. She reaches out, her mass of dark hair tumbling over her shoulders, and traces the veins under my skin until my hand tickles. "I can be such a cow, can't I?"

We smile. I'm a bit pissed though. Why would she say those things? What's wrong with the – what's that she called it – yeah, the Jess and Minty show?

Mum comes over, butting into my thoughts so I push Jess's words aside for now. She takes off her Red or Dead distance glasses, pops them into her Radley bag and says, "Dad and I have been talking. Fancy taking the dogs to Elie this afternoon? The four of us?"

Dad joins in. "Don't worry, we'll still be going to that museum of yours. Next weekend. And no calling off this time. That's a promise. Now, what about that walk? We could set off after lunch. How does that sound?"

Jess looks at me and I catch that twinkle of devilment behind her eyes that I know so well. Turning to Dad, she says, all coy-like, "But what about the restaurant, the Italian meal you said we'd have? We were sooo looking forward to that." She grins, winks at me. "Weren't we, Minty?"

Ata girl, J! I'll say this for my sister – she doesn't stay in a mood for long.

"Yeah, we've been thinking of nothing else all week," I say, and wink back.

With a smile flickering over his mouth, Dad pulls his car keys from the pocket of his navy chinos and, jiggling them in one hand, says, "You'll still get that. Meantime why don't we pick up some pizza later for dinner tonight on the way home?"

"Nice one," I say.

Yeah, Dad, good recovery – one slice and Jess won't even remember what she was narked about!

"Count me in," I say. I can already taste the tang of pepperoni and the sweetness of pineapple on my tongue.

Jess scoots out of her seat to pat Dad's paunch. "But maybe you should stick to the salad, Dad."

"Hey," he says, drawing back his shoulders and sucking in his belly, his relief at being let off the hook splashed all over his face. "I'm a fine figure of a man, I'll have you know."

She pinches the flab on his bicep. "So this isn't fat then?"

Mum snorts with laughter.

Dad tucks his mobile into his shirt pocket and chuckles. "Ha, ha! Stop it, Jess, you're cracking me up." Then chortling to himself, he puts the keys back on their hook.

She can be a right cheeky mare, my sis. But Dad loves it really. I do, too. And that's only one of the things I love about her. And why, despite her being the most annoying girl on the entire planet at times, I flippin' couldn't exist without her.

As it happens, Dad has to go into work for a while so it's well after three by the time we get to Elie. We're just pulling into the car park at Ruby Bay when his mobile goes off again.

"Blast," he says and cuts the car engine, then fishes his iPhone out of his shirt pocket to check who's calling. He frowns and looks at Mum, his expression tinged with guilt. "It's work."

"Again? I thought you said the problem was fixed?" Mum says, her immaculately-waxed eyebrows hitched skywards as she unbuckles her seatbelt.

He shoots her a half-baked smile. "I'd better take this."

Mum sighs. "Oh, all right then, but be quick," she snaps, and stares out of the front window, muttering to herself. "It's late enough as it is."

"Uh oh, someone's not happy," Jess whispers to me. "Think Mum's got the hump with Dad."

Yeah, you know all about getting the hump, don't you, J?

I smile to myself. Bite into the banana I brought with me.

It's then that I notice the sea with its little white horses crashing onto the sand down on the beach. So it's no surprise when Jess opens her door and says, 'Whoa, it's windy!' the second she's outside.

I polish off my fruit, dump the skin beside my bag on the seat and clamber out, too. "Wow! You're not wrong about the wind." The wind whips at my face and tugs at my clothes until it finds the bare skin where my t-shirt's ridden up. "So much for it almost being spring!" I remove a strand of hair from my mouth.

While I'm tucking my top into the waistband of my skinny jeans, I notice Jess fish a scrunchy from her jacket pocket and arrange her hair into an untidy ponytail.

Wish I'd thought to bring something to tie *my* mop back.

Mum stretches across to the back seat, opens the car and leans out to give us our jackets. "Better take these." The breeze tugs at her door.

"I won't bother with mine," I say. "I don't feel the cold."

"Doesn't mean to say you won't catch your death," Mum says and bundles them into my hands. "Now put it on. You as well, Jess."

I pass J her scarlet zip up and slip into my red military jacket.

Holding the door steady with one hand, Mum says, "You two go on. I want to have a quick word with your dad once he's finished his call. We'll catch you up."

As the door closes, Jess and I exchange looks.

"No prizes for guessing what 'the word with Dad's' going to be about," Jess says as she lifts the tailgate to release our retrievers. They leap out before it's even halfway open.

The second their paws touch the ground, they're off, going scatty as they run round and round the car, up onto the grass and back again. Giggling at the dog's antics, I pull the hatch down. It shuts with a dull thud.

Once I've fastened the last of the oversized buttons on my jacket I hitch up the wide lapels and go to help Jess round up the dogs.

As I pass by Mum's window she puts it down again and signals for us to come near. She gestures to the dogs then looks at us. "Girls, I want them on their leads," she says, glancing at Dad who's still jabbering away on the mobile.

Dad places a hand over the telephone and leans across to add his words of wisdom. "Stick to the paths. OK? We'll be with you in a minute." He points a thumb at his phone. "Won't be long with this. Two minutes tops," he says then goes back to his call.

Jess says something to him but her wisecrack is whisked away by the breeze.

Just then Remus bounds up to me and nearly knocks me over. "Yeah, yeah, Remus, I love you, too," I say, laughing at my dippy mutt and trying to dodge his great slurping tongue as I clip on his lead. Ruffling his muzzle, we set off on our walk.

"I hope Mum and Dad aren't going to argue," I say, looking at the Renault Espace parked snugly in the car park while we brave the East Neuk winds.

"Nah. You know what Mum's like: anything for a quiet life. She just gets a bit narked now and then."

I grin. "Yeah, like someone else I could mention."

"Watch it," Jess says with a snigger, nudging one of my Converse trainers with the side of her boot.

By now Remus is straining at his lead so much it's a struggle to hold on to him. I can see J is having the same trouble with Romulus.

Poor things, they need a good romp about. They'd be much happier if we freed them. Jess must think so too because once our parents are out of sight she unclips Rommy's leash.

"Look at him go!" I laugh as I watch him dash up over the grass and onto the path leading to Lady's Tower.

Then I let Remus loose so he can catch up with his pal, and within seconds they've both disappeared.

"Hey, come back!" Jess shouts. "Where're you going?"

"Like they're gonna answer!" I say with a snort. "Leave them, they'll be OK."

Jess slows her step and gazes out over the wild water. "Suppose so."

Her cheeks are bubblegum pink, her wide eyes sparkling with pleasure as she breathes in the salty air. But, ah, those lips of hers could do with some gloss to protect them from the wind.

"Here," I say, rummaging around in my jacket pockets and pulling out a tub of Lip Therapy. "Put some of this on."

She stares at it then snatches it from me. "Hey, that's mine!" Holding up the little yellow and white tin she says, "Why've you got it? What's wrong with your own Vaseline?"

"Yours has SPF15 in it, mine hasn't."

"Like you need a sun protection factor in March. Specially on a day like this," she shoots back.

"Well, it was nice this morning," I say in my defence.

"Tsk!" She shoves her hands in her pockets and scowls. "You've got some front."

"Why're you making such a fuss about it? Lighten up. We always borrow each other's things—"

"You see, that's what I've been trying to tell you." She shoves the tin to my face. "This belongs to me. Can't I have just one thing that's mine?"

"I don't know what you're on about. You borrow my Armani perfume. Geez, we always share stuff, J."

She looks at me, holds my gaze for a moment, then slowly shakes her head. She lets out a weak laugh. "I really love you, Minty, but I'm beginning to feel suffocated. Can't we just behave like normal sisters?"

"Sisters share stuff all the time."

"But not like us!" She cradles her head in her hands. "I just want to be my own person, what's wrong with that?" Then she shoves Romulus's lead into her jacket pocket and yells, "We're not little kids anymore. Give me a bit of space!"

She glowers at me. I glare back. In spite of the blustery wind, heat floods my face. "Fine. You can have all the space you want." I break into a run.

Cos, know what? I'm all done with Jess and her moods.

"Drop dead, Minty," she yells after me.

I whip round and bawl at her, the wind billowing up through my jacket. "Drop dead? Yeah, you'd like that wouldn't you? You wouldn't have to worry about being a twin any more. You could pretend I'd never been born."

And with that, I stomp off to get the dogs. At least they don't give me hassle.

"Aw, Minty, I didn't mean to say that. Sorry," she calls after me.

But I've heard her sorries before, so I keep running.

I hear the barking before I even get there. Loud, insistent, frantic, the wind providing an eerie background music to the awful din.

"What's going on?" Jess shouts at my heels as I take the steps leading to the old ruin two at a time.

We look at one another and I can see from the anxious look on her face that she thinks the same as me – the time for squabbling's over. Something's well wrong here.

"Rom? What's all the racket?" I say, almost bowled over as he launches himself at me the instant I walk through the tall doorway.

Framed by the brown stone arch of the window behind him, Romulus's coat is a shivering mass of golden fur. In the background, the sea batters at the rocks.

Rom's bark has become a terrified whine. Panic rushes to my throat. "Where's Remus?" I look around.

But, Jupiter, look at Romulus! He reminds me of a cartoon cat I once saw on telly – maybe it was in Itchy and Scratchy. I don't know, but I remember creasing with laughter because the cat had stuck his paw into an electric socket and every hair on his body stood on end. Yeah, I laughed then but I'm not laughing now.

The blood drains from J's cheeks at the sight of our terrified dog. Romulus looks at her, leaps onto the windowsill and barks through the empty space where the glass once was. His body tenses and it's like every bit of him strains towards the shoreline. But he doesn't move off the stone ledge, just whimpers and yelps.

"Omigod! Look! Remus – he's down there," Jess says, her voice tainted with fright.

I peer through the window and see Remus, perched on the rocks at the edge of the sea.

We call out to him but he gives no sign that he's heard us.

"What'll we do?" Jess asks, biting fiercely at a nail while drumming her feet on the ground. "Omigod, look at him, he's petrified. See how near the water he is? What if he falls in?"

"He won't. We won't let him," I say, trying to squash the fear inside me. I balance myself against the window frame, lean forward and try to coax him back. But Jess's right – he *is* petrified. It's as if he's frozen there, glued to the rocks. "Remus! Here b—" My voice breaks as I struggle to keep it together.

I swirl round to ask Jess to call him but she's fumbling with her phone, hopping from foot to foot.

"Dad. Got to get Dad. He'll sort it," she says, her voice trembling as much as her fingers.

Leaving her to it, I concentrate on attracting Remus's attention.

Then, cutting through Romulus's whining, I hear her curse. "I can't get a signal," she wails. "Try yours. Quick!"

With a sinking feeling, I dig inside all my pockets. No phone. But then I knew there wouldn't be – I'd have noticed it when I was ferreting around for J's lip therapy.

"I must've left it in my bag!"

"Omigod, what now?"

"We need to do something!"

Do something. Do something? Yeah, yeah, of course we should. But what? There's no way I'm going down there to fetch him. Then Remus turns his head, his melting brown eyes meet mine and I know what that something is.

So, even though the thought of going anywhere near that churning water terrifies me, I lower myself onto the window ledge, swivel my bum on the rough stone and drape my legs over the side.

"Minty, what're you doing?" Jess bellows.

"We have to go down there. Come on."

"Are you mad? Look at the water – it's crashing over the rocks. It's too dangerous!"

Omigod, I know, but what can I do? My dog needs help.

"Come back – please!"

A pitiful yowl from below causes Romulus to bark even louder. I glance over my shoulder and poor Rommy's running about like a dog possessed. Then he stops. Barks once. Whines. Looks right at me.

Yeah, I know, boy, I have to do something. We can't let Remus end up in the sea.

I turn back to Remus. He looks so lost and afraid. But that water…

"Minty, leave it. Let's get Dad. He'll know what to do."

She's right. I know she's right.

Then Rom howls. Remus yelps. Lets out this terrified whimper.

That decides it.

"I have to help him," I whisper to myself more than Jess.

And with that I drop onto the rocks.

Chapter Two

"Minty! Stop! Don't go any further. Wait until I get help!" screams Jess, though I can barely hear her above the crashing waves. "I'm going for Dad!"

She hares back to the car, Romulus tearing on ahead. Meanwhile Remus is whimpering and scrabbling to get a grip on the rocks. So, even though I know Dad'll be mad at me for leaving the path, I've no choice; I have to keep climbing down, I must go after my dog, I just have to!

Soaked through by sea spray, looking small and terrified, Remus stands there shivering but, as I draw near him, he backs away, stealing closer and closer to the water. Suddenly, a massive wave booms over him. He jumps back a step. Yelps. Looks at me with frightened eyes and whines, his claws scraping at the slippery rocks.

Shit! He's far too close to the edge. "Remus! Keep away!"

My stomach lurches. What to do? What to do?

Calm it. Gotta keep cool, Minty.

"Remus. Here boy."

I try to persuade him, but the roaring waters of the Firth of Forth overpower my words. He stares at me but takes another step backwards, nearer and nearer to danger. Gripping onto a jagged piece of rock with one hand, I stretch out the other.

"Here, Remus, come on, boy." I try to grab hold of his collar but, instead of the red nylon, my fingers snatch a handful of air and snarling sea foam.

Blast!

He whimpers. Quivers.

"Please, Remus. Come here boy," I say, carefully checking my footing on the surface as I get within a metre of him.

The blood races through my veins. Hammers in my heart.

The dog looks at me, the trust in his toffee-coloured eyes torn away by the fierce wind that's whipped up. I call again. He retreats even further. I inch towards him. He moves away, his ears flat against his skull, his body bristling with fear. He steps back. Back onto the last scrap of land between him and the sea. My skin creeps. Goosebumps ripple up my arms. He's too close! Then a wave crashes over the ridge and snatches him.

No!

"Remus!"

I watch in horror as the sea sucks my pet into its clutches. One minute his head's above water, the next he's gone without a trace.

"Remus. Omigod, *Remus*."

Weak in the legs, dizzy, snivelling with tears, I scramble to the water's edge, my feet fighting not to slip on the slimy rocks. The spray soaks my face, hair and skin and the sharp stone rips at my hands. The sea roars like fifty thousand Man U supporters protesting an own goal in a cup final. Sea salt stings my eyes as I peer into the water, desperate to glimpse Remus.

There! There he is! Oh, thank Jupiter! I catch sight of his head as it bobs above the surface. Then he's gone. By now, I'm so sick to the stomach I think I'll honk up. Where is he? I scan the sea, desperate to catch sight of him again.

Chill, Minty. Don't panic.

He can't be far away.

Is that him?

Yes!

"Remus?"

I have to grab at him. I need to…

Wait! Stand back. The sea's treacherous. Stay where you are. Jess's right – wait for help. I try to talk sense into myself, but all I can think of is how to get at Remus. How to get him out of danger, double-quick.

So, stepping as carefully as I can, I climb right down to the water's edge, stretch out my arm and gesture with my fingers, willing him within reach. I can barely see for the mixture of tears and another drenching of sea spray. And I don't know if it's the chill running through my body or what, but suddenly

I stop, look around me, my eyes clamp tight and I shudder, my feet rooted to the spot.

Why did you climb down here, you nutcase? Are you crazy? Get back to safety.

Then I think of Remus and how freaked out he must be.

"Where are you, boy?" I cry, looking for him through my tears.

And then I catch a glimpse of his nose peeking above the crest of an incoming wave. I stretch out an arm but, as I do, I lose my footing.

And before I can even take in what's happening, I'm falling down, down towards the water, banging against rock after rock until, head-first, I tumble into the sea.

Omigod!

"Help! Somebody help!"

God, the water's cold. Freezing, freezing cold. An icy cold that knocks my breath away. I struggle to breathe. I gasp, gulp for air. A wave smacks me. I take in a huge mouthful of seawater. I cough and cough. Harsh, racking coughs that really burn inside. My chest tightens. My nose stings with salt. Water spews from my mouth. Another wave crashes against me. And another. And another. On and on they come. Waves that, only minutes ago seemed like nothing, are now monsters. Roaring. Howling. Rearing up. They clutch at me. Tear at my jeans and jacket. Yank at my trainers. Pull me further out. Suck me down. Hurl me back up, to pant for air.

How did the sea get like this?

Now it's *my* head that's struggling to keep above water. In an effort to stay afloat, I flap my arms and kick out my legs. Screaming with terror inside, somehow I manage to turn my body around to face the shore. Fighting against the current I strike out towards land.

Safety, got to get to safety.

But – God no! Remus! I can't leave him in this. Can't let him drown. I can't live without my dog.

So, even though my instincts yell at me not to, I turn back and search for my boy.

Omigod, where are you, Remus?

Half-blinded by the spray, my body thumped about by the waves, I search and search. My salt-stung eyes dart everywhere, and then I spot him again.

"Rem—"

I swallow another ton of water. Puke it out. Cough. Gasp. Splutter. All at once. One shoulder aches where it struck the rocks as I entered the water.

Remus is tossing about on the water like an empty Coke bottle. His frightened eyes meet mine, pleading with me, begging me to help him. And I can, I can rescue him, I *will* save him. If only my legs weren't so heavy.

Swim! Keep swimming, Minty.

I try to get to him, I really do, but the sea has other ideas. It's like some vicious snake that's thrashing around, throttling me, wringing the life from me.

My throat stings from the sea salt, I try to call out again but gag when the Firth of Forth rushes into my mouth.

Remus?

Vanished – he's… Where is he?

There he is! Some metres out to sea away from me, frantically raking the water with his paws. But, in an instant, he disappears again beneath the surface.

Omigod, Remus! I have to get to you, I just have to.

Ignoring my screaming muscles, I strike out towards him. But I haven't reckoned on the weight of my clothes. My jacket and jeans feel like chain-mail. My trainers are like two dumbbells on my feet.

In a frenzied version of the front crawl, I swim to him, a searing pain ripping through my chest.

His front paws are like a hamster's in a wheel. They go faster and faster as he struggles to stay afloat. And then a wave claims him and he sinks below the surface.

My arms ache. My legs too. But I keep going. One stroke. Two strokes. Three. Four. On. And on. To save my dog. The closer I get to him the more my heart thunders, the more my lungs crave air. I gulp. Take in water. Cough. Retch. Try to hold my breath, to stop more flooding into my mouth. But still I push on, ignoring the fire in my lungs, until there, ahead of me, Remus's head is just within reach. With strength I didn't know I have, I lunge at his collar. And grab him.

Oh Remus! Oh Remus, boy. I've got you!

But then the current tugs at him.

Desperately, I yank on his collar, pull him to me. His head disappears beneath the water, shoots back up. The force of the waves almost wrenches him away. I think my heart will burst. There's no feeling in my fingers, but I grip onto Remus like never before. I turn on my side. Make for the shore.

My hair wraps itself round my face like a scarf. The water crashes about us. Over us. Under. But I fight on. And then, upon almost reaching land, a huge surge spews us against the rocks. Then I hit my head on something.

And black out.

Chapter Three

I come to, buffeted about in a mass of swirling foam. Where am I? How long have I been lying here?

Omigod – Remus! Where are you? What's happened to you?

I lift my head and realise that I'm lying on the shore. The current has swept me well away from where I fell in: I reckon I'm about half a mile further along the coast, towards St. Monans.

And then I see him, up beyond the beach on the coastal footpath, barking at me, running back and forward like all of this is some sort of game. But, he's safe. Daft dog! Stupid dog! Nearly got us both killed.

I put a hand to my brow; check all over to see that nothing's bleeding. Blimey, no cuts – not one. How jammy is that? And, considering the last thing I remembered before passing out was getting bashed against the rocks, nothing seems to hurt. Laughing and crying all at once, I pull myself upright and tramp across the wet sand and pebbles, almost stumbling over a lump of driftwood.

Woozy with relief, I reach Remus. His tail wagging madly from side-to-side, he bounds over, rears onto his hind legs and flings himself at me. He must've been out of the water for a while because his coat isn't even damp.

"Remus! You're OK!" I cry and bend to cuddle him. His slobbering tongue flicks over my face and, laughing, I wrap my arms round his neck.

Giving him a kiss on his head, I look around. Instead of the snarl of the sea, it's peaceful on this beach. And like totally safe. Just imagine what might've happened to us in that water! To think we were caught up in all that madness. It's unbelievable.

But it's over now. Though it's left me feeling really weird. Numb even. Why do I feel so numb? So...so...unconnected? As if I'm floating? Up there. Somewhere in the still air. Is this what it's like after you nearly drown?

I shake my head. Shrug off the uneasiness. "Come on, boy, let's find the others," I say, giving Remus a final scratch under his collar.

With my dog circling about me, I cross the beach, climb onto the coastal path and head back to find Jess and my parents. Despite the spaced-out woozy feeling, I have never felt so glad to be alive.

As I pace along, I take in everything: the Bass Rock out in the Firth of Forth, with Berwick Law behind it; how the sky has changed from grey to blue with streaks of wispy cloud; the rabbit droppings dotted through the greeny-yellow grass; the mud and trodden-in sand under my feet; the jagged black rocks and the gunmetal sea with its frolicking white horses, the sea that nearly made me a goner. I watch the gulls in the air. Gaze as one breaks away, soars upwards, letting out a high-pitched cry.

Wowza! I *am* alive!

Twirling round, I catch sight of the Isle of May in the distance. Jess is always banging on about going there one day. To see the puffins. Why wait? We'll do it. We'll do it soon. Tomorrow. Next week. We can do anything we want; we're alive!

"Isn't life just brilliant!" I punch the air, and drum my feet on the ground. Remus barks and scampers round me, looking just as happy as I feel.

"Look at you, you mad dog," I say, through a giggle. I lean over, catch his front paws and we do this dippy dance for a bit until I drop him and say, "Come on, we need to get back." Then I shove my hands into my jacket pockets, and run.

And then, as I'm pounding towards Lady's Tower where this all started, it strikes me.

The insides of my pockets are dry.

Huh? Dry? No way!

I stop. Touch my jeans, my jacket.

They're dry too.

I put my fingers up to my hair. Dry. Eh? How can that be? I've just hauled myself out of the water. I should be wet – drenched. But I'm dry, like I've been in a tumble dryer. My mind whizzes. What's going on? This is crazy. Completely, absolutely crazy. And the wind, it must still be strong; I can see the effects of it on the marram grass, I can hear it whistling, howling really, but I can't feel it. It should be plastering my clothes to my body. Its cold breath should be stinging my face. But it doesn't. What's that all about?

My head's full of it. But then, there, up ahead, I see my dad racing along the path from the direction of the car park with Mum and Romulus running behind. They're dashing over the grass to Lady's Tower where Remus clambered through the window and down onto the rocks. And all thoughts of whether I'm wet or dry slip away.

I wave to grab their attention. "Mum! Dad! We're here!" But they don't hear me. Cupping my hands over my mouth, I holler again. "Dad! Mum! Yoo-hoo! Over here!" They're too far away. The wind steals my words. "Come on, Remus!"

Remus and I sprint as fast as we can, trying to catch them up. I know I'm in for a right rollicking from Dad. Wasn't 'keep to the paths' the last thing he'd said before me and Jess went on our walk? But right now I'm not bothered about that; I have to let them know I'm OK.

Dad tears up to the old ruined tower, dashes inside and seconds later darts out yelling something to Mum who, by now, has caught him up.

I run faster.

When I draw nearer, I see Dad scramble down the rocks closer to the water's edge.

Hear him bellow something at Mum.

See Mum scuttle over the rocks towards him.

Hear Romulus let out an unearthly howl.

See Mum peer over Dad's shoulder.

Hear her scream.

What's going on? What's happened now? And where the frig is Jess?

When he twists round to Mum, Dad's face is the colour of turned milk. "Phone an ambulance! Quick!"

Then he swings back. Slithers to where the sea meets the land. Holds onto a ledge. Reaches out into the waves. And, with a mighty heave, pulls something out of the water.

It's a person, a teenager, I guess – a girl probably. Dressed in torn blue denims and a red jacket that's ripped and sodden. A teenager whose long dark hair dangles over one shoulder like tangled brown seaweed as Dad struggles to pick her up.

So it's not just us, Remus. Somebody else's fallen in, too. How unlucky can one day get?

"Help me, Mary!" Dad bawls.

Mum drops her mobile on the ground and, crying, sliding and stumbling, she reaches Dad and helps him haul that poor teen up onto dry land.

They've just managed to get the girl up off the rocks onto the grass when I catch up with them.

"Omigod! What's happened?" I shriek, my gaze trained on the bruises behind the woven-leather bracelets on the teenager's upturned wrist.

Mum is beside herself, crying and shaking all over like she's the one who's just come out of the water. Romulus lies at the foot of the tower's steps, eerily silent, his golden head on his front paws. Why isn't Jess with him?

"What's going on, Mum?" I say, trying to catch her arm. But she doesn't seem to notice me. It's probably the shock of seeing that poor sod getting dragged out of the sea.

I shiver. God, that could so easily have been me.

By now, Dad has got the kid on her back and is giving her mouth-to-mouth. He puffs air into her lungs, leans back, counts, and tries again. And again. And again. But it's no good.

"No!" he yells out across the water.

He shakes his head. Sits back on his heels, panting. Mum falls on him, moaning and sobbing.

I can't get a good look at the girl's face from this angle; don't know if I want to, really. But I move round to take a look anyway.

Then Mum screams, and I mean really screams. They must be able to hear her across the Forth in North Berwick.

"Mum," I say, reaching out to comfort her. But already she's on her knees, bending over that poor lifeless kid.

But…where's Jess?

Why isn't she here? What can have—

Then it strikes me – that girl's wearing a *red* jacket.

A black t-shirt!

Skinny jeans!

God, no, it can't be. They're Jess's clothes. The ones she was wearing today!

No! It's just a coincidence! Jess went for help. Didn't she? This isn't her. Is it? God, don't let it be.

Mum's hunched over the girl, stroking her hair. Hair I recognise. Dark hair just like—

"It's not Jess. It's not Jess," I say over and over until I find my legs buckling under me and I fall to my knees. "She wasn't even near the water. It can't be her," I tell myself and to prove it I force myself to look at the teenager again. Such long hair. Long *loose* hair! Didn't Jess tie hers up in a scrunchy? So this can't be her! Please say it isn't.

Behind me speaks a voice, a voice that's as familiar as my own. "Mum? What's happening? Tell me she's OK. Tell me she's not dead."

I twist round and there she is, emerging from inside the tower, shaking, crying, hugging her sides. Jess!

Thank God! Thank God she's safe. But if this isn't Jess, then who is it?

Don't think about that right now. Jess is alive!

I rush to her, moving as quickly as the slimy rocks will allow. "Oh, Jess," I cry. "I thought that was you!"

But when I draw near, she doesn't acknowledge me, she just keeps scrambling down to where Mum and Dad are. Once there she tries to drag the kid away. "I need to ..." She can hardly get the words out, she's panting so hard. "I need to catch her breath. I need to catch her last breath."

Too late. Even I can see it's too late. The kid's chest is as still as those models you see in shop windows. She's breathed her last.

"Don't, Jess," Mum whispers, as Jess puts her mouth to the girl's blue lips. "She's gone."

A sudden shaft of sun breaks through the clouds causing the ring on the drowned girl's right pinkie to glimmer in the pale light. It sends a sliver of unease sparking through me.

Because that's when I notice the massive buttons on the kid's jacket.

Clock the huge lapels.

Check out the Converse trainers.

That's when I get a good look at her face, her bruised and bloodied face.

That's when it hits me.

That poor drowned kid is me.

Chapter Four

"Stop it, Jess. Please, stop it," Mum says, her face gritty with tears as she tries to draw Jess back from the kid – me.

Me?

Jess shoves her aside. Sobs. "I need to get her last breath."

"Let her be," Mum says.

"I'm her nearest relative."

Mum grasps her gently by the shoulders. "Love, there's nothing you can do." Her voice is broken, full of pain. "Minty's gone."

Gone?

Jess shakes her head, shrugs her off. "No. I have to."

"She's gone, Jess," Mum murmurs.

I don't understand. How can I be gone when I'm here?

"But that's just it. Don't you see? She can't go anywhere if I can't catch it." Jess's face is scrunched up; tears flow down her cheeks. "Please. She needs me."

She bends down and brings her lips to mine. Then she begins calling out my name. "Minty." She says it over and over. Each time her voice grows calmer.

Slumped on the ground, Dad turns to stare at her, a look of complete disbelief on his face. "What..." He turns to Mum, hauls himself onto his feet. "What is she doing?" he whispers.

"Oh, Geoff." She holds her arms out to him but he ignores her.

Instead, his voice becomes a bellow. He lunges at Jess who's now yanking the gold ring from my pinkie. "Put that back."

Dad!

Omigod, he sounds so angry with her.

"I must do this. It has to be me," Jess says, her tone steady as the ring slips off in her hands. She stares at it for a moment, puts it in her jacket pocket then reaches for my face. With amazing gentleness, she smoothes a hand over my eyes until they're closed. Then she does the same with my mouth, all the time chanting, "Minty. Farewell. Minty. Farewell."

That does it for Dad.

"Leave her alone," he cries and snatches Jess's hands to tug her away. He peers into her face, his sludgy-green eyes full of confusion. "Why are you doing this?"

Jess stares at him. "It's the custom. It needs to be done." Her voice is scarily cool.

Dad groans. Tugs at the hairs on his balding scalp. He jerks his head back. Turns to J. "Oh, Jess, this isn't the time for games." I can barely hear him.

He seizes her hands and peers into her eyes. "You think some ancient rituals are going to bring Minty back?" He looks at my battered body. Crumples over. Clutches his belly. "If only they could."

Then, against the sound of waves breaking on the rocks, Mum lets out a long, deep moan. Dad looks up. Reaches for her. She falls into his arms, sobbing. "Our baby's dead, Geoff. Our baby's dead."

I'm watching all this like it's some movie at the Odeon in Dunfermline. Then I realise – really, totally understand. Omigod, those *are* my clothes that kid's wearing. That *is* my body lying on that grass. That's *me* Jess's calling for. It really is me who's dead. Me. Me. Me. The words beat in my head like a big bass drum. My mind's whirling and yattering and clanging and racing. Dead. I'm dead! I let out a scream. But no one hears it, just Remus who whines and spins around, jumping up at me.

His whining snaps me out of my trance. How can my life be over? I've hardly lived. Kids shouldn't die. It can't be true. And anyway, I'm still here, aren't I? I mean – where's the ferryman? He'd have come for me if I was dead. Yeah? Or shouldn't there be a light? A big bright tunnel to go down? Something – anything. No – this isn't happening! I'm still alive.

"Jess. Jess. Look. It's me."

I drop to the ground beside her. I have to make her understand. If anyone can, it's her. She's my twin after all.

"You don't need my breath. I'm here!" I bawl, pointing to myself. But she doesn't look up.

Can't she hear me? She *must* hear me.

"It's OK. I'm not dead. See?" I wave my hands in front of her nose, grin my special daft grin that always makes her laugh. "I'm all right. J. Look. It's OK. *I'm* OK. See?" But she just sits there, stroking the girl's – *my* - face.

I shift nearer. Peer into her eyes. "Jess. Please. Look at me." But she carries on stroking. I go to shove her, punch her, whack her on the arm again. "Look, J. I'm..."

A needle-sharp rush of electricity shoots up my arm, coursing through my body and into my head. I clutch my chest, and as I look at Jess the words trail away and are replaced by a jolt of sheer terror that slices through my mind.

Noooo!

Because omigod – my hand has gone right through her.

I stare in horror at my fingers, tap my face, pinch my skin, check the solidity of my so-called dead self, glance at the lifeless girl lying on the ground. The world swims before me. And that's when I see it, a golden head tossed by the waves below and crashing time after time onto the rocks. A dog in the clutches of the cruel waters. A dead dog. My dog. That's when I know for sure that I *am* dead – and that Remus is dead as well.

Chapter Five

"Come into the house, love," Mum says from the front passenger seat of our people carrier, her gentle voice hoarse from crying.

She glances out of the window at Dad and Romulus walking up the floodlit garden path with the policeman who drove our car home.

"Poor Remus," I say to myself as I watch him trot alongside his pal. "Do you even realise you're dead?"

Do I?

"Let's go," Mum says, dragging her gaze back to my sister and leaning over to pat her knee.

"I can't," Jess whispers, huddled into the corner between the seat and the door, face hidden in her splayed hands, like it has been ever since she got into the car.

I guess it's her way of coping with everything that happened back there.

God, I know I still can't believe it, that I'm dead. And why *am* I here? Shouldn't I be sailing along the River Styx, on my way to the Underworld? I ought to be – Jess did all the rituals, even though Dad didn't get what she was doing.

Yeah, she did everything right – so why am I here? I mean, OK maybe I don't know for sure where I *should* be, what should have happened…but this? Hanging around like a gas, watching the mayhem: the cops and their questions, checking to see if it was an accident; the arrival of the ambulance guys; the undertakers taking away my body; me climbing in the car, sitting next to my sister on the way home as if this was just another normal day.

Jess's moans interrupt my thoughts.

"We shouldn't have left her." In the dim evening light I see her throw her head back against the dog guard, detect the huge wet tears in her eyes as they stare at the roof. She lets out a stuttering gasp. "*I*…" She thumps her breastbone. "*I* shouldn't have left her. With those…people."

"She had to go to the funeral home. You know that," Mum says.

"But she should be at *our* home. She should be with *me*!"

"I *am* with you, J. Right here," I stretch across to comfort her but as I do my hand brushes against Mum and I get that same weird electric shock again.

"Ow!" I squeal and pull back into my seat to shake the tingling heat and nipping pins and needles from my arm.

I glance down at my hand and from the corner of my eye, there in the shadows, peeking out from under my bum, is the skin from the banana I ate earlier. I try to pull it out but my fingers won't grip, instead they slam together leaving the discarded peel right where it was. And even though I try to lift it again and again, it's still there – I can't friggin' budge it.

Omigod, what's happening? Nothing's like it should be. Am I stuck in some kind of grisly nightmare? Yeah, that'll be it, I'm dreaming – I'll wake up in a bit.

OK, be cool, Minty. Relax. Close your eyes. It's only a dream. OK, it's the most realistic dream ever but…chill. Sit back in your seat and rest. Take deep breaths, let your mind float. Sleep. Sleep. Sl—

But at the sound of Jess's sobs my eyelids spring apart.

"I…I want Dad," she says. "I need to explain."

Mum looks over to the two figures huddled in conversation by the kitchen door. Under the harsh glare of the security light I can see that one's Dad, the other's the policewoman who followed us home in the police car. The cop takes the house keys from him, unlocks the door and tries to usher him inside. Dad shakes his head and staggers against the rough-cast wall, crushing the ivy. I glance at Mum. She's still watching him. Then, holding back the tears, she looks away and gathers Jess in her arms.

Jess pulls away, gazes at her. "I can't stop thinking of Minty all alone." Her voice breaks. "She hates being on her own." Fresh teardrops trickle down her ashen cheeks.

"Try not to dwell on it," Mum says in a choked voice.

Jess takes a shuddering breath and clutches at her throat. "It's my fault. We were…on the footpath. We were arguing. I…I…" she sobs. "I told her to drop dead."

Mum gasps.

The memory of our squabble flashes through my mind. I moan. "Oh, God, J."

Why did we have to have that stupid fight? Why?

Jess's cheeks are streaked with tears. "I didn't mean it, I didn't. Oh, Minty, I'm sorry." She covers her eyes. Sobs into her hands.

"I know." I groan. "We say stuff like that to each other all the time. It was just a dumb argument."

"I never meant what I said," Jess says. Her chin wobbles. She looks at Mum. "I'll never forgive myself."

"It's… Of course you didn't." Mum pulls a folded tissue from the back pocket of her jeans and dabs at Jess's eyes. "Don't do this to yourself. Come into the house, sweetheart." Screwing up the used hankie, Mum climbs out of her seat, walks round the car and opens Jess's door.

Instead of getting out, Jess grabs her by the hand; she squeezes so hard that Mum's rings must be digging into her fingers. "I can't go in there without Minty." She begins to cry again.

When Mum leans in to comfort her, the light in the car makes her lipstick stand out against her white skin. I notice how her mouth quivers, check the tearstains under each eye. Her mascara has run.

"Love, come inside," she says. "You have to sometime. May as well get it over and done with."

Jess stares at the back of the driver's headrest. Not that she's seeing anything, to be honest – her eyes are so unfocused. And her mouth is all lopsided, like she's had a stroke or something. Even her skin seems slack, as if it's the skin of a ninety-year-old, not a teenager. I hardly recognise her. I shut my eyes and try to block out what I'm seeing.

"I can't go inside. Not without Minty. Please don't make me," she mutters.

J, if you could only know the truth: you don't have to go inside without me – we can go in together.

So come on, Minty, do something. Let her know you're still around, it's just that she can't see you.

I stretch out a hand to touch her. "Jess," I say, her name fizzling out on my tongue at the memory of how my fist punched straight through her this afternoon, of how weird it felt a minute ago when I tried again. So, I snatch my arm back.

Face it, Minty. She doesn't know you're here.

And face something else, too – this ain't no dream. This is…what? What is this?

"Are you ready to come in now?" The cop who drove us back joins Mum by the open door, one ginger eyebrow raised, an uncomfortable expression on his freckled face. Omigod, he doesn't look much older than me. I wonder if this is the first time he's had to do something like this?

"Jess?" says Mum, kissing her on the brow and gesturing for her to climb out.

Jess nods. Lets Mum help her from the car.

They stand for a moment, as pale and still as those marble statues we saw in Rome that time. How I wish we were back there. Anything but this.

Mum hugs her, runs a finger across Jess's hairline, brushes back the straggly wisps that've escaped from her ponytail. "Let's go, love."

They begin making their slow progress up the gravel path, but all of a sudden Jess comes to a halt, her gaze fixed on Dad who's still propped up against the doorframe with the police lady murmuring into his ear. With a Remus-like whimper, Jess bolts towards him, sobbing.

"Oh, Dad, I let her down – I missed her last breath." She lets out an agonised moan, throws herself onto him and says into his corduroy jacket, "Now what'll become of her?"

But Dad offers no answer. Instead, he stares at Jess for a long moment, and then peeling her hands from his chest, he turns towards the house, and with heavy shoulders, stumbles inside.

It's not until he disappears into the house that it dawns on me – Dad's the only one of my family who hasn't cried.

Chapter Six

Jess gazes at her reflection in the mirrored wardrobe, the dusky shadows under her almond-shaped eyes the only colour on her face. Her hair hangs past her shoulder blades, unwashed and unbrushed. It's as limp and lacklustre as Jess herself. She pulls down the cuffs of the brown woollen jumper that swamps her slim body and a single tear rolls down her cheek. She doesn't bother to wipe it away. She's wearing the same PJs she put on the night before I died and a dirty toenail peeks through the hole in one of her socks.

This is not the Jess I know. My Jess is gorgeous – way prettier than me, even though we're supposed to be identical twins: her face has a fullness to it that mine doesn't. It's like God made me, studied my upturned nose and thin lips and thought to himself, "Hmm nice, but I can do better". So he did.

Geez, look at her – where did that slave to shower gel and hair straighteners go? But I know the answer to that: she disappeared exactly a week ago, on the day I drowned.

"J, I can't hack seeing you like this," I say, standing right behind her. She's close enough to hug – so I do.

Or at least, I try. But like every other time, since that day in Elie, my arms pass through her body as if she was the ghost and I'm the living, breathing one. Reeling from the weird electricity that surges through me, I shrink away and steady myself by the window.

I can see our street through the gap in the drawn curtains: a couple of little guys on their bikes, the woman from across the way arriving home from work, the old man from three doors up taking his yappy poodle for a walk. It's all so...ordinary.

I glance over at our single beds, at our matching crimson duvet covers with their black and gold pattern and, as I do, a million scenes from the past play out in my head.

"J. Remember that time we nagged Dad to paint the headboards?" The memory makes me smile. "Antique gold so that they'd match the curtains and our duvet covers. Yeah?"

Then I notice the murky stain on the fluffy red carpet. "And remember when I dropped that navy nail polish? How mad Mum got at me?"

My gaze flits across the room. "And what about the desk? How long did it take Dad to assemble it? Four hours or something – and it's still wonky. Isn't it, J? Poor Dad. Mr Can't Fixit."

I take in each item in the room – the holiday souvenirs, our bookcase crammed with paperbacks and DVDs, our saxophones, the stereo and the stack of CDs, the pinboard studded with pics of us and our mates, the posters, desk, chair – all just as it was that day we set off for Elie, the day that ended in my death. Nothing here's changed; it's just the same.

"Everything's like it was – except us," I mutter, turning round to Jess.

Yep, everything's as normal as ever, apart from that photo of me that Jess now has on her bedside table.

I turn to my twin. She hasn't moved.

Normal? Huh! Who am I kidding? Where's the crashing sound of music blasting through the stereo, the bleep of incoming texts, the sound of Jess yacking on her mobile?

"God!" I yell. "It's too quiet in here! It's doing my head in!"

She cocks her head to the side and frowns.

Omigod!

What's she looking at? Who's she looking at? Me?

"Jess?"

It *is* like she's watching me, though her expression remains dead. Even so, she must sense something. Surely? Why else would she have turned around, frowned like that – be staring?

"Jess, it's Minty," I say, raising my voice, holding my hands up to my chin and wiggling my fingers. "See?"

But, though her gaze remains fixed in my direction, she does nothing.

"Look, it's me," I yell.

She stares through me.

How can I change this? Make her see that I haven't gone anywhere, that I'm right here? There must be a way.

And then she comes over to stare out of the window and I remember how sometimes, as little kids, we used to breathe on Mum's make-up mirror and write our initials. Could I do that now? On the window? Write my initials – or my name even? I could try…

I lean forward right next to her, really close, and expel a huge puff of air onto the glass.

Swinging round to face her I say, "Jess, watch this!"

But when I go to scrawl my name there's no sign of condensation there – nothing. I purse my lips. Blow on the glass again and again and again. Zilch! Not a drop of moisture.

"Why is that?" I say more to myself than Jess. "Air's coming out…I can feel it on my hand." I blow on my palm to check. Feel the warmth of my breath on my skin. "Why doesn't it show on the window?"

But, what I don't say out loud is why then, if I'm supposed to be dead, do I even have any breath?

No! Bury it. Bury that thought. Try again. It'll work. It has to.

However hard I try, the outcome's always the same.

"Oh, Jess, what's going on?" I say, lying down on my bed. "Am I dead? What am I? And what're you – you're not J anymore, that's for sure."

I sit up and look at her. "What's happening to us?"

Jess steps back from the window and sits on her bed, hunched up against the pile of pillows. Littered on her duvet are the photographs she's just spent the last hour studying. She picks one up – taken last year in Ibiza.

"Do you remember this, Minty?" she says.

Wait a minute! She's talking to me?

I scramble onto my knees, stretch across the gap between our beds. "Jess? So you *do* know I'm here."

Thank Jupiter!

"Remember when this got taken?" she continues in a whisper. She gazes at the pair of us posing on sun loungers. Tears fall onto the photo.

She looks into my eyes and, with the ball of her thumb, smoothes the moisture from the photograph's glossy surface.

"Course I do." I say, smiling at her.

Smilebacksmilebacksmileback… Please.

She drops the pic and I lean across and touch it. Or I try to.

She scoops up another. "And this one outside St Peter's Cathedral? Look at us, we're grinning like a couple of ginger toms," she says, and it's like she waves it in front of my eyes. "Wasn't Rome just amazing?"

It's *like* she's waving it? What am I talking about? She *is* – so she *has* to be aware of me. Or…is she?

"It was cool that holiday, wasn't it? Miles better than Ibiza," she says. Her lips droop, her eyes have a sad, faraway look. "The catacombs were beyond spooky, do you remember?"

Is she actually speaking to me? Like, does she think I'm here?

"Yeah." I nod. Search her face for a clue, something that tells me she knows she's not alone. "Jess, look at me."

Please hear me.

No reaction.

She picks up another one, of us in the Roman Forum. "Poor Dad…"

Is she speaking to me? To herself? What? I have to know.

"Yeah, he hated Rome," I say, raising my voice to gain her attention. "And having to print off all these photos when we got back."

I smile at her again. No response. She just puts the picture on the bedcover and selects one that's lying face down. She turns it over. "Look at us lolling about. We – no!" She drops it as if it bit her.

I glance at the photograph. Me and J smiling into the camera. On a beach somewhere. At— "Shit! It's Ruby Bay. Elie. Oh, Jess, no wonder you can't look at it. Neither can I." Images from last Saturday flood into my mind. I can almost taste the salt water. Feel it sting my throat.

She sweeps the photographs onto the carpet. "Why did my mobile lose its signal? Why did you leave yours in your bag? If only we could've phoned Mum and Dad, then I wouldn't have had to run for help." She tilts her head to the ceiling. "Oh, Minty, why did you have to climb down after Remus? This is all your fault. It's all right for you, I'm the one who's left behind."

"It's all right for me?" I yell in her ear as a rush of pure anger fills me. "Oh yeah, so it is! Do you think this is fun? Me here and you not knowing I exist?"

Exist? This is existing?

I wring my hands together. "It's so unfair! I can't stand it!" I leap up. "Come on, J, you have to see me. You have to! Please."

By now she's really bawling, sobbing harder than ever.

"No, no, don't cry. Don't crydon'tcrydon'tcry."

Come on, you eedjit, think of something else… So the window thing was a disaster but something else might work.

Think! The photos on the floor. Grab one. Show her it.

"See this, J. Watch." I scoop up the photograph. Hold it between my fingers. Flap it in front of her eyes. "It's me holding it. Me. Minty."

But – dang! – when I look at my hand, instead of the picture, there's just emptiness.

"Don't give up. It'll work," I mutter and bend down and start all over again.

Cos I'll do it. I will. Even if it takes all night.

I must make a trillion attempts at picking up that photo, not that it does me much good.

But why is that? I can touch the flippin' thing – I can, I'm sure I can – but whenever I go to pick it up...disaster!

I'm just about to try again when I'm distracted by raised voices coming from the bathroom. Jess must notice them as well because she looks out into the hallway and her body goes all tense.

Mum's voice wafts into the room. "Enough. Not tonight again. Please." She sounds tired.

"But I can't take it in," I hear Dad say. "I've been over and over it all week. Why were they even near the rocks? That's what I don't understand."

Everything goes quiet. Apart from Dad pacing up and down the bathroom. It's so quiet I can hear the creak of that wonky floorboard by the sink that Mum's always nagging him to mend. He groans. Then he says, "I told them to keep to the paths."

"Stop torturing yourself," Mum says.

"I told them." His voice is really loud now. He sounds like some kind of wild man.

"Geoff. Please. Jess will hear you," Mum shushes.

"Too late for that," I say through clenched teeth, because Jess is bunched up against the pillows, her eyes trained on the wall opposite.

"And what I don't understand, Mary, is why Jess did leave Minty there. She knows Minty is – was – impulsive." He pauses. "You don't think – Minty wouldn't..."

What? Minty wouldn't what?

"She wouldn't have jumped in deliberately? Gone into the water to save Remus?"

Surely he has to be joking?

"No, I bloomin' wouldn't!" I shout. "D'you think I'm a complete idiot?"

"She wouldn't have done that, would she?" Dad says, his voice rising.

"No way!" I get onto my feet. "I was trying to reach him, that's all. And I would've, only—"

"Oh, love," Mum says. "Please stop this."

"Yeah, good idea," I say, as I watch Jess cup her hands over her ears. She begins to tremble and quiet sobs escape from her lips.

"If only Jess had stayed with her," Dad says. Then he makes this strangled kind of gasp and adds, "Oh, why didn't she?"

At that, Jess brings her knees to her chin, a mass of fuzzed-up hair tumbling over to hide her face.

"Jess," I say. "Don't listen to him."

Yeah, Minty, like she can hear you, like that's going to help.

I tear to the door and hiss into the hall. "Cut it out, why don't you. Don't you realise she can hear you?" I know it's pointless yelling at him, but I can't help myself.

Dad grows even louder. "Why? I need to know why," he says.

Jess begins to cry.

"That does it!" I say and stomp into the bathroom. "Stop it! You're upsetting her! Stop! Just stop. OK?" I grind my teeth; punch a fist into my belly. How *can* I stop this? Oh God, I'm sick of being The Invisible Teen!

Dad tugs off his jumper and throws it on the wooden stool by the bath. "It's killing me, Mary. Why did this have to happen?"

He sinks onto the toilet seat, his face scrunched up with so much grief that it makes me gasp.

"Oh, Dad," I say, wishing I could take that raw pain away from him. "Mum's right, stop tormenting yourself. It doesn't help anybody."

Mum wrings the water out of her face flannel, grabs the edge of the sink and turns to speak to him in a whisper. "Jess isn't to blame."

"No," Dad says. "I really don't..." His words escape in one long, slow puff. He massages his jaw. "God, Mary, I'm not blaming her, really, I'm not. How can you even think that? But I can't fathom why she would leave Minty in danger, like that."

Mum yanks the guest towel off the rail and leans back against the basin. She pauses, takes a deep breath. "She came for us. For help." She looks at Dad and says, "She did her best." Then she pulls out the plug and carefully rubs the towel in between her fingers as the water gurgles down the drain.

"It's not Jess's fault. If it's anyone's fault then it's mine," Dad murmurs. "If we'd gone to Edinburgh. If I hadn't taken that last call—"

"No, Geoff, let's not go there—"

"But if I hadn't we'd have gone on the walk with them and Minty would still be alive."

Mum folds the towel and places it on the lip of the sink. "Geoff, there's no point in going through all this again, hour after hour. What good does it do?"

He covers his eyes for a moment, then looks up at her and holds out his hands. "But I need to understand, Mary. Otherwise I'll go mad."

"Please." She moistens her lips. Swallows. "I know you feel guilty. God knows I do. I've asked myself why I suggested Elie in the first place. Why I stayed in the car. Didn't go with them. But…what good does any of this do?"

She clears her throat, lets out a massive sigh.

"Geoff, please. You have to keep it together for the funeral on Friday. Help us through this." Crouching down, she laces her fingers through his. "I need you to be strong. So does Jess." She draws a long breath. Gazes into his bloodshot eyes. "Please, love."

Dad says nothing. The hot tap drips rhythmically in the background, like torture by water. Eventually, he brings their linked hands up to his mouth. Squeezes Mum's tight. "Yes. And I will be."

Mum brings her lips to his knuckles. Attempting a smile she kisses them and says, "I know you'll be there for us. You always are." She hauls herself onto her feet. "I'd better check on Jess." Then tightening the tap, she walks out.

When Dad leaves too, I stay in the bathroom, perched on the side of the tub. It's peaceful in here and I don't have to see what I've done to my family. Because it's all too much, seeing Jess so upset,

Mum and Dad struggling to cope. Is this it? Is this my punishment? Is this what I get for ignoring Dad, for thinking I could rescue Remus? God, I still can't believe I climbed down onto those rocks, went anywhere near the water.

If only I could turn back the clock, think things through before I acted. Like any normal person would've done.

I bang the heel of my hand against my thick skull – once, twice, over and over again. "What kind of nutter are you, Minty?" I roar. "Why did you do it?" I whack my head harder, expecting to feel pain – anything. Something. But I don't. I crash onto the tiled floor. Hug my knees. "Idiot, you stupid, stupid idiot."

And right that second, I hear the dogs bound upstairs and Remus runs into the bathroom, lips pulled back in a typical Remus grin.

My dog, my lovely, crazy boy.

"Look at you," I say, bending over to run my nails through his coat. "You've no idea what's going on, have you? I should be real angry with you. We'd still be alive, if you hadn't legged it."

Remus gives himself a shake, his identity disc clattering against the metal buckle on his collar. He licks at my fingers. "But how could I ever be mad with you?" I whisper, stroking his wet snout.

He allows me to pet him for all of a nanosecond before pulling away and padding out, to find his pal, I guess.

Maybe I'd better go and find *my* pal – my sad twin sister. And even if it takes all night, somehow I must work out how to make her happy again. And maybe if I do that I can do the same for our parents.

Chapter Seven

For the next hour I perch on the edge of the desk chair, gazing at Jess, thinking of a plan. There's got to be a way to get to her. She's my identical twin, we have a special bond. So, how hard can it be?

But when I look at Jess stretched out on her stomach across the bed, head tilted to the side, eyes closed, I admit to myself that what I'm hoping to do is beyond hard – maybe it's impossible. But I won't give up. No way.

The door cracks open and Mum comes in. Her eyes are glossy with tears, her face so, so white. Geez, she looks – what's the word? Haggard. And I'm to blame for that. She looks at Jess then inhales, pulls back her shoulders, and crosses the room to sit beside her.

"It's almost teatime," Mum says, brushing stray strands of pet hair from her black trousers. "Aren't you going to get up, love? Have a shower?"

"No," Jess mutters into her pillows.

"Come on, sweetheart. Let's be having you," Mum says, and draws back the bedclothes. I can tell she's trying to keep her voice light, but she's not fooling me. I doubt if J even notices though. "A long soak under the shower will do you good. I'll turn the water on. Get it nice and hot, just the way you like it."

Jess tugs at the bedclothes. "Leave me alone."

"Love, you need to shower. You haven't had one since…" Mum pauses. "For days." She lifts the quilt, folds back the edge and takes Jess by the hand. "You'll feel better afterwards."

"Mum's right, J. You need to get up," I say, walking over to her.

Jess yanks the duvet out of Mum's grasp. "How can I ever feel better?" Her face is flushed and a bit sweaty. "I was running to get you and Dad and all the time Minty was drowning. I should've known she was in danger, should've felt something – but I didn't." A look of such pain passes over her that I groan. "It's all my fault. Can't you see that?"

I shake my head. "No, Jess, no…"

How can she think that?

"That's why I'm doing this." Jess grabs a handful of her unruly hair, plucks at the baggy sweater over her jammies, and slumps against the headboard. "To mourn her properly, to make it up to her."

Mum worries at the huge diamond on her engagement ring, her grey eyes filling up with tears. "I need to ask. Is there…"

She takes a deep breath and peers at the *Gladiator* poster on the wall above Jess's bed. It's as if she's trying to draw strength from just looking at Russell Crowe.

Mum clears her throat. "Is there anything..." She twists her ring round and round on her slim finger. "About the funeral..." She clasps her hands together and stares at Russell again. "Is there anything you want us to include?"

Jess turns round to see what Mum's been looking at, and then she sits up. Glances around the room. Pauses when she comes to our Roman stuff. "What would the Romans do?" A smile stretches across her cheeks. She scratches her jaw. Nods. "Of course. How could I have forgotten? I need to get Minty's things together. Those she loved the most." Her eyes look brighter. "At least I can do that for her. That might help."

Mum lets out a whoosh of breath and cups Jess's chin in her palm. "And darling, it might just help you, too."

"No. Absolutely not. You're not putting pizza in her coffin."

I lean against the big American fridge-freezer, like some creepy bystander, listening to Mum and Jess discuss my cremation.

"But it's pepperoni with extra pineapple. Her favourite. I ordered it specially," Jess says in a monotone, laying the cardboard box on the kitchen table and taking out the hot take-away.

Her coffin, Mum said. I groan and put a hand to my chest. How can they be planning my funeral? It's surreal. Yet, though my mind kicks against the fact that it *is* my funeral they're discussing, I can't help but smile inside when Jess mentions my all-time fave food, even though her tone of voice really freaks me out.

But Mum's not smiling. Her face is all pinched and washed-out as she stares at the pizza. Maybe she's thinking about the one that I never got to eat. And that I'll never eat pizza again.

The thought of that kicks me in the guts.

Mum looks at Jess. Frowns. Sighs. "Sorry, love. It's not going to happen. Neither's the perfume."

A spark of rebellion ignites behind Jess's eyes. She slaps the pizza down. It slides into the box at an awkward angle, the cheese slipping to one side. "But…I missed her last breath, so we need to do this," she yells, banging a fist on the table, clipping the edge of the cardboard box and sending the contents spinning to the ground. "We *have* to send her to the Afterlife with her things around her."

Mum looks at the mess on her clean floor. She rifles through the pile of my belongings scattered on the wooden table and holds out the Emporio Armani City Glam spray.

"Oh, Jess," she says, "You've got to stop this obsession with all these rituals. We're Church of Scotland, not ancient Romans."

"That has to go in," Jess mutters, gripping the back of the chair in front of her.

God, J, no – you love that perfume as much as I do. Just keep it.

"This?" Mum brandishes the shiny pink can in the air; frowns. Her expression softens. "Be reasonable. Minty's being cremated. The perfume's in a canister. It would explode with the heat. Anyway," she says, dropping her voice to a murmur, "the undertakers won't allow it."

Jess yanks the can from Mum's grasp. "Well, I'm putting her make-up bag in. And that banana," she says, her voice totally manic. "And her pinkie ring."

I catch my breath. Whoa! Wait a minute! This is way too weird. I hold my right hand to my face and there on my pinkie is the same ring that's in the pile on the table. How is that possible?

But what Jess says next causes Mum to draw in her own breath.

"And a copy of *I Capture the Castle,*" Jess says, her eyes filling up.

Mum wobbles a bit on her heels. "Minty's favourite novel." A single tear trickles down her cheek. "Oh, it's all so…unfair. It's…" Now her tears are really flowing.

"Oh, Mum," I say. "Don't cry."

She moves closer to Jess and wraps her arms around her. Jess clenches her jaw, stiffens.

"I'll give the perfume to the undertakers and ask them to spray it on her…body." Mum says, gulping back a sob. "After they've rubbed in the lavender oil you gave them." She gently strokes Jess's arms. "And I'll ask them about the pizza."

"Mum," Jess whispers. She hesitates. "Can I have her ashes?"

Her words crash through my brain. "No, J. Why would you want to do that?" I say with a moan.

"I want to keep them in my room," she continues. "After the..." She goes limp, as if she's going to faint.

"J!" I cry, running to her.

Mum's arms tighten round Jess. She speaks into her hair. "We'll see. And I'll make sure there's a photo of Minty to go on top of...the coffin."

They stand there in the middle of the kitchen wrapped in each other's grief.

And here am I, invisible, watching them crumble in front of my eyes and praying that, somehow, I can do something to change that.

Chapter Eight

The day of my funeral dawns. It's a warm, bright Friday early in April, the kind of weather for a wedding, not a cremation.

It's been twelve days, nineteen hours and three minutes precisely since I drowned.

In keeping with Ancient Roman tradition, Jess wanted the funeral to be at night but my parents weren't having any of that and arranged it for eleven in the morning.

The crem is overflowing with mourners: the pews are packed so tight that there's hardly room for a gnat and loads of people are standing at the back of the room and in the hall outside.

I never realised I'd been that popular.

And now, here is my family entering the crematorium to the sound of Robbie Williams's *Angels*: Dad, head up, an unnaturally grim expression on his face, fiercely gripping Mum by the hand; Jess, face lowered to the dull slate floor. And me, of course. And Remus.

We walk to the front, where my burnished oak coffin lies, a large silver-framed head and shoulders photograph of me grinning inanely on top. Mum sobs when she catches sight of it and Dad pulls her to him. Jess keeps her eyes on the ground but Dad looks at my photo, then shakes his head, swallows hard and rips his gaze away. Slipping into the front pew, they take their places, me beside them with Remus at my feet. The sun's streaming through the wall of windows in front of us and I can hear birds singing and calling to each other.

The room is still, apart from a few sniffs and coughs and the shuffling of feet. I swing round to check out who's here. There are relatives, neighbours, friends of my parents, and friends of me and Jess: Iona and Kirsty, and quite a few others. But what gobsmacks me is how many other kids from school there are. And how many teachers. Even the Head's here, sitting in the back row, his lanky frame looking unusually smart in a black suit.

I blink, rub my eyes, and look along the row again at Jess and my parents. And for the millionth time I ask myself surely this can't be happening? Maybe this is all some crazy nightmare? Or a cruel joke that someone's playing on me? I hide my head in my hands. Yeah, it's cruel all right. I can touch my skin, my hair. But I can't touch Jess. Anyone. I look around me. God, I just can't take it in. This all *has* to be a dream.

I hug my sides, blotting out everything except the strains of the organ music. But the constant rhythm of Jess's weeping makes me look up. I stare at her grief-stained eyes, at Mum's drained face, at the determined set of Dad's mouth. No, this is real all right – no mistaking. Suddenly, there's such a jumble of emotions in my mind that I think my head'll explode.

Just as the music stops, a lad skids in beside me. He grins at me, displaying gleaming white teeth; they're a bit crooked but on him they look right.

"Just starting? Didn't want to miss anything," he says to me, flicking back an untidy blond fringe. His eyes are as blue as an early summertime sky and they twinkle as he speaks.

I sit up sharpish. Swivel round to look at him properly. "You talking to me?"

He grins again, his mouth lopsided, his eyes crinkling. "Sure."

"But…but…" I stutter. My mind buzzes. "But I'm…"

"Dead. Yip, I know."

All of a sudden, he stands up. He strides over to the coffin, tucks his shoulder length hair behind his ears, bends down and sticks his head inside. And I mean… inside. I sit and watch his whole head disappear inside the wooden box. And then it pops out again and he straightens up. I can't keep my eyes off him.

"Spitting image," he says, nodding over to Jess as he retakes his seat. "Identical twins, huh? Cool. Your mouth's hanging open, by the way. Not a good look."

"How d'you do that? Who are you?"

If I still had a heart it'd be battering my ribs by now. As it is, my mind's going crazy trying to work out what all this is about.

"Jack," he says, holding out a long, slim-fingered hand. "Jack Muir. Welcome to The Club."

The minister stands up, clears his throat and begins to speak. But my eyes are on the guy. This guy who can stick his head right inside a coffin. My coffin. He sits back, his hands behind his head, long legs sticking out before him.

"What's with the coin in your mouth?"

"Huh?"

"Why d'they put a coin in your mouth?" He nods to the coffin.

"To pay Charon. The ferryman. For passage across the river Styx," I say in a daze.

"Right." He flashes another of those grins. Stretches out his legs. God, they're long. And so skinny – about as skinny as mine. "And the pizza? Book? The other gear?"

I keep staring at him. Who is he? What's he doing here? What did he mean by "Welcome to The Club"? I want to ask him all sorts of questions but the words won't come.

The minister's voice drones on. I can hear folks crying, blowing their noses. It's all so unreal. And here's this guy, appearing from nowhere and scaring the shit out of me.

Organ music soars through the room. Everyone stands up. Remus begins to whimper. I soothe his head and stand up myself.

"Didn't get to Rainbow Bridge then?" the guy says, pointing to Remus.

"Eh?"

"Rainbow Bridge. Where pets go. After they die." He bends over and chucks Remus under his chin. "He won't wanna go, I suppose. Won't wanna leave you. Not now you're stuck here."

All of a sudden a white flame bursts in my mind. I clench my fists. "Stuck? You think I don't know that by now? But why? Why am I still here? What's all this about?"

"It happens sometimes. It's a bit of a drag but you gotta deal with it."

"So what…how?" I gape at him as he looks at me, one eyebrow arched, a self-important smirk lighting up his features. "Right, get up." I grab his shirtsleeve and pull. "You've got some explaining to do."

And unlike with Jess, this time my hands don't go through.

We sit outside on the stone step next to all the floral wreaths and bouquets from previous funerals. I wish I could smell those flowers; I've always loved the fragrance of freshly-cut blossom. The ground is a carpet of rainbow colours and blooms of every size. I see one floral tribute, in the shape of a name. I have one like that too. Suddenly the brilliant colours – pink, yellow, orange, red – blur as one, burn into my brain. I tear my eyes away and look down into my lap, forcing myself to concentrate on my interlinked fingers.

"Feel the cold, does she?" the guy – Jack – says.

"Who?" I say, glancing up.

"Your twin," he says, flexing his bare toes and rubbing his ankles. He's wearing these tan leather sandals that would look just right on a gladiator, and his toenails could do with clipping.

I manage a smile. I can see why he asked, for Jess is still wearing that thick brown woollen jumper. "It's the custom. They wore dull woollen clothes when they were grieving."

"When who were grieving?"

"The Ancient Romans." I shrug. "Mum tried to get her to wear something else for the funeral. But Jess insisted. She's had that jumper on since I... died."

"She must be sweltering." He sits back. "What's with the Roman vibe?"

I sigh. "She's obsessed with that stuff. So am I – well, was. We've both been since primary school – don't know why, we just have. That's why she put my favourite stuff in the coffin. But I never thought she'd take it this far..."

I look out at the grass and the trees swaying in the breeze, thinking of poor Jess.

"It's hit her bad, your sister. She'll be why you're stuck."

"Yeah, yeah, I can see I'm stuck, but where should I be? And what's this to do with Jess?"

"She wants to hold onto you. Can't accept you're dead. And you're trapped here until she does."

He says it so matter of factly that I want to punch him. I press my nails tight into my palms but I feel no pain. Nada. What's going on here? And how can he be so...so casual? Talking about being stuck. What does that mean, exactly? And is that such a bad thing? At least this way me and Jess can still be together – sort of. But then I think of her back there in the crem, how she's been each minute since I drowned. I look up and clock the smug grin on the boy's face.

I pounce on him, curling my fingers to stifle the urge to slap away his smugness. "How come you know about all this?"

I try to hold his gaze, but his face clouds over, an unfathomable expression behind those piercing blue eyes. He looks at the ground and his voice is so soft I can barely catch what he says next. "Cos I'm stuck too. Because of...my mother. She's never got over my death. Kinda couldn't forgive me for dying."

"How did you die? And how long've you been stuck here?"

He flinches, still won't look up. "Thirty years. Three decades of watching. Waiting. Hoping she'll get on with her life. Let me go."

"Thirty years?" I slump back. Jess would be forty-four if she waited that long. Practically ancient.

"Yip. That's what I said." He jumps up. Smiles again. "But it's not that bad. You learn to be patient."

"But what do you *do*?" I say, looking up at him. "What'll *I* do?"

"Hang around. Wait for them to change. To get over it," he says with a shrug.

Hang around for how long? A year? Ten? Thirty, like Jack? And let Jess waste her life?

"I can't do that."

"You don't have much choice," Jack says, with a brittle laugh.

"But you must be able to *do* something. Get in touch with them somehow. Let them know you're all right."

He stares at me, that inscrutable look back in his eyes. "As I said, you learn to be patient. Now come on. We don't wanna miss any more of your funeral, do we?"

He lopes off, the flares on his blue denims flapping against his calves. He looks so real as he strides through the door back into the crem that I quiver. And, not for the first time, I wonder: is this nightmare actually happening?

But when I follow him in and see Jess's stony face as she sits in that front pew, I know for certain. I am dead. This is real. But I also know something else. There's no way I'm allowing Jess to grieve for me for the next thirty years. There's no way I'm letting her ruin her life. I'm dead, nothing can change that. But I can change how she deals with it. And even though the thought of leaving her and going God-knows-where scares me, I know that somehow I have get through to her. Let her know I'm OK. And that it's fine for us both to move on.

I just have to find a way.

The chandeliers suspended from the ceiling of the function room are colossal. Just as well really because it would be right gloomy in here otherwise cos just as we left the crematorium the sun disappeared behind dark rainclouds. Big black clouds that match the way I've been feeling since Jack told me all that stuff about being stuck.

Thirty years he's been here, thirty years of this horrible phantom life. And he says that's what I'm in for unless Jess stops grieving. What a thought! Shaking it from my head, I rub my eyes and look around me.

It seems as if most of the mourners have taken up Dad's invitation to come to the hotel for the funeral tea. The place is crowded. At every dining table there are people in sombre clothing, so with them, and the big fake candles in the overhead lights, it makes me think that this is what a Goth wedding might be like. Because in a weird kind of way it does seem like a celebration; in the crem it was hushed and tense, but here the air is alive with murmured chatter and the occasional burst of laughter. I've never been to a wake before but no way did I think it'd be like this!

And no way was I expecting to meet that boy. I still can't believe I have. Maybe things are looking up. After all, he's been a ghost for ages so there must be loads of stuff he can tell me.

Smiling to myself, I watch a couple of guests go up for more food. Blimey, check that out: pizzas, teensy rectangular sarnies stuffed with all kinds of fillings, bite-sized sausage rolls, individual bannoffi pies and lots and lots of the scrummiest looking scones I've seen – ever. Plus countless bowls of thick clotted cream and others with glistening raspberry jam. There's even a heap of bananas with perfect yellow skins, not pockmarked with those brown spots that I hate so much.

Yeah, so much grub. But I can't have any of it. God, being dead stinks!

"Nice spread," says the boy sharing the window seat with me.

Dragging my eyes from the buffet, I turn to my new friend and smile. "Yeah, too nice."

OK, being dead sucks but at least I'm not on my own any longer.

Out of the corner of my eye I notice Remus mooching around the tables, looking for scraps. He's ignored, of course. I nudge Jack. "Look at my poor dog. This must be so confusing for him because – heck – it sure is for me."

I call Remus over and when he trots up I reward him with a pat on the nose. "It's pants, isn't it, boy?"

Wheeling round to Jack I say, "Doesn't all this just freak you out? Don't you wonder why nobody can see us and yet we're..." I tap a hand, lift a lock of my hair and look up at him. "We're still like skin and bone and stuff. We're breathing and talking. And, here's the thing; when I go like this" – I smooth my cheek – "I can *feel* it, Jack. I can feel the pressure of my hand on my skin. I can even feel this. See, here?" My forefinger brushes along the rough, zigzag scar above my top lip. "Why *is* that?"

As he watches me tracing the outline of my scar, his face is totally impassive and he doesn't utter a sound.

Leaning towards him, I grab his arm. "Heck, I can even feel you. Feel the warmth from your skin through your sleeve." I glance down at Remus. "And it's the same sort of thing with him. It's like we're still alive. I just don't get it."

I hug my knees. "How am I able to just sit here?" I demand. "Why doesn't my bum fall through the seat, the way my hand goes through Mum or Jess?" I frown and press my fingers to the windowsill.

Jack bends over to stare at his sandals, his blond fringe obscuring his features. Geez, is he even listening?

"Come on, help me out here," I snap. "You must've some idea of what's going on. There's so much of this that seems normal – interacting with our environment. Yet...when it comes to real live people, or when you try to move stuff – well, you know what happens, don't you? What's that about?"

Still no response.

I shift my position to dangle my legs over the sill. "See these?" I say. "Solid, yeah? Yours, too. Our bodies seem like they always were, but they aren't."

He sits up.

"We've no sense of smell. Or taste. We aren't able to sleep. Or feel pain. And – whoa!" I yell as a waiter carrying extra buffet food walks past, sending a tingling fire up my calves. Putting a hand to my leg, I look at Jack. "OK maybe we can't feel pain but I sure as heck felt that! And it's happened each time I've tried to touch my family. Why is that?" I close my eyes for a second. "Oh, I don't understand any of this. None of it makes any sense."

"No, I don't reckon it does," he says eventually, in a lazy drawl.

"But doesn't it drive you nuts – being stuck in this crazy limbo?"

He shuffles his feet. "I guess you could call it limbo." He scratches behind his ear, then says, "I don't know for sure what it is, it just is. That's all. You have to learn to accept it."

I look across at Jess sitting between my parents, with a plate of untouched food in front of her, staring into space. "Just like I have to accept what's happening to my sis?" I say, fury suddenly boiling up in me. Then he turns to me and when I look into his eyes, his gentle blue eyes, the madness vanishes.

"Oh, Jack. You should see Jess as she really is: funky, funny – annoying." I falter, casting my mind back to my last day and the fight we had. I heave a huge sigh. "She's enough life in her for the two of us and now she's turned into some sort of zombie."

Jack puts a hand on my shoulder. "It's tough, kid, I know."

I stuff my head in my hands, bite on my bottom lip. This is when the tears would come...if I were alive.

"Why can't I cry, dammit?"

He drops his arm.

"I just want to understand," I say through gritted teeth.

"Look," Jack says, stroking the wavy fur on Remus's back. "I don't know for certain what this is all about but I have a theory."

At last! Some answers!

"When you're alive, you're part of this." He glances around. "The physical world." He leans against the doorframe, opens his hands with a flourish. "You sit, stand, walk, run – that sorta thing." He pauses. "So, when you die, and you're stuck here like us, well, I reckon your mind tells you that you can still do all that stuff because it's what you know, what you're used to. What's familiar, if you like. Maybe it's some sort of coping mechanism, the mind's way of helping us deal with the situation we're in."

"But...the mind? Isn't that just the brain? And my brain – and yours – is dead," I say, playing with the bracelet round my wrist. "Heck, my body's at the crem." I shudder. "I...*euch*..." I screw up my face. "You know what happens there. I won't have a brain any more. And if you were cremated, neither will you."

Remus looks up from my feet. His tail swishes across the plush navy carpet.

"Yip," says Jack. He pauses, as if to gather his thoughts. "The brain is dead. But I think the mind isn't. It's all we've got left." He sounds as if he's picked his words very carefully.

"The mind? Don't you mean the soul?"

He laughs. "The mind *is* the soul, I reckon. It's the part of you that lives on." He knocks on his head. "It's what's up here that counts." He shrugs. "Maybe, the soul isn't even in here, I dunno, but I do know that the thinking part of you lives on."

"Let me get this straight – the mind fools us into thinking we're flesh and blood, even though we're not, yeah?"

"Give the girl a coconut!" Jack says with an exaggerated groan, though he looks at me through amused eyes.

"But at school, in science, they told us that thinking was all to do chemical messages between synapses, or something. So how come we're dead – our brains are dead – and yet we can still think? I don't get it. And that doesn't explain everything. What about when I go to pick things up, or move things, why can't I do that? And what about Remus? What's the deal with dogs? And—"

All of a sudden, I remember what he did in the crem.

"How did you shove your head inside my coffin? Don't tell me you could do stuff like that when you were alive?"

He adjusts his collar. "Er, no."

"Well?"

"So many questions," he says with a sigh. "Dogs first – maybe they have no concept of death, or life for that matter, maybe they just are." He peers at Remus for a sec, smiles at him, then shrugs. "I dunno what the score is with them..." He laughs, bitterly. "Or with us, if I'm being honest. One thing's for sure, you won't find an explanation in any of your school textbooks."

"But the coffin thing, could I do that as well?" Although the very idea of it makes me shudder, at the same time it'd be kinda cool, I guess. "OK, not with a coffin but...could I walk through doors? Or walls? Crikey, how cool would that be!"

"No, you can't," he says. "Or maybe some day. But not now. Not yet."

"Why?"

"I have no idea," he says, staring at the buffet table as if he's trying to memorise every item on it. "All I know is that it was a long time before I could do it. Years. Perhaps it's a time thing. Maybe you need to be dead for a while before—"

"That's rot! I'll bet I can do it right now."

I dash over to the door that the waiter guy's just closed behind him.

"See?" I say jumping to my feet to push myself through it.

Jack glances round just in time to see me thump into the expanse of wood. Blasted door!

He walks over, trying to hold back his laughter. "Told ya."

"Well, at least it didn't hurt."

Well, it did hurt, but only my flippin' pride. Although I'm not telling him that. Anyway, he's still got some answering to do.

"But forget that – what about shifting things about? I've tried to do that – tried to pick up some photos, to let Jess know I'm still around. But I couldn't manage it. Is there a way to do that sort of thing?" I clap my hands. "Cos – wow – if I could then I'd be able to help Jess. Contact her—"

"It's impossible," Jack cuts in. "The dead can't communicate with the living."

"But—"

"But nothing," he says, sharply. I try to hold his gaze but he won't meet my eyes. "It can't be done. Final."

"No, listen to me! Us ghosts, we can communicate with each other so why can't we do the same with those who aren't dead?"

"Maybe that's because ghosts *are* dead," he snaps back at me. Then he writes inverted commas in the air and adds mockingly, "In the same dimension." He rakes his hands through his hair. "Perhaps our minds connect." He tuts. "Oh I dunno." He sighs. "Let's give it a rest for now. OK?" he says, a pleading note in his voice.

Then I hear Jess's words, the ones she said to Mum in the car outside our house on the day I drowned. 'I'll never forgive myself'.

How can I possibly give it a rest?

"Oh, Jack," I whisper, clasping my hands to my chest. "She's so unhappy. I need to help her."

"Look," he says, offering me a weak smile. "I'm sorry, I truly am. I know this is hard on you. Remember I've been there, I know what you're going through right now. I asked myself loads of questions, too. But, believe me, there is no way to contact your sister. None whatsoever."

"There must be."

"You can try all you want, kid – but, trust me, it's not going to happen."

"I have to do something to help her."

"There's nothing you can do." His eyes find the floor. "I'm telling you the truth."

But – is he?

Chapter Nine

Jack sits on the chair by the desk, singing some weird song to himself and tapping the rhythm out on his thighs. He runs his gaze along the stack of books and DVDs on the gold-lacquered bookshelves and, as he does, I smile to myself – another of Dad's DIY disasters, those shelves; must've taken him ten attempts before he got them level.

Abruptly, Jack stops his singing and drumming, looks at me and says, "Pity we couldn't watch one of your movies right now, eh?"

I ignore him.

"Admit it, man, you're bored," he says, and crosses his lanky legs to lean against the chairback. "We've been hanging around here for what, three weeks? Four? You gotta be fed up. I know I sure am."

"I'm fine. I need to be with Jess."

I furl my brows and narrow my eyes at him because somehow that bizarre shirt he's got on really bugs me. What kind of boy wears a shirt like that? I mean, the colour's OK, I guess – a washed out pale blue that matches his jeans – but check the material:

it's crinkly – flippin' 'eck, that's well girlie! Did guys in the seventies think that was cool?

"Why don't we split for a while?" He nods over at Jess lying in the bed opposite me, coiled under the duvet, her dark head almost hidden beneath the covers. "She'll still be here when you get back."

"How many times…? I'm staying put. Got that?" My eyes flicker to the *Ben Hur* poster over my bed as I hoist myself up on one elbow. "Look, who invited you here, anyway?" I jab an index finger in his direction. "Haven't you got somebody of your own to haunt?"

Blimey, that was a bit nasty, Minty. Just cos you're peed off, that doesn't mean you have to take your frustrations out on him.

I'm just about to apologise when the front doorbell rings.

"Come on," Jack persists. "Let's beat it. A change of scene'll do ya good."

"Shh!" I say, as the sound of familiar voices filters up from the downstairs hall. "I'm sure that's Kirsty and Iona." I check to see if Jess realises who's here. "J. Do you hear that? It's our mates."

Jess doesn't budge so, after a second's hesitation, I head out to check.

"Hey, guys," I yell when I reach the landing at the top of the stairs, forgetting for a moment that this isn't some ordinary Saturday and our friends aren't here to collect me and Jess for our usual mooch around Kirkcaldy.

"Am I glad to see you," I say with a full-throttle grin on my face, taking the stairs two at a time. But then reality punches me in the guts, slapping the smile off my gob and I come to a standstill halfway down.

Iona glances up the stairs, then addresses Mum.

"You sure it's OK – us coming round?" Iona says, toying with a wooden coat button as Mum closes the heavy front door behind her. "It's just, everybody at school's asking for Jess. Wondering when she's coming back."

She looks around nervously but her gaze wavers when she comes to the staircase. She frowns and draws in her chin, blinks a few times. Then she gives a little shrug of the head and goes back to Mum.

Why's Iona acting so peculiar? Duh, Minty, think about it – how would you feel in her position?

"It's been so long," she continues, and I can hear the nervousness in her voice. She sneaks a look upstairs again, massages the back of her neck. "And she's not answering our emails. She's ignored all our texts, every one—"

"We don't want to intrude," interrupts Kirsty, her voice ringing out in the silence of the hall as she pulls the blonde strand of hair she's been sucking on out of her mouth. Tiny worry-lines ripple across her brow. "But…"

"You're not intruding at all. In fact," Mum says, fingering a lapel on her beige linen shirt, "I'm glad you came." She moistens her lips, smoothes back her hair and glances up the stairs. "Jess could do with her friends right now." Then she sighs, lowers her voice, and leans against the console table, almost knocking the telephone off its cradle. "I can hardly get her to leave her bedroom. She won't eat or bathe. All she does is stay in her room."

Iona glances at Kirsty, looks at Mum with worried eyes. "That's awful."

Mum adjusts a pearl earring and her eyes film over with moisture. She pulls out a tissue. "Sorry. It's...just..." She splays her hands. Swallows a sob. "It's difficult."

"Oh, Mum," I say, rushing downstairs to comfort her. "I'm here. Please don't cry." I'm right beside her, close enough to smell her perfume, only I can't – I can't smell anything. I step back and almost crash into Kirsty.

"Did the school tell you," she says to Mum, shuffling her feet on the parquet floor. "They're holding a memorial service? In two weeks' time."

"They've asked if we'd say something," Iona adds. She tucks back a tuft of curly dark hair, a perplexed expression on her face. "About Minty."

"Yes. Your Headteacher told me," Mum says, with a quick bob of her head.

"He wondered if Jess would play her sax." Kirsty fiddles with the clasp on her shoulder bag. "But maybe she won't want to."

"She might. For – Minty," Mum says, my name sticking in her throat. "Maybe you could persuade her." She gestures to the stairs. "I'll tell Jess you're here. Make her come down and talk to you. Why don't you wait in the living room?"

When Mum goes to fetch Jess, Kirsty turns to Iona with tears spurting through her fair eyelashes. "Oh, Iona, I'm not sure this is such a good idea. You saw the state J's mum's in. We really shouldn't be here."

"You heard what she said: Jess needs us," Iona says, yet her voice sounds really odd.

"Yes, you're right," Kirsty says, drawing back her shoulders and opening the glass-panelled door leading into the living room. "We have to do this. That's what we came for."

Nevertheless, Iona hangs back.

Kirsty beckons her over. "Well come on then." She plumps down onto the leather sofa, muttering to herself, "Right. This is it. Be cool, yeah? We're here to help. OK?"

With a backward glance, Iona follows Kirsty into the room. Yet when I pass by, ready to settle myself in Dad's armchair, Iona comes to a stop. Her eyes widen until they're like two glossy back marbles.

Geez. What's up with her?

Wiping the remaining tears from her eyes with the back of her hand, Kirsty looks at Iona and says, "I know, I'm nervous, too."

"It's not that. It's…"

"It's what?" I say, moving towards her. But before I do, in a flash of golden fur, Remus bounds into the living room and lunges at me. I lose my balance and my shoulder merges with Iona's, sending sparks of what feels like static electricity through my torso.

Iona shudders. "God! Somebody just walked over my grave." She looks around her. "There's… there's something spooky about this house."

"Don't be silly, you've been here lots of times. It's lovely," Kirsty says.

Iona frowns. "Yeah but, don't you think there's a funny atmosphere today?"

Kirsty's just about to speak when she catches sight of Jess, framed in the doorway, so her answer dissolves on her lips.

Turning round, Iona catches sight of Jess, too. "J," she gasps, grasping the arm of the sofa.

She goes to say something else but, like Kirsty, the words just get stuck – and no wonder. For there Jess stands: that shapeless thick woollen jumper; the mass of matted dark hair; enormous black smudges under her eyes; dirt under her fingernails; shoulders drooped; back bent. But it's the expression on J's white face that does it; she looks so… blank, so out of it, like she's in another world – one that one no-one else holds a passport to.

"I thought I'd know," Jess murmurs. "She was in the sea but I never felt it. She drowned, yet I didn't feel a thing. Why was that?" She swallows a sob. "We had a link. I should've felt something."

"I know. I don't understand it either," I say, stuffing my head in my hands. I look up, hardly able to bear what I'm seeing, hearing. "But please, J, don't blame yourself. You didn't make me fall into the sea."

"She must've been really struggling," she continues. "But I never knew. Why? Why didn't I feel anything? Why didn't I know she was dead? I should've…I could've saved her." She sways, steadies herself on the doorpost.

"J. We're so sorry." Kirsty cries, and puts her arms around her.

Then, tears ruining her black mascara, Iona joins them, and there they remain huddled on the thick shag-pile carpet, with Jess circled in their grasp, their sobs punctuating the silence.

And, although it's another in a series of sad, sad scenes since I died, I can't help wondering – did Iona sense me just now?

I collapse into Dad's chair.

Oh – my – God… Could she be psychic? She must be – look how she reacted when I banged into her. Why else would she have acted like that?

And then Jack appears and I remember what he told me at the funeral tea, what he's been telling me ever since we met.

And I admit to myself … Iona isn't clairvoyant.

She's just upset.

Chapter Ten

The saxophone's sad, sweet music hangs over everyone like an invisible mist. Jess, her dark hair plaited down her back, her eyes closed in concentration, wrings each poignant note from the gleaming instrument, oblivious to anybody else in the hall.

When it's over, she glances up, gives a slight shrug, places the sax on its stand and walks down the steps to her seat. The only sounds are the clip-clop of her heels on the wooden floor and a couple of junior kids crying in the second row.

The Head stands up. He's wearing that same black suit he wore at my cremation. With a quick nod and a half smile, he thanks Jess. He doesn't mention that this is the first time she's played solo in public. Nor does he mention that it's the first time Jess has ever performed without me. But most people know that anyway. What they don't know, however, is that this is the last time Jess will ever play. Although she agreed to do it for my memorial service, she told Mum and Dad that would be that. No more saxophone. She couldn't bear to play again, now that I was gone.

"That was cool." Jack swings round, uncurls his long legs and dangles them over the assembly hall stage.

"She was always way better than me," I smile, watching Jess pick her way to her chair in the front row. "She's mad about the sax. Thinks Tommy Smith's God. Wanted to play in his Youth Jazz Orchestra – we both did. And she's good enough too. She's really talented. But…now…" I watch the empty expression behind Jess's eyes. Look at the saxophone gleaming away, up on its stand, never to be played by her again. I swivel round to Jack. "Now you see why I have to get through to her? She's just going to give up on life otherwise."

"Shh. I wanna hear what they're saying about you."

Iona and Kirsty have moved to the front of the stage. Kirsty goes first. Her small, heart-shaped face is white except for the blotches of blusher high on her cheeks. I can tell she's been crying, for her normally sparkling green eyes are dull and red-rimmed. Even her lovely fair hair looks lifeless; it's as if all the colour has been bleached out of her. What's more upsetting is her voice. Although Kirsty's tiny, she has this big, deep voice, a voice that's got her into tons of trouble in class cos it carries round the room even when she's trying to whisper. But this morning it's as small as she is, thin and tinny, hardly a squeak.

She says some awesome things about me; if I'd been alive I'd have had a lump in my throat. Then she stops. She stares out at the kids, gulps back a sob and steps back to let Iona say her piece.

Iona towers above her, with her glowing mahogany skin, model-girl height and a figure to match. I can see some of the sixth year guys nudging each other. God, their tongues are nearly at their knees! Have they no respect? It's my memorial service, after all.

"Minty," she says. "What can I say? That she was pretty? Yeah, she was, you just have to look at J to see that." She tosses her chocolate brown corkscrew curls and smiles at Jess. "What else can I say? That she was bright? Funny? Talented? Kind? Oh, she was all that. She was pretty kooky too, just like Jess. Sorry, J, but you know that it's true, with all the Roman stuff and that."

Jess nods. A ripple of laughter wafts through the hall.

"And she was special. Just like her sister. A true and loyal friend." She stops and smiles again at Jess. "A bit bossy though, especially when playing board games. And don't start me on that bloomin' Roman game, Monkey in the Middle. You so do not want to go there! Isn't that right, Kirsty? J?"

A smile cracks Kirsty's solemn expression and she nods; yet Jess just gnaws her lip.

"But what set Minty apart was that she was brave." Iona's voice wavers. She takes a deep breath, tugs on her shorter than regulation grey skirt. "She was the bravest person I ever knew. She was never scared to speak her mind. Never held back." A few of the teachers smile to themselves at that. "And she couldn't stand kids being bullied. She always stuck up for them. Yeah, she was brave all right. So it was no surprise that she tried to save Remus that day. She loved that dog. Loved both her dogs – her cat too. She always said she'd do anything for them. And, well, she did, didn't she? I wouldn't have done what she did; I'd have been too scared. Too worried about saving my own neck. Not Minty though, even though she was scared of water. But that was Minty. I'll miss her." She pauses. "We all will," she ends in a whisper.

By now lots of kids are openly crying and quite a few of the teachers too. Even old Stinky Reid, our tyrant of a maths teacher, is sniffing into her hanky. Who'd have thought it?

"Touching," Jack says, jumping off the stage. He thumps me on the back. "They gave you a good send off. You should be pleased."

Pleased? Oh yeah, right. I am just sooo pleased I died. I am so pleased to see my twin shrink away from living. So pleased to watch my mates tearing themselves apart with grief. Not!

"What?" says Jack, looking at my thunderous face.

"It's not a joke, you know."

"Hey! Hey! Cool it, man," Jack laughs, holding his hands up in surrender.

I stamp my foot. "Cool it? When everybody's so upset? Have you seen the state my sister's in? Do you think I enjoy seeing her like this?"

I motion towards Jess, who is looking so white-faced and lost. I want to run to her, tell her a stupid joke, tickle her till she screams with laughter. Make her face flushed with giggling. I want it to be like it was. I close my eyes for a second.

"And I can do nothing to help her. According to you." I yell, snapping my eyes open and glowering at him. "How do you think that makes me feel? Eh?"

Remus starts whimpering. I pat his head, look up at Jack. "Now look what you've done!" I shove past him, my dog circling my heels. "Come on, Remus," I say with a click of my fingers and I join the throng of senior boys who're bunking off early.

Jack catches up with me by the main gate. He lopes over, a suggestion of that lopsided grin on his face. Leaning against the metal railings, he runs a hand through the unruly mess that passes for hair, and looks suddenly serious. "You OK?"

I know if I were alive I'd be crying by now. I never was one for the waterworks; I left that to Kirsty. God, she'd cry at a wasp getting bashed against a car windscreen. But, oh boy, I could do with blubbing right now. At the thought of Jess back there in that hall, swarms of emotions buzz in my mind. I just can't get them out. Express them.

Funny then, how I can feel Jack's arm around me. I look up and sure enough he's slipped an arm across my shoulder.

"Better now?" he asks.

I stare into his face. A ghost's face. The face of a boy who died thirty years ago. And somehow his face becomes Jess's. Mine. And the horror hits me. What if he's right? What if this is it? What if I really am stuck in this limbo for as long as Jess lives? What if I have no other choice but to watch Jess throw her life away? What then?

I'm so busy stretching this idea round and round in my mind that I barely hear the end of day bell ring. Hardly notice the kids spewing out of the building. Don't take much notice of Jess and our mates coming out a while later. Don't really register them until they're only a few feet away.

Then I hear it. In the now empty playground, I hear Iona gasp. My thoughts freeze as I realise that she's standing as if she's nailed to the concrete. Then, slowly, she turns round and looks into the distance, and I notice how dilated the pupils in her dark eyes are, the strange look on her face. And – oh God – she isn't peering into the distance at all, she's looking right at me. I could swear it.

"Iona, come on, J's mum and dad will be bringing the car round soon," Kirsty says, tugging at my friend's sleeve with her slender fingers, as Jess rests her saxophone case on the ground.

"Can't you feel it?" Iona says.

"Feel what?" I ask, skipping in front of her.

Omigod! Omigod! Am I right? Is she looking at me? Does she sense I'm here?

She steps forward and jabs a finger in the air. Actually, she jabs a finger through *me.* Then she lunges forward, into me – through me. Like a sandstorm in a desert, a blisteringly hot wind rushes from my spine to my belly, from the tip of my toes to my head. I gulp and my mind's pierced by a million exploding white hot rods of the thinnest steel. Everything goes blurry.

"Whoa!" says Jack, catching me as I collapse.

"Wha..." I wheeze, staggering upright. "What was that?"

"Take it easy," he says in that smug way of his. "It's always like that at first."

"At first what?" I say, shaking my head to get rid of the uncomfortable sensation in my mind.

"The first few times someone moves through you. Someone alive, that is. Or you move through them." He shrugs. "Same-same really."

"It was like when I tried to touch Jess. And Mum. And..." I say. "But...but a zillion times weirder."

He stands back, tilts his head to the side and folds his arms. "Pretty far out, huh?"

I shake down my body. Try to get back to normal, well – as normal as I can get considering I'm dead.

Iona stands by me, her pupils as huge as satellite dishes, hands clasped to her breastbone. Her glowing complexion is not so glowing now and it's definitely several shades lighter than usual. She stands between Jess and Kirsty, like a beautiful bronze statue.

I look at her. "Iona? Can you see me?" And I turn to Jack. "She *can*."

He stares at Iona and his body tenses.

"I could sense someone behind me," Iona says, to Jess and Kirsty. "That's why I turned round. But when I looked there wasn't anybody there." She rubs the back of her neck. "It was the weirdest feeling."

"What are you on about?" Kirsty says, glancing at Jess.

Iona shudders. "Like there was a disturbance in the air. I don't know really. I thought I could feel it during the memorial service. No, I'm sure I did." She looks to Kirsty. "It's the same feeling I had in Jess's house. Remember I told you then something weird was going on," she says, the words tumbling one over the other.

"Oh, Iona," Kirsty says, putting her hand on Iona's arm. "Stop fooling around. Let's go, come on." And she takes a step towards the school gates.

"At my house?" Jess says, pushing Kirsty's arm away and staring at Iona. "What about my house?"

Iona looks at her. "Sorry, I'm not trying to scare you, but I was a bit spooked. I told Kirsty that I—"

"Spooked?" Jess says. "Why?"

"It was like someone was watching us. Listening. The hairs stood up on the back of my neck." Iona gnaws at her top lip. "Honestly, I'm not trying to scare you but…well, have you noticed anything lately?" She wrings her hands together. "Anything unnerving? Like—"

"Don't be ridiculous," Kirsty says.

"You think there's a ghost? Are you telling me my house is haunted?" Jess says. Then she takes in a huge gulp of air and her eyes narrow. "Oh I get it! You think it's Minty, don't you?"

"Could it be? You were so close…"

Jess claps her hands to her ears. "Don't, Iona. I so do not want to hear this!" Her screech pierces the still of the playground, causing a pair of first years, slouching by the gate, to glance over.

Kirsty moves to comfort Jess but she shoves her off and screams at Iona, "Stop it! Are you trying to drive me crazy? Minty's dead. Do you think she's been trying to make contact with you?" She waves a hand above her, eyes blazing. "Is that what this big act's all about? Hmm? Well if she *was* trying to make contact it'd be with me, not you. She was my twin, not yours. You got that?" she shouts and, snatching her saxophone case off the ground, she hares off.

"Oh, Iona. What d'ya have to say that for? You've upset her. Hasn't she got enough to deal with?" Kirsty sighs, rolling her eyes.

Iona watches Jess stride through the school gates, past the first-year pair who have stopped their blathering to see what's going on. "But I felt something. I did..."

Kirsty tuts, swivels on her heels and runs to catch up with Jess, leaving Iona standing there, open-mouthed.

I look at Jess's retreating back. Begin to race after her, Remus thundering after me. Then I stop. Look at Iona. Then back to J. I want to go after Jess, I really do, but I need to know for sure whether Iona can really feel me, hear me. I have to. So, I let my sister go. And follow my friend.

Chapter Eleven

Iona sits on the peach and brown striped bedspread, her knees scrunched under her chin, her dark curtain of curly hair tumbling over her face. The daylight is fading, and the orange glow from the streetlamps casts murky shadows around the cavernous bedroom. She sighs, shakes her curls and gets up. With a couple of long-legged strides, she crosses to the wooden shelves by the door and picks up a large zany-patterned silvery-pink box.

Placing the box on her bedside table, she rummages inside and extracts four cream pillar candles and a book of matches. One by one she lights the candles and arranges them round the room, then she slips the box back on the shelf.

She pads back, props the pillows against the pine headboard, climbs onto the double bed and leans back, legs crossed, eyes closed, fingers outstretched, her wrists turned to the ceiling as she begins to meditate.

"Ohm, ohm," she chants, on and on in such a pure, clear tone I just stand where I am by the window and stare.

Neither me nor Jack say anything until Remus starts running up and down, yelping.

The spell is broken.

"Oh man." Jack whistles through his teeth. "She's one of those hippy chicks. Meditating, huh? Never did see the point of that."

"Maybe she thinks it'll help get through to me. You know – chill her head," I say, crouching down to calm Remus.

"Yeah well, she's kidding herself. And so are you."

He leaps up, makes for the door. Unless I can get him to change his mind, Jack will be out of here, double-quick.

"Come on," he snaps. "This is a waste of time. We've been here long enough."

"No! Wait!" I flick a look in Iona's direction, looking for some sign that she knows I'm around.

"What for?" He stops at the gap in the door and swings round to me. "You've yelled at her. Screamed at her. Jumped up and down. Stamped your feet. Sat here in this dumb room for hours," he says, counting each one off on his fingers. "You've done it all. I told ya, it won't work. She can't see you. Never will."

"But what about today? At the service? She sensed I was there. She *knew* I was. And that time in my house? What about that?"

Jack's eyes drill into mine. His voice is harsh, scathing. "Get real, kid. She did *not.* She was doing it for the attention. Chicks like that need it—"

"Chicks like what?"

"Drama queens. Face it, man, your friend Iona here was doing it purely for attention. Nothing else to it."

"You think all that was just to get attention? No way! She *did* know I was there. She *felt* me. Besides, I know Iona – she's not like that. She's *never* attention-seeking."

Jack spits out a laugh. "She's a nice enough gal, I'll give you that. But not attention-seeking? That isn't how I see it. Think of her giving that eulogy. What was she like! She was lapping it up. Standing there in her skimpy skirt all sad and beautiful, speaking in that sexy voice, all eyes on her. She loved it, man."

"But the playground! What about that?"

He sniggers. "She was milking it. Hooked on the attention."

"You've got Iona all wrong," I say, distracted for a second by the dream-catcher spinning hypnotically above her bed. I drag my eyes away and scowl at Jack. "Why're you being so mean?"

"Why're you being so thick?" He turns his gaze back to Iona, stares at her as he slowly strokes his cupid's bow with an index finger. "I've seen her type before."

"What's that supposed to mean?"

"Your pal reminds me of a girl I knew. She was gorgeous, too. Blonde, though. A real looker. And man, did she know it." He frowns. Glances back at Iona. "Now, come on, let's get outta here." He nods towards the door. "You coming, or what?"

Right at that moment, the chanting stops. Iona gives a little grunt, wiggles her shoulders, gets up, has a stretch and walks to the door, as if to close it. But then she pauses, her fingertips on the brass handle. Now I'm standing right by her. Right by her side, so close I could blow into her ear. So I do. Don't ask why. I just do. I blow as hard as I can.

Jack explodes with laughter. "What d'ya think that'll do? You think she can feel you doing that? Oh boy, oh boy."

I glare at him. "Shut up. Just shut up." Then I bellow at Iona, "For God's sake, it's Minty! Come on, Iona, what you playing at – you must know I'm here. Please, you've flippin' got to."

But she doesn't.

"Iona, see. It's me." I reach up and peer into her eyes. Once, twice, three times, I snap my fingers. Snap them right under her nose.

It doesn't make any difference.

Then, slowly, she massages her neck and stares round her blankly, like a blind person checking out a new environment.

Yes! That's more like it, Iona!

"See that?" I say to Jack, my mouth split in a grin. "She's reacting to me. Look."

He frowns.

Hah, Jack! You've got this contact thing all wrong! Just look at my friend, I'm getting through to her.

But when I turn back to Iona she's yawning, pushing back her hair and rubbing her brow, looking one hundred per cent knackered, just like any regular girl who's had such an emotional day.

Yet she did act funny when I yelled at her. Didn't she?

So, looking for an indication that I'm right – however small – I watch her pad over to her night light and switch it on. I scrutinise her as she goes round the room snuffing out the candles. Wandering to the window, she glances out, draws down the roller blind, then goes back and sits on the bed. She leans over, opens the top drawer of the bedside table and takes out the latest copy of *Cosmopolitan*, which she flicks open and begins to read.

Aw, who am I kiddin'? There *are* no signs…there never were. Just because you want something badly enough, it doesn't make it true.

"Come on," Jack says, catching my hand.

"But—"

The frown has faded from his face. He looks at Iona. Then he turns to me and smiles: a gentle smile, an understanding smile, a smile that tells me that's he's been there. Been there all those years ago, when he died. Of course, he'll have tried everything too. To communicate – get through to the living.

"Time to go," Jack says.

Iona's engrossed, lost in a world of the latest fashions, of make up and glamour, and how to bag yourself a hot date. The real world, one I'll never ever be a part of again. So, I might as well face it, I can jump up and down as much as I want to, I can scream and howl and beg to be heard, to be seen, but I'm dead. I am dead and there's nothing I can do about it. And, watching Iona as she thumbs through that friggin' magazine, I know deep inside that there's nothing I can do to get through to her, to make her realise I'm still around.

And, with a lightening flash of clarity, I understand now that goes for Jess too.

Chapter Twelve

Head down, eyes glued to the pavement, I slouch along the dimly-lit street, keen to get back to my twin, wishing that we'd never followed Iona home after the memorial service this afternoon. It's late, past midnight for sure, and we're the only ones about, except we're not actually here, are we? We're not really here at all.

I sneak a peek at Jack with his shiny blond locks; look down at Remus running around sniffing the ground as usual. Why's Rem doing that – can he still smell things? If he can, why can't I? And look at him, he looks so real…so solid. Jack too.

Heck, they seem so *normal.* I can't get my head around that: why things seem just as they always were…but they aren't.

"You OK?"

With a start, I glance up. Even in the shadows I can see the questioning look on Jack's face.

I smile, but it's not much of a smile. "I'm fine. Just thinking."

"Yip. Guess you've a lot to think about." He flicks a thumb over one shoulder. "Sorry. It wasn't cool, what I said about your pal."

"Yeah, well."

I stop, wave my hands about and nod to the rows of houses with their tidy front gardens, at the cars parked in their drives.

"I was just thinking how normal this all seems," I say. "I mean, here we are, in the street, in my neighbourhood, my house only minutes away. OK, it's like way too late for me to be out, but apart from that it's so – ordinary. And. And, I feel so real. The pavement feels rock-hard under my feet, I can hear that telly blaring."

I gesture to the semi across the road where the loud din of some TV programme pours through a half-open window.

"Bet their neighbours love them," Jack says.

We exchange a smile.

From far off comes the sound of some saddo doing his boy racer bit along the high street. A few doors down, a dog barks. Remus pricks up his ears and, for a moment, I wish I could be like him – just exist in our phantom world without really questioning it.

"Blimey, Jack," I say, with a sigh. "I really thought Iona could see me. I really, really thought she could help me to get through to Jess. But it's hopeless, it's friggin' hopeless. You're right – the dead can't communicate with the living. I realise that now. I was clutching at thin air thinking that Iona could see me, but Iona hadn't a clue we were in that bedroom, she hadn't a friggin' Scooby."

He stops walking, looks at me, licks his lips and blinks. "This isn't *Ghost*. No one's gonna help ya communicate with Jess—"

"*Ghost*?" I frown at him. "The movie? How do you know about that? It hadn't been made when you died."

Jack pulls a face. "Gee, man! I *have* been hanging out around here for the last thirty years." He shrugs, smiles. "I've seen it at my old dear's. She bought the video when it came out. Watched it once, then stuffed it in a cupboard somewhere." He sighs, takes his hand from my shoulder and kneads his neck.

A middle-aged man with an enormous belly staggers past us, and clutches at the fence of the house we're standing by. Mumbling to himself, he totters to the gate, yanks it open then closes it behind him with a thud and weaves his unsteady way up the garden path. When he stops at his front door to hunt for his key he's swaying so much it makes me giggle.

"She isn't a big film-buff," Jack continues. "Not like me and the old guy. We used to go to the local fleapit every Saturday. Loved it." He slaps his thigh. Grins. "And I still like going the cinema, especially the Odeon in Duloch Park. Well, gotta do something to pass the time." He winks at me. "But now I just slip in. Watch anything I want. Don't pay a bean."

I hear the man cursing to himself and then the sound of his door banging shut.

"Yeah, well, maybe this isn't *Ghost* but...Jack, I can't help thinking back to the playground this afternoon. Iona was so insistent. I totally thought she could feel me there."

"She couldn't, though." He shuffles his feet. Looks away. "And she didn't this evening."

"But – maybe she was just tired. Maybe the memorial service got to her. Stopped her from—"

Suddenly, with a screeching yowl, a cat darts out from under the gate and scoots in front of us, the hairs on its jet-black fur standing on end, until it gets to Remus. Then it whips round to face him, arches its back and lets out a fierce hiss, but my dog just wags his tail and trots towards it.

"Oh Remus," I say laughing, as I move towards him. "It's not Octavius." Over my shoulder, I grin at Jack. "He must think it's our cat." For a second, I forget that we're dead and try to pull my dog away from what I'm sure will be a massive swipe from the cat's claws. "Here, boy."

As I bend over to grab the dog's collar, I smile at the moggy, will it to calm down. "Hey, puss," I murmur, reaching out a hand. "Don't worry about Remus. He won't chase you or anything."

All at once, the poor wee animal goes berserk, spitting and meowing and arching its back even further. Then, with a childlike whimper, it gallops off down the street.

"What the...?" I jump back, staring at the cat flying into the night, then turn to Jack. "Omigod, that cat knew Remus was there. That I was, too!"

But Jack's nowhere to be seen.

Like the cat, he's disappeared.

Chapter Thirteen

For the next ten minutes or so, I run up and down the deserted streets searching for Jack.

Still no sign of him. Where *is* he? He can't have got far. Why did he disappear like that? What did I do, or say? Or is he just a great big scaredy and gets freaked out by cats? And what about that cat? What was going on there? It saw us. I'm sure. Or felt us near. So, there *is* some way of getting through. Is there?

Like a litter of yapping pups, the questions snap at my thoughts.

And what was all that crap I told Jack about feeling normal? Did I really say it? That is what I said, isn't it? Then, how come I don't feel cold – it's the dead of night, for Jupiter's sake. How come I'm not hungry? Or tired. Or—

"What kept ya?"

I swing round. Jack's standing there, leaning against the window of The Golden Fry, head to the side, arms folded, eyebrows arched, looking like Mr Cool himself. I've got a good mind to scratch his bloomin' eyes out for going off and leaving me the way he did.

"Get lost, then?" he says with a laugh as he offers a hand for Remus to lick.

I chuck him a filthy look. "What you doing jumping out on me like that? And what's with the disappearing act?"

"What disappearing act?" he says.

Geez, he's one slippery eel; he can't meet my eyes. His gaze settles on Remus for a while, then he glances up and there's something behind those baby blues of his that I just can't read. But I don't have time for this right now – I have to go home to Jess.

Stuff Jack. Who needs him?

Clicking my tongue, I stride off.

"Kid! Wait!" he shouts, catching up. He backs in front of me. I try to swerve round him but wherever I move, he's there.

"Leave me alone," I say, skirting round a bus shelter.

"Look," he says, "I'm sorry I split like that. But..." He looks around him. "I, er, needed – need – to, er, be somewhere. See someone."

"Oh yeah?" I say, my voice loaded with sarcasm. "So why d'you come back then? Get scared out on the streets all on your own? Saw another cat, did you?"

I watch a lorry trundle past and turn right at the mini-roundabout.

"Look, Minty, I said I was sorry."

I come to a halt. "That's the first time you've called me that," I say, my voice as sad as I'm suddenly feeling.

"What?"

I bend down to nuzzle Remus's neck. "Minty. It's kinda nice. Normal. As if we're friends."

"What ya talking about?" He grins at me. "We are friends."

"Are we?" I say, straightening up. "OK then, answer me this – why did that cat go mental back there? Why did it act as if it saw me? Did it see me? Eh? And why did you run out on me like that?"

Jack drops his gaze; shuffles his feet. Lifts his shoulders a fraction, releases them again. "I got things I need to do."

I cross my arms in front of me. This I've got to hear. "What?"

He traces a line on the paving stones with his right foot. He seems to find the pavement fascinating all of a sudden. "Just things. Bit of this. Bit of that."

"Just what the heck does that mean?" I snap, fury rising inside me. "Well?" He ignores me. "Look at me, for God's sake."

He keeps his eyes to the ground. Finally, he stares up through his fringe.

A siren pierces the quiet of the night and an ambulance whizzes past.

I sigh. "If we *are* friends then we've got to be honest with each other. So, come on, tell me what you're on about. Who's this someone you need to see?"

Jack slumps against a lamppost. "My old lady."

"Your mother?"

He nods and casts his eyes back to the ground. "She's sick. Dying, I guess."

"So why're you here? Why aren't you with her?"

He throws his head back, stares into the neon-lit sky. When he speaks, there's none of the cockiness I've come to expect from him. Deep lines are etched in his brow.

"I dunno. I wanna be. But—" All at once, his shoulders hitch up in a half-hearted kind of shrug and his face falls. When he sucks at his lips, he's like a little kid on his first day at school.

"You're scared, aren't you?" I reach out to him. "Do you want…"

No! You can't, Minty. You have to get back to Jess. I grab my hand back. Then I catch the sad droop of his eyes. "Would you like me to come with you?"

There! I've said it.

He gazes at me for a while. Then he smiles. "Yip. Why not?"

Jack halts at the huge wrought iron gates pulled back against the fringes of the wide drive. A car passes on the road, its headlights slicing through the dark and illuminating a brass plaque on the high stone wall to the right of the driveway.

Inchgauldry, the plaque says.

"We're here," Jack says, hopping from foot to foot but making no move to walk on.

He takes a step, hesitates, then with a gruff, "Let's go," begins trudging up the long gravel drive, me and Remus hurrying after him.

We walk on. Bushes and tall trees loom up on either side, until we come to what seems to be a huge park, and there, ahead, sits an enormous three-storey house with a fancy porch for a front door, a massive conservatory to the left and a separate garage big enough for four or five cars. The place is in darkness except for a light at a window upstairs and one filtering through the triangular window above the entrance door. A dark four-wheel-drive is parked at the foot of the short flight of steps leading up to the entrance.

Jack hangs back by a rose bed steeped in moonlight and stares up at the first floor windows, but he doesn't speak. Somewhere in the trees, an owl hoots, breaking the silence.

"This is your parents' house?" I say, walking up to him.

He drops his head. Examines his sandals. "My mother's." He glances up at me, turns away. "My old man's dead."

"But…it's flippin' gigantic! She must be loaded."

Wait a minute – did he just say his dad's dead?

"Yip. She has it all. Everything money can buy," he says, with a huge sigh.

"Except you," I whisper, chew my lip. "Sorry about your dad."

He nods.

The huge front door creaks open and, through the burst of light that floods from the entrance hall, there comes a slim, smartly dressed woman and a tall middle-aged guy carrying a briefcase. They walk down the steps, murmuring to each other, and stop at the car to continue their conversation.

As the man unlocks the car – a Range Rover – Jack grabs my hand. "Let's go."

I hang back, shake my head, amazed that the Jack I know once lived in a place like this.

"I never took you for a posh boy – the way you talk and everything."

But Jack's not listening. He pulls me up the steps and in through the open door.

Inside, the house is even grander than I imagined. The front hallway is really impressive with loads of rooms leading off it and a sweeping staircase to the next floor. The walls are decorated with this powder blue silky wallpaper, there's fancy gold cornicing with cherubs and everything, and there's these ancient looking paintings of geezers in weird clothes. But what really grabs me is this gigantic crystal chandelier that hangs from the high ceiling. Wow! I wouldn't want to have to dust that!

I whistle, forgetting for a moment why we're here. "You royalty or something?"

But Jack's already half-way up the stairs. Remus and I bound after him and follow him along a long corridor until we come to a door that's slightly ajar. Jack stops, shoots me a nervous look, and slips in.

It's a big, big room – a bedroom that's six times bigger than mine. A high window with fussy floral curtains looks onto the flower beds and rolling lawn, and there's a large white fireplace made of marble or something. More of those old-fashioned paintings break up the pink striped wallpaper and the room is crammed with cream-painted wooden furniture.

I wouldn't want to live in here – no way – it'd be like living in a museum. I grimace, thinking of the visit to the museum in Edinburgh that I never got to go on.

"Oh!" I cry as I suddenly notice the motionless figure laid out on the bed.

"Mother," Jack whispers.

She's wearing a mask over her face so I can't get a good look at her features, but I know that Jack's mum's in a bad way. As well as the drip she's attached to, there're all these wires and stuff stuck to her wizened skin, and they're hooked up to this scary machine thing. With every shallow breath she takes, it rasps like some mechanised Darth Vader.

His mother has company: a small, tubby woman, kinda ancient looking, who's hunched over the bed stroking the sick old lady's pale hand. Where the skin on Jack's mum's hand is so thin that I can see the blue blood in her veins, the other lady's is plump and pink and splashed with big brown blotches.

"Who's she?" I say, pointing to the stranger, trying to speak as quietly as possible.

"You don't have to do that – whisper. She can't hear you," Jack says, a smile flitting across his mouth but vanishing just as quickly.

I pull a sheepish face.

"Mrs Fuller, the housekeeper," he says. "Not that she does much housekeeping now. She's too old and there's other staff to do that. But my old dear keeps her on. Mrs F's been here since before I was born. Her husband was the odd-job man. Died five years ago."

"Wow!" I blurt out, glancing at the chubby woman, half expecting her to tell me to shush. "Your mum has servants? You really are royalty, aren't you?"

Jack doesn't reply but just keeps his gaze fixed on the bed.

The housekeeper budges round in her chair then, leaning heavily on the bedside table, struggles up and shuffles to the window to peer down at the drive.

"This could take a while," Jack says, sinking into the vacant seat.

The contraptions by the bed continue to beep, huff and wheeze. Suddenly the one with the drip attached utters a stuttering whine that causes me to jump.

Omigod – is she dying? Please don't die! Omigod, what if she does? I don't want to see that. My gaze darts to Jack, to his mum, to the machine, the housekeeper. Don't let her die, don't let her die, don't let her die…

And then the machine rights itself, the high-pitched drone disappears and it starts to beep like before.

Phew.

"Shouldn't she be in hospital, or something?" I ask, squinting uncertainly at the machinery.

"She's got everything she needs here." Jack stares at his mum, at the equipment. His tense body's as still as his mother's, and the hoarseness in his voice mimics the breathing machine. "Like you said, she's loaded. Money talks."

We sit for a while, neither of us saying anything – just us two, plus the old housekeeper. And, as I listen to every artificial breath that Jack's mum takes, it strikes me – where is everyone? Where's the rest of Jack's family?

"Jack? Why aren't the others here yet? Surely they should be here, too?"

"What others?" he says, his eyes not leaving his mum's face.

"Your sister? Brother?"

"There's no one else. Only me," he says in a tone that's hard to work out. I notice then that his hands are shaking, that even though he's not flesh and blood he seems pale and drawn.

God, what a selfish cow I am! Why have I never asked him this before? And how must he be feeling right now with his mum so sick and all?

"Look, Minty. Why don't you go back? I know you wanna." He smoothes a straggly clump of hair from his eyes. He tries to smile but his lips twist like someone who's about to cry. "I'll hang out here awhile. Hitch up with you later."

"No, I should stay with you," I say, though I'm thinking of Jess lying on her bed at home.

"It's OK. I'm cool. Look, she's not gonna die yet," he says, looking down at his mother. "Else she'd have…" He rubs the flat of his hands over his face, sighs, and gestures to the door. "Go back to Jess."

I really should stay. What if his mother *does* die? Won't he need me then?

"Are you sure?" I say, despite myself.

He flashes me a smile. I wonder how much effort it took him to do that.

"No worries," he says. "You go, I'll catch you later."

Chapter Fourteen

By the time I arrive in my back garden, it's almost light.

As I recline on one of the wooden steamer chairs, thinking at first of Jack and his mum, then wondering how long it'll be until I get inside the house, the back door squeaks open and Dad appears, carrying a sack of rubbish. He's in his half-mast jammie bottoms and the scabby denim slippers he will insist on wearing around the house. His thinning brown hair's standing on end in wispy tufts like he hasn't combed it for a fortnight, which is so, so weird cos Dad is the world's vainest man about his barnet – or what's left of it – even at this hour of the morning.

Scratching his stubbly chin, he stifles a yawn and, with another quick scratch, ambles down the three steps to the black plastic wheelie bin.

In a flash, I spring up off the chair, whip across the back garden and stop right under Dad's nose. He's standing by the bin, his hand on the lid handle, poised to lift it. His face has a faraway expression and I gasp at the huge black blotches under his greeny-brown eyes; I reckon he didn't get any more sleep last night than I did.

Hah! Me get some sleep? I wish!

By now, I'm so close to Dad I can see the hairs sprouting from his nostrils. Oh my, things are bad cos Mum can't stand bushy nostrils. At the first sight of any hair she nags him to use his nasal hair trimmer.

Our moggie, Octavius, appears at the back door. He stretches his neck, rubs it against the wooden door frame and peers out into the garden. With a thumping tail and a bark of delight, Remus bounds over to him and stops at the bottom step, panting and slobbering. Octavius takes one look in his direction, straightens his back, splays his paws and gives out this strangled high-pitched cry that snaps Dad out of his daydream.

"Octavius?" he says, dropping the rubbish bag onto the paving stones. "Are you OK?"

But Octavius isn't OK. The poor thing's completely freaked out. Why is that? How come he can see Remus now but he couldn't before? That's like beyond weird.

With an ear-splitting meow, Octavius turns on his paws and darts back into the house with Remus charging after him.

Shaking his head in puzzlement, Dad tips the rubbish into the bin, slaps down the lid and stands there. He closes his eyes. Breathes in. He sways a little and grabs the bin to steady himself. His hands clasp it so tightly it's as though he's terrified he'd fall over if he let go.

He looks so sad. So empty and sad.

"Dad?"

I know he won't hear me but I can't help it, I need to do it, I have to comfort him.

"Dad. It's me. Minty."

My voice is hardly more than a whisper but the morning is so still and clear you could almost hear pollen fall. And then I do it. I do it because I can't do anything else: I just have to try and touch him – to console him. I stretch out a hand. But, before I make contact, he spins round and strides back into the kitchen.

I'm just skipping up the steps after him when he shuts the door.

"Blast! Now what do I do?" I say, frowning.

Yet as I finger the jagged line of the scar above my lips something Jack said last night comes back to me. *This isn't Ghost ...*

"I've watched that movie," I say to myself, scratching an ear as I remember Mum telling me and J how she had the hots for that Patrick Swayze bloke who played the ghost. Yeah, that was way too much information, Mum!

"What was that Swayze guy's character called?" I mutter. "Yeah, Sam, that's it. And wasn't Sam stuck, like me?"

No one's gonna help ya communicate with Jess...

But he got through to his wife, didn't he?

I whack my forehead. "You Muppet, Minty, you've been acting like a total wuss. Time to get a grip. Be like Sam – take control, instead of floating round here feeling sorry for yourself."

Then I recall the failures I've had trying to communicate with Jess – like that time with the photos – and I think to myself, what's the point? But hey, wait a friggin' second…

I cast my mind back to Jack popping his head inside my coffin and I remember the times when *my* body moved through things – like when my hand dived down into the car seat as I went to pick up that banana skin. Or how my fingers passed through that snap Jess had been looking at.

"Something doesn't add up," I mutter, as I tuck and re-tuck a strand of hair behind my ears.

And as I play about with my hair I'm reminded of how, when I question him, Jack sometimes won't look at me, how he shuffles his feet. And more of his words come back to me – *I'm telling you the truth.* And I remember him asking me to trust him. It's just what I've done, isn't it? But should I? After all, I hardly know the guy.

Mulling this over, I climb to the top step and tentatively touch the kitchen door. "According to him, I can't walk through this," I say to myself." But if my hand can pass through other stuff what's to stop it going through this?"

I press my palm in as hard as I can. Yet though I press, press and press again, my hand stays right where it is.

"Dang it!" I say, shaking my fists in frustration. "There must be a way to do this. Think, Minty, think."

Of course – think! That's it, use your mind! Jack said it's all we have left, that the thinking part of us lives on. Could I just think myself through it? OK it isn't rational but – I snort – nothing is these days.

So, screwing up my eyes and really staring at the door, in a slow steady voice I talk myself through it. Perhaps it helps to talk out loud? I don't know, but I do it anyway.

"Visualise. Focus your mind on putting your hand in through the wood, out to the other side. You can do this."

My head's in a flurry, trying to take in what I'm telling myself. For a moment I remember how I reacted when Iona walked through me. Will this feel the same? Even the thought of it makes me wince.

But so what if it does feel the same? It'll pass. So, keep cool, Minty. Don't freak.

"Easy, easy," I say. "Let your mind meld into the moment." My voice is automatic, hypnotic. Willing me on. Coaxing me. But there's a storm in my head. A whirling, whooshing hurricane of thoughts. Thoughts that scream and shout and tell me this isn't possible.

"Come on. Focus on your hands. Focus on the door."

The storm in my head dies. Where there was fuzziness, there is now calm.

As my mind finally locks on to what I have to do, the early morning sounds melt away. Until there's only the door. And me.

I imagine my body passing through it and a tingling stream of fire spreads up my fingers, seeps into my hands. I watch mesmerised as they disappear into the wood. As I step forward and thrust my forearms in through the door, the air about me crackles and snaps with energy. I plunge further. My arms are on fire. My shoulders burn. My chest is filled with flame. There's a roaring wind in my head. I'm almost overwhelmed by the sensations rippling throughout me. But my mind urges me on.

And then.

I'm through.

On the other side.

In the kitchen, in a heap on the floor, tingling, shivering, laughing.

"Holy sh—" I whisper through the buzzing in my head, my brain exploding with what I've done. "I did it!"

I close my eyes to let the weirdness subside, but all of a sudden I feel Remus by my side. I look up and he's standing right by me.

"Remus?"

I haul myself up and look over his shoulder at the big, hard mass of oak that took me such determination to pass through.

"How did you do that? Oh forget it, come here boy," I say, slapping my thighs for his attention, hysterical laughter erupting from me. "Hey, Remus, aren't we clever?"

He comes over and licks my face and I smile at him, big time, and tickle him under the chin.

"And Jack said it was impossible. Why d'you think he said that, boy? Why did he lie?" I snuggle into his rough coat and glance at the door – the door that Jack said I couldn't walk through. The smile slips. "Cos he did lie, didn't he?"

Chewing on that thought, I slump against a kitchen cupboard, going over and over every little thing Jack's told me since we met. And I ask myself: what else has he been lying about?

I spend so long inside my head, debating the Jack thing that it's a while before I become aware of my surroundings again. It's the sound of running water that does it. I look up and clap eyes on Mum at the Belfast sink, filling the kettle. With her sallow skin and baggy eyes, she doesn't look any better than Dad did back in the garden, and the sight sends chills through my brain.

"Have you seen her this morning?" Dad asks her as he shoves a fresh black bag into the rubbish bin.

I can't get used to the fact that I can earwig my parents' conversations but I kinda can't help myself from doing it, so I scramble onto my feet and hover by the washing machine.

"Yes," Mum says softly, setting the kettle on its cradle and snapping on the switch.

Dad collapses onto a chair. Puts his hands to his face. "Is she still clutching that...that thing?" He spits the last word out as if he loathes it.

"Yes, yes she is," Mum says, tightening the tie on her thin cotton robe and going over to sit beside him.

Dad places his hands on the table, drums a manic tune with his fingertips. Jerks back. "It's not right, Mary. It's just not right. To behave…like that." Again, he spits out the last word, his voice laced with revulsion.

"It's little more than two months since it happened. Give her time, Geoff."

"Time?" explodes Dad. "Give her time? How much time? How much?"

"It's early days," Mum says, tracing an invisible pattern on the table.

"God, Mary, you sound like a bloody counsellor!" He jumps up, pulls at his hair. Thumps a hand with a fist. "So we're supposed to like the fact that she sleeps with it? We're supposed to accept that? It's every night for Christ's sakes."

Why's he mad at Jess? What's she done? Surely he's not still harking on about her leaving me to go for help. This is my fault, not her's.

"Geoff. Please." Mum leans across and winds her arms around Dad's neck. She rubs the back of his head and looks up into his eyes. "Don't wind yourself up like this."

Dad wrestles himself from her grip. "God, Mary, take a reality check. Our daughter, the only daughter we have left…" Mum gasps. Dad glowers at her. "First she refuses to go to school. Then when she does, she comes in every afternoon, goes up to her room and lies there day after day, night after night. With…that thing."

Mum stands back, catches her breath. Utters a sob. "That thing is all that remains of Minty."

"Mary, love, I'm sorry, so, so sorry," Dad says, reaching out to her, his anger becoming a whisper. "It's just…when was the last time Jess showered? Or had a bath? Brushed her teeth? And as for that… that…jumper… God, Mary, what's happening to our little girl? It's as if we've lost Jess, too."

Mum bites her lip. "It's Jess's way of coping, Geoff. We have to respect that."

Dad closes his eyes. Puts a hand to his brow, drops it to his chest. "But for how long?" He sighs. "Tell me that."

"For as long as it takes," Mum says.

He draws in breath. Swallows. "It's just…I don't know how to deal with any of this." He looks at her, his eyes pleading with her to understand. "Look at me, I haven't even shed a tear for Minty – my own child. I wish I could, but I can't. What sort of man does that make me? God help me, I hardly recognise myself any more."

Dad holds out his hands to her. With a sob, she goes to him. They stand there, huddled together with the early morning sun filtering through the closed Venetian blinds. There's not a sound in the kitchen apart from the buzzing of the fridge freezer, the kettle coming to the boil and Mum's muffled weeping.

And somehow, being able to walk through a blasted door doesn't seem all that helpful any more.

Chapter Fifteen

That's the thing about being dead: you get to see what people are really like. I mean *really* like – and that includes your parents. When I was alive my mum and dad were so cool about everything; nothing much got to them, not even when Jess used to get the hump. But now, seeing stuff like that, back there in the kitchen. Geez...

And Jess, what am I going to do about Jess? What *can* I do about her? I mean, look at her, lying there sound asleep in her bed. Dad's right – she's still wearing that stupid woolly jumper. She looks so pathetic, so unlike Jess that I can hardly bear to look at her. It really does my head in.

All of a sudden, she lets out a piggy snore, such a typically Jess snore that it brings a chuckle to my lips.

"God, J, you and your snoring. It's as loud as Kirsty's voice, and that's saying something."

The drawn curtains cast purple shadows across her face. She snorts again, wriggles a bit and the duvet slips to the floor. Remus, who's curled into Romulus at Jess's feet, lifts his head and turns in my direction. He thumps his tail when he catches sight of me.

"Here, boy," I whisper, and hold out my hand.

He takes one sniff then snuggles back up against Romulus.

Jess groans and flips onto her back, revealing a lump of wine-coloured plastic that rolls along the bed a little. I groan, screwing my eyes up in revulsion at the sight before me. My urn!

Dad's right, it's just horrible seeing her with that. I couldn't get over it when Jess asked Mum if she could have my ashes. I mean – why would she want them?

"Oh, Jess, what d'you get from doing that?"

Jess's eyelids flicker wildly, her mouth twitches and she moans louder and louder.

Suddenly, I want to give her a slap.

"Wake up, damn you! How long are you going to act like this? Dad's not the only one who wants answers. D'you hear me? How long's this going to go on?"

Remus turns around, a baffled expression on his doggy face.

But me – inside I'm so pent up. I need... Oh why can't I just burst out crying? Why can't tears pour down *my* face? Why can't... Why? I scrunch up my eyes. Clench my jaw. Stamp my feet. Why won't she wake up? By now I so want to thump Jess; anything to get a reaction out of her.

"So come on then, J? How long? Another week? More?"

I'm towering over her. Yelling. Laughing manically. Desperate to cry. There are tears behind these eyes of mine – somewhere, I know there are.

"Six months even? That long? Come on." I flop onto my bed, fling my head back, laugh another crazy, crazy laugh. "You know you're allowed it. That's the maximum period, isn't it? For mourning a kid? In ancient Rome, yeah? Well, isn't it? Or is it a year? I don't know – you tell me!"

I'm screaming. Willing her to wake up. To notice I'm here. But Jess just rolls on her side again, flings an arm out, whacking the urn further along the mattress, and curls up like one of those petrified figures we saw in that museum in Pompeii.

God, look at her! You're such a dolt, Minty. You thought you were the Big I Am just because you walked through the friggin' kitchen door. You thought that changed everything. Hah! Just shows what you know! It doesn't change a thing. Look at her, there's the proof.

And as I think this, a combination of fury, frustration and revulsion bubbles up inside me like the waters in a hot spring.

Just then, Jess gets really restless, flopping around on her bed, kicking out her legs, thumping Romulus in the process. The urn rolls off the foot of the bed and lands on the carpet with a thud. Romulus looks up then nestles down again but Remus drags himself off the bed and, with a little whine and a wag of his tail, comes to sit next to me.

"Oh, Remus, what am I going to do?" I say, stroking his ears. I heave a sigh. "How can I get Jess back to normal? How I can take away her sadness?"

He cocks his head to the side.

"You wondering that too, eh? If only I was right about Iona. I could work on getting through to her, get her to help me. But Jack said... Well, we know what he said."

I screw up my face. "But he's wrong, isn't he boy? Or lying. Cos why would she do that to J?"

Remus looks at me with his big innocent eyes and something about that look reminds me of my friend.

"No, that's not what Iona's about. She must've been telling the truth. Yet..." I bury my face in my palms. "Oh I don't know what to think anymore," I whisper, letting my hands fall into my lap.

It's only then that I notice Octavius purring on top of the wardrobe on the other side of the room.

His name escapes from my lips.

"Octavius."

My voice is barely more than a whisper, but it's enough to make him look up.

I put out a hand, beckon him towards me. "Puss, puss, puss," I say, beckoning him towards me.

Look at you, my lovely wee cat. If only Jess was as contented as you.

All at once, the purring stops, his body stiffens. Then his head sinks into his shoulders and he stares at me through orange eyes. He just stares and stares and ogles some more.

"Octavius?" I say, glancing over my shoulder.

What's he looking at?

I turn back to him. His glittering eyes are as round as hubcaps.

Cos of me?

"Can you see me watching you?"

He pricks up his ears, yet he doesn't scarper like he did at the back door. He just continues gawping, his head stretched out towards me, his teeny pink nose twitching slightly. I don't want to startle him, so I gingerly pad back across and take my place on the edge of Jess's bed. Nice word that, gingerly, a good word for Octavius cos he's a ginger tom. Well, ginger except for those creamy-white stripes on that fluffy fur of his.

Omigod, you eedjit, why're you wondering about that? Something massive's going on here: first Iona, then that cat in the street, now Octavius here, and then that thing I did with the door. Wow!

Octavius springs up and jumps off the wardrobe, vaulting over my urn on his way out of the door.

At the sight of the ugly plastic jar my spirits plummet.

"I hate that thing!" I say, getting up to kick it but seeing my foot sail right through it.

I stoop down and make a grab for it but it's like I'm snatching nothing – maybe I should be used to that by now.

I fall back against the wall, glare at my sister and point at the urn. "You're so dumb, J. You think I'm in there? Well I'm not!" I thump my breastbone. "I'm here! Look at me, dammit! You said it – we're identical twins and we're supposed to have this super-special connection. So why can't you see me? Why don't you realise I'm still with you?"

I stride up to the bed, hover above her and screech. "Did you think I'd leave you like this? Listen to me. You must know I'm here beside you. Please, look at me!"

But she just lies there, motionless.

"Wake up, for God's sake! You're really pissing me off now, J!"

The face – my face – smiling out of the photo frame on her bedside table seems to mock me.

"What're you grinning at?" I say, clipping the frame with the side of my hand, willing it to topple over with a crash and wake my sister.

It doesn't.

So I walk away, leave Jess to herself.

As I'm stalking out of the room, she moans and mutters a stream of gobbledegook. I turn around and notice she's begun to breathe out really noisily. She throws an arm out over the edge of the bed, her dark brown hair spread out over the pillows; suddenly I don't feel so mad.

"God, Jess, what are you like?" I say, going over to sit by her. "Your hair's a mess. All matted. Look at the tugs in this. Have you been practising backcombing? Heck, Jess, you look like friggin' Russell Brand!"

I try to brush a few tangled strands from her brow but my fingers slip straight through. Blast! I grit my teeth in frustration: I can't stand not being able to touch her.

Jess mutters. Yawns. Turns. Rolls over onto her stomach. Then all of a sudden, she gags. And gags.

Again and again. Her eyes snap awake, she hauls herself up onto her knees and takes in the air in big greedy gulps, like a fish that's just been landed. Then she coughs. Her breathing goes all peculiar and this ugly sort of rattling comes from her throat. It's the sound of a drain emptying. She attempts to get out of bed but her breathing's gone totally haywire, like she's choking on something.

I look on in horror. "Jess? What—?"

Her eyes widen. She clutches her throat. Rasps. "I…I…"

What the hell's going on?

"Jess?"

She's sobbing and coughing and gasping for breath. And I can't bear it. What if she dies? God, no.

"Jess. Please. Omigod, somebody do something! Mum! Come quick!" I say, putting my arms around her and rubbing her back – or trying to anyway.

And then, like someone's flicked a switch, the coughing, fighting for breath, the rattling in her throat, stops. Just like that. Then she bursts into tears.

"Oh man, she's sure got some problem. One big, fat problem," drawls a familiar voice behind me.

Ripping my gaze away, I whirl around.

"Jack, did you see that?" I cry, my attention snapping back to Jess who is perched on the bed, panting like Remus after a run. Tears stream from her eyes, her skin's all sweaty and her face has a foul green tinge to it. "Jess? Are you all right? What happened?"

"She can't hear you. Remember?"

Jess hunches over, the dogs at her feet, her hands on her thighs, taking short, shallow breaths. The greeny tinge on her skin has paled to a yucky creamy-grey. She rubs an arm across her forehead and coughs. Romulus whines, crawls up the bed and shoves his muzzle into her lap.

"It's OK, Rommy," she says, her voice like a chain smoker's as she puts out a hand to stroke his neck. Then, taking a stuttering breath, she gets up, slips her feet into her slippers and staggers towards the bathroom.

Instead of going after her, I turn to Jack, wondering how much of Jess's choking fit he saw. "Well? Did you? Did you hear what I said?"

"So much for welcome back, Jack," he says, hitching up an eyebrow.

"Sorry," I say, but the image of Jess fighting for breath forces everything else out of my mind. "Well?"

"Yes," he says, propping himself up against the wardrobe. "I saw."

"What was it? It was frightening, watching her struggling like that."

"You know, I've heard about this." He taps his bottom lip, lays a finger across his chin. "Never actually seen it, though."

"What? Come on, tell me."

"This twins thing. I dunno that that *is* what it was. All I do know is, it's bad news."

"Bad news? How? Explain."

"She was experiencing everything you did. When you died. Happens sometimes with identical twins. Not that often but it does happen. That's what I was told, anyway."

"What?" I sink onto the chair by the desk. "The choking. Gasping." Remembering what it felt like in the sea, I put my elbows on the desk and bury my head in my hands. "Oh, this is awful." I look up. "That" – I jab a thumb in Jess's direction – "was because we're twins?"

"Looks that way." He shrugs. Won't meet my eye. "As I said, I've heard of it. But never seen it till now."

This is too much. Hasn't Jess got enough to cope with, without this?

I sigh, rake my hair with my fingers and glance up at him. "How do you know all this?"

He still won't look at me. The shifty sod.

"Someone told me."

Someone told him? And was this before he died? After?

"Who?"

"Does it matter?" he says, swinging on his heels and striding into the hall.

"Wait!" I cry. "Where're you going?" I catch his arm. Pull him round to face me. "Will it happen again?"

He shuts his eyes. Nods. "Maybe. Probably."

"But when? And is this it, until – whenever?"

"I dunno."

"She's like that until *she* dies?" I latch onto his shoulder. "You have to tell me. I need to know what's going on here."

"For the last time, I dunno," Jack grunts, shrugs me off and stomps out.

"Come back! I'm not finished with you! You're hiding something, I know you are."

Yeah…that guy knows more than he's letting on, and not only about this. I'm not stopping until he tells me everything.

So, with a backward glance at my twin, I chase after him.

Chapter Sixteen

The classroom's buzzing with gossiping girls and boisterous blokes, all making the best of the fact that, for once, Stinky Reid is late. One gang of boys – a couple of them perched on tables, others sprawled over grey plastic chairs – roar with laughter at some sick story one of them's told. Three girls huddle by the windows giggling, and another bunch loll around, brushing their hair and plastering on another layer of forbidden mascara.

One of the girls takes a can of hairspray from her bag and squirts it over her fringe; a mist of sticky particles floats in the sunlight streaming through the windows. I can just imagine the stench of Elvive filling the room and I must be right cos some of the guys pretend they're choking. That's a good one! As if they'd notice! I remember the stink of all those unwashed armpits! Boys' underarms, yeah, they're the pits all right – *euch!*

But I don't know why I'm making lame jokes because there, in the middle of the classroom mayhem, sits Jess and her friends. Amongst the sea of grinning, laughing, joking faces, they make a right grim threesome. And no wonder; Jess is telling them what happened this morning.

"Maybe it was an asthma attack."

"Kirsty, I don't *have* asthma!" Jess snaps.

Her hazel eyes are all puffed up and her skin still has that sickly sheen to it. Heck, she looks terrible.

"No, but it could've been brought on by stress. That can happen, you know," Kirsty says, her face full of concern.

"No. I told you. My lungs were…bursting. Like they were on fire."

"Asthma gets you that way," Kirsty says in a soothing voice as she rubs Jess's back.

"Kirsty's right. My cousin has it and she says it's like her lungs are bursting," Iona adds, twirling a coil of brunette hair round a slim brown finger.

"No, no. You don't get it, do you? It was like… it was so real…as if I was…drowning. I could feel water. Cold water. All around me."

So, Jack was right – about this, at least. But, Jupiter, I wish to heck he'd been wrong.

Jess shudders as if an icy draught has swept in. "It was… I was living it. As though I was in the sea. Fighting for my life." She drops her voice to a whisper. "Just like Minty."

"This is a nightmare," I whisper to myself.

Iona squeezes Jess's hand. "How awful."

"I was gasping. Choking. Drowning. Going through what she must've gone through. I *was* Minty," Jess whispers, her voice disappearing into the din.

I groan.

"Oh my God," Kirsty says, her eyes filling with tears. Her hand flies up to her gaping mouth. "Did you tell your mum?"

Jess shakes her head. Her barely-combed hair swings out like treacle-coloured candyfloss. "How could I? She'd flip. Hasn't she got enough to cope with?"

"But, you must tell her!" Kirsty booms.

The girls by the window look up in surprise.

"Shh. Keep your voice down. I don't want everybody to know. They think I'm a freak as it is," Jess hisses.

"No they don't," Iona says, hitching down her miniscule skirt.

"Yes they do. They think I'm la-la. Because of this." Jess tugs at the thick woolly jumper. "But I *have* to wear it. I have to. You understand, don't you?"

Kirsty raises her eyebrows at Iona. "Course we do," she says, kindly. "But maybe—"

The room falls silent as Mrs Reid strides in, brows drawn, face as dark as a blackcurrant, her silky brown skirt billowing around her like a parachute. Someone titters nervously, but one by one every single kid, even the toughest, takes their place, pulls their maths books and stuff out of their bags and sits nervously, waiting for the tongue lashing that's surely coming. For the first time ever I'm sorta relieved nobody can see me: Stinky Reid sure is terrifying.

⚜ ⚜ ⚜

Jack is stretched out on the chair at the end of the only unoccupied desk in the room. His eyes are closed and he has an expression of total boredom on his face.

But he's not fooling me! He isn't bored; he's being bloomin' evasive. Well, your time's up, boyo – I want answers and I want them now!

"So, come on, Jack, tell me. No more ducking out of my questions," I say, jumping up and pacing to and fro in front of him. "What's going on here? I need explanations."

The instant I open my gob, Iona looks up from her desk. Chewing on her pencil, she turns towards me, frowns, gives her head a little shake, then goes back to work.

Crikey, get her! Either she's developed a nervous tick since I died or she senses something. Yeah, and I know what that something is – me! I knew I was right about her!

I scrutinise Jack. Why did I ever doubt myself? Why did I let him talk me into thinking I was wrong? She flamin' does feel my presence.

And just to prove it I peer at her, centre my determination on making her hear me. When I call out, "Iona? It's Minty. I'm right behind you," she glances round again, bewildered.

Yee hah! See Jack, I *haven't* got it wrong – no way. I'm going up there to talk to her, yell even. Yeah, I'm...but...no... That'll have to wait until you tell me what's going on with J.

"Jack, enough of the silent treatment – for the zillionth time, what does that choking thing mean for Jess?"

He opens an eye. "Ya know something, kid? You're like a dog with a bone."

"Yeah, just call me Fido," I say, putting my hands on my hips. "So? Speak to me. I'm waiting."

Before he gets a chance to answer there's a tentative knock at the door.

"Come in!" says Mrs Reid in her usual irritated way.

The door cranks open and a weedy wee first year with a bad case of the jitters sidles in, clutching a crumpled sheet of paper.

"Don't just stand there," the teacher says. She marches up to him, the long rope of wooden beads that dangles from her neck clacking against her spectacle chain. She glowers at the poor boy and snatches the note out of his grasp.

Remus slinks over to me, shoulders down, tail hanging limply to the floor and cowers into my legs.

Jack walks up to her, and with a snort of laughter says, "Man, she's one scary lady. She'd frighten you to death." He winks at me. "If you weren't already dead, that is."

So you're talking now, Jack?

"She cried at my memorial service," I say, tartly. "Who'd have guessed?"

And then Mrs Reid looks up from reading and with a loud tut barks, "For goodness sakes, lad, go and shut that door."

All at once, before the kid gets a chance to react, Jack skips out of his seat. "Let's split. Never could stick maths." He looks at me. "You coming?"

"What about Jess?" I say, glancing over at J who's bent over her textbook.

Come on, Minty, how's hanging around here going to help her? And anyway, you and Jack need to talk.

I catch him eyeing up Iona and my mind's made up.

"On seconds thoughts, why not?" I say, looking pointedly at my gorgeous mate. "It'll take you away from any distractions."

Look at him – he has the nerve to laugh!

Well, tell you what, Jacko, I'll wipe that grin off your ugly mug, I think as I push past him.

"What you doing?" he says.

I wait until the kid's shut the door then I stand with my back to it.

"Now you've done it," Jack says. "We're stuck here till the end of the period now."

I take a look at Stinky Reid scanning the note she's been given, watch my classmates all slouched over their desks, busily working away on some dumb exercise she's set them, and an idea rushes into my head.

Crikey, there'd be a riot if they could see what I'm about to do!

I turn to face the door. "Here till the end of the period? I don't think so."

OK, girl, just do what you did last time. Show this smart ass that he's not the only one holding onto a secret.

Flattening down my clothes, I empty my mind, square up to the big hunk of wood – and I don't mean friggin' Jack – take a step forward and really, really focus until I've pushed into the door and am in the corridor on the other side, tingling with needle-sharp heat.

Remus appears. He bounds over to me, his tail whirling in the air like a helicopter blade. Then Jack arrives, leaping through the door like Billy flippin' Elliot.

He towers over me and gives me a round of applause. "So you've got it all sussed," he says, his voice thick with sarcasm. "So now you know – you *can* move through things. Was it mentioning *Ghost* that did it? Did that get you thinking?"

"No, I haven't got it *all* sussed," I say, sitting up and brushing myself down. "Yet I'm not as dumb as you think. There's more to this being dead thing than you're letting on and you sure as hell are going to tell me. And yeah, for your information it was *Ghost*."

He scratches his chin and grins. "Yeah well, I never said the movies didn't get it right sometimes." He lets out a cackle.

"Oh shut up, Jack!" I snap as Remus shoves his snout in my lap. I rough the dog's coat with my fingertips, shove him gently to the side and glare at Mr

Smug. "Maybe I have been thick – so what? At least I don't lie!"

"Meaning?"

"Meaning I don't hold out on people. Spin them tales."

He stares down at his hands. "And I do?"

"Yeah, you know you do." I hobble onto my feet; walk up close to him, jutting my face into his. "Geez, you must've been cracking up when I asked you about that thing you did with my coffin. When I pressed you to tell me if I could walk through walls and the like. Worried I was on to something? Worried that I'd catch you out in the rest of your big fat fibs, were you?"

He backs off. "What fibs?" he says.

The cockiness in his voice has gone; all of a sudden he's deadly serious.

"Lies about being dead," I say. I nod to the classroom we've just left. "About the fact that we have more…oh what's the word…?" I bang the heel of my hand against my forehead. "Yeah…interaction. More interaction with our environment than you acknowledged." I point to the door. "Random stuff like what we did there, for instance."

I watch for his reaction but he hides his face from me.

Taking him by the chin, I say, "Remember that night coming back from Iona's – when we saw the cat? I asked you why it freaked out like it did, whether it could sense me."

He tries to slink off but I bar his way.

"You never did give me an answer to that, did you?" I cross my arms, hitch up my eyebrows. "Geez, you did a right number on me with Iona." I snort. "I guessed that she was the key to it all – to getting through to Jess. But you almost had me convinced. Had me believing that I was imagining her being able to feel me around the place." I stare him out. "But I could – I can – no use you denying it." I pause. Wait for a response. He looks away. "So come on, Jack, what's the deal? What else is possible?"

He thrusts his hands in his pockets, shuffles his feet. Says nothing.

"Come on, it's time to quit stalling." I swirl a hand in the air above me. "I want it all, every last detail."

"What's to tell?" he says.

"The truth, Jack!" I grab him by the shoulder and turn his face to force him to look at me again. "I'm not giving up till you tell me. So, start talking."

He leans back a little and whistles through his teeth, a faint smile flickering around the corners of his mouth. His eyes meet mine. "Bossy little chick, aren't you?" He laughs, weakly. "OK. You win. I'll tell you all I know."

He puckers his temple, shakes his head like a horse shrugging off a fly, and lets out a big whoosh of breath. "You're right, I haven't been exactly straight with you. There *are* things you should know."

His face takes on that dead serious expression that Dad gets when he's checking the lotto numbers. He taps his forehead. "And the magic's in here. It's all in the power of the mind. Our ability to make decisions." He points to the fire extinguisher fastened to the opposite wall. "Like taking that out of its bracket, say. Picking it up." And gesturing to Mrs Reid's door, he adds, "We didn't even have to walk through that just then, we could've used our minds to open it."

"OK," I say, slowly fingering the jagged line of the scar above my lips. "Or could we just turn the handle using our hands, like we're used to?"

Jack tickles the dog beneath his collar and chuckles. "Turn the handle? What fun would that be? There've got to be some advantages to being dead, right?"

"So I *can* manipulate stuff to show Jess I'm still around." I grin. "And there's Iona…" I jump in the air, clap my hands. "I can do the same with her – yeah? Whoopee – double whammy!" I throw my arms above my head. "It's really going to happen, I'm going to help Jess get back to herself." I look at Jack. "Yeah?"

He stares at me for what seems like forever, then he slides down the wall, rests his elbows on his knees and tucks his balled hands under his chin. Then taking them away from his face, he massages his thighs. "Yip. And you're the only one who can."

"Go on," I say, and flop onto the floor beside him.

Jack twists his bottom lip between his fingers, his gaze glued to the wall across from him. His right foot looks as if it's keeping time with some tune playing out inside his head and Remus can't take his eyes off it. Jack sighs and his fingers drop away from his mouth; when he begins to speak his voice is hesitant, measured, as if each word he uses has been tested out in his mind beforehand.

"You've gotta remember, I've been doing this stuff…" He falters but with a flick of his wrist carries on. "Hanging around. Waiting. For years." He puffs his cheeks, tugs at an ear as if it's a piece of elastic, and fixes his eyes to the ground.

"Then you came along." His voice has dropped to a whisper and it's a bit of an effort to hear him above the low level noise coming from the surrounding classrooms.

He pulls back his head and looks at me, his eyes meeting mine. "You gotta understand, I'd convinced myself into thinking I was cool on my own." He begins to fidget, and then his gaze slides away. "But I wasn't, I was lonely – there are only so many movies you can watch on your tod without it doing your nut in. I needed the company." His voice tightens. "Didn't want it to happen again."

"What?" I say, wishing he'd just spit it out.

He cups his hands over his lips. "Didn't want you to go off. Move on."

Move on? Did I hear that right?

"I thought you said I couldn't move on?"

Jack nibbles his bottom lip, rubs it with the tip of his tongue. "Mmm, well, that's where I haven't been exactly straight with you." He ruffles his hair, massages his cheeks and gives me a strange kind of look. "Thing is. You probably can."

"What?" I explode.

Remus gives a start. I offer him an absent-minded pat on the head.

Jack holds up a hand. "Hear me out!"

I slap his lying, cheating face – not that it'll hurt him, but it makes me feel good. "You pig. You told me I couldn't—"

"Yeah. Yeah. I know. And I'm sorry," he says, arms crossed in front of his face to defend himself. "But..."

"How did you know I could?" I yell, battering his arms. "And for how long? Tell me, you stinking rat."

He throws his head back against the wall. "It was Iona, then the cat on the street. They *did* sense you."

"But you said..." I sit back on my heels and put on his voice, "Don't waste your time trying to get through to her. The dead can't communicate with the living." I hit him again. "How could you?"

"I know. I know. But I told you. I was lonely."

"Huh! Lonely? What kind of excuse is that? You knew there was a chance I could move on. And you lied to me. You had no right!"

"I guess not," Jack nods. "But before that I thought...I thought you couldn't. Romulus – Octavius – look, they'd never reacted when you were around. But then when Iona came into the picture... and then that cat..."

He shrugs, pauses, his lips clasped.

I lunge forward and poke him in the ribs. "Oh no you don't, Mr Jack Whatever-Your-Name-Is, don't stop now. You said you were my friend? OK then. Prove it. Tell me everything. Spill."

Two classes down, a door opens and a skinny little guy with ears like Mr Spock's comes out, the hubbub of classroom chatter spilling out into the corridor behind him and breaking the silence between Jack and me. Jack's eyes trail after the boy, as if he's desperate to go after him, to get away from having to explain himself to me. The kid opens the fire door. It swings behind him and closes with a thud.

A burst of laughter erupts from the classroom opposite Stinky Reid's. The teacher – Mr Stewart, I reckon – calls to the class to pipe down.

I glower at Jack. "I'm waiting."

He nods. "You're not the only one I've met since I died. Ghost, that is," he says. "There've been a few over the years. Adults mostly. A couple of kids. When I met the first one, I didn't realise he was dead. Until he spoke to me."

"Like you did with me. At my funeral?"

"Yeah. He was about my age. Geeky type. Not the sort of guy I'd normally hang with." He shuffles his bum, looks up at me through his brows. "But what choice did I have? It was the first time I'd spoken to anyone for nearly a year."

"A year? Blimey," I say, wondering how I would feel if that was me. "How come?"

Jack lets out a half-hearted laugh. He runs his palms down his thighs and looks at me, one eyebrow up, like that Sean Connery bloke in the old Bond movies Dad loves so much. "I'll ask you a question: how many other dead guys have you seen since you met me? Before that even?"

"I…I… None?"

"That's what you think." He pauses, looks up and down the corridor, and back to me. "They're out there. All around us. Not many, but they are out there."

"But if they're dead then… Well, I thought you said our souls connect – and that's why we can see each other?"

"Reckon they do. Without us knowing it. We see other ghosts but they just look like regular people to us."

"Then why haven't I seen any?"

"You saw me, didn't you?" Our eyes lock. "But if I'd met you on the street and hadn't spoken to you, would you have known I was dead?"

Holy moly! He's right! My mind goes into overdrive.

"Anyway, this guy – Pete – he was stuck, too, but another ghost had told him it doesn't have to be like this." He leans away from me, looking like he's anticipating another thump. "That it *is* possible to communicate with the other side. There are ways…" He pauses. Drops his head. Examines his toenails. "So, he showed me. I learnt the techniques." He rubs his hands together, shrugs. "He showed me and he left."

A sliver of fear cuts into my thoughts. Left to go where? Heaven? Hell? What?

Enough of the speculation! Concentrate on Jack.

He's trying to act as if he doesn't care but his face is as sad as I've ever seen it: still, I'm not falling for that 'poor old me' act. He held out on me. The skunk.

"How did he work out you were dead? How did you know I was, that day in the crem?"

"It's not rocket science. You only have to watch – study." He glances along the corridor. "Look for the loner. Watch how they interact with others. See if they actually do."

I follow his line of vision, half-expecting another ghost to appear. "So, if those other guys left you – moved on - why're you still here?"

"Because." He groans, wipes a hand over his eyes. "It, er, doesn't work for me. I can do everything he taught me. All of it. But when I try it on my old dear, try to communicate with her…well…it just doesn't work."

I furl my temple. "Why doesn't it, though?"

But when I see his sad face my expression softens.

"Oh, Jack," I whisper.

Poor guy, he looks so… Hey, hold on there, Minty, this is the boy who's lied to you for weeks – don't feel sorry for him!

"OK, why are you telling me all this now?" I say, my tone now harsh and demanding. "Why not keep on lying? You're good at that."

Jack stares at the wall. "It was seeing my mother again." He runs a finger over an eyelid. "Look, that night, I didn't really run off because of her. It was the cat thing. When it reacted like that and then with Iona acting the way she did, I knew you'd start asking questions. Would want to know why Iona sensed you, how the cat knew you were there. I knew I'd have to admit that contact is possible. And..." He shrugs again. "I didn't want that. As I said, I was lonely." The corners of his mouth droop. "You were the only friend I had."

He chucks me a thin smile and tries to take my hand but when I pull it back he nods at me, as if to say, 'It's only what I deserve'.

He continues. "So then I thought what a coward I was being, disappearing like that. That's why I came back."

"So you used your mum as an excuse?"

He squirms a bit. "Sorry." His eyes take on a sort of faraway look and his voice becomes hushed. "Then when we got to my old girl's that night and I saw her lying on that bed – well, I thought back through all these years since I" – he clears his throat – "died. I thought about how lifeless she's been. Remembered how she used to be when I was alive. How she's wasted her life since."

With an apology written across his face, he reaches for my hand again. This time I let him take it.

"And it made me think of your sister. I knew that could happen to her as well. So, when I came back to your place and saw her choking, how low she'd already got..." He looks at me. "Oh damn... I've been trying to think of a way to tell you this. I knew

I couldn't do that to her. To you. Finally accepted that you deserved the chance to save her. Save yourself. Because, you're the only one who can, Minty. Then you can both move on. And I can help you with that."

So it's definite – I can make contact! That's what he's saying. There is a way.

A grin bursts from my lips and I have this massive urge to kiss him. I don't though – no way!

"No holding anything back this time?"

He sighs, nods his head.

"OK, teacher," I say, crossing my arms. "Let's do it. Tell me all you know." A slow smile slithers along my face. "Only, don't go all Stinky Reid on me. Deal?"

He breaks into a gentle smile. "Deal."

CHAPTER SEVENTEEN

"So?"

"Where do I start?" he says, rubbing the nape of his neck. He gestures with his chin towards Stinky Reid's door. "You've already worked out that we can walk through things but, as you suspected, you also can use your mind to do other stuff – almost anything. Manipulate electrical equipment, for example."

His eyes look to the strip lights in the ceiling, back to me. "Lights. Radios and the like. TVs. Even those mobile phones you have these days. Hard to believe, but you can even conjure up smells. Alter your shape. Get into people's heads – right inside their thoughts." He raps his knuckles against the side of his skull. "All this, just by channelling your mind power."

Another gale of laughter erupts from Mr Stewart's room, causing Remus to run to the classroom door and bark.

"Come on," I say, as I jump to my feet, smiling at my dog. "Let's find somewhere quieter. This is a lot to take in. I could do without the interruptions."

Skipping along the narrow passageway, I call to him over my shoulder. "Get off your butt, Jack. You've got work to do."

When I come to the fire doors, I spin round and head back the way we came because I really don't fancy walking through them – I've had enough weird sensations for one day. A few minutes later, we arrive at the main staircase.

"We need to find an empty classroom," I say, looking up the steps and taking them two at a time.

Turning at the top of the stairs into the English department, I peer into one, two, three rooms until I find one that's empty. "In here. Quick."

With Remus at my heels, I bound into the classroom, check all around me until my eyes settle on the notices pinned on the wall to the right of the whiteboard.

Jack pauses at the door.

"Stop wasting time." I jab an index finger at an A4 timetable tacked up with what looks like the world's biggest lump of Blutac. "According to this, there's a class here in twenty minutes."

As he comes into the room, my eyes are drawn to a huge, garishly colourful poster advertising *Julius Caesar* at some theatre in Edinburgh. I find myself smiling at that cos, even though I think Shakespeare stinks, I really get that play, what with it being set in Rome and all. Pulling back my attention, I notice the two PCs tucked into the far corner of the classroom.

"We can use our minds to do almost anything?" I say, walking over to them. "What about one of these? Think I can get this to work?" I rap on a monitor. "Type a message on the screen, or something?"

Jack strides up to the computer. "These things are a bit of a mystery to me." He grins at me, tucking a strand of fair hair behind one earlobe. "They weren't around when I was alive. Sure you wouldn't rather nip back to the Music department? Try playing an electric guitar, or the like?"

I slap his back. Giggle. "Let's just get on with it."

He sniggers. "All right, keep your shirt on," he says and sits down in front of one of the PCs, flexing his fingers in the air above the keyboard as if he was a concert pianist getting ready to perform a concerto. Then he crooks his neck to one side. "Ready?"

I lower myself onto the chair next to him, Remus nestling by my ankles.

"Now before you bombard me with more of your questions, I don't really know any of this for sure. It's just my theory, plus what I've been told, though I doubt anyone knows for definite…there are far too many anomalies for that."

"Anomalies? What're they when they're at home?" I ask with a frown.

"Inconsistencies," he says, smiling. "Got that? Yip?"

I nod. Though why he couldn't have just said that in the first place, I don't know.

"OK," he says. "You'll have heard of mechanics?" His lopsided smile flickers into life. "You know –

reacting to forces, movement, that sorta thing? Science, yeah? Not that I was ever much cop at that. All I know is we can't move any of these inanimate objects, like a computer key, a door handle, unless we harness our mental energies."

He knocks on his skull again, wiggles his eyebrows and nods at me like a demented donkey. "The power of the mind, yeah?"

"But, Jack, isn't mechanics about how *physical* bodies interact? But we don't actually *have* a physical body, do we?"

He spreads his hands. "Like I said, science isn't my strongpoint. And if you think about it, even in the living world science can't explain everything. It's the same with ours – some things just defy explanation."

"OK, but let me get this straight, it's our minds that allow us lot – ghosts – to interact with each other, you know, like physically?"

"Reckon so. It's as if our minds lull us into thinking we're still living, even though we're not physical beings."

"And what about the living? Why can't we harness our minds to touch them? I mean properly touch them?"

"God knows. But I think our emotions cloud our ability to focus properly."

"You mean they get in the way?"

"Yip. That's what I reckon, anyway. But, as I said, who knows for certain?"

"Aren't your emotions part of your thinking?"

"I suppose. But you gotta put them to one side. Forget about your feelings. Use the pure energy of your mind." He smiles at me again, showing his full set of crooked white teeth. "Righty-o then, let's get on. Watch this." Jack focuses on the PC tower by his right leg. "First we need to switch on the power…" He turns to me and winks. "Ghost style. You've got to remember to forget the old reality. This is a whole new ball game. OK?"

Brushing my fringe out of my eyes, I get ready to put what he's told me into practice.

He faces the PC again. Body alert, brows pulled together, he peers at the tower for a couple of seconds and then there's a click and a whine and a green light appears.

I whistle through my teeth. "Cool."

Remus looks at me through one half-shut eye.

"Now, we need to do the same to this thing," Jack continues, pointing to the monitor. He stares at the button underneath the screen and then, seconds later, there's a sing-song whir and the screen flickers into action. "So far, so easy. Over to you now – typing is girls' work."

"You sexist sod! This is the twenty-first century, you know. Boys type, too."

"Not ones from the nineteen-seventies, they don't," he says with a laugh, his blue eyes twinkling.

"Yeah, well I'm glad I live now," I say with a shrug as I think to myself that I'm not actually living at all. "Whatever! So, what do I have to do?"

"Operate it as normal...but by using your mind. Think what needs to be done next. Focus on it really hard. Imagine it happening. Then it will, or it should."

"OK," I say, slicking my tongue along my bottom lip and scrunching up my nose. "I need to enter a password, first. Hmm." I shift around in my chair and look over my shoulder at the entrance. "What classroom is this?"

Jack nips to the door to check. "E4," he says and comes back inside.

"OK," I say, glancing at the monitor, then down at the keyboard. "E4." I depress the E key, forgetting for a moment that my fingers will just plunge down into the board.

"You can do it like that - using your fingers," Jack says, as I shake the tingling feeling from my fingertips. "But it's much trickier. Better to use your mind, to imagine it all in your head. Harness that imaginative power. So, lock your eyes on the key, visualise your finger pressing it down."

"Are you sure this works?"

"Yeah, course I am," he drawls.

Gritting my teeth, I channel my energy into focussing on the E key, willing it to push down. My hands are clenched, my forehead drawn, my gaze bores into the key, willing the impossible to happen.

Push down.

Come on.

Nothing.

"I can't do it!" I say, banging my knuckles against my skull. I look at Jack. "You do it for me."

"Nope. She's your sister – you write the message."

"But I can't!"

"Yip, you can. Concentrate."

My hands are two tight fists. My eyes dart from the E key on the keyboard, to the monitor that's prompting me to enter a password.

"Yeah, I know, you want the password," I mutter to the computer. "I'm trying! If I could just get this flippin' key to go down."

"Concentrate, Minty," Jack says.

But my mind flits from the E to the 4 and back to the E key again and nothing happens.

Come on!

I look up at the screen, screwing up my face as I try to re-focus.

E. 4.

"One key at a time," Jack murmurs. "Visualise one. Then the next. Then the other. You can do this. It's not like when you were alive. It *is* possible to utilise your mindpower."

I crane my neck, fix my eyes on the keyboard, but my gaze wavers, darts from the computer to the wall behind it, to Jack, and back again to the PC.

Sagging into my seat, I tell myself that there's no point in doing this – it just won't work. But then I whack myself on the thighs, straighten up in my chair, and tell myself that I'm talking rot, that I'll make it work.

All of a sudden, there's a commotion behind me that breaks my train of thought.

"Did you ask why? The tickets should be here by now, Derek," says an exasperated female voice.

I look round to see who's come into the classroom and interrupted me. It's that young teacher, the probationer, Miss Hamilton, or Harrington. Oh I can't remember. Anyway, the one with all that tumbling blonde hair down to her bum that the lads in my year drool over. She sashays over to the whiteboard, arguing into the shiny pink mobile that's stuck to her right ear. Dumping a stack of papers on the nearest table, she curses as the pile topples over, some scattering to the floor.

Tsk! Tsk! Language Miss— What *is* her name? God, she's grumpy. And so, so noisy. Enough noise to wake up the dead – or a dead dog at least, I say to myself as I watch Remus get up off the floor and give himself a vigorous shake.

"Trust me to have gone to a school full of crusty old fossils," Jack says, getting an eyeful of Miss's cleavage when she leans down to scoop up the mess. "Male ones at that. No wonder I failed so many exams." He wolf-whistles and Remus's ears prick up. "I'd have been top of my year if we'd had teachers like her."

"Oh, get a life, Jack," I snap, scowling at him, till I realize what I've just said.

Jack grins and we both start laughing. Then, to the sound of Miss Whatshername arguing away on her mobile, we go to find another room.

Chapter Eighteen

"Where now?" Jack asks, as we amble along the corridor heading downstairs with my dog, me trying to figure out why I had so much trouble typing into that computer.

Maybe it just takes practice. But what if it doesn't work? What if I never manage this communication thing? And even if I do, what good will it do me? After all, Jack can do most of it, yet he can't get through to his mother.

But why is that? Surely that's not right? Could this be another of his lies?

"Jack?" I say, stopping at the top of the stairs as he trudges down the steps. "Why doesn't it work for you? How can you do all that stuff yet your mum still doesn't realise you're there?"

He hesitates, one foot poised in mid-descent. When he turns round he won't return my gaze.

"Well then, what about your dad? Does he?"

Suddenly he goes all sort of rigid, grabs onto the railing on the half-landing.

Remus stares at him.

"My old man's dead," he murmurs.

"Oh!" Me and my big gob! I stuff a fist in my mouth, suddenly remembering he already told me that when we were at his mum's house. How could I have forgotten? "I... When?"

Jack looks at me, his face clouded by such sadness that I just have to run down to him. "It was..." He turns away. "He died." The next bit's said so quietly I barely catch it. "And I couldn't deal with... That's why I..."

He shakes his head, puts his back to the turn in the banister, and gazes out of the wall of windows looking onto the playing fields. "He was forty-nine. Heart attack. Never had a day's illness in his life."

"Oh, Jack, I'm sorry," I whisper, touching his arm. He flinches, as though I've given him an electric shock. "Sorry, I should've asked you that..."

I fidget with the leather bracelet at my wrist, wondering what he's going to tell me next.

"My parents tried for years to have kids," he says. "Then, when they'd given up hope, I came along. Maybe that's why we were so close, my dad and I. Why we did everything together. He wouldn't even let the old girl send me to his boarding school." His tone is oddly monotonous. "Generations of Muir males went to that place. But not me. He wanted to keep his boy near him, I guess. Then when I was fifteen - he died. Went to sleep one night, and didn't wake up. And that was it."

"I had no idea. It must've been awful for you and your mum." I gulp, squeeze my eyelids shut. What sort of self-centred monster am I? I haven't even asked him how his mother is. Me, me, me, it's all about me. Isn't it?

"Omigod, Jack, Your mother... You know... Is she? What happened after I left?"

I'm sure if I was alive my cheeks would be burning with shame.

"It's cool. She's still alive." Jack sighs, swinging off down the stairs. "Now let's go and find another compu—"

The changeover bell drowns him out. As it grows silent, a new noise whooshes through the empty corridors: laughter; bawling; bellowing; the sound of a rumbling, seething mass of kids escaping from one classroom and moving on to the other.

Look at them, so full of life. I'd give anything to be like that again. They don't know how lucky there are.

I sigh.

Oh wise up, Minty, there's no place for you in their world, so get over yourself.

And with that thought in mind, I dart after Jack with Remus bouncing along beside me, weaving through the sea of pupils, eager to avoid as many of them as possible passing through my ghostly body.

We're just heading past Business Studies when I notice Jess, head and shoulders slumped so low that I can't see her face, sandwiched between Iona and Kirsty while they trail after the rest of their class to the next lesson.

A pair of older lads I don't recognise bursts out of one of the rooms, having a right old lark about.

One of them punches his mate in the guts and he topples back into Jess, knocking her schoolbag to the floor. She utters a startled cry as her legs buckle under her and she falls to the ground.

Iona and Kirsty spin round and when they see her laid out across the corridor they crouch down to help. Not that those boys care – they just smirk and carry on their way, messing about like two daft nursery kids.

"Nice manners, man," says Jack, glowering at the boys as they disappear from sight.

"Omigod, J, are you OK?" Iona asks as I run up to Jess, Remus yelping behind me.

I bend over to see how Jess is. When my body merges with Jess and our friends, I do my best to ignore the searing sparks of heat pulsing through me.

"I'm… Don't worry, I'm fine," she says, but her voice rasps like an old man's.

My head spins, every cell of me tingling with the human contact. I close my eyes for a second and it seems to amplify Jess's quick and shallow breathing, her hoarse voice – Jupiter, it's like she's got tonsillitis or something. Opening my eyes I find myself face-to-face with her, staring at skin that's bleached the palest white, as if a vampire had just feasted on her blood.

Iona helps her onto her feet, moving into my body and sending another shuddering bolt of electric through me. I shrink away, rubbing at my forehead.

She holds J at arms' length and stares into her bleary eyes. "You sure you're OK?" she asks, brushing Jess's hair off her face to peer at her.

All at once, Iona takes a sharp intake of breath and staggers back, the mahogany skin on her cheeks turning this weird, mucky puce.

"J? What's that on your neck?" she says, her pupils dilating alarmingly as she gawps at a ghastly bruise that starts beneath Jess's ear and spreads to her throat.

Then she rolls up the left cuff on Jess's jumper and peels away the other to reveal more ugly brown and purple marks on the insides of her wrists.

Jupiter! What're those?

Eyes widening in dismay, Kirsty says, "God, J. How did you get those marks?"

"I don't know. I've never seen them before. Honestly," Jess says, a note of panic in her voice, her eyes wide with worry. As she holds her arms out to inspect the horrid multi-coloured smudges, my gaze falls to my own arms, my unblemished wrists, my – but wait! Mine weren't smooth and flawless when… when … God no – it can't be! Can it?

I grab Jack by the elbow. "I know those bruises. I've seen them before."

As he examines Jess's skin, Jack's brow creases. His jaw drops. He gasps. "Oh shit. I really don't like this," he says, in a tone that sends an arrow of ice through my heart. "She's a lot worse than I reckoned."

"Are those what I think they are?" I ask. "Tell me they're not."

Please let me be wrong. If they are, what'll I do, omigod, what *can* I do?

Jack draws closer, stares at the hideous misshapen blotches on Jess's skin.

"They might be – they – yeah," He nods. "I reckon they are," he says. His eyes are wide and full of dread. "I never thought this would happen." Suddenly he sounds as if he's as much out of his depth as I am.

And all at once, I'm back at Elie, reliving the awfulness of seeing my dead body spread out on the grass. "They're mine. The ones I got when I… drowned." I waver, fall against the wall. "But, they can't be. How is that possible?"

"I dunno." Jack shuts his eyes, smoothes a thumb over his cheek. "Oh, man, I got a feeling this is not good. Maybe Jess's too far-gone. Maybe no one can help her now."

I don't want to see those bruises again but I force myself to. When I can't bear it a moment longer, I drag my eyes away and find myself staring into Jess's face again.

Oh sis, you're so pale!

But it's not only that, she's so – expressionless, her face devoid of shock, fear, feeling of any sort. Where seconds ago the horror of her discovery was etched in heavy worry lines, now there's…nothing. Her features are blank. Lifeless. Her whole body is. Jess, why aren't you screaming? Bawling? Why retreat into yourself?

She looks at our friends with eyes that are as lifeless as mine.

"Bruises don't just appear without reason," Kirsty says. "Oh!" Her hand flies up to her chest as Iona gently lifts the mass of Jess's lank hair and exposes another glaring bruise on the other side of her throat.

"You should show these to your parents." Iona says, her temple crinkled in alarm. "Get them to take you to the doctor."

Jess rolls down both sleeves and tugs up the collar of the jumper to cover the marks on her neck. "There's no need."

Oh, God. The tone of her voice, it…it really *is* as if she's dead inside. As if she's given up, doesn't care why these bruises are there, or how she got them.

"But you must," Kirsty says. "Maybe you're sick."

"I told you I don't need to!" Jess cries, the words shooting out into the surrounding hubbub like a silver bullet.

At last! A reaction.

Remus runs up to her. Kirsty and Iona exchange looks. Two kids up ahead glance over their shoulders at us. A passing Sixth Year flings Jess a disapproving look. Well, stuff you, matey! You don't know what my sister's going through, do you?

"I know *exactly* what they are," Jess says, dropping her voice, the spark inside her replaced by brimming tears.

Kirsty's gaze is still locked on those bruises.

Jess twists her arms and thrusts them out to display her inner wrists. "I know what they are," she repeats, and points to her neck. "Punishment."

"What?" says Iona, in a strangled whisper. "What do you mean?"

My thoughts exactly. Punishment for what?

"They're punishment for hurting Minty." Jess says in such a soft tortured tone that I could weep – if I was able to. "For letting her down, complaining and for..." She pauses for breath, her lips trembling. "For moaning about having to share everything. To punish me for what I said..." She looks at them with anguished eyes. "Don't you see? It's only what I deserve. Minty used to take care of me: tell me to remember my keys, my homework – you know what she was like...she had to be in charge. But sometimes it got too much and I just needed a bit of space." She releases a bitter laugh. "Now look at me." Then she buries her face and, from behind her hands, mutters, "Be careful what you wish for."

Kirsty and Iona look as gutted as I'm feeling. They also look...mystified. I can tell that they don't realise the significance of those bruises, have no idea of what J said to me on my last day, what we said to each other. My mind backs away from recalling that stupid argument, at remembering how angry I was.

Cos, geez, it doesn't seem that important now.

Jess glances up. "All that stuff I told her." She sniffs, dabs her nose. "If only I could take it all back. Let her know I'm sorry."

"I *do* know that, Jess," I murmur. "I do."

She pulls up the sleeves of her jumper and brandishes her bruises again. "So I'm glad. Don't you get it? I'm glad I've got these. They make me feel nearer to her somehow." Jess rests her head against the wall. "In spite of what I told her, I really loved her. We were one, me and Minty. One person."

She snatches a handful of jumper. "I'm so lost without her. That's why I've been like this." Her moist eyes are fiery once more – lively. "That's why I'm wearing this ugly old thing. Yeah, it's a Roman custom – for grieving and all that. But I thought it'd bring me closer to her, that maybe, if I wore it, I'd sense her around me."

Then her body seems to deflate, the fire dies behind her eyes. Remus starts whining, his ears and tail flat against his body, as though he senses the distress Jess is in.

"Jess, please, listen to me," I say to her, putting a finger out to shush my dog. "You have nothing to punish yourself for."

"J, I'm so sorry," Iona says.

Jess looks up at her. "I really wanted you to be right." Her eyes mist over. "You know that day? After the memorial? When you wondered if Minty was still around. That's why I was so mad at you. You said you could feel something." Tears flow down her cheeks. "But I knew I couldn't."

Kirsty begins to cry too.

"She died and I don't even know what she went through, how much it hurt, how scared she was – nothing," Jess says, covering her face with her hands.

"J, don't torture yourself," I say.

I'm doing enough of that for both of us

"Minty was always there for me," she says, running her fingertips under her eyes. "But when she really needed me I wasn't there for her. Now she's gone. And I don't know what to do without her." She yanks down a sleeve and uses it to wipe away the remaining tears. Then, hoisting her schoolbag onto her shoulder, she mumbles, "I'm going to the loo. To wipe my face."

"We'll come with you," Kirsty says in a hoarse voice as she dabs at her own tears.

"You don't have to. I won't be long," Jess says, pulling a hankie from her skirt pocket to blow her nose. She attempts a smile. "Go on, I'll catch you up."

Stuffing the snotty tissue back into her pocket she says, "Tell Mr Cosgrove I'm feeling sick." She makes a face. "Or say it's my time of the month – that should stop him from asking too many questions." And with that she walks away, leaving behind a stunned silence.

"Should we go after her?" Iona says as J disappears down the corridor.

"Of course you should," I say running up to her, my concern for my sister revving my voice into a high-pitched wail. "Quick. Go." I turn to Kirsty. "You as well."

If I'm expecting Iona to react to that she doesn't even flinch. What's wrong with her?

"Hey man, pipe down." Jack says, putting his hands over his ears. "It's a wonder half the school didn't hear that. Cool it."

Cool it? Of course! I should calm down. I'm too emotional. Jack said...oh what was it? Our emotions cloud our ability to focus properly. That'll be what's happening here. And – of course! – that'll be why I couldn't get through to her in her bedroom! Cos I was too worked up about it. Yeah, I need to take control of myself.

So freeing my mind of everything that's just gone on, I focus on Iona and say, as coolly and clearly and as I can, "You saw the state Jess's in. Go find her."

And I've no sooner said it than she looks straight at where I'm standing. She stares blankly for second or so, and then smiles in my direction just like she used to smile at me when I was alive. Then she turns to Kirsty, grabs her arm and says, "You saw the state Jess's in. Let's go find her."

It worked!

"Jack, did you hear what she just said? Those were my words."

"I heard." Jack smiles.

He knows it, too! Thank Jupiter for that!

The thought of what I've done, what it might lead to, makes me break into a manic dance of joy. I shake my bum and wave my arms around, singing a tuneless rendition of 'Crazy Right Now'. Remus joins in dashing to and fro like one of Beyoncé's backing singers – until he nearly knocks me over. Putting my superstar act on hold, I drop onto my knees and smother him in kisses. Then I look up at Jack, and treat him to the biggest grin I can muster. "I got inside Iona's head, just like you told me I could."

As Remus's tail swishes over the floor, I watch my friends vanish from sight, off to join Jess. Then, after planting another kiss on my dog's golden head, I smile at my ghostly friend and add, "And if I can do that with Iona, what's to say that I can't do it with Jess as well? All I need to do is to get a proper handle on channelling my mind power. How hard can it be?"

Chapter Nineteen

Because there's something I want to mull over which I need a clear head for, I decide that Jack and I will wait for Jess and our friends outside the toilets.

A while later, they emerge, Jess first, her face all red and shiny from washing away the tears, no doubt. Kirsty and Iona bring up the rear. She must've reassured them that's she's OK cos they look much more composed than when they went in after her.

As the three of them head for Mr Cosgrove's class, I turn to Jack and voice something that's been taking shape in my mind while we were waiting. "You know what you said about Jess choking? I'm sure you're right – it *is* a twin thing. I'm surprised I didn't cotton on quicker. It *is* all to do with that. And the bruises are cos we're twins, too. Jess's right. Some funny stuff happened to us. We used to think it happened to all sisters. Till we found out it didn't."

"What sort of things?" Jack asks.

"Like she fell off her bike one day and I got a pain in my knee. In the same place where she fell.

And when I got this." I show Jack the scar above my lip. "Jess had a twinge there for months afterwards."

"Could you read each other's thoughts?" Jack asks.

"Yeah. Sometimes," I say, remembering how it used to be. "Quite a lot actually."

"Cool," he says, nodding in approval.

It was cool – then. But when I think of Jess back there in the corridor, recall her bruises hidden beneath the folds of that horrible jumper, well – God – that's anything but cool. It's a catastrophe. And…I can barely put what I'm thinking into words but…did she cause those marks to appear? Subconsciously? And the coughing fits, too? Are they some cruel distortion of the bond we have? If so, it has to stop. All the more reason to get cracking then, to make contact with her as soon as I can. Because I *have* to stop it. I must.

When the girls arrive at class it's just like Jess said it would be – pretending to get her period is the perfect excuse for being late. The very second Iona mentions it, poor Cossy turns slightly pink in the cheeks, stops her in mid-explanation and tells the girls to sit down and get on with their work.

The teacher's embarrassment brings a much-needed smile to my lips. However, as I watch Jess and the girls log in to their computers and think out my plan of action, Jack says something that churns my guts.

"Getting back to what we were talking about," he says, tapping a finger against his chin. "I've been contemplating your sister's bruises and the choking fits. Maybe they mean she's too far-gone for help, that you can't do anything for her now. And nothing's gonna change that."

I swallow hard and close my mind to the sad, serious note in his voice.

"I'm sorry, I know ya don't wanna hear this." He touches my shoulder, offers me a smile halfway between sympathetic and nervous. "But I'm worried too much time's gone by. That you might've lost your chance with Jess."

Why's he saying that? What proof does he have? Nobody knows anything for sure about this crazy world of ours – he said it himself.

He leans against the bank of wall cupboards, picking at his fingernails. It's done so casually, as if he hadn't a worry in the entire universe, that it makes me thunder inside.

"No," I say lunging at him and poking him in the belly. "You're wrong, I know you are. OK, maybe that's what happened with you and your mother years ago, maybe *you* gave up on connecting with her, I don't know. But I *do* know that *I'm* not giving up on Jess."

I blink and turn my back to him to shut out the sudden hurt that flashes across his face.

No. Don't worry about him, don't think of anything except—

Wait a flippin' minute! Is this another of his delaying tactics? Is he trying to distract me? Put me off trying, like he did before? But why would he do that now?

My eyes search his, but he's giving nothing away.

"I don't care what you say, I'm doing it," I say, marching up to Jess's workstation. I pause, glance round, my gaze challenging him. "Just watch me."

He smiles, but it doesn't quite reach his eyes. "I hope you're right. I just don't want you to be disappointed, is all I'm saying."

Disappointed? That word's no longer in my vocabulary.

I look at Jess, sandwiched between Iona and Kirsty, staring at the blank computer screen. She seems so frail that it makes me want to gather her into me and hold her tight. But I can't. I can, however, try to speak to her, give her the comfort of knowing that she hasn't lost me for good, that she doesn't need a woolly jumper, bruises – anything – to keep me near. So, I close my eyes, let her image drift away, and little by little I rid myself of all emotion. Then, opening my eyes again, I say, "Jess, talk to me. It's me, Minty."

Jess gazes at her computer. She doesn't even flinch.

"J. I'm right beside you," I say. "Can't you see?"

Jack must catch the desperation in my voice cos I hear him say, "It's no good, kid. You're making no impact."

He's not wrong; even I have to admit that. I look at Jess, at the way she clutches on to her sorrow like a malevolent comfort blanket. And it shreds my confidence to pieces. I glance at my balled fists, am aware that I'm grinding my teeth. Huh, so much for ridding myself of emotion!

Relaxing my hands, I resolve to try harder so, one by one, I let my thoughts glide from my mind.

But…

They're punishment… Needed a bit of space… Only what I deserve…

I can't expel Jess's words.

She needed me—

"Stop! Why's it so difficult? Why doesn't she hear?" And I realise that my hands are curled into claws again.

Too emotional. I'm way too emotional. But then Jess's my twin – I love her so much, maybe—

From the corner of my vision I catch Iona thumbing through her worksheets, poised to begin her assignment. When she opens a blank Word document on the PC, it occurs to me: Jess might well be part of me, but Iona's not. Yeah, she's an awesome friend and all but she isn't my soulmate.

I'm such an eedjit. I'm way too—

"Cocky. Didn't you tell me once I was cocky?" I say to Jack with a bitter laugh. "Well maybe I am. Maybe I'm being too ambitious. I'm too worked up by everything that's happened to Jess in the past twenty four hours." I motion towards Iona. "So – change of plan. I'm sticking to Iona for today. I'll get to J through her."

But…what to say to Iona? Something – anything – just get it done!

"Iona," I say, gritting my teeth and tuning everything out: each sound, every person, distraction by distraction until there's just me and her. "Tell J that Minty's here. Please."

There's a fraction of a second and then she looks up from her computer. Her features tighten into a frown.

"It's me, Minty," I say, forcing my words into her mind. "Tell J I'm right beside her."

To me, it seems an age before she reacts, but it's probably less than a couple of seconds. Then she stares at me, swings round to Jess, and in the exact same tone she used before, she says, "Minty's beside you."

Snuffing out the flicker of excitement that ignites inside me, extinguishing the sound of Kirsty's gasp, I talk to Iona once again.

"Tell her I've never left her," I say.

And as Iona does what I suggest, I detect the bewilderment on my sister's face.

"What're you saying?" Jess says, her confusion distorted into something like fear.

Don't be scared, J.

"Tell her not to freak, that there's nothing to be frightened of," I yell at Iona. But Iona just sits at her PC, her expression matching the shock on Kirsty's face.

"Have you lost your mind?" Kirsty hisses at her as she gives a silent Jess a hug.

"I…I don't know what came over me," Iona says in a dazed voice.

Jess's complexion loses colour. Her eyes teem with moisture.

"You're really putting the wind up them, I reckon you ought to tone it down a little," Jack says, as he watches Jess dip under the computer desk and fumble around in her bag – for a tissue I expect, though she's taking a long time about it. It's then I realise that she's stopped searching through her schoolbag, and is hugging her sides instead.

Now look what I've done!

"God, Iona, you sure do pick your times for fooling around," Kirsty says under her breath. "What on earth are you playing at?" She scowls and turns her back to her.

I don't wait for Iona to answer. It's time to sort this out.

Frowning, I focus my mind on the blank document on Jess's computer, rehearsing the drill that Jack talked me through in the English room. I picture the pads of my fingers pressing down hard on the caps lock key.

Click!

After a second or so has passed I'm rewarded by the gentle tap of the keys as one letter, then two, three – more, appears on the monitor.

CARISTA.

And yes! By the power of my mind, the word I've chosen is there on the screen.

Jupiter! I can do this.

"Carista?" I hear Jack say. "What's that about? Couldn't you have made it simpler? Typed Minty? Or, I'm here? But hey, with all that Jess has had to deal with today couldn't you just leave it? Try again tomorrow?"

I try to tune him out.

But he's right about one thing – what was I thinking of? I *should* type my name.

So I knit my brows again, purse my mouth and will my mind to type the next word.

MINTY.

Jess, please look up, I say to myself as I glance down at her. But she's back to rooting about in her schoolbag again.

Kirsty grabs Iona by the hand. "What the heck are you doing writing that?" she asks in a fierce whisper, gesturing to the words on J's monitor.

Iona's pupils bulge. Her jaw drops. She peers at her computer screen.

"I...I didn't," she says, in a real gobsmacked voice.

"Is that supposed to be funny?" Kirsty says, more in a hiss than a whisper.

"I didn't type it," Iona says.

"Well who else did? I didn't," Kirsty says, speaking as quietly as I've ever heard her, though her anger's unmistakeable. She jerks a thumb at Jess. "Well, stop that right now and get rid of it before J sees it."

However, Kirsty's gutsy voice has let her down again because Jess seems to have heard her anyway. She looks up from under the desk, frowns, then goes back to searching her bag.

But hey, ignore all that, Minty, fade it all out. Get on with it!

So, channelling my energies into adding another word to my message, I select the relevant keyboard letters and will them to flash up on the monitor.

Yet as I do, that awful searing heat returns to engulf my eyeballs and spread into my forehead, fogging up my concentration.

IMHEREHELPJ.

Crikey, what kind of word's this? They won't understand that. Where's the apostrophe? Why didn't you press the space bar? Why didn't you finish it?

Omigod, the blistering agony! "My skull, it hurts," I gasp, as I try to rub the pain away. I screw up my face and tip backward, clutching at my head. And as I tumble, my body glances off Iona's shoulder, earning me a sharp bolt of that horrible electricity again, just to add to the unbearable agony that's already swamping me.

Through it all, I hear Kirsty's voice. "What're you doing?" she says. "I told you to get rid of those words, not add more."

I close my eyes against the scraping sound of a chair being pushed back and in the background I can just hear Jess say, "Please don't argue."

In the distance somewhere, Iona says something, but I don't catch it because of the fiery intensity that overwhelms me. It's all I can think of. The pain rips everything from my mind, and I find myself fumbling my way across the classroom until I end up by the window.

As the searing heat dies down, Jack joins me.

"What just happened?" he says, his voice thundering in my head.

"Cut the shouting," I rasp, propping myself against the ledge.

"I'm not." He gives me strange look. "What's with you?"

Somehow I manage to drag myself upright to face him and, finally, the storm in my head subsides.

"Jupiter, that was scary," I say, massaging my temple. "I thought my brain was about to catch fire. The harder I concentrated, the worse it became."

He squints at me, touches my shoulder. "You OK?"

"Never been better." I attempt a smile.

"You're a plucky little thing, aren't you?" He grins. "But perhaps you should try out one thing at a time, huh? Till you get the hang of things. But tomorrow, yeah? Leave it for now." He drops his hand. "Now tell me," he asks in a false let's-change-the-subject kinda way. "What does Carista mean?"

"It's a festival," I mutter, reluctantly, cos I'm determined not to let him sidetrack me.

He crouches down until his eyes are level with mine, then he makes an inquisitive face. Smiles. Nods. "And?"

"The ancient Romans used to have them."

Tell him anything to shut him up.

"Go on."

"It was one of these three special ones they held in February," I continue. "A family thing. That, and the Parentalia and—"

"But why type that particular word?" Jack asks.

I sigh.

"Look, I was trying to think of something easy to write. Something that Jess would instantly recognise. Would make her think of me. OK? I dunno why I thought of it. I just did. It just popped into my head."

I touch my forehead, half-expecting that it'll be hot and sweaty. But, it's not. Guess that figures. Why would it be? The burning was all in my mind.

Even so, the words on the screen were real!

I look across at Jess and my friends. They're huddled over J's computer, whispering to one another and although I can't see their faces I know by their body language that they're excited about something. No, not about something – about *the* thing. The thing I just did.

"And you said I'd be disappointed? You said I should leave it?" I say to Jack, not even trying to hide the smugness in my voice, nor the self-satisfied smirk on my face. I point to the girls. "Look at them, it *is* working. I don't care what it costs, I have to write some more. Even if it kills me."

Kills me, when I'm already dead? Hah! Is that what my English teacher calls irony, I think with a wry smile. Even so, the idea of all those disturbing feelings rushing through me again doesn't exactly fill me with joy. I so do *not* want to experience that again. But I have to – what choice do I have? I need to see this through. So, pivoting on my heels, I make my way back to J and the others.

Nevertheless, before I'm even halfway there, I realise that something is well wrong. The girls are huddled together right enough, but they aren't excited like I'd thought they were. No – they're arguing!

So much for me reading their body language.

And geez, Kirsty – I've never seen her like that. Yeah, OK, she is still keeping that big booming voice in check but, blimey, there's no mistaking she's mega upset and beyond angry – and it's with Iona.

"How could you?" she says to Iona, the colour high on her cheeks. "All that pretending to feel Minty around us, and now this?" She pokes a finger at Jess's monitor. "Do you get some sort of kick out of that?"

"Watch my lips," Iona says, her mouth drawn in determination. "I didn't write it." She blows out a puff of air. "How many more times?"

"I don't understand you lately," Kirsty says, wiping away an angry tear with the back of her wrist. "You never used to be so cruel." She goes to grab the mouse. "I'm deleting this."

"Don't bother! I'll do it myself," Iona says and gets to it before Kirsty can reach it. In a few clicks, she erases what was on the screen.

Jess watches the words I'd written disappear, her facial expression completely blank, but then she looks at Iona and says, "I don't understand. I thought you were my friend."

"I am your friend," Iona says and grips Jess's hand. "You've got to believe me, I have no idea how that writing got there but it truly wasn't me who wrote it."

"And what about what you said just now? You are bang out of order, Iona McIntyre," Kirsty spits. She shakes her head. "I don't know you anymore." Then she delivers her killer blow. "And I don't know if I want to if you're going to keep acting like this."

"Stop it," Jess says, and though her voice is deathly quiet it fires into my mind like an explosive. "Stop arguing – I can't bear it."

"You've got to believe me, J, I'd never do anything to hurt you," Iona says, appealing to Jess with her eyes. "Even though I've been telling the God's honest truth about all the weird feelings I've had. And yeah, OK, I do wonder if Minty's hanging around." She runs a hand along the monitor. "But I had nothing to do with any of the things that have happened here in this room."

Jess slumps into her seat, looks at both of them and says, "But Minty's gone, Iona. God, I wish you *could* see her. I wish *I* could. You have no idea how much. But I can't. She's gone for good. And d'you know what? Half of me's gone, too. Died along with my twin."

"Please, Jess, don't talk like this," Iona says, biting her bottom lip.

"And you know what else? I wish I had died. I wish it had been me who'd drowned that day. Me. Not Minty. Me. Because, what good is life now she's not here?" Jess's voice is so dull and lifeless it makes me wish I'd never stepped foot inside this blasted classroom.

God. What have I done?

"J. Don't say that," Kirsty says, her mouth quivering as fresh tears well up in her eyes.

"I can't help it," Jess says. "If I've got to live without her, I might as well be dead."

And with that, like a puppet cut from its string, she flops sideways across Iona's keyboard, sparking a volley of random letters onto the computer screen.

That's when Mr Cosgrove comes over to see what's going on.

And when I realise I've messed up big time.

CHAPTER TWENTY

Jack stares at Jess sleeping flat out on the duvet, her long tangled-up locks spread across the pillows. "She's outta it, man," he says, his golden hair tinged with soft evening light. His smile is kind, sympathetic. "Reckon she has an excuse tonight, after the day she's had."

I know he doesn't mean to but his words hack through me like a machete.

And, God, I can hardly look at my sister. Those puffy eyelids and her skin as sallow as uncooked pastry just remind me what a stupid, pig-headed idiot I am. But even though I hate to do it, it's as if I'm torturing myself, because my gaze keeps straying towards Jess.

Jack flexes his long legs as he lounges against the wall.

"Poor kid's in pieces," he says. "It can't help her to bottle up everything inside. She shouldn't hide those bruises from your parents. She ought to tell them about them. And about the coughing."

His gaze meets mine, inviting conversation, but I'm not much in the mood for talking.

Remus stirs, glances over his shoulder at Jack, and then curls back up with Romulus at the bottom of Jess's bed.

How simple it would be to be a dog.

Jack brushes his hands down his faded denims, gives his arms a stretch and studies me for a sec, really stern all of a sudden. Then he ambles over and joins me on my bed.

"Stop brooding," he says. "What's the point of it? Think of something else for a while. Tell me about your school."

"Are you for real? My sister's like that..." I take one more look at her then glower at him. "And you want to chat about school?"

He shrugs his apology but continues anyhow. "All that jostling, running in the corridors," he says, scratching his head. "And the din the kids made. Man oh man! The masters would've caned us for that. Is your maths teacher the only one with discipline in that place?" He grins, raises an eyebrow. "But what I really wanna know is what's it like being co-ed? How do you concentrate with the opposite sex around?"

"They're just boys," I say, already tired of this discussion. "What's the big deal? Now leave me alone. I don't want to talk right now. OK?"

"So, would you rather feel sorry for yourself?" he says. "How will that help?"

"Oh shut up," I mutter, easing myself off the bed. "This is all your doing."

"Hey! Hey!" he says, holding up his hands. "Don't take it out on me. It's not my fault it went pear-shaped."

"Isn't it?" I stare him out. "You were the one who told me what to do."

"At your insistence. And as I recall, I tried to tell you this afternoon that it probably wouldn't work, that Jess wouldn't respond, that you should lay off her for the day. But you thought you knew better."

"I would've got through to her long before now if it wasn't for you. I would've figured it out for myself if you hadn't tried to put me off the scent."

My glare intensifies.

When I think of how he conned me, let me think that there was nothing I could do for Jess I could…I could thump him. This *is* his fault.

I lean right into his face. "You know what, Jack? I wish I'd never bloody met you!"

And with that I'm off downstairs.

Not that I go far because with each step I take I get less and less mad at Jack and increasingly angry with myself until, drained of my wrath, I sit down on the bottom step, thinking what a muddle I've made of everything.

You thought you knew better!

Yeah I did. I thought I had it sussed. I thought all I had to do was to talk to Jess, try out my tricks on Iona, compose a stupid message and Jess would spring back to life.

Seems I got it wrong.

"Minty?"

Jack's voice makes me start.

I turn around and there he is, at the top of the stairs, massaging his chin and looking at me uncertainly.

When he goes to speak, I interrupt him.

"Just leave it," I say. "I don't need…" But the words fizzle out in my throat.

In a few long-legged strides he's by my side. He sits down next to me. Smiles.

"Let's not fight, eh?" He elbows me softly in the side. "Truce?"

I don't say anything.

"You weren't to know how it'd turn out today," he says in the gentlest of voices.

Don't be nice to me. Don't!

I hug my knees. "I'm such a jerk. I've just made things worse."

"Maybe we're both jerks," he says. He bumps his skinny hips against mine. "Look, at the risk of sounding boring I'll say it again – brooding isn't gonna get you anywhere."

"Yeah well … perhaps you're right," I say, looking up.

"Kid, I'm always right. You only just realising that?" he says with a wink. "I'm like the Pope – infallible."

"He's not though, is he? And neither are you."

He clutches his chest, looks all affronted. "How can you say that? I'm crushed."

Eedjit!

"Jupiter! How did I ever get stuck with you?" I say, raising my eyes to the ceiling.

"Admit it, man," he says, erupting into a laugh. "You'd be lost without me."

I squirm, remembering what I yelled at him earlier. "Jack, I'm sorry. I didn't mean what I said." I twist my lips into a shamefaced smile. "I *am* glad I met you."

He shrugs. "No sweat." He looks at me. "So, what you gonna do about your sis now?"

"Take your advice: stop moping about." I fiddle with one of the buttons on my jacket. "Get my backside into gear. Plan things better next time."

He opens his mouth but I cut through whatever he was about to say. "Cos there has to be a next time – you heard what Jess told Iona, she really wants to see me again. And I've got to give her that chance."

But what if it *is* too late for Jess? What if Jack's hunch is right?

No – brush away those negative thoughts.

"So, even though she gets spooked by the things I have to do to make contact, it'll be worth it once she realises what's really going on, won't it?" I stand up, smooth down my jeans.

"The end justifies the means?" Jack says, but he must realise I haven't quite grasped what he's just said cos he adds, "It's for her own good?"

"Exactly." I venture a smile. "Let's face it, she couldn't feel any worse than she does now."

Chapter Twenty-One

I lie on my bed for ages, working out what my next move will be. Heck knows what Jack's up to – I left him downstairs. Eventually, Jess rouses. She pushes back the bedcover, slips her bare feet into her dog-chewed slippers and heads for the stairs. Naturally, I follow her. Well, maybe not naturally given the fact that I'm a spirit and she has no idea she's being tailed.

When we reach the bottom step she lingers in the hallway. A low murmur of voices filters out from the living room. She runs two fingers underneath the frayed sleeve of the manky woollen jumper she's wearing over her pyjamas, then shoves back her mussed-up hair, moistens her cracked lips, and puts an ear to the door. Then she cranks it open and we shuffle in.

Mum's on the sofa watching some late-night TV programme, with the sound turned way down. She looks up from the screen and smiles when she sees J.

"Couldn't sleep either?" Mum says, shifting along the chocolate-brown leather and patting the space next to her.

Jess tugs down the sleeves of the jumper, brings her hair around her neck and yawns. "No, I was asleep but I've just woken up. Wanted a drink of water." She muffles another massive yawn. "What time's it?"

Mum checks her watch – the funky DKNY one that Dad bought her for her last birthday. "Almost half past one."

J flops down next to Mum, kicks off her slippers and tucks her skinny legs under her, rearranging her pyjama bottoms in an effort to get comfy. I don't know who looks worse – Jess or Mum. Geez, my poor sis. But, oh God, what about Mum? Look at her.

She hasn't even been to bed by the look of it; her face's still made-up and she's wearing the smart navy trousers and white cotton blouse she had on to work today, except they're pretty crumpled now. In the dim light of the half-lit room, even under the make-up her skin is horribly grey and there are those huge bags under her eyes she seems to have all the time now.

My family is falling apart. Thanks to me.

"Hey, come and join us," says a voice from the shadows. "You'll like this."

Jack. Curled up in an armchair.

So that's what he's been doing, watching TV. It's then I realise that it isn't some telly programme they're watching. Crikey, why didn't I notice before – it's one of the DVDs from our bedroom: *Quo Vadis.* Oh, Jess, our all-time fave movie! A fleeting smile comes to my lips as I think back to the day we got that DVD, how excited we were, how we couldn't wait to play it.

I ease myself into Dad's Stressless armchair, sit back, and plonk my feet on the cream leather footstool.

"Have to say though, I'm surprised you know it exists," Jack says, nodding over to the television. "It's even older than I am."

He doesn't get a response because I'm too distracted by the worry lines on Mum's face when she notices Jess looking at the screen. Maybe she's expecting Jess to do something, like burst into tears cos the movie reminds her of me.

Mum clears her throat, nods to a half-drunk mug of tea with a yucky, milky scum on the surface and smiles at her. "Want me to make you a hot drink?"

"No," Jess replies with a shake of the head. "I'll get some water in a sec and go back up."

But she doesn't make any move to go, instead she snuggles into Mum and they sit in silence staring at the plasma telly on the wall. They look so peaceful and calm, there in the flickering light; they have no inkling that there are two ghosts sharing the room with them.

Yet, they could do – or at least I could make them realise that I'm here.

I look to the television. What if I switch it off? I could do that, couldn't I? It'd be a start, and after that I could… But then I glance at Mum and Jess tucked up on the sofa, and I wonder should I disturb them? Hasn't J had enough for one day? Then I'm reminded about something else – Jack was worried that too much time had gone by to help Jess. There hasn't, has there? But, omigod, what if I leave it even longer? Then it maybe *will* be too late.

I look at my twin again, remind myself of the real Jess, the one before I drowned, and I realise that the only way to get her back to herself is by acting right now.

Before I can talk myself out of it again, I say to Jack, "Sorry to disturb your viewing but I have to have another try, Jack. I can't put it off any longer." I point to the telly. "I'm going to turn that off."

He arches an eyebrow, gestures to my twin. "You sure this is a good time?"

"Will there ever be a good time? I have to help her, whatever it takes."

He stares at me, and then smiles his agreement. Unfolding his lean body he perches on the arm of his chair, and rubs his hands together like a dodgy second-hand car salesman. He grins. "OK, get on with it then."

So, crossing my fingers behind my back, I stretch out my neck, peer at the telly, and focus my mind on the rectangular screen, keeping my body statue-still. And I imagine my eyes are lasers boring through the plastic.

Then, with a pop, the picture on the TV screen goes blank.

"I did it! First time too!" I say to Jack, a grin splitting my face.

Jack returns my smile. "It's a blast when it goes well, eh?"

Mum sits up with a start. "What happened there?"

She reaches for the remote control, feels about until she finds the right button, and presses it half a dozen times. "Nope. Seems to be something wrong." She makes another attempt. Scowls. "No good."

She picks up the remote for the DVD player and tries that. When nothing works she drops both remotes on the sofa. "Time I was in bed anyway. You too, love," she says, getting up.

Sorry, Mum, but I can't let you do that.

So I stare and stare at the TV until…it flicks back on.

Yah me! Crikey, Jack never said this could give you such a high!

"How did that happen?" Mum says, looking puzzled.

Jack winks at me. Peers back at the screen. All of a sudden the telly switches back off.

Good one, Jack!

"Why is it doing that?" Mum says, scratching her ear.

Just then the television snaps back into action and this time the sound's been turned up and loud theatrical voices blast into the living room.

While Jess and Mum exchange glances, I beam at my partner in paranormal crime.

"That's weird," Jess says, plucking at the neckline of her jumper.

"Blasted thing," Mum tuts. "Don't tell me it's on the blink. We've only had it six months." She goes over to have a look at it, presses the power button a few times and sighs. "I'll get Dad to check it in the morning."

She gives Jess a hand off the sofa. "Come on, get your water and off to bed."

"Wowza, Jack! I haven't had so much fun since I was alive. And it's so easy!" I say with an excited giggle.

OK, ditch the laughter, Minty.

The grin drops from my face and I knuckle down and focus on the telly. In my mind I see my index finger reaching for the hard black plastic of the power button, then pushing it down until the TV bursts into life.

And, as I visualise it, the television really does fire up.

"What?" Mum cries, spinning round.

"I did it again!" I say, clapping my hands and bursting into an on-the-spot jig. I turn to Jess who's gaping at the telly. "You can't blame *that* on Iona, J."

"You switched it off," she says to Mum. "I don't... What's...?"

I blot out the confusion in her eyes. Keep my mind on what must be done.

"It must be faulty. I'd better disconnect it at the mains." Mum walks over, leans down and flicks off the wall switch. But, as she walks away, the TV goes on once more.

"Why did it do that?" Jess says, wringing her hands.

"I don't know. But I'd better unplug it, to be on the safe side," Mum says as she yanks out the plug. "Wouldn't want it catching fire."

She disconnects the DVD player as well then pads over to put out the table lamp but, before she gets there, it snaps off.

Nice one, Jacko!

"Mum?" Jess whispers. "What's going on?"

Jack grins at me. "Thought we'd diversify a little. You up for that?"

I nod my answer but he probably doesn't notice because he's back to focussing on his task.

Instantly, with a loud click, the lamp lights up.

Jupiter! He's wizard at this. How can a guy this good at all this spooky stuff still be stuck here? His mother must be blind, or something.

"I don't understand," Mum says, a frown line creasing her temple. "Why did that happen?"

Well, his mum might be blind but mine sure isn't!

Jack smiles at me. Bobs his head towards the table lamp. "Gonna try it?"

Turning away from him, my eyes bore into it. I imagine my mindpower gathering in my brain, soaring through the air until it lands on the switch and holds it down. In my head, I hear the click, see the lamplight die and, suddenly, it does just that – it blinks off.

Result!

Through the gloom I see Jack giving me the thumbs up.

Flashing him a quick grin, I centre my thoughts on the other table lamp until it snaps off as well, pitching the room into darkness.

Jess jumps back with a screech and clings to Mum, her whole body juddering.

"It's all right, love." Mum gives her a reassuring pat on the arm, for all the good it does because Jess just clings even tighter.

Jupiter! Look what I've done to my poor twin. I freeze.

"Jess, I'm sorry," I say. "But it's for your own good."

Mum fumbles for the overhead light but before she gets to it, I flick it on.

"OK, OK. No more. Maybe she's had enough for one night," Jack says, pointing to the panic in Jess's eyes. "You don't wanna give her a heart attack."

"What's all the racket?" Dad appears at the door, in his pale-blue pinstriped PJs. He doesn't look best pleased to have been woken up.

Jess jerks into the air, her arms flying forward as if she's trying to fight off an invisible demon. She spins round and flings herself into Dad's arms.

"Dad! Something really weird's going on. The telly went off. And the lamp. And—"

"Easy. Easy," he says, giving her a cuddle. He looks over her head to shoot Mum a quizzical look.

"She's right. The electrics have gone haywire," Mum says, glancing back over her shoulder, her eyes darting all around the room.

My poor mum. It's not only Jess who's rattled. But then, my sister isn't the only one who's grieving either. I think of Dad who hasn't managed to cry since I drowned, of the guilt he's feeling – of the guilt Mum's feeling too. And I realise that it isn't just Jess I can help by making contact, I can help all of them. So with that in mind, I redouble my efforts and switch off the ceiling light and we're plunged into darkness again.

Jess screeches with fear.

Mum gasps.

Dad shouts, "What the..."

"Kid? What did I tell you? Cool it," Jack yells.

Above his cry, there's the sound of feet thumping downstairs and Romulus runs in, closely followed by Remus. Suddenly Romulus goes crazy, running into the room towards where I'm standing and scurrying back to the door again. He's yelping and whining and barking. Remus joins in, bounding around the room, yapping and whirling his tail in the air like a rotary dryer caught in a gale.

"You silly dog. Stop that noise," Dad says, and switches the overhead light on.

But Romulus is in a frenzy and before I know it I'm clicking my fingers to distract him. "Here, Rom."

Holding out my hand, I fix my mind on calming him, just as I did with that cat in the street. Suddenly, his body goes rigid. His eyes lock on to me and his hair stands on end, like in those daft Scooby Doo cartoons Jess and I used to watch.

"That's it, boy. Settle," I say, as I crouch down and hold out my hand for him to sniff.

See me, Romulus. See me. I'm here. I roll the thought round and round in my mind, concentrate my energies on calming him down.

Romulus growls. Sniffs.

His tail drops.

His head drops.

His nose twitches.

He inches towards me, pricks up his ears and whimpers a bit. Then the whimper turns into a whine – it's not a sad, frightened whine, but it's a whine all the same. His head tilts up as if to meet my gaze, his eyes never leaving me once.

At this point, the whining stops and Romulus lies on the carpet, quiet and very still. I guess that to J and my parents he looks as if he's staring into space. But he isn't – he's staring at me! My mind does a little dance at the idea.

Yet, although Romulus sees me, Mum and Dad don't: they gape in my direction all right but they look totally mystified. As for Jess, her face is hidden in the shawl collar of Dad's dressing gown.

Seconds later, she looks up. "What's Rom peering at?" she says, the terror in her voice matched by the look on her face. Her hands cling onto Dad so tightly I can see the white of her knuckle-bones shining through the skin.

"Geoff?" Mum says, her voice halfway between a gasp and a whisper. "Why is he acting like that?"

"Something amazing's happening here, Jack!" I say. "Check out their reactions. It's working! All this is working!"

Omigod, is this it? Is this the breakthrough? The moment when Jess accepts that I haven't deserted her?

"Minty, enough," Jack says.

"No! I have to keep going. It's the only way!" I yell back at him.

"Have you gone mad? It's too much for her," he says. "Remember what happened at school today."

But, deaf to his warning, I re-focus on the light and plunge us all into darkness again.

Jess yelps, and even in the dim light I can see her bury her face in Dad's chest, detect the dark form of her body quivering uncontrollably. "I…think I'm going to…" she says. Then she lets out this pitiful little moan and collapses.

"Jess," Dad says, reaching out to catch her just as the lights snap back on.

"She's fainted, Geoff," Mum says, taking the limp bulk of my twin in her arms. "Help me."

And it's those two words that do it – *help me.* I take in the fearful looks that pass between my parents, the dead weight of my sister in my mother's arms and I think to myself, how is this helping anyone?

Oh great, Minty, another disaster.

"You pushed it too far," Jack says, shaking his head as he lowers himself into Dad's chair. He crosses his legs and studies me, his head cocked to one side. "I did warn you."

Yeah, Jack, like I don't realise that.

Dad scoops Jess up and carries her to her room, leaving Mum to follow after them. All the while, he doesn't say a thing, not one word. When he gets to the bedroom he gently lays J on her bed and then drops down onto mine. He stares and stares at her ashen face while Mum makes her comfortable, easing the tangled hair from her eyes and smoothing out her limbs.

Then she lightly pats J's cheeks. "Love, wake up," she says in a tone that matches the wretchedness in her face so precisely that I have to close my eyes and cover my ears to shut out the misery I've caused.

Even so, it's useless: the evidence is tattooed on my eyeballs, imprinted on my eardrums, in every atom of my brain. This is all my fault.

Omigod, why didn't I take Jack's advice?

"What's happening to us, Mary?" Dad asks, clasping the side of his head, forehead knotted as if in discomfort.

"I don't know. That was horribly frightening down there," Mum says in a more collected voice.

All of a sudden, Jess springs up and stares wildly round the room. "Quo Vadis, Minty?" she says, in short rasping breaths.

"What is she on about?" Dad asks, his voice shot through with worry.

"Quo Vadis: whither goest thou – where are you going," Jack murmurs.

"Where are you?" J says.

"Jess, love," Mum says, stroking her hair.

Jess turns to look at her. Well it's more of a stare really, and then a dreamy smile crosses her face. "Minty?" Her eyes mist with tears. "Oh, Minty," she whispers and she moves close enough to touch our mother's cheek.

Mum gulps and says, "No, Jess, it isn't Minty."

Jess looks at her. Her hand stills. "Minty?" she says again, the question hanging in the air as Mum and Dad trade worried glances.

"Sweetheart," Mum says, but she doesn't get the chance to finish her sentence, because at the sound of Mum's endearment Jess gasps and lets out a pitiful cry. Then she jolts backs against the headboard and dissolves into uncontrollable sobs.

And whilst I watch my parents doing their best to console her, I say to myself: My God, Minty, there's got to be a better way of making contact than this.

CHAPTER TWENTY-TWO

Funny how time drags when you can't sleep. The way each minute seems like an hour, and you think morning will never come again. Tonight's been one of those nights. But who am I kidding? Every night since I died has been one of those nights. If I let myself think back to how it used to be – how I used to fall into a coma whenever the light went out, sleep right through until Mum dragged me out of bed the next day – I'd go crazy. I would.

Jess had the same sloth-like tendencies as me – but see her now. Look at her, cuddling my urn, pinched white face peeking out under that mound of duvet, at the dark shadows of exhaustion smudged on the skin around her eyes. She hasn't had the best night either; she never does now I'm gone. Poor J.

Poor J? At least she's been able to get some shut-eye. At least she *can* sleep. Actually exists – not like me.

Enough, Minty! Stop feeling sorry for yourself! But if only... If only I could feel human again.

"Do they still teach Latin these days?"

Oh, Jack, go away. Let me be.

"Well, do they?" he asks, for what seems the ninety-ninth time since Mum and Dad went to bed, having eventually soothed my sister into some sort of sleep.

I pretend that I haven't heard. Again!

"Never was much good at science but Latin – now you're talking. Amo, amas, amat and all that," he says, trying to catch my eye.

I blank him.

OK, Jack, cut out the chit-chat. I know you mean well but I've got stuff to think about.

Yeah, Minty, like how to avoid another flippin' disaster!

He gestures to Jess, to the row of DVDs on our bedroom shelves. "*Ben Hur. The Robe. The Fall of the Roman Empire.* Don't ya have anything else apart from films set in Roman times? Is that how Jess picked up Latin? From watching *Quo Vadis,* and co?" Squinting at a fading drawing of Jess's tacked up on the pinboard, he says, "She's from that flick? Lydia, isn't it?"

"Lygia," I say, correcting him despite myself.

"Hah! I knew you wouldn't be able to resist putting me right on that." He plants his bum on the chair by the desk. "So, you gonna talk to me now?" He smiles his gentle smile. "Look, don't beat yourself up over it – you got carried away, it happens. If it makes you feel any better, I did it, too, at the beginning. So come on, put today behind you. Chalk it down to experience, yeah?"

I glance up.

He overdid it, too? Is that the truth, or is he spinning me a line? Heck, it wouldn't be the first time.

His smile turns into a cheeky grin, and then he blows through his crooked teeth as if he's trying to cool hot tea. "This Roman thing – you chicks really are obsessed, aren't you?"

Yeah, you call it an obsession; I'd call it perfectly normal.

Romulus is tucked up in the crook of Jess's bent legs, snoring quietly, apart from the occasional feeble woof that makes me think he's in the midst of some lovely doggie dream.

Is he dreaming of seeing me in the living room? *Did* he see me?

As if he's tuned into my thoughts, Jack looks at Romulus too then smiles across at me.

"Been quite a night for him. Seeing you for the first time," he says.

My curiosity gets the better of me so I gesture to Romulus and say, "Why then? How come Rom could see me then when he showed no signs of it before?"

Jack knocks on the back of his head. "All in the mind. Remember? You harnessed all your energies on what you had to do. Just as you did with the television and the lamps."

"But I did the same with the PCs at school and we both know how that turned out."

"Yip, but you'd just seen Jess's bruises..." He stretches out those long lanky legs of his. "And it's understandable but maybe you let your feelings pollute your thinking."

"I've already wondered about that. Is...is that why I can't always make contact with Iona – cos I'm too emotional at times?"

"Maybe...probably. Although keeping your emotions in check doesn't always guarantee success. As you've already gathered, sometimes making contact can be unpredictable. It certainly doesn't help if you're over-emotional though." He stops, lost in thought for a bit. Then he dips his head into my eye line, forcing me to look at him. He grasps my hands and says, "Here's the thing..." He frowns. "Too much emotion hampers our attempts at communication, but in extreme circumstances – like where someone alive is in danger, real danger – then... You're not gonna believe this, because I sure find it hard to..."

Romulus woofs again in his sleep. Jack looks over at him.

"Then what? Tell me."

He drops my hands, sits back down where he was. "Then us guys – ghosts – can..." He breaks off for a moment, as if dredging up a long-lost fact. "Get back our physical bodies, just as if we were alive again. Can make actual physical contact. Temporarily." He looks up at me with an uncertain grin, shrugs. "That's what I've heard, anyway."

What? How can that be?

As though he's heard my unspoken query, he adds, "Maybe it's the level of emotion, the intensity of it. Between the dead and the living, I dunno. Look, it probably doesn't happen. It's probably some kinda... Oh what's that expression? Urban myth, yeah, that's it."

He scratches his chin, brows furled in thought. "But then again, it makes you wonder. No?"

"Omigod. It does."

"Yip. Emotions are powerful things." He says it in a strange faraway tone, his eyes fixed on the central light above our heads. "They have to be because even though we can't express them through tears or the like, we can still feel them in here," he taps his chest. "When we're dead."

He slowly shakes his head. "The power of emotion, huh? Remember that guy I told you about? Pete? The ghost I knew?" His expression alters and it's as if his face is lit up from the inside. "Guess that's how Pete's old man appeared to him that day. To tell him he was ready."

"What're you talking about?"

The lines on his temple unfurl. His mouth slackens. "The old guy was near death, maybe that's why he was able to communicate through his mind. It'd be the emotion that did it." He stands up, walks over to the empty bed.

Communicated through his mind? The ghost did? The old man? And intensity between the dead and living – what does that mean, exactly?

Jack stretches out on the bed. "Why don't we catch some zeds? OK, I know us spooks don't sleep, but you know – rest, sneak some quiet time, whatever you wanna call it."

"Yeah, yeah, fine," I say, my head brimming with thoughts of that urban myth.

Physical contact? What if it's true? What if I could get my body back? Could be with Jess again?

Imagine if I could! Jupiter! How awesome would that be?

Chapter Twenty-Three

A gentle rap at the bedroom door brings the night to an end.

"Morning, Jess."

I twist round and there's Mum, one hand on the door handle, an anxious little smile on her face. She goes over and gently shakes Jess by the shoulder. "Love, Iona and Kirsty are here. They're going shopping in Kirkcaldy and thought you might like to join them."

Jess lifts her head a fraction off the pillows. She murmurs something unintelligible and falls back down with a grunt.

"It's such a lovely day," Mum says and strides over to the window to pull back the curtains, allowing brilliant sunshine to pour into the room. "Too nice to lounge around inside."

She gazes out onto the street for a second then turns back to Jess. "Why don't you go with your friends? Get yourself some new summer clothes. What do you think?"

"I told them yesterday I don't want to," mumbles Jess from under the covers.

"Well," Mum says, briskly, "I'm not leaving you here on your own. If you're not going with them you can come to Perth with us. Dad and I really must buy a new bed. That one of ours is totally past its best."

Hey! Hold it, Mum. Too much information!

"We're leaving in half an hour, so make it snappy," she continues. "We want to get there early before all the crowds. You know what Saturdays are like."

I clamp my mouth together to press down the giggle that's risen up at the back of my throat. A day out shopping with Mum and Dad? For a bed? Because they've worn out the old one? I don't think so!

Jess must think that too because she sits up, tugs back the duvet and hunts for her scabby slippers, all without looking at Mum once. "I'll be down in a minute," she mutters.

Before Mum goes out the room, I just have time to catch the smile that flashes across her face.

"Nice one, Mum," Jack chuckles, voicing my thoughts exactly.

But what I see next robs me of any momentary happiness, for as Jess picks up the mirror off the bedside table and pulls back her straggly hair to peer at her reflection, my jaw drops. For there, round her neck are those bruises.

She moves the mirror down a bit so that her gaze locks onto the ugly brown and purple ones on either side of her neck. Then it falls onto the hand holding the glass, to where her jumper's slipped back to expose the inside of her wrist.

She yanks back the other cuff, drops the mirror onto the table and moves about the bedroom in this zombie-type motion, like something from a freak show, fetching clothes, shoes, a bag, money. She doesn't bother to get washed, or tug a comb through the snags in her long hair. It's as if when she looked in that mirror, instead of seeing those bruises again she saw a monster, a monster that sucked the last remnant of the real Jess through the looking glass.

But she doesn't need to stay that way.

"You're so thick at times."

"What?" Jack asks, giving me a strange look.

Blimey, I hadn't realised I'd said that aloud!

"Not you! Me," I say. "You said back in school that I'm the only one who can save Jess." I glance over to her. "But I haven't made a very good job of it so far, have I? I need to box clever. Keep my cool. Be more specific in what I plan. Do things she'll connect with me."

Jack smiles. "OK, but less of the talking, yip? *Gesta non verba* from now on."

"Eh?"

He laughs. "So it *is* only your sis who's picked up Latin."

"For your information I know some Latin, just not that gesture non versa thingy," I say, sticking my nose in the air.

"*Gesta non verba,*" he says, emphasising the A. "It means actions not words."

Well, why didn't you say that in the first place?

But *gesta non verba,* eh? You bet!

⚜ ⚜ ⚜

"Here we are," says Iona and takes three Big Mac Meals off the plastic tray and leans the tray against the table leg.

"How much do I owe you?" Kirsty asks, reaching for her purse.

Iona holds up a hand. "Nothing. It's my treat." She offers Jess an apologetic smile. "To say sorry for being such a pain lately."

"Yeah, and so you should," Kirsty grumbles. Yet as she tears the stripy paper off three straws her face lights up with a sudden grin. "But thanks anyway," she says popping a straw each into the three large-size Cokes and shoving a meal towards Jess.

"And I want to see you eat that," she says, giving Jess a pointed look. "You hear? You're getting way too skinny."

Jess opens the Big Mac carton, lifts up the bun, looks at the burger and pushes the box to the side. "I said I'm not hungry. "

Iona gives her a wisp of a nudge. "Go on, Jess. At least take a bite. You need to eat something."

The burger's oozing with mayo. Despite my worry for my sister, the sight of minced beef, salad and cheese is really getting to me.

"I love McDonalds," I say, licking my lips. "What I would do for just one bite of a Big Mac. Or a sip of strawberry milk shake."

Jack nods. "One of the things I miss most, food. Never had one of those though. Weren't many of these places around when I was alive."

"I wish I could smell it," I say, swooping down to burger level and taking a huge sniff. "No. Nothing."

Jack laughs. "Tough luck, kid."

"This is yummy, J. You don't know what you're missing," Kirsty says, through a mouthful of fries.

"But *I* do!" I say, my eyes on Jess's food.

If only I could have just one fry, just one crunchy, salt-speckled, French fry. Surely that's not too much to ask?

Jack chuckles. "Poor Minty." He turns towards Jess. "Guess she's too exhausted to eat."

"Yeah, thanks to me."

"Cut yourself a little slack," Jack says, with a smile.

He hovers behind Kirsty but his eyes are all for Iona. "She's some looker, your mate."

"Jack. Put your tongue in. You're drooling."

He laughs. "You're one to talk. Lusting over that burger."

"That's different!"

But is it? We both want what we can never have. But stuff the burger; what I really need is to tune in to what Iona's saying to Jess.

"J," Iona says, reaching down to grab her shoulder bag off the floor. "I know it's not your birthday or anything." She glances at Kirsty. "But we want you to have this."

She unzips the inner pocket of the embroidered denim bag, takes out a square gift-wrapped package and hands it to Jess.

Jess holds it between her fingers, rubs the shiny purple paper with a thumb. "What is it?"

"Open it and see," Kirsty says, her gutsy voice suddenly gentle.

Jess gives them a thin smile and begins unwrapping, carefully sliding a finger under the sellotape, stripping back the paper to reveal a black cardboard box with bright silvery writing. She looks up at the girls. Iona nods at Jess encouragingly, her beautiful chocolate brown curls bobbing round her face. Jess peels away a layer of lilac tissue paper and takes out a necklace of tiny lilac stones with a large tear-shaped purple pendant.

I gasp. "It's beautiful."

"Go on, put it on," Kirsty says, her voice cutting through the hubbub in the restaurant.

"We thought it might help. It's made of amethyst. The woman in the shop said amethyst eases grief," Iona says, her warm brown eyes misting over. "And promotes happiness. Those were her exact words."

"The sobriety stone," I whisper.

"You what?" Jack says.

"Amethyst. That's what the ancient Romans called it. The sobriety stone. Me and J looked it up on the Net ages ago – part of our Roman thing, you know." I look at my friends sitting there, anxiously waiting to see what Jess thinks of their lovely pressie.

"Cool," Jack says, eyeing up Iona. "Gorgeous and thoughtful. That's some combination."

I swear if that boy were alive he really *would* be salivating!

"Here," Iona says, gently lifting Jess's frizzed-up, uncombed hair. "Let me help you on with it."

Iona tugs down the neck of Jess's bulky jumper to uncover those evil marks on her neck. "I'll put it on for you," she says with a frown, her eyes flitting from Kirsty and back to Jess's exposed throat.

"Wish she'd touch me like that," Jack says, leering at Iona, not even registering Jess's bruised neck. He groans. "An angel. She's an angel." Another groan. "I'm in Heaven."

"No you're not," I snap. "You're in limbo. Remember? And you're a ghost."

Sometimes, guys just bug me.

As Iona fastens the necklace, Jess rests her elbows on the table, her chin cupped in her hands.

When Iona's finished, Jess just sits there, her fingers tracing the line of her straggly eyebrows and then she sits back in her seat and strokes the largest amethyst.

"Happiness?" she says, so softly it's almost as if she's talking to herself. She looks at the girls, with such raw pain in her eyes that it makes me want to hold her more than ever. "I used to be happy. When I had Minty. We used to do everything together. Crikey, we even used to—"

"Finish each other's sentences," Jess and I say in unison.

Jack chuckles and in spite of myself, I laugh, too.

"Yeah. I remember how you'd both start speaking at the same time," Kirsty says.

"And when you were telling a story you used to yell at her to shut up and let you tell it," Iona says, acting all cheery, to lighten it up a bit.

"The Jess and Minty Club," Jess says, in a hushed tone. Then she looks at the girls with such wistfulness that my laughter dissolves on my tongue. "I was happy with that – honestly – in spite of what I told her." She stares at the table, her hair obscuring her features. "God I miss her."

And I miss you.

Kirsty and Iona exchange looks. Iona picks up her Coke and pokes at the ice in the paper cup with her straw.

"Did I ever tell you about our dreams?" Jess props her elbows on the table and, after sweeping the hair out her eyes, rests her chin in her hands. "Dream sharing, we called it. It hasn't happened since...well, you know. But we used to dream the same dream."

"God, yeah, J. Remember that one we had when we came back from Italy last time?" I say, leaning closer to her.

"I always knew Minty was in mine, too," Jess says, her eyelids fluttering shut. She smiles and looks at our friends. "It was the same for her. Then we'd wake up, talk about it. Work out what would happen next. And go back to sleep."

"Then we'd get on with the dream," we both say.

I grin at the memory.

"Wow. Did it work?" Iona says, a tad too brightly.

"Yeah. There was this one time. Just after we came home from holiday last July," Jess stops, looks right at me and laughs. "When we had this dream where we were these tour guides in Pompeii. Then we woke up, decided it'd be cool to sprout wings and fly to the Colosseum – you know, in Rome."

"So, did you?" Iona asks.

"Yeah. Dreamt we saw gladiators fighting in the arena. Nothing gory though. But it was amazing. We could even hear the clash of their swords, smell their sweat as they were fighting."

Kirsty screws up her face. I scrunch up mine, too, because there's something nagging away inside my head. But what? Another dream we had? I scratch the side of my skull. Think. What was it? Something to do with the Romans?

Oh yeah…

I clap my hands and turn to Jack. "I've just remembered. That necklace they've given her – the sobriety stone – it's supposed to help you sleep. I remember me and Jess coming across it on a couple of websites."

Jack hardly gives me a glance; he's so fixated on Iona. He leans closer and says to her, "Good choice of gift, gorgeous."

I roll my eyes at him and carry on watching Jess, although the memory of some long-forgotten fact still scratches at my subconscious.

She looks across at the queue of folk waiting at the counter, then returns her attention to the girls. "And, you know, even when we weren't dreaming, we used to talk to each other in our sleep. Could carry on some good conversations, as well. But Minty always ended up harping on at me for something."

"You sound a real little charmer," Jack says, the sarcasm dripping from him like melting ice cream from a spoon. There's a smile in his eyes though.

I tut at him. I was so not like that! Was I?

But those dreams we had – God, they were awesome. Hey, wait a sec… Dreams? That's it! That's what I was trying to remember.

"There's something else about that stone – it's sometimes called the dream stone, and – omigod! – it's supposed to give you psychic dreams." I lurch forward, reel him round by the collar until he's facing me. "Psychics dreams, d'you hear me?"

"Hey," he says, shrugging me off. "What was that for?"

I don't reply cos my attention is caught by the way the light glints off the amethyst hanging from Jess's neck. It's such a beautiful stone, it's— My God, that's it! The dream stone, it's meant to have special powers! I read that somewhere didn't I? No! *We* read about it! So…what if she placed the necklace under her pillow, right next to her head. What if I told her…

"Jack, you know how you said yesterday that ghosts can alter their shape, get into people's heads?"

He re-arranges his shirt. "What about it?"

"I know how to get through to Jess! I've worked it out!"

"How exactly?" Jack says, standing behind her.

"I could use the stone to get into Jess's dreams." I grin. "I could, couldn't I? Think you could help me to do that?"

He scratches his chin, frowns for a second and then smiles. "Worth a try, I guess."

"Great!" I run up to Iona and bellow in her ear, "Tell Jess I'm going to meet her in her dreams."

Iona bites on a piece of burger, noisily drains her drink. Then she shoves the remains of her food to the centre of the table.

Look at her, you dumbo, she can't hear a thing you say. And no wonder – you're too bloomin' excited. OK enough already. Fine-tune your game plan, Minty.

So…

Forget the packed restaurant, the little kids tucking in to Happy Meals, the teens picking at fries, the Mum's sipping on coffee. Let them fade from your vision. Close your eyes. Relax.

Tune out the background noise. Slowly. Steadily. Easy does it.

Relax.

Focus on one thing. One person.

Iona.

Centre your thinking.

"Iona," I say, clearly, forcefully. "Tell Jess to put the necklace under her pillow."

Keeping my mind locked on what needs to be done, I open my eyes and peer at her.

Iona looks my way. She crosses her arms, rubs her shoulders. Shivers. Her pupils enlarge.

Don't react. Calm, keep calm.

"Iona, take Jess's hand. Repeat this after me: Jess, put the necklace under your pillow." My tone is commanding, filling up every corner of the room.

Eyes glazed, she looks at Jess. Reaches for her hand. "Jess, put the necklace under your pillow." Her voice is thin, otherworldly.

Kirsty shoots her a warning look.

Don't react to that.

"It'll help you dream of Minty," I say, forcing each word into Iona's head with as much mind-power as I can muster.

Trancelike, Iona mimics what I've just said.

"Why're you saying that?" Kirsty asks her in a voice so loud that the family on the table next to them glance over.

Iona's face is glowing, her eyes shining. She shows no sign of having heard Kirsty.

"You'll meet her again in your dreams," I say to Iona.

She repeats it, her voice unwavering.

"Shut up, Iona!" Kirsty says, banging a fist on the table so hard that the Big Mac cartons bounce up in the air and Iona's empty drink cup falls on its side. An angry pink flush floods her cheeks. "Why're you doing this?"

"Think you'd better quit while you're ahead, Minty," Jack says, "Or else your mild-mannered friend here is gonna turn into the Incredible Hulk."

The family next to us look over again. The mother mutters something to the dad and he looks like he's about to say something to the girls, but at that point Kirsty regains her cool and, blinking, Iona gives herself a shake.

"Sorry," Kirsty mutters, giving the family an embarrassed smile.

"I'm sorry, too," Iona says, but to Jess, not the strangers. She leans across the debris of the burgers and buns and grasps Jess's hand. "J, I can't tell you why I said that. I don't know what got into me. Honestly. Just forget it. Please. Forget I said it."

I can see that Kirsty's expecting Jess to burst into tears – we all are, I guess. Instead she sits, cupping the big stone from her necklace with a look of intense concentration.

Kirsty frowns, shoots Iona an enquiring look. Iona just looks pale and a bit out of it, if I'm being honest.

Jess still doesn't speak.

By now Kirsty looks as drawn as Iona.

Finally, Jess says, "Did you know it was the Greeks that started it? They wore amethysts for all sorts of reasons." She lifts the pendant and gazes at it, a pensive smile touching her lips. "They used it to increase psychic awareness. I remember now."

She squints at Iona. "Do you believe in crystals? Think they hold any power?"

"I…think so," Iona says, warily. Then she glances at Kirsty, back to Jess and adds, more forcefully, "Yes, I do."

Kirsty sighs. Shakes her head.

"We had such a strong connection, me and Minty," Jess says, almost to herself. She scrunches up her face, as if she's working out a fiendish maths problem, then she looks at Iona and says, "Can I ask you a straight question? Do you really wonder if Minty's still around? Seriously?"

Iona takes a deep breath, her body taut with tension. She gnaws on her lip for a moment, sneaks a nervous glance at Kirsty then turns to J and says, "I think it's possible – yes."

I hear Kirsty gasp.

Jess frowns. "Is it possible? Could…" She lets the sentence peter out.

Then she touches the necklace, treats Iona to a weak smile and say, "I think I will put this under my pillow tonight."

Iona exhales, and with shoulders relaxed falls back in her seat.

And by Jupiter, she's not the only one who's feeling relieved.

Chapter Twenty-Four

As soon as Jess arrives home she goes right upstairs and flops down on her bed to stare at the ceiling. I'm not bothered at all cos I can tell by the set of her mouth and the preoccupied look behind her eyes that she's up to something. Something good – I just don't know what yet.

After half an hour of this she suddenly sits up, takes off the amethyst necklace and hides it under her pillow. Then, like a lemming off a cliff, she leaps from the bed and stands in front of the mirror wardrobe and checks out her reflection, scowling. She grunts, tears off her woollen jumper, and chucks it on the duvet.

"Hallelujah for that," Jack says. "I'm sick of the sight of that thing."

That makes two of us. Why has she done it though?

By now, Jess has clocked that photo of me that she keeps on her bedside table. She snatches it, opens the top drawer, rams the snap inside with all the other clutter and slams the drawer shut again. Spinning round to the bookcase, she grabs another photograph of me and another of the pair of us posing with our saxes after a school concert. Eyes flashing, she scans the rest of the room. When she spies the pinboard above the desk, she dashes over and untacks every photo there is of me – us – every single one. Then she takes the whole lot, opens the bedside table drawer again and throws everything in. But, as if she's in two minds about it, she dips a hand back in, gathers up the pics, sifts through them and, with a long, drawn-out sigh, shoves them back and shuts the drawer.

"What's she doing?" Jack says.

I wonder – what *is* she doing?

I watch as Jess's gaze flits around the room: at the posters emblazoning the plain cream walls; at the fake bronze statuettes and the little glass figurines on the tall chest of drawers by the wardrobe – souvenirs of our first summer hols in Italy; at the Roman tragedy and comedy masks we bought in one of those museums we dragged our parents round. At first I think, like me, she's remembering when we bought all this stuff, but when she opens up the drawer once more and takes out a photo of me, strokes it thoughtfully then carefully puts it back in again, image-side down, her face lights up. It's then that I understand.

"Of course, J," I nod. "That's what all this is about."

Jess dives to the door, a girl with a purpose, wrenches it open and hops downstairs.

"Gonna tell me then?" Jack shouts after me, as I tumble down the staircase behind her.

The expression on Mum and Dad's faces when Jess bursts into the living room almost makes me laugh. They watch, stunned, as she strides over to the wall unit, swipes the framed portrait of the two of us off the top shelf and tucks it under her arm.

"Jess? What are you doing?" Mum asks.

"Yeah man, that's what I'd like to know," says Jack, pausing by the door.

"Get that one, get that one!" I say, barely holding in my laughter as Jess steps up to the mantelpiece, stops for a second, then scoops up another photograph – the school one of me taken last term. "You go, girl! I never liked that piccie!"

"Jess?" Dad says, in alarm.

But Jess is not listening. She's a twin on a mission. She's in the dining room now, emptying the sideboard of all the photos of me she can find – and there are plenty; Mum goes a bit crazy with the camera, at times.

"Stop that," Mum says, sounding hysterical.

"Have you gone mad?" Dad says.

"No, Dad, not mad. Anything but mad!" I cry, laughing out loud.

"Looks that way to me," Jack says, leaning against the wall, arms crossed.

"She's doing everything she can to make it possible!" I shout, whirling round and grinning at Jack.

"Looks like she's lost it, mate," he says, nodding over to Jess as she shrugs off Mum's outstretched hands to get to the kitchen. "Gone totally doolally. Mad as a bag of snakes."

"No! She's getting rid of my pictures."

"I can see that," Jack chuckles.

"You don't get it. She's doing it to make contact with me easier."

I follow Mum and Dad into the kitchen. Jess is at the noticeboard, taking down more of my photos. The framed picture slips from under her arm and topples to the floor, smashing the glass on the quarry tiles. She dips down, picks up the broken frame and steps over the shattered glass. The crunching sound makes me chuckle. Just as well she left her shoes on!

"You're as mad as she is," Jack says.

"Well, we are twins!" I holler.

This is good. So, so good.

Dad grabs Jess by the arm. "Stop. Jess, stop," he pleads.

Jess smiles at him and pulls herself out of his grip.

"The painting!" she cries. "I forgot the painting!"

And, she's off. Off out the door, back into the living room, like the Pied Piper with me, Mum, Dad, and Jack trailing after her.

"Will someone please tell me what's going on? Or am I going crazy?" Mum says.

She's crying now. Mum is crying and that would normally do my head in. But not now. Because Mum isn't crazy. And neither is Jess. No, Jess isn't crazy at all. In fact, it's flippin' brilliant! Jess has just done the first sane thing since the day of my drowning.

"That's enough, Jess!" Dad cries, catching her by the wrist and whirling her round to face him.

Photographs fall from her like misshapen snowflakes, littering the carpet with their multi-coloured images.

"I've got to hide them," Jess says, stooping to gather them up. "I don't know why I didn't think of it before."

Dad tugs at her wrist. "I said enough."

Mum glares at him. "Leave her, Geoff." Her face streaked with tears, she crouches beside Jess and smoothes the hair off her forehead. "Jess, love. Come and sit down. Tell me what's wrong."

"Nothing's wrong," Jess says, giving Mum a wild-eyed smile. "It was the necklace..."

"What necklace?" Mum says, frowning up at Dad.

Jess continues collecting the scattered photos. "And there was something else we learned on the Internet. Something important, that I read way back. I've been trying to think of it all the way home." She pauses. Smiles. "Then a minute ago I remembered. And...and... Oh Mum – the photos. If I hide them, I can get Minty back again."

"For God's sake." Dad's face is the colour of black cherries. He glowers at Mum. "Are you actually listening to this nonsense?"

"Geoff. Your blood pressure. Please," Mum says. "Be careful."

Jess gets up, dumps the photographs on the coffee table and takes down the painting of me and her that hangs above the fireplace.

"Leave that!" Dad shouts, striding over and wrestling the picture from Jess's hands.

"It's all right, Dad." She smiles. "I'm not going to burn them or anything, just put them away for a bit. So that—"

"Give it to me," Dad says, tugging on the frame.

Jess's knuckles are bone white as she tightens her hold. "No. Really. I know what I'm doing."

"Jess. Geoff. Stop it!" Mum screams, so loudly that both Jess and Dad stop in their tracks. Mum stands there, her features drawn and crumpled, sobbing like a little girl. Her voice drops to a murmur. "I can't take any more."

Dad releases his grip on the painting, eyes brilliant with emotion, his hands clenching and unclenching. "And, by God, neither can I."

Chapter Twenty-Five

We're back in our room cos Jess has been packed off to bed to calm down. She's lying back against the pillows, the amethyst necklace still tucked under them (she checked!), stroking Octavius with one hand and holding a copy of *Martyn Pig* in the other.

Jess is reading Kevin Brooks? Eh? My face explodes into a grin. Jess is so not into his stuff, his novels are really edgy – much more my bag than hers. It's weird cos we usually went for the same things, except when it came to books – she's much more a Meg Cabot than a Kevin Brooks kinda girl.

I can't stop grinning because, not only is Jess calm and finally reading the wonderful Mr Brooks for a change but, at last, she's dumped that stupid woolly jumper – she's actually slung it in the bin. And she's taken the urn off her bedside cabinet and placed it on the floor inside the mirrored wardrobe. She won't be sleeping with that tonight.

Jess is fighting back. She's fighting back. Taking control. The thought ripples through my mind until I chuckle out loud. Look at her; you'd never think that just twenty minutes ago she'd been storming round the house freaking out the wrinklies.

Octavius crawls out from under J's hand, shakes himself, sending a flurry of gingery hair into the atmosphere. Then he jumps down off the mattress.

"That guy's an absolute fluff factory, man. I wouldn't have been able to go near him when I was alive," Jack says, watching the cat slink out of the door. He clasps his chest, like some hammy actor. "Allergic, you know? Not now, though. One advantage of being dead, I reckon."

I grin.

"Hey, that was a heavy scene back there," Jack says, shaking his head. "Specially when your mother said your sis could take the photos to her room."

My grin grows so wide I could almost whisper in my own ear. "Suppose."

"I know why you're so happy but, hey, what about your poor ma? And as for your old man. Phew! Thought he was going to hit the road. He just couldn't handle it, could he?" He nods over to Jess. "She was far out." He puts a finger to his head. Rolls it round and round. "Totally Loony Toons United. Lost it, she did."

"No way." I smile over at Jess. She looks as relaxed as a Buddhist monk, with the dogs all snuggled at her feet as usual, snoring their heads off. "It was genius."

He glances under the bed, at the big plastic box where J's stashed all my piccies, facedown. "What good is hiding all those photos gonna do? And that painting of you both. Nice painting by the way."

My grin fizzles out. I chuck Jack a look of total disgust. "Very funny. We're like something out of a freak show in that. We hate it. Both of us."

"Nah. I think it's sweet," Jack says, with a wicked grin. "How old did you say you were when it was done?"

I scowl at him. "I didn't."

"Looked like you were about ten, to me."

I tut. Give him evils. "No, Jack. We were eleven. Some old hippy did it. In Ibiza. When we were there on holiday. And it's the pits. OK? Now, can you leave it?"

He scratches his head. "But go on, tell me. How's getting rid of that supposed to bring you and Jess back together?" Then he snorts with laughter. "Oh, I get it – some sort of R.O.M.A.N. thing? Yip?"

I nod. "It's what they believed. When someone died. They surrounded themselves with paintings of the dead person. Thought it kept their ghost happy. So it wouldn't haunt them, you know? Had to be a good likeness though."

"So why go ape getting rid of those photos?"

"Cos if Jess gets rid of all my pictures, and that" – I glare at the painting propped up against the wall with an old t-shirt of Jess's draped over it, and roll my eyes in disgust – "my ghost *won't* be happy. And if my ghost isn't happy, it'll haunt her. Don't you see? By doing all that she's inviting me to!"

"Right. Got ya." Jack says. "Not that you need the invitation, of course."

"Yeah, but she doesn't know that." I beam at him. "She's really going for it, isn't she? Thank Jupiter the girls gave her that necklace. I mean, look at her. It's wicked. She's taking control. She's determined to make it happen. Through her dreams. She's desperate to talk to me. Just like before. And that, my annoying friend, is where you come in."

Blimey, if I thought this was going to be easy, then how wrong was I?

"Right. Teach me one more time," I say, my nails digging into my fists, every muscle in my body tense and my eyes locked on Jack, just as they have been since we started nearly an hour ago. "No, better still, you show me how to get into her dreams, then I'll try it after you."

"OK. OK. But chill first. It won't happen if you're all worked up. Release the emotion. Remember?"

"Just do it, Jack!"

"Show me. Teach me. You're getting to sound like a long playing record," Jack says, smiling.

"A what?" What is he on about? But never mind that – I need him to show me this. "Just do it, Jack!"

His corn-coloured fringe flops across his eyes. "OK. OK," he says, shaking his hair back like a model in a shampoo ad. He straightens up. "Now watch. Don't talk. Watch and learn. No questions. I need to focus."

He shuts his eyes. Stands completely still. And then, his shoulders sag a bit, and it's as if his whole body is hanging loose, as if it's melting right in front of my eyes.

"Wow," I whisper.

I forget that Jess is here with us, that Octavius is back in the room, that the dogs are slumped across the foot of Jess's bed. My mind is mesmerized by what's happening to Jack.

As I watch, every millimetre of him – his glossy hair, his head, his lean body, his long denim-clad legs, his skinny arms – shimmers, wavers, loses substance, until he's almost a shadow, a shadow of mist and air that's in the shape of the solid boy that once was Jack.

And, as I gaze in wonder, the mist begins to glow with a dull white light that spreads and swallows up every morsel of the boy I know, till all that's left is a ball of energy that glows faintly through the real shadows in the room.

"You've done it," I gasp, as the sphere of light floats up in the air and comes to a stop, nestled in the corner of the ceiling above my old bed.

I look around the bedroom. Romulus and Octavius are snoozing away, while Remus watches me, his bushy tail flicking over the duvet. Jess lies on her side, trying to drop off to sleep. Her face – my face – lit up by the streetlights outside, totally unaware of Jack up there, glowing like a night light.

Then that question crosses my mind again: how come Jack can do this – can do all these things he's shown me and yet he can't move on? I really don't get it.

But why am I wondering about that? What am I waiting on? If I follow his lead, I can be up there, too.

So do it, Minty. Just do it!

I slip off my chair, close my eyes and shut it out, shut it all out. The purring cat, Romulus's snuffling, the constant rhythm of Jess's breathing – it all disappears. There's just me, standing here. Just being. I let my mind float. I let my body float. I am energy. Pure energy. Energy that my mind can mould into any shape or form I want it to.

A lovely, warm gorgeousness takes over. I'm light and fuzzy. I am a warm, shimmering mass. I am me.

Up, Minty. Go up.

And I drift up, up, up to the ceiling.

I can see. I can see it all. I don't need eyes. I have no eyes. I have no body. I have only me, my mind, my spirit – I don't know what you'd call it. All I know is – I am me. Minty. And I'm up here, on the ceiling. And down there, is my sister.

All of a sudden Romulus jumps off my duvet and begins padding up and down between the single beds. Remus drapes over the edge of the bed, his head resting on his paws, watching him.

"Romulus," Jess says, hauling herself up to see what the dog is up to. "Settle, boy."

Romulus plonks himself down in the middle of the floor and stares up at me.

"What're you looking at?" Jess says, following his gaze.

She's staring right at me. Can she see me? Omigod, can she?

Octavius uncurls himself. He stretches out his back legs and repositions himself on Jess's pillows. Then he looks up and gawps at me.

"Octavius? What are *you* looking at?" Jess asks, glancing back at him. And she lifts her eyes to the ceiling. Catches her breath. And gasps. "Oh my God. What is *that*?"

Chapter Twenty-Six

"Still awake?"

Jess rips her gaze from where I am on the ceiling and swings round. Mum and Dad are at the door, two dark shapes framed in the hallway light.

"Can you see it?" Jess says, in a shrill voice. "Can you see it? That light?"

Mum steps inside. Glances around the room. "What light, love?"

"There. See? Up there. In that corner," Jess says, pointing a finger at me.

Suddenly everything goes dazzlingly bright as Dad switches on the overhead light.

"Dad!" Jess cries. "It's gone now. Turn off the light."

Mum walks across and sits on Jess's bed. Octavius jumps off and slinks over to the window. "There's nothing there," Mum says. She tries to hold Jess but Jess's having none of that.

"Yes there is." Jess stares at where I am on the ceiling. She frowns. "Well, there was, it was there. Right there. A little ball of light. Fuzzy. Not very bright. But it was there. I swear." She nods to Romulus who's now sitting at Dad's feet. "He saw it. So did the cat."

Oh Jess. Jess, you *can* see me. My mind reels. The warm weightlessness in me grows and grows until I think I'll explode. Jess can see me! I look over at Jack. Even though the room's lit up I can see his energy. But, why can't they? And why can't Jess see me anymore? Why can't my mum? Dad?

"You're overwrought. Tired. Still upset."

"No, Mum, there *was* a strange light." She makes hand gestures in Octavius and Romulus's direction. "I told you – they saw it too. They were staring and staring at it. That's what made me look up. And I saw it, this blurry ball of light. Up there. I'm not imagining it. It was real."

Mum smiles. Runs a hand down Jess's arm, straightens out her pyjama sleeve. "Maybe you did see something. But it was probably a reflection. The streetlight seeping in. Bouncing off the wall."

"No! I've never seen anything like it before. It was eerie," Jess says.

Mum looks at Dad.

"But I think I know what it was – no, I'm sure I do," Jess adds.

Mum looks puzzled but it's hard to tell what's on Dad's mind.

"All the way home this afternoon I couldn't stop thinking. Trying to work things out. Then I finally began to understand," Jess says. "Minty's been trying to make contact all along."

Dad flinches.

Listen to her, I can tell by the tone of her voice that she believes what's she's saying – she really does! I've finally got through to her! Yippeeeee!

I don't know if I can grin, being a ball of light and all that, but I sure can feel the rush of joy whizzing through me. Yah!

But hey, Minty, keep cool – work to do. Tune in to what J's saying now.

"The telly, the lights, Iona – it all adds up," she says, the words tumbling out in excitement, her hazel eyes flashing. "Minty's not gone away. She's still with us."

Dad groans. Presses a hand to his forehead. "Haven't we heard enough of your theories?" He crumples onto my bed, glaring at her.

Jess's face sparkles with animation. She bounces up and down on the mattress. "Think about it, Dad. Think about all the weird stuff that's been going on around here. But only since Minty died…you know that's true. So you see, Iona was right all along. She knew that Minty was – *is* – still around. She's here." She looks around her. Glances up at where I am. "Somewhere. So, that's why I hid all the pictures – to help her get through to us. And maybe…maybe we'll… Oh, what if we can see her again? What if that light's only the start?"

Dad shakes his head and gets up, clucking his tongue against his teeth in disgust.

"This is too much, Jess," he yells and then his words catch in his throat. "I can't handle any more of this. You've got to stop. Learn to deal with Minty being gone."

All at once, his face scrunches up like he's got toothache. He blinks a couple of times, gulps, then in a soft, broken voice adds, "You're not the only one who's mourning." Then he stumbles into the hallway.

Mum half gets up off the bed to go after him, but slumps back down again. "Oh Jess," she mutters. "Jess, Jess, Jess. What are we going to do with you?"

Jess grasps Mum's hands. Looks at her with an electric smile. "Oh, Mum, imagine if I'm right though."

Jack lies on his belly, hanging off the end of my bed, drawing swooping circles in the air with an index finger. Remus's shaggy head swivels round and round, in a trance as he follows the lazy patterns Jack makes. I am perched half-on, half-off the seat by the desk, with a big, smug grin on my gob, thinking over and over again, 'Jess saw me!'

"She's dropped off at last. Thought she'd never fall asleep. Man, was she high," Jack says, and pulling himself up the bed, he rolls onto his side and sits up.

As I listen to Romulus snoring away at Jess's feet and watch the way her eyes flutter as she sleeps, I think of her face just an hour or so ago, of how the life flooded back into it. And suddenly I'm like that woman in the *Sound of Music* movie – Maria I think she's called – where she's high up in the mountains and so happy she wants to sing, sing, sing. I skip over to Jack. Spread out my arms like in the old film and whirl round a couple of times.

"Jess saw me up there, Jack, my energy. I really, really think she saw me. I honestly do." I fall onto the bed with a bounce. I feel as light as cappuccino froth, as keyed up as a lottery winner. "Jack, I'm getting through to her. Isn't that amazing? Fantastic?"

He just sits, watching me, saying nothing, a strange, empty expression on his face. And I remember what I was going to ask him.

"But she didn't see you, did she? She didn't see *your* light." I poke a finger to the ceiling. "Jess only saw me up there. Why just me? Why didn't she see you too?"

He scrunches his knees up to his chest, folds his arms and props his chin on them. He won't look at me – this is getting to be a bit of a habit. Instead, he watches Octavius chasing an imaginary mouse across the carpet.

"Why, Jack?"

He rubs his head. Shrugs.

"You never have explained. You said before that when you use your powers on your mum they don't work. Ever. Why is that? Crikey, look what you did with the lights and telly downstairs. But then, just now, Jess didn't notice your light. I don't understand."

"What's to understand? Sometimes it just doesn't work. OK? Isn't that enough? And what's the big mystery? All this stuff I'm showing you, sometimes it won't work for you either. You shoulda gathered that by now – it's not like I haven't told you. That's just the way it is. Right?"

Fair point.

He springs up and stands between the two beds. He turns to me, lips drawn in a harsh line, eyes glinting as he spits out his challenge. "Look, you gonna go through with this dream lark, or not?"

"Yeah, yeah, of course," I mutter, suddenly feeling guilty. After all, this must be really bad for him.

And yet…I get that feeling again that there's something he's not telling me.

With his hands behind his back, Jack moves closer to Jess's bed. He looks round at me, nods, and in a soft, sure voice his words float in the air, talking me through what I need to do.

"OK, remember what I told you."

I latch onto his words, relax into the moment.

"Alter your thinking. You are not flesh and blood. You are not skin and bone. You are energy. A mass of pulsating, travelling energy."

His words seep from his mind to mine, his thoughts are my thoughts.

"Put your energy into Jess's head. *Be* in her mind. See what she sees. Feel what she feels."

All of a sudden, I'm aware of this blinding, blazing heat. A million burning needles prick me. I throb, fizz, prickle. Then there's this massive tug. A whoosh. And a sensation of being drawn out of myself, of being sucked through the air, atom by atom.

It's black, intensely, frighteningly black. An inky, suffocating darkness that brings with it such a feeling of despair I can barely take it. Then, like an exploding star in outer space, from the centre of this darkness shoot shafts of vibrant colour. Neon yellow, cobalt blue, dazzling shades of green, red, orange. Colours that spark and cut through the gloom until, swirling and throbbing, they form into pictures:

Me lying on a cold, marble slab.

A body swept against the rocks at Elie.

Blue lips.

A wrist without a pulse.

An empty bed.

Someone screams. Yells.

Voices. Lots and lots of voices.

Chanting. Accusing.

Your fault, Jess, all your fault.

Why? Why?

Jess's voice:

No, stand back…

I'll get help,

get help,

help,

help.

Iona swims into the technicoloured mist, her voice confident and determined.

She's there, J. Can you feel her?

The school playground looms before me. A shadowy shape wavering at Iona's side; a shape that grows into a teenager with a sodden jacket and trousers. A girl with no face, just a mass of bruises.

And through it all, such pain. Such sadness.

Away! Take it away!

Then, just when I think I can't bear any more, the pictures fade, the sensations abruptly stop, and I find myself sitting, half propped up against the closed bedroom door.

Smiling. Solid. Whole.

Me.

Minty.

Is it you?

"Minty?"

Chapter Twenty-Seven

"Minty?"

Jess?

That voice! It's her. Can she be... Is she? Omigod, she's calling my name – as if she's actually speaking to me, as if she knows I'm here. Is it possible after all? Surely not!

Yet I look up and there she is, leaning over me, tears welling up in her eyes as she searches my face, checking it's truly me.

"Minty? Is it really you?" Jess says, blinking.

She rubs her eyes, holds out a hand. Then she squeals, flings herself down onto the floor beside me, pushing me up against the door as, laughing and sobbing, she smothers me in her arms.

"Oh, Minty! Minty! You've come back!"

Whoa, she smells pretty musty – sweaty, if I'm being frank – feels it, too. But I don't care.

Wait a minute – I can smell her? Omigod! It's really happening: me and my sis are back together again!

She pulls back, squints at me.

"I thought I'd never see you again," she says, dabbing her eyes with the sleeve of her PJs. The corners of her mouth twitch, then she grins. "What an eedjit, eh?" She slaps her forehead and laughs. "A stupid, stupid eedjit. A total dafty. Of course you'd come back. You're Minty! My twin. I should have known you'd find a way. You just needed a little help. Thank God for our friends. And— Oh, why didn't I think of the pics thing earlier?"

Oh, Jess, that's not how this happened – but it'd take too long to explain.

Straightening up, she grabs my hands and tugs me to my feet. "We need to tell Mum and Dad. They wouldn't believe me when—"

I pull her back. "Later. We've got so much to catch up on."

"OK then," Jess says, dragging me to the bed. Legs crossed, she squats on her messy duvet and smoothes out the rumples. "Tell me everything."

I sit down on my own bed and stare across at my sister's happy face. Then the penny drops – she touched me. She really, really touched me! My hands didn't go through her! I actually connected with her. Physically. I stretch across and put out my fingers, desperate to see if I'm right. My heart skips like a spring lamb: I can feel the damp tears on Jess's cheek. I run the side of my hand down her warm, smooth face. I *can* touch her. Jupiter – I even smelt her! A lump rises in my throat.

"Oh, Jess. Oh, Jess. It's over, the nightmare's over."

"Don't cry, Minty," Jess says. "You're safe now."

Don't cry? Am I crying? My hands fly to my face. Hot teardrops tumble over my cheekbones. I catch a blob with a finger, put it to my mouth and taste it. Salty? I can taste things? Yah! I'm real. I'm real and I'm here! And I'm with Jess. This must be what Jack meant – that urban myth thing. Except it isn't a myth at all. It can happen. This proves it!

"Oh, Jess!" I scream and bounce up and down on the bed. "I've missed you so much. I was so worried about you."

"And I was worried about you," Jess says, and we both burst out laughing and cuddle each other to pieces.

"What're we like?" I chuckle, taking in every inch of her face.

"I'm so glad you're here," Jess says, squeezing my hands tight enough to hurt. A shadow falls across her features. "I thought I'd lost you. After it happened, I put the coin in your mouth. For the ferryman, you know? I didn't want to do it. Didn't want to let you go. But it was – you know – well, I had to. So, I thought that was it. You'd gone for good. And I couldn't bear it. I just couldn't."

I smile, eager to take that sad look away. "But I've been here all along."

"Have you?" Jess says, a ripple of happiness appearing on her brow.

"Yeah." I put my hands on her shoulders. Peer into her eyes. "I've been with you since Elie. Watched you every day since...well, you know, since I...died."

An apple-sized lump swells up in my throat. A sob gurgles from my lips. "God, J, you've been so miserable. It was terrible seeing you like that. So, so terrible." I pause. Look pointedly at the bundle of sludgy brown wool draped over the rubbish bin. "Seeing you in that awful jumper."

"You know about that?" Jess says.

"Yeah. And the necklace under there," I say, nodding to Jess's pillows. I glance across to where her saxophone sits on its stand in the corner. "And I heard you tell Mum you'd never play that again." I grab her by the chin to make her look me in the eye. "But you've got to. D'you hear? You've got to start playing again. OK?"

"OK." She shakes her head. Smiles. "You know everything?"

I grin. "Everything. But things are gonna be different now. You've got to do something for me. Yeah, Jess? Get rid of that." I scowl at the urn that's back by Jess's bed again.

"But...but..."

"Promise me," I say, in as fierce as tone as I can. "Promise?"

Jess looks from it to me. She smiles. "I promise."

"Good," I say, brushing the moisture off her forehead. "Cos, know what? You don't need to keep that anymore. Cos, I'm here now. Me, not a load of old ashes. Me. It's me and you – just like before."

The tiniest of worry lines appear on her forehead. "The Jess and Minty Club?" she says, in an unsteady voice.

"You bet!" I say with a huge grin.

"I'm sorry about the club thing – I never meant to—"

I put my hand gently over her mouth. "No apology needed. All that matters is that you've got me back. And we…" What? Never have to be apart again?

You can't promise her that, Minty! But…why not? What harm could it do? I'm here, aren't I?

I must have said that last bit out loud cos her face lights up with delight and she says, "Yeah, you are here. I can't believe it, but you really are!" She bounces on her mattress. Grins. "Well then, what're you waiting for? Let's talk!"

And so, just like the old times, we lie on our beds, resting against the headboards, and get set for a blether fest.

"Oh, Jess, I've so missed being together. Haven't you?"

"Mmm," Jess says, flexing her arms and sliding down the bed.

"But you're not together again, are you?" a voice says.

I jump with a start. "Jack!"

Jack is standing by the window, frowning at me, with Remus at his feet, staring at me too. I glance over at Jess, half expecting her to register that there's someone else here, but she's stretched out on the bed, a sleepy grin plastered across her face, totally oblivious to the fact that there's a cute guy in her room.

"Forgot about me, had you?"

"I…"

"You need to tell her, tell her to move on. Live her life," he says, looking as serious as I've ever seen him.

"But..."

"It's just a dream, Minty. Remember? You're in her dream and that's cool but it's not a girlie get-together. You haven't suddenly sprung to life. You're still dead. You know what you have to do. You need to pass on your message. So. Do it."

"But...it's so real. I can feel things." I smash a fist against my chest. "In here. And these, see these?" I tap the damp skin under my eyes. "These are real tears."

"No, Minty. They only seem real to you because Jess is dreaming them."

I wail. "No, that can't be true. It's—"

"Minty," Jack says, gruffly. "Tell her. There isn't much time."

I turn to my sister. She's so happy, so ecstatic to have the nightmare over at last. And isn't that what I told her? That it was over? Suddenly, I'm disgusted with myself. Disgusted that I allowed myself to get carried away. Disgusted that I lied to Jess. Because I did lie. I knew this was a dream – this *is* a dream.

"Jess?"

"Mmm?" she says, yawning.

"You know this is a..." I whirl round to Jack. "I can't!" I cry, my lips quivering. "I just can't."

"You have to. Tell her she's dreaming. Tell her to move on. Live. Have a good life. That you won't forget her. That you'll be waiting for her when her time comes." His words are blisteringly direct. "Do it, Minty!"

"Minty. What were you saying?" asks Jess, scrunching the sleep from her eyes.

I turn to Jess, "You're drea—"

"Eh?" Jess says, slowly sinking down into the pillows. "Oooh, Minty. I'm so happy. So…" Her voice is slurred. Her eyelids flicker.

"Jess," I whisper, threading my fingertips through a tangled lock of her hair. "I'm happy, too."

My gaze lands on the candyfloss strands. Please stay with me, J. Please. I need you. I love you. Stay.

"She's falling into deep sleep. Quick. Tell her," Jack snaps.

I look at his sombre face. Look back at Jess, at the way her features have relaxed into unconsciousness. Omigod, Jack's right. I dip down and bawl in her ear. "Jess. Wake up."

Her eyelashes flutter once, twice, and a smile crawls across her lips. Then with a tiny shake of the head, she sighs, shifts onto her side and begins softly snoring.

"Too late. You've blown it," Jack says with a groan.

Then, before my eyes, Jess's image gets fuzzy with those wavy, black and white lines you get when the telly loses reception.

"Please, Jess, wake up. I need y—"

Fireworks go off in my skull. My body feels as if it's being gobbled up by flames. The room begins to spin and it's as if I'm caught up in a tornado, like Dorothy in *The Wizard of Oz*.

Then, there's another massive whoosh and I find myself back on the chair by the desk, feeling so sad and empty that I wish I was dead.

And then I remember – I already am.

Chapter Twenty-Eight

"Why, kid? Why d'ya do it?" Jack says, his features scrunched in puzzlement. "Why d'ya bottle out? Thought the idea was to tell her to move on. That's what you want, isn't it?"

I glance down at my twin sister tucked under the bedclothes, her lips puffing out and in as she breathes, the worry-lines smoothed from her face.

"Is it?" I whisper.

Jack sighs, swipes a hand down his cheek. "What gives, Minty?"

What does give? Why didn't I just tell her? Tell her to stop grieving. To carry on without me.

"Well?" Jack asks.

What to say? How do I explain what I don't even understand myself? Yet he deserves some sort of reason – yeah? But, as I'm searching for an answer, I'm side-tracked by Octavius sitting up on the window ledge and stretching himself. He lets out an enormous yawn, jumps onto the carpet and pads over to Jess's bed. Then he squeezes his body into the space between the headboard and her head, and begins to purr, louder and louder, all the time pawing at the cotton pillowcase.

I smile at the memory of how hopeful I felt the first time he sensed me. It felt so good, but it was nothing compared to the way I felt when Jess looked at me in her dream, how brilliant it felt to laugh with her, talk to her again, to really be with her. That seems like a lifetime ago, now. Was it really only minutes?

Jess, you have no idea how hard it was when you slipped back into sleep – the ache I felt. How can I ever bear to be parted from you for good?

"I can't leave you, J. I don't have the bottle." My lips barely move as I say it, but Jack hears it all right.

"What are you saying?" he says, his voice tinged with disbelief. "That I've been wasting my time teaching you that stuff? You don't want to make contact after all?"

"No. Yeah." I throw back my head, stare at the ceiling. "I don't know. I just want it to be like it was." I blow out a plume of air. "Maybe it'd be enough to do what I just did. Be with her in her dreams." I hug myself. Add in a whisper, "That was so real."

"Oh, and that's gonna work. Not." Suddenly, he's crouched down by my side, rubbing a thumb along the inside of my wrist. When he speaks he takes the volume down several notches so his tone is almost tender. "Think about it. It would drive her nuts. She'd never do anything then. She'd be living some sort of half-life, waiting for the next dream and the next. What kind of existence would that be? Is that what you want for Jess?"

Outside in the street, a vehicle draws up and, piercing the stillness of the night, there's the sound of two car doors clunking shut and some girls giggling. That'll never be me and J. We'll never get the chance to come home in the early hours, like a pair of dirty stop-outs. I'll never learn to drive. I groan. But she could. God, what've I been saying? Wanting to hang around so me and Jess can be together in her dreams?

A picture forms in my mind. I see her as some sort of creeped-out robot who spends each second of every day longing for sleep. And slowly I meet Jack's gentle blue eyes, and see that he's thinking that same thing.

"No. Of course not," I sob, burying my face in my hands. "What kind of monster am I? Thinking I could do that to her."

"You're not a monster," he says, his voice soft with compassion.

I look up, appealing to him with my eyes. "Really?"

He nods, and when he smiles two teensy dimples form in his cheeks. Funny – I've never noticed them till now.

"I lived my whole life as a twin. I've never really been a 'me', only an 'us'," I say, watching Jess fast asleep on the bed. "I'm scared, Jack, scared to be on my own."

He rubs my arm. “I know you are,” he says and pulls me into a hug.

A movie reel plays in my head, of me and Jess and all the stuff we used to do together. Then, re-focussing my mind, I glance over his shoulder and my gaze falls on her saxophone, at the coating of dust that’s dulled the once-shiny metal. “She used to polish her sax like a fiend,” I whisper. “Now look at it.” As I turn away, I catch a glimpse of the CD player. I point to it. “She used to love playing Tommy Smith CDs on that – full blast, too. And she was welded to her iPod.” Then I gaze into his eyes. “Will she ever do that stuff again?”

He holds me at arm’s length and peers at me. “She could, if you help her to. And you’ve already begun.” He finishes with a smile. “You just have to keep going.”

He’s right. Of course he is. That’s all I can do. But what if I’m not able to? What then?

And so, with my voice cracking with emotion, I say, “Oh, Jack, I only hope I’m up to it.”

Chapter Twenty-Nine

On Monday morning, Jess bangs through the changing room door and looks around the sea of chattering girls until her eyes alight on Iona and Kirsty.

"Look, J's not wearing the jumper," Kirsty whispers to Iona as Jess strides over.

"Yep, and that's why I'm smiling," I say to Jack, as we traipse in after her, me with such a massive grin on my gob that you'd think I was advertising toothpaste. "And that's not all – gerra load o' that," I say to Kirsty and gesture to Jess's glowing hair.

Jack nudges me, grins. "She's only had a shower this morning, not swum the channel," he says and squeezes into the space between Iona and the girl next to her. A tight space, I might add – he's surely not fussed then about getting a dose of that horrid electricity, or whatever it is.

"Omigod, you're right, and she's washed and brushed her hair," Iona whispers back and then, when Jess plonks herself down beside Kirsty, Iona pipes up in a bright voice, "J. At last." She budges up the wooden bench to make room for her. "We thought you weren't going to make it."

Jess dumps her grey Nike rucksack on the bench, unzips it and pulls out her PE kit. "Got caught up in traffic." She rolls her eyes and grins. "You should've heard Dad. The language!"

Iona's eyebrows shoot up. A smile travels across Kirsty's mouth.

Ripping off her white blouse, Iona says, "We didn't know whether to get on the bus, or wait for you." She adjusts the lacy strap on her skimpy white bra.

Jack whistles through his teeth at a girl who's adjusting her teeny pink thong, then goes back to checking out Iona, his tongue lolling over his jaw like a mangy old dog's. "All these half-naked chicks," he says, leaping onto his feet and rubbing his hands together. He struts about and letches at the girls. "Oh man, who needs Heaven? I'm already there."

What is that boy like? It's like letting a randy bull loose in a field of dairy cows! Sad really.

"Shut up, you perv," I say, as Remus finds a nice spot for himself under an empty bench.

Jess tugs on a pale blue polo shirt and flicks her glossy ponytail out from where it's trapped under the collar. "Sorry. I meant to text you but there was no time."

"Lucky we phoned you then, wasn't it?" Iona says, winking at Kirsty as she finishes changing into her PE gear.

Kirsty fastens the button on her shorts. "Hope you never got hollered at for being late. How come you slept in?" She reaches down, takes off her socks and catches a look at Jess. "God, J, you look knackered."

I'm surprised it's taken her this long to notice the tell-tale charcoal smudges under Jess's eyes.

"Didn't get much sleep the last couple of nights," Jess says, though she doesn't sound too bothered about it.

"You've not had that horrid choking thing again, have you?" Kirsty says, scrunching her socks into a ball and popping it into her bag and tugging on her trainers. She's just about to lace one up when she stops, her eyes flitting to Jess's wrists. "Or those awful bruises?" She checks out Jess's neck.

"No. They disappeared this morning." Jess opens out the neck of her polo shirt and shows Kirsty the creamy skin on her throat. "See?"

"Jumping Jupiter! So they have. God, Kirsty, it's not just you who doesn't notice things! Why didn't I realise that?" I say checking to see if Jack's seen them. But no, he's not paying one scrap of attention, of course. Not with all these girls around.

Iona slings her scarlet and white Juicy Couture backpack under the wooden bench. I love that bag; it's the University Shoulder Backpack, and it's way cool – *so* Iona.

"Why couldn't you sleep?" she says. "Didn't you put the necklace under your pillows like I…er…" She clears her throat, hides her face from Kirsty. "Suggested?"

Jess lowers her voice. "Yeah, but listen…" She beckons to the girls to come closer. "Something awesome happened to me on Saturday night."

Iona and Kirsty hang on to Jess's every word as she describes each detail of her dream. When she goes on to tell them about seeing the ball of light, Iona begins humming softly.

She stops, a faraway look on her face. "Robbie Williams. 'Nan's Song'. I love that. What you've just said reminded me of it." She turns to Jess and touches her elbow. "J, those spheres of light. I'm sure they're some sort of paranormal activity. Spirits." She squeezes Jess's arm.

"Iona!" Kirsty says, tossing back her blonde shoulder-length bob. "You're getting carried away."

"No I'm not. I bet I'm right," Iona says to her.

"Guys," Jess says, taking a deep breath. "There's more."

The three of them huddle together like Macbeth's witches – but way prettier ones.

"Wait till you hear the next bit, Kirsty," I say, leaping off the bench and dancing with excitement. "Then even you'll have to admit that Iona's right."

Kirsty's pupils are like two black marbles as she listens to Jess describing her dash round the house hiding all the pictures. As she concentrates on what J has to tell them, Iona bends down to tug up a sock, giving me and Jack an eyeful of cleavage.

"And it was just as I was nodding off that I saw that weird light," Jess rounds off.

The rest of the girls have left the changing room by now but my sister and her mates don't seem to have noticed – they're too caught up in Jess's story.

"That's just amazing," Iona says.

"The dream was wonderful. I thought about it all day yesterday, and last night. It reminded me of the ones I told you about at Macdonald's – you know, the ones when Minty was alive," Jess whispers, staring into the distance. "It was like Minty was actually there."

"She was J, I'm sure she was," Iona says.

Kirsty gives Iona a sharp look.

"It wasn't just... What's that called...?" Jess says, looking at each of them in turn. A strand of hair falls into her eyes. She puts a hand up to brush it back but stops half way. "Yeah, that's it – wishful thinking. That's what I wondered when I woke up on Sunday morning."

"Yes. My mum says things always seem different in the morning," Kirsty says.

At that, Jess goes quiet and just sits there looking at her knees.

"Oh shut up, Kirsty! Do you have to be so damned sceptical all the time?" I yell. "Don't listen to her," I holler to Jess. "The dream was real."

Iona frowns, slips a hand under her chocolate-brown curls and rubs her neck.

Jess stands up. "We'd better get into the hall before Mrs Jennings sends out a search party. I'll just nip to the loo first."

When J's left the changing room, Kirsty verbally pounces on Iona. "Why'd you have to encourage her like that? It's cruel."

"No, it isn't. Jess did everything possible to see Minty in her dreams again – and it worked," Iona says.

"Yeah, I admit it's weird what happened to her on Saturday night," Kirsty says, with a glance at the toilet door. "But there has to be a rational explanation. Think about it. She's knackered. Then she had that asthma thing. Plus you've been putting all those ideas in her head about Minty. Then there's all that Roman stuff she was talking about the other day, and…" She pauses, giving Iona an exasperated look. "It's no wonder she had such a vivid dream."

"But you're missing the point – Jess made it happen."

Kirsty leans back against the wall. "Iona, I know it's been awful for her since Minty drowned – no one was as close as her and Minty. But it was just a dream. Believe me." She sighs and gets up off the bench.

"You're not going to let her get away with that, are you?" I say to Iona.

She shivers, strokes her neck again and takes a long, puzzled look in my direction.

"Listen," she says to Kirsty. "Some things just can't be explained away rationally. Why're you so unwilling to believe that? How d'you explain all the things that have happened to J? Or the voices I've heard…" She looks around. "And the odd feelings I've been getting?"

Kirsty tucks her polo shirt into her shorts. "You, Iona? That's easy, you just have a very vivid imagination. I'm not trying to be mean, but it's true." Then she bends down to tighten her laces. "J's been through such a lot and she misses Minty so badly that, well…" She straightens up, gives an apologetic shrug.

Iona stares at her without uttering a word, a host of emotions flickering across her face. Then she purses her mouth and says, "She made it all up? Is that what you think?"

"No! That's not what I'm saying."

"Then what do you mean?" Iona asks.

Tears well up in Kirsty's eyes. "Oh, I don't know what I mean. Look, I want Minty here, too." She takes a breath. "But she's never coming back. Jess said it herself – remember? I can't understand why you…" She swallows. "I'm not trying to be harsh but there is no life after death. We just want there to be. To make sense of our loss." She drops her voice to a whisper. "But when you're gone, you're gone."

Iona gasps.

"Oh, Kirsty, you're so way off the mark," I say.

Jack shakes his head.

Iona wheels round to Kirsty with a challenging stare. "No, it's not the end when someone dies. There's more to us than that. It's just that some people won't accept it, that's all."

The toilet door swings open with a squeak. The girls look round. At the sight of Jess the blood rushes to Kirsty's cheeks and, eyes fixed on the floor, she dabs her eyes and starts nibbling on the skin around her thumbnail.

Once Iona adjusts the waistband of her navy shorts she walks over to Jess.

J smiles at her but addresses Kirsty. "I know you don't believe what I've just said," she says. "But remember I told you about all those amazing things that happened to me and Minty just because we were twins? Well, think about it." She sighs. "How can our connection be broken? It can't. That's why I know now that she's still here, somewhere. I told my parents that." She shrugs. "Not that they believe me either."

A look of embarrassment passes over Kirsty's face as she joins J and Iona. "It's not that I don't believe you, it's just that I…er…think there's a reasonable explanation, that's all."

"Well, you know what? There isn't," Iona says, face serious, her tone firm. She squeezes Jess's fingers. "We know that Minty's still hanging around, don't we? And I think I know why. She's trying to tell you something."

When Jess bows her head and nods, Iona turns to Kirsty, a look of triumph on her face.

"I think you're right," Jess says. "That night, in my dream, she told me that she couldn't stand to see me so unhappy. That's why I'm not wearing my jumper – she hates seeing me in it." She smiles to herself. "OK, I know that I'll never actually see her again for as long as I live, but somehow it's enough to know that she's around, watching over me." She looks at them, squares her shoulders. "She wants me to be happy. And I will be. It'll be hard." She peers at both girls, her lips set in determination. "The hardest thing I've ever had to do in my life."

She juts out her jaw. "But I'm going to do it. You'll see."

Chapter Thirty

After school, Jess lets herself into the house, and when Romulus does his usual leaping about to welcome her home, instead of pushing him off like she's done every day lately, she roughs his coat, laughing and kissing him just like she always used to. And Remus hasn't ignored Rom either; he's leaping around the kitchen, yelping with pleasure at being reunited with his friend.

If I was a dog, I'd yelp with pleasure too. After all, that wasn't hot air back in the changing room, Jess really is making an effort.

Getting herself a drink of Tropicana, she takes it through to the living room where she lolls about for ages idly changing channels on the TV until, with a burp worthy of Dad, she giggles then gathers up her school stuff and nips upstairs, the dogs bounding after her.

When I hang back by the bottom step to watch the dogs disappear round the top landing, Jack asks, "Aren't you going after her?"

I beam at him. "You know what? I think I've earned myself a rest. I'm tired out."

He snorts. "Tired? You wish. You and I don't get tired anymore. We don't actually get anything. How can we when we don't have a physical body?" he says, following me back into the living room.

I ease myself into Dad's Stressless chair and, plonking my feet on the leather footstool, I slide down the seat until I'm almost in the sleeping position. "Oh, button it," I say with a grin. "You know what I mean. So shut up and park your bum, Peeping Tom."

I smile to myself at the nickname cos that's the title of one of my fave Tommy Smith albums, the first CD of his me and Jess ever bought.

"Hey, man, you calling me a voyeur?" Jack says, squinting at me with an amused smirk as he sits on the edge of the sofa.

I laugh at the face he's pulled – the daft sod. "You're a real letch, d'you know that? I saw what you were like this morning in the girls' changing room."

He chuckles and settles down properly on the sofa, one leg tucked under him. "Give a guy a break, will ya? The place was chock-a-block with half-naked chicks – I might be a ghost but I am male."

I shake my head, beaming. "You're still a letch though."

"Your sis is doing OK today, isn't she? Pretty upbeat, I'd say," he says, changing the subject.

He's not wrong: in my mind I see the smile Jess had on her face as she went up to her room – yeah, *her* room, not ours anymore. Not really, however much I might kid myself that it still is.

Note to self, Minty: Do. Not. Go. There. Don't spoil the day by feeling sorry for yourself. The sparkle's back in Jess's eyes, think about the way she walked home with a spring in her step. Be happy. Be chuffed about the fact that she did normal stuff like channel-hopping and slurping her juice.

Yeah, it's all good.

I close my eyes, try to relax, and as I let my mind drift, the image pops into my head of the dogs greeting each other at the door. I glance out of the window into the back garden, wishing that Jess would react to my presence like that. I turn to Jack.

"Hey, you know when we came in? Well, did you see Romulus? He realised Remus was around, didn't he?"

"Doubt it. Think about it: he never really responds to Remus."

"But when you see them together, curled up on the bed, or running about and stuff, it looks as if they know each other's there."

"Nah. It's Remus that does all that. He's the one who makes all the moves, not Romulus. Like, it's Remus who snuggles up to Romulus at night, not the other way round. And back there, in the kitchen, Remus just joined in with Romulus's excitement at Jess coming back." He straightens out his leg. "I guess it looks like they were doing it together because that's the way they behaved when Remus was alive. Because you're seeing them as they used to be. But, no, Romulus doesn't know Remus is there."

Oh Remus! Poor dog. Though you seem to be handling it well enough. But I wonder – are you trying to make contact with Rom, like I'm doing with J?

I'm still thinking this through when I hear the sound of vehicles coming up the drive. The engines cut off and first one car door clunks shut, and then another. Footsteps crunch over the paving chips. There's a rustling, scratchy sound at the kitchen door as someone turns a key in the lock, and the door opens with a rusty creak – looks like Dad needs to get his can of WD40 to those hinges.

I just get to the kitchen as Mum and Dad step in. They've just come back from work and, geez, they look whacked out, especially Mum. And they're both so thin – gaunt, I think the word is. No wonder – there hasn't been a lot of eating going on in this house lately. I suppose I should be happy to see Dad lose his belly – he has high blood pressure after all, but I'd rather see him back to his greedy-guts self instead of picking at his food the way he has since he hauled me out of the water.

"You honestly think so? Or are we reading too much into it?" Dad asks Mum as she puts the kettle on.

Jupiter! Is that a note of hope in his voice?

"I don't believe we are," Mum says. "I've noticed a difference in her over the weekend, haven't you? She seems less gloomy somehow."

"She's still not right though, not by a long chalk. I'm worried about her."

"I know, love. I am as well," Mum says. "But at least she's showering again. And she was more engaged yesterday, I thought. It's a start, isn't it?"

"She *was* a lot brighter in the car on the way to school this morning," Dad says, unknotting his tie with a pensive expression on his face.

The tie makes me gulp; me and Jess gave it to him for his birthday. It was just before I died. He howled with laughter when he pulled it out of its wrapping paper and saw the picture of the grinning Tasmanian devil.

"There you go now."

"She even told me off for cussing," Dad says, sounding the cheeriest I've heard him in a long time.

"Now why doesn't that surprise me?" Mum says, her lips twitching. "I guess the roads were busy then?" She chortles. "I hope your language wasn't too choice."

How great it is to hear you laugh, Mum.

"How can you say that?" Dad says, putting his hand to his throat in a theatrical gesture of hurt.

Oh, Dad, don't give up your day job!

"Experience, my love," Mum says. "You can be like Attila the Hun behind the wheel at ti—"

All at once there's a deep, sweet, musical sound above us. They look up at the ceiling.

"The sax! She's playing her sax!" I say, and I rush upstairs.

Sure enough, when I get to our room, there's Jess standing by the window, running her fingers up and down the saxophone, picking out notes. Then, she plays a few bars of the number she played at my memorial, the sad, jazzy tones swirling unseen into the air. And then I notice her bed: it's littered with Tommy Smith CDs. My eyes snap to the Youth Jazz Orchestra's CD, *Exploration.* Tommy Smith's Youth Orchestra? My mind freezes, hurls back to the past. Jess's ambition! She so wanted to play with them. Planned to audition for a place one day. Does this mean…she still does?

Mum and Dad come into the room and the music stops. Jess takes her plump pink lips from the mouthpiece, blows out some air and stands there, legs slightly apart, holding onto her sax.

"I had a dream," she says, in a trancelike voice. "About Minty. She told me to begin playing again."

"Oh, Jess," I whisper.

"Minty would have wanted you to carry on. You know that. She would have wanted you to keep playing," Mum says.

Jess carefully places the saxophone back on its stand.

"Love, your hair smells glorious," Mum says, scooping up a handful of J's ponytail and breathing in the scent.

"I washed it after you left this morning. Didn't Dad say?" Jess says.

Mum smiles and draws her into a hug.

"Oh, Mum," Jess says, her eyes shining. "I know that Minty wants me to play again – she told me to last night. And that's not all she said..."

All of a sudden I'm conscious of Dad, as still as Trajan's Column, by the bedroom door. His lips are so thin and tight you'd think a cartoonist had drawn them. A muscle below one eye goes in to spasm and his face is flushed such a funny shade of purple, it's as if all the blood in his veins has gathered in his head. He stands there, listening to Jess tell Mum about the stuff me and J talked about in her dream, and one of those veins I'm talking about throbs just above his left brow and his lips grow more and more twitchy. It's like he's simmering. Crikey, it's like watching a kettle boil. Is this angry man my dad? He was joking with Mum a minute ago, so why's he being like this now? Why can't he just accept what Jess is telling him? I can't bear it.

"Minty told you? Minty told you? I don't believe this," he says, his voice contorted by something that would pass for rage.

Please, Dad, hear her out. Don't get mad.

"Uh-oh! Another heavy scene," Jack says, lying back on my bed and crossing his ankles.

"Why don't you butt out?" I say, rounding on him. "And take that stupid grin off your face. It's all right for you. This is my family."

"Get you, Little Miss Angry," he says.

Jess's face has whitened by several shades.

"Wouldn't you be?" I point at her. "Look at her, she's well upset." I scowl at Dad. "Why's he being like this? She might even give up again. Just when I thought I'd got through to her."

Jack folds his arms behind his head. "Do something about it, then."

"Like what?" I say, eyes flicking to Mum. I glance back to Jess, then at Jack.

"Try something else. Use your powers."

"What? Now?"

"No time like the present," he says, stretching out those long legs and wiggling his bare toes through his leather sandals.

"Right, I will!" Do something, he said. Yeah, well, I'll show you, Jacky-boy!

Right.

Do something then, Minty. Show Dad she's telling it how it is.

Concentrate. Concentrate. Put yourself into the moment. Concentrate…

On…

Bananas.

On huge, ripe, yellow bananas.

One perfect blemish-free banana.

A great big, curvy banana forms in my mind.

I peel off the soft yellow skin.

Taste it, Minty.

Smell it.

In my mind, I bite at the pale, creamy flesh. Hmm.Yummy. Banana-y and sooo scrummy. It tastes so good. It smells so good. A smell that seeps up my nostrils and oozes through my pores. A good, strong banana-y scent that filters into the air, wafts round the room, and splits into two swirling snakes that hover under Dad and Jess's noses. Two curling, dancing whiffs of banana that they suck in with every breath they take.

J's nostrils quiver. She shuts her eyes. She moves her head from side to side, a puzzled expression on her face. She sniffs. Her hazel eyes fly open. She tilts her nose upwards. Looks at Mum.

"That smell," she whispers, jerking back her head. "Bananas. Can you smell it?"

Mum crinkles her forehead and glances nervously at Dad. "Bananas?"

Yeah, bananas, I think to myself. And here's another one.

I rip off the skin and bite into it.

More banana-y perfume drifts over to Dad and my sister, floating up their noses one more time. The powerful, unmistakable whiff of my all time fave fruit.

"A-hah, bananas." Jess nods excitedly, takes a deep breath. "It's really strong. Reminds me of Minty. Do you remember, every time she was starving, she used to wolf them down?"

Mum smiles but, when she looks across at Dad, her face falls.

A slow smile flickers across Jess's face. "This proves she's here. Right now. Why else would I be able to smell it?" Jess says, taking in another sniff of banana-y air.

Dad steps back, clutches the door handle, and with a growing look of sheer bewilderment, his nose twitches at the air again like a spaniel tracking down drugs at an airport.

Jess stares at him. "Dad? Is it just me? Or can you smell it, too?"

It's as if the world has stopped breathing. Everything has frozen as I wait to hear what Dad's answer will be. His gaze is fixed on Jess's hopeful face, his fingers still wrapped round the handle. Then he moves his head a little to one side. His nostrils twitch as he takes another sniff of air. A frown creases his brow and the lines at either side of his mouth deepen. All of a sudden he shakes his head, like the dogs do after a bath. Backing out of the door, he peers at Jess as if it's the first time he's ever seen her.

"You almost had me believing it," he whispers. Then he sighs and walks back into the bedroom. "But this has to stop. This talk of Minty. It's not healthy." He starts off so quiet that it's hard to catch what he's saying but with each word he utters, his voice gets louder and louder, his face floods with blood again and little specs of spittle fire into the atmosphere.

"There is no smell. Minty is not trying to make contact. It's all in your imagination. Please, Jess, you have to accept that." He's shouting so loud now that the neighbours must hear him. He pauses, stares over to where I am and shivers. Then he seems to lose his footing. Mum's arms shoot out to steady him and at that he moans and his next words come out as a croak. "And that's the end of it."

Then his body sags; his anger, frustration, whatever it was, is replaced by shallow, rapid breathing. And wrenching himself from Mum's grip, he stumbles out of the door.

"Hmm, that went well," Jack says to Dad's retreating back.

This is so not the time for jokes, I think as I look at Mum's worried expression.

"Please, Jack, no more of your smart comments. OK?"

"My lips are sealed," he says and presses the fingers of his right hand together, running the tips along his closed mouth.

Like me, he watches Mum whisper something to Jess before sprinting off after Dad.

"Bananas, eh?" he says, once they've gone. "Thought you'd have gone for mint. Being named Minty, that is."

So much for sealed lips.

"Purleeze, I'm not that obvious," I say, looking at him down my nose. "It had to be bananas. I knew they'd recognise that, connect it with me. Like Jess said, I ate tons of the things."

I watch her putting away the CDs. Just seeing her doing such a normal, everyday sort of thing brings a wee smile to my face. So Dad's outburst hasn't affected her like I fretted it would.

"And it worked," I say, smiling. "He definitely smelt them, not just Jess. I'm sure of it."

"Reckon so. Even if he did end up reacting like an exploding bomb. And then breaking down like that. Man, he's living on the edge, that guy."

The image of Dad's stormy expression flashes in front of my eyes. Oh, Dad. Furiously, I rub my thumbs over my eyelids, trying to blot out the picture.

"Yeah, well, that's why I wanted him to smell it," I whisper, choking back the memory. "I thought if he did he'd know she was telling the truth about the dream and the light and all. He'd know something was going down, so he wouldn't flip."

"A bit flawed, your logic. Though I catch your drift."

I slip my bum onto the desk chair. Release my breath. "You're bang on about Dad though. He was way pent up. And did you see how angry he got? He never used to be like that. It's like he's taking it out on Jess. It's as if he blames her for what happened to me."

"Nah. I've seen it all before," says Jack, his eyes on Jess too. "The guy's cut up. He's feeling guilty about what happened to you. That he wasn't there to protect you. That you drowned. Parents are like that. They expect to die before their kids."

"But why be so mad with Jess?"

"Don't reckon he is. Reckon he's angry with himself. Didn't you say he cancelled your trip to Edinburgh that day? And that's why you went to Elie? It'll be destroying him."

I never thought of that!

"Poor Dad." I gaze at Jack. "I should've realised. It's tearing me apart. Why shouldn't it be doing the same to him?"

"The thing is, Minty, just remember: it's not only Jess you can help. Keep working on your sister and once he sees her totally back to herself again, he'll be fine, too."

Chapter Thirty-One

By seven thirty next morning, Jess is showered, dressed and downstairs in the kitchen looking for her breakfast. To Mum and Dad's surprise, she pours herself a mega bowl of Bran Flakes and wolfs down the lot. Not only that, but when Mum leaves for work Jess even manages to polish off Mum's left-over fruit salad! But she won't touch the stewed tea Dad offers her, no way; it's a weak coffee with loads of milk and one sugar for Jess.

Situation normal. It's incredible.

All through breakfast and in the car on the way to school Dad mentions nothing about last night, and neither does Jess, though from time to time throughout the journey I catch him sneaking a peek at her out of the corner of his eye, puzzlement wrinkling his brow.

I see that same questioning expression on a lot of people's faces at school all day. It begins with Kirsty, and ripples through Iona to every teacher Jess comes into contact with, and some of the kids, too. But Jess just carries on, quietly trying to be herself, just like she used to be.

So given the way she's been today, I guess it's no real surprise that when Iona suggests that the girls hang out at hers after school, Jess says she's up for it. Although it is a bit of a shock when J suggests a game of Monkey-in-the-Middle. Well, it is to me anyhow. Because, like with the sax, Jess has never played it without me.

So here's me and Jack sitting on the wall that separates the paved terrace from the neatly cut lawn in Iona's sprawling back garden, watching my sister and our mates play their game.

They leap about on the grass, their laughter soaring into the clouds that pepper the brilliant-blue afternoon sky. It seems even the weather's in a good mood today. And so is my dog: he's running up and down chasing the ball. Poor thing, he did love a good game of Monkey when he was alive.

Iona raises her arm, ready to launch the ball through the warm summer air to Kirsty, who's trying to shade the sunlight from her eyes while Jess hops up and down between them, looking to snatch the ball.

"Check that out," I say to Jack, with a nod to J. "She's actually having fun."

He cocks his head and looks at me. "Wish you were playing?"

"What d'you think?" I say with a wistful smile. Stretching my limbs, I glance skywards. "It sucks being dead. Wouldn't it be good to feel the sun on your skin?" I look over my shoulder to the white iron patio furniture, to the pitcher of iced juice cooling under the shade of the massive green umbrella. "Or to have a drink of that OJ? Specially with a humungous slice of pepperoni and pineapple pizza?"

Jack just grins.

"OK, catch!" Iona shouts to Kirsty and lobs the ball high into the air.

I don't know if it's because of Jack's question or Iona's excited challenge, but before I can even think about it I'm up off the wall and darting in front of Kirsty to catch the ball. But it sails through my hands and, as it passes overhead, Jess springs up and grabs it.

"Dang!" I yell, scrunching my fists in frustration. Remus barks.

"Gotcha! It's mine!" Jess says and does a little dance. The ball cupped in her palm, she throws it up in the air and catches it a couple of times before running up to Kirsty and with a hint of smugness on her face says, "OK, swap. That's you Monkey-in-the-Middle now."

"I've had enough," Kirsty pants, wiping a bare arm across her sweaty forehead. "I need to get my breath back. I'm going to sit it out for a while."

Jess tosses the fluorescent yellow ball into the air again, then snatches and brandishes it. "But we can't play without you. Just five more minutes, yeah?" She pulls one of her daft faces.

"Come on, Kirsty," I say, smiling at seeing my sister so happy and chilled.

"The chick's spent," Jack says. "Give her a break."

And right enough, Kirsty tucks her damp hair behind her ears and says, "Nope. Sorry. I've had it."

Jess chucks the ball on the sun-parched grass and it rolls under a rhododendron bush, my dog darting after it. "OK, time out then." She walks up and flings an arm round Kirsty's neck. "But ten minutes, no more. OK?"

Iona laughs. "Now *that's* the Jess we know and love." She turns to Kirsty. "Give her half a chance and she'll have us playing till after dark. Better grab a drink while we can."

"Oh ho, very funny," Jess says, slapping Iona's backside.

But, hey – Iona's not wrong; knowing my sis they could be there all night!

The girls plonk themselves down at the table and Iona pours each of them a long glass of iced juice. Remus appears and nudges my leg. I reward him with a pat on the head.

"Is anyone else hungry around here?" Kirsty says, raising her eyebrows at Iona and grinning.

Iona chuckles and says, "There's a bunch of bananas by the fridge and a multi pack of cheese 'n' onion next to the cooker. Go and get them. But leave some for us. Right?"

Bananas? I think to myself, recalling last night's events.

Kirsty laughs and trots off to the kitchen, leaving Jess and Iona lounging back in their chairs, their faces to the afternoon sunshine.

While Jess closes her eyes and stretches out her limbs in full sun-worshipping mode, Iona glances over at her and smiles. Then as Iona drains the rest of her drink Jess says, "Minty came to me again last night." Her voice is muted; her eyes remain shut.

The glass almost slips from Iona's hand. "What happened?" she says and Jess goes on to explain.

When Jess finishes, she opens her eyes and smiles at Iona.

"That's incredible, J," Iona whispers. "And that banana thing – fantastic!" Then, sounding concerned, she adds, "What a shame about your dad reacting like that, though."

Jess sits up, leans towards Iona, her elbows on the table. "Funny thing is, I could swear he smelt it as well."

"I thought that, too, J!" I say, not that she's aware of it. Neither's Iona.

"Wow!" Iona says.

"Not that he'd admit it," Jess says, and lapses into silence, observing three starlings on the grass rooting around for worms. She continues watching them until, chirruping noisily, they fly into the trees. She looks at Iona and says in a gentle, hopeful voice, "D'you think Minty's watching us just now?"

Iona holds J's gaze, smiles. "Yeah, I do."

Jess smiles back. "Me too – and the thought of it's amazing, comforting…but…" Her eyes cloud with apprehension. "You know the dream I had – how I told you about Minty saying she wants me to be happy?" Her brow knots together. "What about her? I can't imagine what it must like for her. Cut off from everything."

"She has you," Iona butts in, voicing my exact thoughts.

Jess shakes her head. "She hasn't though, just like I don't really have her."

"You do. We're still together," I say.

"But think about it – at least I've got you guys, and Mum and Dad. Who does she have?" She gasps. "God, I hope she's not lonely! You know Minty, she hated – hates – to be by herself. Oh, Iona, what if she's miserable, scared. If only I knew she was happy." Jess gazes out over the lawn, glances to each side, behind her. "Minty," she says, lowering her voice, her tone tentative. "Can you hear me? Are you? *Are* you ha—"

"I bring sustenance!" Kirsty says, bursting through the patio doors, a bunch of bananas in one hand and flaunting a huge bag of crisps in the other.

Remus shuffles on to his paws and his nose twitches in her direction. I wonder if he misses food, like I do? I expect he does. He surely can't smell it though?

"So, *do* you think she's happy? Is Minty OK?" J whispers quickly to Iona.

Iona grins at Kirsty and under her breath she replies, "She is. Believe it." She reaches over and gives Jess's hand a quick squeeze. "As long as you're happy, she's happy."

How right you are, my friend.

The worry lines relax on J's forehead. "Thank you," she mouths to Iona, then in a bright voice says to Kirsty, "Well, pass me some crisps then."

Kirsty opens the multi-pack and tosses a couple of bags over and the three of them sit munching on their snacks until Jess badgers the girls for another game of Monkey.

As they troop back to the lawn for round two, with Remus bringing up the rear, I give Jack a gentle dig in the ribs and nod to the patch of grass where Jess is retrieving the ball from under the bushes. "Wanna join in?"

"Er, no." He snorts. "I'd rather throw acid in my eyes. But you can suit yourself."

Maybe he sees my look of dejection, I don't know, but his voice softens and he says, "Sorry, kid, but we've got as much chance of joining their game as we have of being alive again. We'd just be leaping around like idiots with the ball whistling though us every time we went for it. What fun would that be? It'd be like torture. I've got a better idea – why not relax, yeah?" With that, he swings his hips and shuffles round and lies along the top of the wall, eyes shut, like he was sunbathing on a padded lounger, leaving me to watch my sister and our mates muck about in between glugs of orange juice.

And I wonder if my dog agrees with Jack cos minutes after the game resumes he soon gives up. I look down at him, spread out at my feet, and I smile to myself. "Jess wondered if I was lonely?" I say in a whisper. "How can I be" – I give Remus a pat – "with you around?" Then I look at the boy on the wall who looks for all the world as if he's asleep, and I mutter, "And you."

And for the first time since he spoke to me at my funeral, I truly appreciate just how lucky I am that I met him.

And the voice inside my head says, 'Mysterious, frustrating, annoying Jack Muir – you're not J, but crikey, how would I cope without you?'

Mum and Dad are still at work when Jess gets home. The second she walks in, Romulus springs up off the tiled floor yapping, yelping and lunging at her as though she's been away for a fortnight. Then Remus bounds up to him, his tail wagging double-time as he supplies a few barks of his own.

"Have you missed me?" Jess says, roughing up Rom's coat.

Oh, Rommy, I wish I could do that. I sure miss our cuddles. Do you miss that, too? Do you miss *me*?

Jess takes a can of Coke from the fridge and goes into the dining room with the dogs traipsing after her. Dumping the stuff she's carrying onto the table, she calls Romulus over. The dog doesn't budge; his gaze is set on where I'm standing.

"What're you staring at, boy?" she asks him, sounding puzzled.

But I know what he's staring at – me. He's gazing right at me! A gust of delight rushes through me.

Jess glances around the room, looks at Rom again. "Is…is it Minty? Can you see her?" Her face takes on the slightest smile. "You can, can't you?

Clever boy." She looks at him again, sighs and adds, "I wish I could."

"You saw me in your dream."

And she could again. No! Don't even go there!

With one last scan of the room, she sits down and gets started on her homework.

But look at Rom, he's still gawping at me. Lovely boy. I wonder…I wonder whether…if Jess dreamt of him – and me – could we meet again?

I look at my sister. What harm could one more dream do? One last dream to be with her again? Maybe even be with Rom, as well?

Just as Jess opens her French textbook, the door squeaks ajar and Octavius brushes past it on his way in. Jess looks up, puts her pen down and tries to coax the cat over. He stands for a second or two, surveying me and Jack, who're now sitting on the table, our feet dangling over the side. He gives a wee meow then leaps onto the sideboard. And there he sits, wedged between a vase of wilting flowers and the ugliest ornament the world ever saw – some present Mum hasn't had the heart to get rid of – drilling into me with his massive round eyes. I try to stare him out but he's not giving in, no way: whilst I swing my legs and scoop my hair back from my face, he watches my every move.

"Come here, Octavius," Jess says, and when the cat glances over at her and then turns his head back to me she strolls across to him. "What's so fascinating?"

She bends down to stroke him, but when she's halfway there she stops. Slowly, she straightens her spine and her mouth falls into a perfect sphere. "Could it be…? Yes, of course," she says, her eyes shining. "You can see Minty as well, can't you, Octavius?" And for the second time in the past few minutes she says, "I wish I could."

Oh, Jess, you know there's a way for that to happen, for us to be together like we used to.

One more dream… Stop! Quit even thinking that!

She takes a quick look around the room then hunkers down beside the cat. She's smiling as her hand runs along his back, but I can still detect the wistful expression on her face.

Suddenly, she's distracted by the rhythmic bleeps of a text coming in on her mobile. She pulls the phone out of her jeans pocket, checks her message then punches in a rapid reply. All the while Octavius's eyes remain on me.

Giving the cat an absent-minded stroke, she goes back to the table, lays her phone by her notepad and resumes her work. Or at least she does for all of ten seconds, because then another text comes in, which, of course, she just has to check.

"I wonder who's texting her?" I mutter, getting up to take a look.

When Jess opens her message I have my answer: Iona.

So wot r u planning? her text says.

Jess grins, starts typing her reply.

Planning? Planning what, I wonder? But then my eyes fall on Jess's notebook and there, at the top of the page in block capitals is my name. And underneath that she's scribbled Carista with an elaborate question mark.

What does that mean?

But when I catch J's message to Iona, I find out.

A carista. That's all i'm telling u 4 now.

Ah! Now I get it!

"She's planning a Carista," I say to Jack. "It's party time."

Chapter Thirty-Two

Next day, when Jess gets home from school, she dumps her stuff upstairs, gets changed and curls up on an armchair in the living room, scribbling like mad onto her A4 Pukka Pad.

"Isn't she done with that yet?" Jack says, sprawled out on the sofa as if he was a Roman at a feast. He holds up a hand and looks at it as if there was a big bunch of grapes dangling from it. Then he lets it fall and inspects his nails.

I know what he's on about because she spent the remainder of yesterday evening beavering away, surfing the Net for Carista facts and scribbling heaps of notes into her notebook – not that I could catch a glimpse of them because of the way she was sitting.

I go up behind her to see what she's written today but right at that moment she hunches up further, an arm curled round the notepad as if she's hiding the answers during a school test.

"Would've thought she'd have planned enough last night," Jack says in a bored voice. "What on earth is she writing? Can't you tell what with your extra-sensory twinny whatsit?"

"I haven't got a clue." I say, faking a scowl. He is so not funny! "Jupiter, I'm not a mind reader."

"Jupiter?" Jack says. "You like that guy, don't you?"

"He's—"

"A god. I know, I did Latin at school, remember?" He raises an eyebrow. "So you're not an atheist then?" Gaze falling to his fingers, he picks at a nail. "Think this Roman guy's gonna be waiting for you once you're done here?"

Done here? If I ever am. How can I be when Jess needs me? And she does cos, blimey, what would she be like now if I *had* moved on? Who'd be helping her out of her grief then?

"Minty," he says almost under his breath, as he shifts onto his side and leans an elbow against the arm of the sofa. Pulling up one knee, he presses his lips together, his eyes serious all of a sudden. "Think your Jupiter's waiting for me?"

"I..."

My ears prick up as I hear car tyres crunching over gravel.

At the sound of a key unlocking the back door, Romulus and Remus rush out of the room, barking and woofing at what they no doubt imagine is some evil intruder. I laugh as their crazy woofs and growls turn into excited yelps when Mum greets them (well Romulus anyway), though I frown at the tone of her voice as she tries to get Rom to cool it – she sounds completely whacked.

"Jess? Are you home?" she calls but J doesn't acknowledge her, she just sits there bent over her notebook, writing furiously.

Moments later Mum comes in. "Oh my goodness, Jess, you gave me a fright!" she says with a startled cry. "I thought you were out." She pauses for a moment, hand on her chest, then she crosses the room and squats down by my sister.

Jess still doesn't acknowledge her.

"Love, are you all right?" Mum says.

There are so many fine lines on Mum's face you'd think a toddler had been let loose on it with a brown felt tip pen. That same kid must've coloured in the horrible dark patches under her eyes, as well. Crikey, my mum seems to have aged twenty years since I died. She cranes her neck to see what Jess is writing, and the movement's enough to make Jess glance up.

"Mum?" she says, a note of surprise in her voice.

Jess hides the notepad with her hands. Mum goes to peck her cheek but at the same time Jess looks up and Mum ends up kissing her nose. J's face breaks into a smile and then she laughs, a throaty laugh that makes me think of Kirsty. Mum returns J's grin, and the apprehension behind her eyes disappears.

"You were totally absorbed there. What with?" Mum says.

"It's a project I'm working on. But it's a secret. I'll tell you all about it once it's done," Jess says, snapping the notebook shut and replacing the cap on her biro.

She looks up. "Mum, I know I've been a pain since Minty...but, well, I... Remember that I told you I'd let her down? Well I had. But I've thought of a way to put it right."

Jess jumps up. Hugs the pad to her chest, sucks on the pen and shakes her head just the teeniest bit. She holds the notepad aloft. "That's what this is about. It's all in here and – oh, Mum, I can't wait to tell you about it. Just not now – OK?"

Mum brushes back Jess's hair. "My darling, you take as long as you like." She hesitates, her hands dropping on to J's shoulders as her face takes on a hopeful expression. "Are you feeling a little better now?"

Jess looks into Mum's eyes. "It's hard to live without her, Mum."

Mum caresses J's cheek. "I know," she whispers.

The lines on Mum's forehead deepen, her mouth sags.

Jess must notice this as well because she blurts out, "But I'm trying, honestly. And Minty's still..." She glances down, pats her breastbone. "Here." She beams at Mum, sweeps a hand through the air with a flourish. "She's everywhere – hasn't left me, really. And that's good. So don't worry about me. Please."

A huge sigh escapes from Mum's lips. Mine too.

We smile.

Chapter Thirty-Three

"Are you ready yet?" Dad hollers up the stairs the following evening as he paces the hall.

"Just coming!" Jess shouts down from her bedroom.

Smiling to himself, Dad wanders back into the kitchen, jangling his car keys as he goes.

"It almost feels normal, doesn't it?" Mum says, rinsing soap suds out of the washing-up bowl. "Her hogging the bathroom. The hairdryer going. You hanging around waiting." She turns off the tap and looks out the window into the early evening sunshine.

Geez, I say to myself with a sigh, I remember it well.

"Hard to think that just days ago all she did was hide away in her room. What brought about the change?" She pauses. Frowns. Gives a little shrug. "Not that I'm complaining. I'm just glad to see her more like herself again."

Yep, I'm with you on that one, Mum!

She reaches for the hand towel but, as he watches Mum dry between her fingers, Dad's smile falters.

"I don't think I could take it if she went back to how she was," he says, his face twisted with concern. "Hell, all that about Minty trying to contact her..." His grip tightens round the car keys. "I'm telling you, Mary, I just couldn't deal with it."

Mum folds the towel and threads it through the handle of the oven. She walks up to Dad and hugs him.

"Don't worry, Geoff, I think she's going to be fine. I really do. She's still terribly sad. She misses Minty so much – we all do – but she's making the effort now. Let's just be grateful for that, eh?"

Dad winds his arms around Mum's thin waist, drops his chin on her shoulder. "You're right. But I can't help worrying she'll have a relapse."

"Then don't," Mum says, squeezing him. "She's got this big secret now, this project she's working on. It'll give her a focus. Something to put some meaning back into her life. She's been beavering away on it for over a week now. You've seen her, she's definitely more like herself. Look – she's even going out tonight. When's the last time she got dressed up and went out on a Friday evening?"

She rubs at the corners of Dad's mouth as if trying to put the smile back. "It'll work out. You'll see."

For a moment, they're quiet. The only sound in the room is the stutter and buzz of the fridge and, all at once, I'm reminded of the last time I saw the pair of them here like this. They were so distraught then, so lost. I hope they never have to feel like that again.

"OK, I'm done now," Jess announces, hurrying in, the heels of her shoes clip-clopping on the kitchen floor.

When I swivel round and see her, my eyes pop. Her long brown hair, freshly washed and dried, hangs loosely down her back like a sheet of finest silk, and she's wearing a gorgeous star-print dress that Mum bought her from Top Shop a couple of weeks ago in an attempt to cheer her up. And check out the killer heels on those shoes! Jess has *never* worn heels like that; she's supposed to be an Indie girl, for Jupiter's sake!

"Jess, love, you look wonderful," Mum says, tearing herself away from Dad and going over and taking her hand. She inches closer, sniffs and laughs. "You smell nice, too. Is that one of my perfumes?"

"D'you need to ask, Mum?" I say with a laugh, remembering all the times J nicked my Armani City Glam.

Jess dips her eyes and purses her plump lips. My God, she's wearing lippy! When did she put that on? Things really are looking up if J is wearing lip gloss again.

"I don't mind," Mum says. "It suits you. You can have it, if you want. I've plenty more."

"She scrubs up well, your sis."

I look up and there's Jack filling up the hall doorway, like some nineteen-seventies throwback.

"Where've you been?" I say, wondering what exactly kept him upstairs for so long. "You'd better not have been perving my sister."

"Moi?" he says, clutching a fist to his chest, bottom lip stuck out in a gross exaggeration. "I'm gutted that you would think that."

I shake my head, chuckle. "You are *such* a saddo."

He staggers back a step or two, in a show of wounded pride. "Such cruelty from one so young," he says in a deep, overly posh voice.

"And you're a crap actor," I say with a giggle. Then I hear the back door opening, the jiggle of Dad's car keys and the dogs running past my legs as they escape into the garden.

"Jess's going. Come on, but behave. OK?"

He strolls up and drapes an arm round me. "Would I do anything else?"

"That's some vehicle," says Jack, as he gets out of Dad's car. He whistles. "Man, it's more like a bus than a car."

"It's a people carrier, Jack. What's to get excited about?" I say, watching as Jess waves Dad off and catches up with Iona and Kirsty hovering outside the multiplex.

"Incredible," he says, shaking his head as his gaze follows the Renault driving away. "So much space inside."

The second Kirsty's through the automatic doors, her nose sniffs the air like a pointer on the scent of a grouse. It reminds me of how Dad reacted that night I conjured up the scent of banana. I gulp at the thought.

"Smell that popcorn," Kirsty says, inhaling deeply. "Fancy sharing a tub?"

"Hmm, why not?" Iona says, skimming her hands over her hot mini dress and leggings.

"That girl should be in a film, not watching one," Jack quips, eyeballing Iona as she adjusts the skimpy straps on her dress.

"Cool it, you," I say, cuffing his ear.

We laugh.

As they walk towards the box office Kirsty takes her purse out of her shoulder bag, fishes out a tenner and looks up as if to say something to Jess. But then her jaw slackens and her gaze sweeps over Jess's face.

"Wow! Would you look at you," Kirsty says, her voice at the max as she takes in Jess standing there, grinning like an X-Factor finalist.

"Yah!" Iona says, letting out a scream of pure pleasure. "The old J is definitely back."

A bunch of guys in the games' zone look over, snigger and get back to playing their stupid, noisy game. I notice one of them glancing round and giving J the once over, though. And no wonder – her skin's glowing and she's giving out so much energy you'd think she'd been wired up to the national grid!

"Right, J, spit it out," Iona says, laughing. "What's going on? This got something to do with this huge secret you've been keeping from us?"

Jess bounces up and down like a toddler full of e-numbers. She grabs Iona's hand.

"It's all thanks to you guys," she says, her eyes shining. "If you hadn't given me that necklace – well..." She lets out a whoop causing the middle-aged couple walking past with their tickets to smile at her. "Omigod, I've been so thick. I should've realised the second the message flashed up on my computer." She smiles. "Oh, I've been dying to tell you. But I wanted to wait till I had it all planned." She releases Iona's hand. "Listen up."

J goes on to fill them in on how she's been finding out everything she can about a Carista.

She jumps back, hugs her elbows. Rocks on her heels. "And the reason I've been boning up on it," she says, the words coming out all in a rush, "is that I'm going to ask Mum and Dad if we can have one. I'm sure that's what Minty wants. A proper goodbye."

Eh? I've never said that. And anyway, she already said goodbye on the beach.

"I'm sure you're right," Iona says, beaming.

But Kirsty isn't smiling, she's biting her lip. She clears her throat. Gawps at Jess.

"And I want you guys to be there, too," J says. "Will you come?"

"Try and stop us. Oh, that's just the best. I'm so glad for you, J," Iona cries, clapping her hands together. "Of course we'll come." She leans over to Kirsty and whispers out of the corner of her mouth, her perfectly-shaped eyebrows arching spectacularly, "And you said Minty wasn't around." She prods Kirsty's side. Smiles. "You said I was imagining things."

Kirsty glances at Jess's happy expression and hisses back her reply. "What does it matter what I think, Iona? Look at how J is, that's all that counts."

A trio of lads bowl in through the entrance, guffawing and slapping each other on the back and generally making a noise. Iona does that thing with her eyes again.

All of a sudden she grins, swings her hips and strikes a supermodel pose. "I feel another visit to the teenage temple coming on."

Kirsty frowns. "The teenage temple?"

"Yeah. McDonald's. Forget the movie. I wanna know more about this Carista thingy. You up for it, J?" Iona says, linking arms with her.

Jess laughs. "What d'you think? We've got tons to talk about," she says and she offers Kirsty her hand, links arms with Iona and the three of them march outside.

As Jack and I skip after them I can't get a good look at Jess's face, but from the sound of her voice, I know she's grinning big time and that makes me smile, too.

But here's the thing – although my sister might be beaming all over her face, a question rushes into my mind like a blast of frosty air: what does Jess mean by a proper goodbye?

Chapter Thirty-Four

That Saturday morning, Jess sits on her bed putting the finishing touches to her plans. At her feet, in the gap between the divans, is Remus, panting away like he always did whenever he was overheated – when he was alive. It must be so hot outside to have come up to the cool of Jess's bedroom. I expect Romulus is still basking in the sunshine in the back garden, but I reckon it won't be long until he comes in, too.

Pant! Pant! Pant!

Oh boy, Remus, that's some racket you're making. I suppose it makes a change from your snoring. But… how can you feel the heat when I don't? Or do you? Is the panting just from habit? Oh, it's all too confusing!

God, *everything's* confusing. I mean, doesn't J want me around anymore? Didn't she say to Mum that she was glad I was? So, has she changed her mind? She wants me gone, wants to be free of me? Is that what she meant by 'goodbye'? And if I want to know so badly then why haven't I entered her dreams yet? Why don't I just ask her? What's to stop me? Just the once.

As I'm pondering this, she leans over and puts a hand out to pat Remus's head. "There, there," she says. "Are you too hot, Remus?" She chokes back a cry. Her hand freezes, fingers outstretched. "Remus?" she whispers and looks down to where he sits. "Remus, is that you?"

On hearing her say his name, Remus wags his tail. He stops panting, sits and holds out a paw, waiting, I guess, for Jess to pet him. But the poor dog is disappointed because Jess just stares for a second, her face scrunched in consternation, tapping her bottom lip with the biro.

"Is Minty with you?" she says, looking up. She scans the room, stops when she gets to my bed. "Minty, if you're there, I just want to tell you that I'm OK." She grimaces. "Well, not OK, not really. It's...well, it's shit most of the time but I'm beginning to work through it. Somehow..." She swallows hard, looks around the bedroom again. Her eyes glisten with tears. "But you know that, don't you?" She puts her writing stuff on her bed. Looks at my pillow. "Thank you, Minty – for the dream, and the other things you did. For looking out for me..." She holds back a sob. "Even though you're dead. But you don't have to—"

Pant!

"Quiet, Rem!" I let him lick my fingers, go back to Jess. "Don't have to what, J?"

"I miss you, too, boy," she says, looking to the spot on the carpet where our dog is.

Then she picks up her pad and pen and slips out of the room.

"Wait!" I say, and skip after her.

When we reach the garden there's Jack lounging on the steamer chair I spent the night on that time I left him at his mother's. Thinking back to how lonely I felt that night, I realise just how much I've come to depend on that guy. He's a bit of normality in this crazy world I've found myself in. I hate to admit it but I don't know what I'd do without him.

As if he's reading my thoughts he glances up, gives me a cheeky salute and grins, flashing those dazzling white teeth of his.

The garden is filled with the sound of summer: birds twittering, a lawnmower cutting grass a few gardens along, while the three little kids from next door giggle and scream as they splash about in their paddling pool. Octavius lies, in all his ginger and white glory, sunning himself right in the middle of Mum's bedding plants – it's a miracle she hasn't shifted him. Romulus is fast asleep under the shade of the copper beech at the bottom of the garden. And there's Mum hauling out weeds by the gazebo, while Dad leans against the garage wall as he chats to someone on his mobile.

He looks up at Jess as she strides across the lawn and smiles. When Mum sees Jess, she places her trowel on the ground and walks towards her.

"So, have you finished your project now?" she asks J with a gentle smile. "Do we get to know what it's about?"

"Maybe," Jess replies, with a tint of mystery in her voice.

The two of them cross over to the wooden table and four chairs. Mum pulls one out, adjusts the green seat cushion and plonks herself down, letting out a sigh.

"I hate gardening in this heat," she says, running a thumb along the fine line of sweat that's collected above her top lip. She points to J's notepad. "So, are you going to tell me what you've been up to?"

Jess sits down and spreads her pad open on the table. Her greeny-brown eyes dance in the bright light.

"Well," she says, spinning out the word. "I really wanted to tell you and Dad together." She glances over. Dad's still in deep conversation. She looks back at Mum and her face splits in a grin. "But I can't wait any longer!" She taps the pad. "I've planned it all. It's all down here. Everything." She pauses. Takes a breath. "I want us to have a Carista."

Tiny wrinkles form above Mum's eyebrows. "You'll have to explain."

"Of course, we should wait till February cos that's when it should be held – but I can't wait till then! Oooh, it'll be so good." Jess lifts the pad and reads. "I thought we'd invite Iona and Kirsty. And there'll be you and Dad. And me – obviously – and—"

"Hey! Hey! Hold your horses," Mum laughs. "You haven't actually said what it is yet."

"A Carista? It's a kind of Roman party. A family party. Of course, Iona and Kirsty aren't real family, but they're as good as." Jess runs her eyes down the page. "I thought we'd hold it at six o'clock. Have a dinner. A buffet. I've even thought of the menu. Listen: olives, eggs, grapes, mushrooms, cheese."

She grins at Mum. "It's all traditional Roman food, by the way." She checks what she's written. "And nuts, we need to have nuts. And pork. I thought, maybe fish too?" She raises a brow. "And some chicken?"

"Whatever you say," Mum chuckles, squinting against the strong sunlight.

"No forks though. Just spoons. Or eat with your hands. To keep with the Roman theme. OK?"

"All right." Mum leans back, crosses her arms and stretches out her legs, her eyes full of amusement.

"And," Jess puts on a sweeter than sweet smile. Her words shoot out like gunfire. "I thought we could have some wine. Mixed with a bit water. You guys like wine. And it's traditional you know..."

"All right! All right!" Mum laughs, holding up her hands. "You've convinced me!"

"And we should serve fruit. And cakes an' sweet stuff. And we'll need to dress up. Dad can wear a toga. And us girls'll need a tunica. Maybe a stola too."

"What are you two talking about?" Dad says, tucking his phone into his shirt pocket and pulling up a chair.

"Apparently," Mum says, with a huge grin, "we're going to have a party."

Dad takes a white cotton hankie out of his shorts pocket and begins polishing his sunglasses.

"A party, eh?" He blows on a lens and continues polishing.

"It's all Jess's idea," Mum says. "She's just been telling me all about it."

"What's the occasion?" Dad says, examining his shades then putting them back on.

"It's a Carista. The ancient Romans used to have them. It should be in February, only we're having ours in June. But that's OK," Jess says, sliding the notepad across the table so Dad can have a look. "Look, I've planned it all out." Dad glances at the open pages. "I thought we'd have the Parentalia on the Saturday and the Carista the day after. We should really leave a week between the two. To reflect. Think of Minty. But—"

"What's this got to do with Minty?" Dad says, the relaxed tone of his voice tightening.

"That's the whole point," Jess says. "It's to honour her. Strictly speaking, the Parentalia should be to honour a dead parent. And Minty never mentioned having a Parentalia, she just told me to have a Carista."

"Minty mentioned?" Dad says. His body goes rigid. He takes off his sunglasses. Holds them by the legs, grasping them so tightly that you can see the bones shining through his skin.

The excited, confident expression on Jess's face fades a little. "Well I…er, yes."

"I can't listen to this," Dad says, moving so quickly out of his chair that it topples over and clatters onto the decking. Setting it upright, he puts his sunspecs back on and says, "You two plan what you want, but leave me out of it."

"Geoff! Sit down. Listen to her," Mum says, rising halfway out of her seat to pull him back. "It's not what you think." Her eyes are pleading as she holds his gaze. "Stay. Please."

He sinks back down into his seat and rests his elbows on the table, his hands cradling his head. And under his breath, I hear him say, "A Carista. What the Hell next?"

"I'm sorry, love," Mum mutters to Jess, and briefly touches her shoulder.

Jess looks at her, glances at her Pukka Pad and then she sits up and talks to Dad in a cool, clear voice. "Dad, it isn't what you think at all." She swallows and carries on in that same steady manner. "I need to do this. I really do. For Minty. For me..." Dad flinches but J carries on anyway. "And I need you to be part of it. It'll really help. Please understand."

I gape at her, turn to Jack, my chin slack with shock at her awesome confidence. Jack's looking at Jess, too, but I have no idea what he's thinking. I turn back.

Mum stares at her, a host of emotions flicking over her face. She takes a deep breath, her eyes on Dad's bowed head and, like Jess, waits for his reply.

Eventually his hands slip back across his balding scalp. He studies Jess for a minute and then says in a strange, tight tone, "You honestly think it will help? If we have this Carista you'll cope better?"

"I'm sure of it."

He nods. "All right then, if that's what will make you happy again then we'll do it."

She grabs his hands and smiles. "Dad, it'll make us all happier."

Way to go, J!

"It's just what you said, Jack!" I glance at Dad. "OK, he's not happy yet, but he will be – the way Jess is improving."

When I grin at Jack, he smiles back but it's a really weird one, sort of sad. But what's there to be sad about? J's having a party – for us both! 'I need to do this... For Minty. For me...' That's what she said – my brave, amazing sis!

"Omigod, J, I'm so proud of you!" I say. "You don't know how much."

But she could – if she dreams tonight. And, heck, telling her how one million per cent brilliant she is, how brave and gutsy she was persuading Dad, well that would hardly be messing up her head or driving her nuts, like Jack warned me about. Would it? And while I'm about it I might as well take the chance to ask her about the other stuff. Cos, geez, I'd be crazy not to.

"It's your ball, Minty!" Jess yells and hurls it at me.

It soars high over Kirsty's head, a bright yellow blur against the cobalt sky, and lands with a thud at my feet. Kirsty spins round, spies it and, like a Jack

Russell after a rat, she dashes over, dives down and gets to it at the same time as I do.

"It's mine, Minty, you're out."

"In your dreams," I say, trying to prise the ball out of her clammy paw. But in the midst of our tussle my foot slips and we end up rolling on the grass, rocking with laughter.

My muscles feel heavy and warm, my pulse races as my heart pumps double time against my ribs.

"Cor, you're boiling," I say, my hand on Kirsty's hot, damp forearm. "And, sorry, but you smell a bit rank, too."

"Blame your sister. I'm sweating like a hog. I wanted to pack it in hours ago."

"Me, too. Can we stop now?" I say, twisting round to Jess, my own sweat cooling on my skin, giving me a sudden case of the shivers.

Jess stares at me for moment and then she smiles. I gasp; feel the blood drain from my face. My hearts pounds and bile races up my gullet. That smile – it's the same one I saw today – on Jack.

"I—"

"Shh," she says, putting a fingertip to my lips. "It's for the best."

And she walks off.

I turn back to Kirsty.

"Why'd she do that?" I say but – hey – where's Kirsty gone?

She's disappeared.

"Where're they going?" I say turning back to Iona.

However, I can barely see her for the shroud of dazzling mist that rises from the ground and spirals upwards to cloak everything in a shimmering grey-white blanket. And, before I even get a chance to question what's going on, the fog gushes up my spine, licks at my neck, pours into my mouth and into my head, blinding my vision. And all I'm left with is this throbbing heat building up inside me and the sensation of being tugged and pulled towards the brightness.

And then, like I'm in the world's fastest, scariest elevator, I'm hurtling through time and space until – thump – I'm on my knees on the floor in my bedroom between our beds, wondering what the hell went wrong.

"Back to Earth with a bump?" says a familiar voice above. "Kinda serves you right."

When I look up there's Jack towering over me.

I scramble to my feet, fighting off an intense, lingering sadness.

"What happened?" I say. "I'd only just entered her dream."

Jack's eyes drill into me. "What happened? I could ask the same thing of you. Why d'ya do it? I thought we'd agreed the dream gig's a bad idea."

Back off, Jack!

"It was only this once." I glance across at Jess asleep in her bed, the suggestion of a smile on her lips. "She walked away from me. Why?"

"No idea," Jack says, turning to stare at the wall.

"Well, I want to know. I'm trying again," I say, standing upright and shutting my eyes to blot out the distractions surrounding me, in preparation for another go at entering Jess's dreams.

But Jack says, "No point. Look at her."

Opening my eyes, I look at Jess and Jack in turn. "What about her?"

He points over. "See her eyelids. She's in too deep a sleep. You won't reach her when she's like that. Not that you ought to."

Sure enough, there's no fluttering or twitching of her eyelids.

"Oh God, there's no REM," I say in a flat tone.

"REM?"

"Rapid eye movements. That's when dreaming occurs." I move across and hunch up on the bed. "She's probably dog-tired. It must've taken a lot out of her to speak to Dad like that today." I look up at him. "I should've remembered – she never dreams when she's whacked." I sigh. "So you're right, there's no point in trying again tonight. Better just leave it...for now."

I pretend I don't see Jack grimace and shake his head at me.

Yet as I watch her sleep, I can't get that interrupted dream out of my mind, of Jess's sad, sad smile – or what she said before she vanished into the swirling mist. And overriding it all hangs the notion that maybe there's more to the aborted dream than an absence of rapid eye movements.

CHAPTER THIRTY-FIVE

All through the night and into the brilliant sunshine of the next day, the nagging doubt in my head takes hold. I should be the happiest ghost haunting the globe because my twin seems even more like her old self today; but I can't let it go, the feeling of something not being right. I try to shake it off, to enjoy watching Jess relax on her sun bed – seeing her pack away two desserts at lunch. But it's no use, the misgivings persist.

By sunset, the weather has deteriorated into a wintery gale. But then you never know what to expect in a Scottish summer: howling rain, rolling mist and bursts of warm sunshine all packed into a few short hours! Even so, it's beyond wild out there tonight. Heck, even above the telly you can hear the wind rattling against the windowpanes. Blimey, you'd think it was the middle of flippin' November, not early June. No wonder Jess and Mum are snuggled up together on the sofa.

They've just watched *The Robe* and are settling down to view *Quo Vadis* again. It was Mum's idea to have a DVD evening – Jess's choice – and although

Dad wasn't keen on a Sunday night of old movies, he let Mum have her way. I guess he knew that it would please my sister.

"What a night," he says, looking up from some game he's playing on his iPad. "It's tipping down out there."

"Shh," say Jess and Mum together, their eyes never leaving the telly.

Look at them, they're so chilled. What a difference from the last time they were tucked up together on the sofa, when I used my powers to switch off the electrics.

Dad smiles over at them and gets up to shut the curtains, then he comes back to his armchair and switches on his table lamp before swopping his iPad for the news section of *The Sunday Times*. And it's the lamp that makes me think: why don't I do it again? Why don't I turn off that light, prove to myself that I still have my powers, that the failure with Jess's dream was only a fluke? And Jess's bound to know it's me who's done it, sure to realise that I'm still watching. It might even prompt her to dream tonight. And she must – cos I *have* to talk to her, squash my fears about her plans for the Carista.

Right! Enough with the talk, Minty, rev up those powers – do it!

Forcing back the spark of excitement that's ignited inside me, I run the routine through in my head and get started.

Craning my neck, I peer at the lamp and really, really focus on it, telling myself I can switch it off.

The light remains on.

OK, so try again, concentrate harder!

In my mind's eye I watch my hand reach for the button, see my finger push down onto it and – snap! – the lamp goes off.

Yah!

Except...what's this? It hasn't. Eh? How come?

Oh stuff the light. Try something else.

Turn off the plasma screen! Yeah, that's it. That's what I'll do.

Gathering my willpower, I ignore the actors' voices blaring from the telly, blank out their faces and each and every movement to concentrate on the power button underneath.

But...but – dang and blast, the TV doesn't even flicker!

So forget the telly, try something else.

I spin round, my eyes scanning the room all the way to the ceiling.

What to try next? What to do?

Yes, that's it – put the overhead light on! That'll really get J's attention.

I walk over to the wall switch and picture my fingers on it, feel the pressure of my hand on the cool chrome. But though I'm doing everything right, nothing happens. Drawing down my brow, forcing myself to keep calm, I go over the routine one more time.

Still nothing.

"Gonna tell me what you're up to?"

I swing around and there's Jack, watching me.

"Oh! I get it. You're attempting to make contact again," he says.

"Nothing works, Jack," I say, my voice betraying the panic I feel. "I can't do it." I lunge at him, grasp his shoulders, searching his face for an answer. "Why can't I do it?"

"Why even bother? You've got through to her, haven't you? She's happier now. Isn't that enough?"

My gaze darts around the room as I decide what to try next. "No, I want her to know I'm here."

He frowns. "I woulda thought you'd already established that," he says and gazes at Jess for a moment. "Look at her," he says as he shrugs me off. "Take a long hard look. She's gonna be fine."

I watch as, eyes riveted to the screen, Jess fishes a couple of tortilla chips from the bowl on Mum's lap and crams them into her mouth, crunching on them noisily.

"Isn't this what you wanted, to see her like that?" Jack says.

"But I need to get through to her again."

Jack looks at me like he's discovered a slug in his salad. "It isn't all about you, you know." He challenges me with a gaze that hits me square in the eyes. "Have you never considered that maybe she doesn't want you to contact her anymore? That she wants her life back?"

"But she needs me!"

"Does she?" he asks in a low tenor. He looks at Jess. "Does she look like a girl who wants to be haunted?"

I shield my ears. "Shut up! You're just jealous that I've got her and don't need you any more."

His cool stare forces me to drop my hands to my side.

"Maybe I am," he says in a whisper. "But that doesn't make what you're trying to do here right." With a shake of his head, he leaves the room.

And OK, I'll admit it, something about what he's said makes me squirm. But he's got it all wrong. He just doesn't understand how it is between me and Jess. She wants me near her. She can't survive without me. I know she can't. So I'll be damned if that's going to stop me. Even if it takes all night I'm going to make Jess know she's still got a sister – and she's right here.

It's not until much later that evening, when Jess is in her room sorting through her bag for school tomorrow, that I work out what went wrong. It'll be the emotion thing again, just like before: I need to cool it if I'm gonna be successful. How thick am I not to have realised earlier tonight?

"But enough already with the thinking – action not words, that's what you need. Just like Jack told you," I mutter to myself as I watch Jess take a heap of Tommy Smith CDs and dump them beside the stereo.

She picks up the copy of *Exploration* that's on the top of the pile, takes the disc out of its case, inserts it into the machine and presses play. The instant the first track bursts into life she flits around getting everything she needs for her homework, her head nodding along with the beat.

Come on now, Minty – action! But what should I do?

It's when she presses the stop button, leaving the CD in the stereo as she gets ready to go downstairs, that I think to myself, it's still inserted so I could…

I could… I can…

Switch…

It…

Back…

On.

Moving forward a step, I straighten my spine and fix my eyes on the CD player. I peer at the play button and gather all my thoughts, my hopes, wishes. As I focus, in my head I see the button push in, see the laser inside the machine hover over the disc. I run it over and over again in my mind.

Willing it to happen.

Hearing the CD begin to play.

Letting the moody, smoky notes blast into the silent bedroom once more, filling it with life.

I imagine the melody washing over me, that there's only me and Jess in the room and it's any normal day. I can hear the sax already. Oh how I love that vibe, I remind myself as I close my eyes for a sec, my hips swaying in time to the rhythm.

When I look over at Jess, I expect her to be doing the same, but instead of gyrating to the music she finishes packing up her schoolbag and takes a pair of clean PJs from her drawer.

Jess? Haven't you noticed? Can't you hear the beat?

All at once, my mind is polluted by the image of her walking away in the dream last night.

And the music stops.

"Why all the dancing?" Jack says, his voice cutting into the silence as he gestures in my direction.

"Didn't you hear the music?" I say, looking at Jess disappearing from the room.

"Music? What music?" Jack says.

"That music," I say, motioning towards the CD player.

"Kid," he says, parking his backside against the radiator under the window. "There *was* no music."

"Yeah, there was. I—" Oh heck, was I just imagining it? Surely not! I look at Jack, check his face for signs that he's kidding.

His runs his fingers through his unruly fringe. "Ah, I get it – another attempt, yip?" When he looks at me his eyes are sorrowful and so is his voice. He glances over at Jess. "You've gotta let it go now, kid."

"But why, why have my powers failed?"

"Leave her be—"

"I can't."

"Anyhow, it's time to split – give her some privacy," he says, pointing over his shoulder to Jess pulling her top over her head, ready to strip off into her pyjamas. "Contrary to what you might think about me, I'm no Peeping Tom."

Then, in a few loping strides, Gentleman Jack's out of the room and heading downstairs.

"Hey, come back! Tell me what I'm doing wrong. Do you know what's happening with my powers?" I say, following him. "Why couldn't I get the CD to play?"

Jack stops on the bottom step and the sadness in his face evaporates. His lips hitch up in a cute grin and, with a twinkle in his eyes, he says, "I'm kinda glad it didn't – I don't reckon much to your taste in music."

"Philistine," I say, though I can't help but smile – guess not everyone's into Tommy Smith like me and J are. But he's not still answering my question, and I need him to.

I can hear Mum and Dad chatting in the living room, above the low volume of the telly, so I decide that the calm of the kitchen is the perfect place to probe Jack for information. Mum's left the down-lights on under the cupboards when she was setting out the breakfast things earlier. It makes the kitchen look cosy. But cosy's anything but how I feel at the moment.

I get right to the point. "That's twice it's happened, three times if you count what happened in J's dream," I say to Jack.

"Leave it," he says, easing himself onto a worktop.

"So what gives? Was I too distracted?"

Jack sighs, massages his temples, but if he's trying to evade me he's got another think coming.

"Or could it be that I need to get some extra practice in – somewhere quiet, like here." I spot the kettle. "With that, for example."

I crane my neck, peer at the switch, intent on turning it on. Yet as much as I try, I just can't do it. "Come on! Work damn you!" I say, shaking my fists at the stupid thing. "No, come on. Make it boil. Now," I mutter to myself, then unfurl my hands, letting them hang by my side to refocus. But I can't make it do anything.

I feel a hand on my elbow. Jack swings me round to face him. We're so close I can see little flecks of navy amongst the sky blue of his eyes. He loosens his grip. "It's no use. I reckon you're losing whatever power you had because... Look, there's something I should tell you."

That heart-breaking smile's back, the one I saw in the garden on Saturday! It gives me the heebie-jeebies.

"This Carista Jess has planned." His voice is tender, his expression full of pity. "It's more than a party, I'm sure of it." He touches my cheek. "I saw her notepad, managed to sneak a look at it—"

"So? I saw it, too."

"*Farewell*? Did you see she'd written that? At the bottom of a page. Scribbled in miniscule writing."

I look down, twist my pinkie ring round and round. "I never saw that," I say, about-turning. "You're making it up."

"No, Minty, it's true."

"So what if it is?" I say, swivelling round to him again. "Farewell's what she called out after I died. She'll have been thinking about that."

He hesitates. Takes my hand in his. "And scrawled beside it… Oh, kid, I'm sorry – there were more words."

"Yeah – liar, cheat, fraud!" I say, slapping his hands away. "How's that for more? Describes you perfectly!"

A pained look flickers across his eyes but he carries on regardless. "She'd written *Minty at peace*, and that's not all. She'd—"

"Yeah, whatever!" I say, poking a finger in each ear and la la la-ing out loud. I stop my noteless tune and add with a glower, "Why don't you go play with the traffic or something? I've got work to do."

Put a block on his words – the kettle, concentrate on the kettle.

"Listen to me," he says, drawing my hands from my head. "She'd also scribbled *proper goodbye.*" He peers into my eyes. "Don't you get it?" What he utters next is spoken so gently, yet the words might as well be spikes rammed into my heart. "She's letting you go, Minty."

No, this is all a joke – he's mucking about. Or putting a twisted spin on what Jess actually meant. But…what exactly did she mean? I've never had the chance to ask her about what she's got planned.

I force my eyes shut, but when I open them again Jack's still gazing into them. "I think the Carista's her way of saying goodbye to you," he says. His voice is tender, not the voice of a joker at all.

Goodbye? She wants me to leave?

No, Jess! You can't want that for me. For yourself. Don't you need me anymore? But I can't leave. I really don't think I can. I need to stay here. With you. Me and you together, J. Always. That's how it should be, yeah?

I close my eyes; rest my face in my hands. Then I feel Jack's arms around me. He whispers into my neck, "I'm sorry, Minty, but I really think it's true." I hear him swallow. "It looks like your work here is done. You've done your bit to release Jess from her grief, the guilt she was feeling. Given her the strength to carry on. And now – she wants to do the same for you."

Chapter Thirty-Six

Ireallythinkit'strueIreallythinkit'strueIreallythinkit'strue Ireallythinkit'strue—

"Stop it!" I scream, breaking away from Jack's hold, and lurching out of the kitchen to take the stairs two at a time.

Got to get away from him. Got to get back to Jess.

Ireallythinkit'strueIreallythinkit'strueIreallythinkit'st rue—

With Jack's voice pulsing through my mind, I stumble into the bedroom and fall onto my bed.

"I didn't know how to tell you," he says, entering the room. "I'm so sorry."

Don't listen to him, concentrate on Jess's steady breathing.

She's letting you go, Minty.

I screw my eyes up tight, grind my teeth.

Your work here is done.

It isn't. He's mistaken.

Then ask her. Find out for yourself. Look, she's sleeping! Do it now. Prove him wrong. Talk to her.

Jack lowers himself onto my bed, looks at me, and sighs. "It's a lot to take in, I know, but you've done what you set out to do. You did great. But it's time to—"

He's interrupted by a soft, questioning voice.

"Minty?"

I gesture to her, blot out the sympathy written in Jack's eyes. "D'you hear that? She's calling to me. She wants me in her dream." I drop to my knees, by her side. "Jess?" She's still asleep, but her eyeballs are rolling under her partially closed lids, her lashes flapping wildly, and from time to time her nose and lips give an occasional twitch. "You're dreaming," I whisper, gazing at her lovely face. I stand up. "Wait for me, J."

Moving to the foot of her bed I close my eyes and will myself into her dream.

Relax. You are spirit: weightless, timeless, energy.

Feel your energy alter. Feel yourself float.

Travel through space and time. Seek out her dreams.

Enter her mind. Feel what she feels. You are one.

You.

Jess.

One.

A soft summer wind carries me upwards. Girls' laughter rings out into the air and is carried away in the breeze.

A seagull.

Mum and Dad smiling.

Minty, farewell.

A glass of red wine.

Happy tears.

And Jess on a sun-kissed beach.

"Jess?" I run to her yet before I get there I slip on a patch of seaweed. I bite my lip. "Ow!" God, that hurts.

She turns around and when she spies the trickle of blood that I can feel dribbling down my chin, the smile on her face cracks.

"It's OK, it's only a scratch," I say, catching the drop of warm liquid with my tongue and making a face at the tangy taste of iron. I hold out my arms. "Well, help me up then."

"You dope," she says and hauls me onto my feet.

Blimey, is she trying to pull my arms out of their sockets?

Rubbing my shoulders, I laugh. "Have you been eating porridge or something? Or spinach, maybe?" I draw her towards me and it muffles her giggling response. She pongs of too much Armani City Glam.

I shove her hair back off her face. It feels as soft as the duck down feathers that sometimes escape from my duvet. I smile. "God, J, you do love that perfume of mine, don't you?" I pinch her cheek. "But you can keep it, if you like."

"It's mine now anyway. I snaffled it when Mum wouldn't let me give it to the undertakers."

"Ow," I say, rewarding her with a cuff. "Do you have to remind me of that?"

"Well, you are dead." She looks up at Mum and Dad. And, hey, Iona and Kirsty are there, too. They all smile over. "That's why we're here. For the Carista," she adds.

I grip her arm. "Why're you having it, J?"

She pushes me away and rubs her forearm. "Ouch, Minty, you're hurting me."

I touch her fingers. "Sorry. But I don't understand. What's the Carista for?"

"But, Minty, it was your idea. You told me to do it."

"You still want us to be together though. Yeah?"

Right then a yellow ball, the size of a double-decker bus, comes rolling down from the headland, heading straight towards us.

"Jess, scarper!" I say and break into a sprint.

But however fast I run the ball travels faster. As it gets nearer, its colour changes to shades of blue and green mixed up with sleety grey – the colours of the Firth of Forth – and I realise that its one enormous, terrifying wave.

And soon it's on me, crushing me into the sand, sweeping the shoreline into the sea.

Goodbye, Minty.

Suffocating.

Blinding. Deafening.

Until there's only blackness.

Then I open my eyes and I'm staring at Jack.

He just puffs his cheeks, shakes his head and sighs.

"Wow, that really suits you, Minty. It's totally funky."

I survey myself in the changing room mirrors.

"You think? It's not the wrong colour?" I wrinkle my nose. "Hmm, not so sure the cream works. Maybe try it in purple?" I scrutinise my reflection, run the back of my hand over the lacy skirt of the dress I'm trying on. "This lace is sooo scratchy." I extend an arm, pluck at the sleeve. "And these are like far too long."

A bundle of grey and black creased cotton slaps me in the chest.

"Try that one then; you'll look hot in it," Jess says, clasping the empty hanger of the dress she's just lobbed at me.

"No way. Too grungy."

"Yeah way. It's cool."

"Yeah, if you're a Goth, or like ninety-four."

Jess laughs. She glances at another of the dresses she's brought in, holds it up to me. "Want to try on this?"

"Er, strapless? Fuchsia? You outta your mind, girlfriend?" I rest my hands on my hips, in my teenaged-girl version of Gok Wan. "I'm Indy, remember? And so are you, or you used to be."

"Not any more, time I grew up. Got sophisticated." She shrugs on a neon orange floaty number. "Time you did, too." Halfway to pulling up the zip, she yawns. "God, I'm whacked." Her voice sounds drowsy. "Need to lie down for a min."

She drops the dress onto the floor and parks her bum cheeks onto the shelved seating.

I tug her up but she falls back down again. "Don't go to sleep. Please."

She curls into a ball, a woozy smile on her lips. "Have to. Bye, Minty."

And as I go to drag her back onto her feet her image blurs, the light fades to the palest grey and my head – my entire body – feels like it'll explode. Soon, the all-too familiar heat sears through me and I'm being sucked and spun through the air to the sound of Jess's drowsy voice telling me goodbye over and over again.

"Wake up, J!"

I open my eyes and we're in the school dining hall and Kirsty is stretched across the table, trying to rouse a sleeping Jess who's hunched over in her chair like an old lady in a nursing home.

Jess blinks, her eyelids flutter open momentarily and her chin droops onto her torso.

"Jess, you can't sleep here. You're in the dinner hall," Kirsty says, looking across the table at Iona, her face full of alarm.

Jess looks up, squints at Kirsty through puffy eyes.

Maybe it'd be enough to be with her in her dreams…

Still think what you're doing's right, Minty?

I squirm, shrug off the thought and turn back to Jess.

"God, J, you look terrible," says Iona.

It would drive her nuts… Some sort of half-life…

Look what you've done to her, Minty.

No! Can that thought. You're doing nothing wrong here.

Some sort of creeped-out robot… Longing for sleep…

I'm not hearing this!

Is that what you want for Jess…?

Kirsty nudges Jess's arm. "People are looking," she whispers, looking over at a table of senior girls who are staring at us with interest. "Do you want to go? Get some fresh air?"

Jess shakes her head. "No, I'll be OK. It's just…" Her face breaks into a smile but just as quickly, it disappears. She massages her eyes. Exhales.

"What's got you so zonked?" Kirsty asks.

Jess's smile resurfaces. "Not sleeping great. Well, I am. Sort of." She yawns.

"J," Iona says, fiddling with her fork. "You were out of it. If you can fall asleep in the middle of all this din then you are far from OK. What's wrong?"

"Nothing." Jess sighs and traces a thumb along the side of her tray. She looks down at her lap and her hair flops forward until it obscures her face.

"You having trouble sleeping at night?" Iona asks.

Jess sits up and tucks her hair behind her ears. "No, the opposite in fact." She glances at the untouched food on her tray. "And I have such lovely dreams, where I'm…I'm with Minty again."

When she looks up there are tears cascading down her cheeks.

God, J, why are you crying?

"Jess, don't cry," Kirsty says.

Iona delves into her bag for a tissue. She hands it to Jess. "You only said about the one dream. You've had more?"

Jess takes the hankie. "Yeah, every night for the past couple of weeks," she says, mopping up her tears. Then, thank Jupiter, she smiles once more. "Look, just ignore me, I'm being silly. Those dreams. They're the best – I'm not alone anymore, I'm a twin again. It's just…when I wake up I want… Well, it brings it all back to me. I *am* on my own. It's just me now. And it's so hard."

"Oh, man," Jack says, kneading his temple and shaking his head.

It doesn't take a genius to know what he's thinking.

But when I notice the wistfulness in Jess's eyes, catch the sudden smile on her lips, I know that he's wrong: Jess needs me, and if those dreams are the only way for us to be together, well, so be it. After all, I'm doing it for her own good.

Chapter Thirty-Seven

When we arrive home from school there's a note from Mum and Dad on the kitchen table to say they've gone to Tesco. Jess reads it, pours herself a cranberry juice and takes a packet of ready salted crisps from the cupboard. Then, she fixes herself a cheese and pickle sarnie, shouts for Romulus and takes the snack to her room.

I don't know why she bothered because she only takes a bite out of the sandwich, doesn't even look at the crisps and leaves the glass of juice barely touched. She should be famished because she ate like one chip at lunch and only played with her cereal this morning.

After her half-hearted effort at eating, she feeds the rest of her sandwich to Romulus, then opens the wardrobe. She bends down to pick something off the floor. When she straightens up and I see what she has in her hands my eyes almost pop out of my skull. It's my urn!

"Why've you still got that?" I say to her, as she shoos Octavius off the duvet, settles on her bed and sits cross-legged with it in her lap. "I hate that thing. It's not as if I'm really in there."

She unscrews the lid and stares at the contents.

"I'm so lonely without you, Minty," she whispers, her eyes glistening.

In the background, I hear Jack tut.

To my horror, she dips a hand into the wine-coloured plastic and scoops out a handful of my ashes. Her hand trembles as, with huge round eyes, she peers at the little mound in her palm. "Is this all that's left of you?"

"Jess, what're you doing? Put them away. Please."

She nestles the urn against her stomach, holds her palm up to her face and scrutinizes the grey layer. Slowly, she brings up her other hand, sticks out the index finger and prods around in the gritty dust. And, as she does so, a single tear springs up in the inside of one eye. It gathers in size and hangs there above the bits of me in my sister's splayed hand.

"Jess, no," I plead.

Jess snorts, swipes the tear away with the back of her free hand and shakes the ashes back into the urn.

Thank Jupiter for that!

"Oh, Minty," she says, fastening the lid and stroking a hand down the ugly plastic tub. "Why did you do it? Why did you go after Remus?"

"God, Jess, you know I had to," I say, leaning back against the wall.

"You had to be a bloody hero, didn't you?" Jess spits. "You couldn't leave it. Couldn't wait till I got help."

She lifts the urn up to her face and begins shaking it so hard that the skin under her nails goes white.

"I told you I was going to get Dad but, no, you didn't listen, did you? Oh no, you knew better. And I hate you for it." She sobs. "I hate you for leaving me."

And then she lobs the urn at the window.

The dogs yelp and run for the door. Octavius screeches, arches his back and vanishes.

"Whoa!" Jack cries, as the urn sails right through him and crashes against the bottom rim of the window ledge, marking the white paint. One of the bronze figurines teeters on the window sill then topples onto the carpet.

"I hate you for dying! You never thought of me, did you?" she screams, thumping her chest. "You never thought of me!" And quivering, she bursts into floods of tears.

"J, I'm sorry, I'm so, so sorry." I fling myself down on the bed next to her.

I hear Jack clear his throat. Then he begins to speak. "Minty—"

"Please, Jack, back off," I say and hold my hand out in an attempt to stop him. Then, turning round to Jess again, I run my hand down her hair as if to stroke it and incredibly, as I do, she flinches and her body stiffens. She touches the back of her neck and trembles like an infant with a fever.

"Jess?" I whisper, moving even closer to her.

Slowly, she twists round. Her tear-stained eyes peer into mine, questing, unsure.

My God, look at her. This is not how I want her. Not like this. I just want us to be together. Please, Jess, please, please can't you see that?

I move nearer. "J," I say, so close to her that I'm sure she can feel me brush against her skin. "I'm here. Right beside you. Everything's going to be all right," I say, making my voice as soothing as possible.

Then her body seems to relax.

She heard me?

"Sleep, need to sleep," she mutters. "Got to be with Minty." And she wraps the duvet around her legs and closes her eyes.

Through it all Jack doesn't say anything, not a word, yet in my mind I hear what he's thinking as clear as if he'd uttered it:

Yeah, Minty, your sister is handling things just fine, you got it all worked out.

You must be feeling really proud of yourself.

CHAPTER THIRTY-EIGHT

It's the perfect summer's night: a clear, inky moonlit sky dotted with stars, everything around us quiet and calm – it's perfect, just perfect. Except, I'm here in my back garden with a dead guy and Jess is upstairs in our room in a heap. And try as I might, I can do nothing to help her. Where have I heard that one before?

"Penny for them," Jack whispers.

"Oh, Jack," I say, and look up for the thousandth time at the light in our bedroom window. I think of how exhilarated Jess was when she was planning the Carista, of how distraught she is now. "I only want her to be happy."

Jack follows my gaze. "You sure about that?"

"You have to ask?"

"You really want what's best for her?" Jack says, stretching across the wooden table to reach for my hands. "Then you know what you have to do."

He's wrong, I don't. There's nothing I *can* do. I wish there was but I—

I? And then it dawns on me, the truth crashing through my thick head: I'm selfish.

Yeah, Minty, it's all about you, isn't it? Yeah, just you muck about with Jess's mind. Carry on invading her dreams. Never mind what happens to her. Why should you bother if she can't hack it? As long as you can snatch back that feeling of being alive again. As long as you get what you want. It's OK if you do – cos you're scared, aren't you? Poor dead Minty.

Jack.

The sudden sound of another person in the garden makes me jump. I look round and there's a tall, skinny old woman of about seventy standing and smiling at us. Under the night sky she looks a pale silvery grey – hair, skin, clothes – but her wrinkled face has the most beautiful smile I've ever seen.

"Jack. It's time," she says, and before either me or Jack can say anything, she fades away before our eyes.

"Jack?" I say, stunned by the look on his face: delight, expectation, fear – it's all there, all plastered over his features. And there's something else, something round the eyes, something about the set of his jaw, his long limbs.

Then I get it. "That woman… She's…"

Jack spears me with his gaze. He nods. "My mother."

"Yeah," I whisper. "I thought that. Even though I didn't get a good look at her face that time we were at yours…"

His expression steals my words away. Geez, his eyes. They're enormous. Dark. Deep. Troubled even. And his mouth's gone all droopy, like it can't carry the weight of what he has to tell me.

"Jack? What? Why did she appear like that?"

"You heard her – it's time," he says, elbows on the table as he runs his nails through his hair.

I nod. Look over to where, only a split second ago, the Pale figure of Jack's mother had stood. "Of course. You told me about this. I remember. It's because—"

"She's on the point of death."

She's dying? But why is she here? Why has she come for Jack? He said she couldn't forgive him – has she changed her mind? Omigod, what if she has?

Chapter Thirty-Nine

We hurtle through the town, past shops, the taxi rank, a couple snogging at a bus stop, past some yobs hanging round the chippie, on and on and on we run – running, running, running till we're on the outskirts, where the houses thin out and countryside takes over. This is serious running but Remus thinks it's great fun, charging ahead, stopping, dashing back, swirling round our legs and almost making me fall, then tearing into the distance like he's doing the hundred metre sprint in the doggie Olympics.

Our feet pound along the tree-lined narrow footpath by the side of the main road leading to the neighbouring town and, just when I think we're going to be running all night, Jack slows down in front of the wide driveway that leads to his mother's house. This time, one of the huge wrought iron gates is pulled halfway across the drive.

"Inchgauldry," he says, his fingers tracing the letters on the brass name plaque on the boundary wall. "Wonder if I'll ever be back here?"

Jack squares his shoulders and begins walking up the gravel path. When he turns to speak to me, he's right twitchy and there's a real edge to his voice. "Quick, Minty."

With Remus at my side, I hurry after Jack as he strides up the path. The tall trees loom over the drive, their branches rustling in the slight wind that's whipped up. Through the bushes I can hear the scurrying and flapping of nocturnal creatures and, as we near the house, an owl hoots, just like the last time we were here.

And then it's in front of us: the huge mansion that Jack spent most of his life in. Even though I've seen this place before, I can't help but gape at the grandness of it all – the park, the sweeping driveway we've just rushed along, and the house itself. Crikey, it's even posher than I remember.

Jack takes the front steps two at a time, but comes to an abrupt stop a couple of paces away from the closed door. He stands there and it's as if his body collapses in on itself.

"You OK?" I ask, rushing up the steps to put a comforting hand on his shoulder.

He gives a jerky nod, glances back at me. "Sure," he says, but his tone is grim.

He doesn't make a move, just stands there, motionless, gazing up at the skylight above the door.

"Come on," I whisper, and reach for his hand to pull him through the door with me.

Our fingers interlink and, at that instant, the most incredible sensation ignites inside me – in my head and throughout my whole being. Relentlessly hot, yet not burning. Amazingly powerful, but comforting with it. Tingling, although soothing. An awesome, fearsome feeling of connection with Jack, the world, the universe, that grows and grows – an exploding atom bomb of emotions, thoughts and feelings.

"Wow" I say under my breath, clutching Jack tighter, scared to let my grip loosen. Scared that the sensation, feeling, whatever it is, will splutter out. Disappear. Yet as I squeeze his fingers, everything intensifies. "What *is* that?" And as my gaze falls on our entwined digits, there's such a torrent of joy surging through me that I think I'll explode with happiness, and I have to clamp my mouth together, to stifle the yell that springs to my lips.

I gaze at Jack. He stares back at me with such amazement that – omigod – I know he feels it, too.

But then, with a huge sigh, he yanks his hand away and the next instant he's swallowed up by the door.

No! Jack, no! Where're you going? Come here! Give it back! I want it back! I need to experience that again. I just *have* to!

I stumble around like some old wino and my legs are so weak that I have to prop myself up against the front door.

"What just happened there? I have to know," I mutter, rubbing my temple, blinking to clear my head.

The fierce heat I felt only moments ago has now cooled to a warm sleepiness.

"It was fearsome, so fantastic," I murmur, smiling to myself, crossing my arms before me in a hug.

I must sit down. No, I need to lie down. I'm tired, so, so tired.

But as I crawl onto my hands and knees, intent on resting on the hard stone steps, the warmth turns to an arctic iciness that leaves me wanting to weep. I drop my head, hide it in the crook of my crossed arms as I curl up into a ball by the door. And, as I do, my happiness is hijacked by an unbearable emptiness that's so powerful it causes me to cry out.

Then, through the vacuum, I remember why I'm here.

Jack's mother's dying. He needs me. Stop it. Get up. Focus on going inside. Find her bedroom. Help him. Do it, Minty.

Dragging myself off the steps, I lurch to the door, force myself through it and try to remember my way from the last time I was here.

Yet as I head upstairs, the questions bombard my mind – demanding, insistent. What went on back there? What caused it? And why now? Why didn't I feel it when Jack touched me in the garden tonight? Or before? What's changed? Though overriding it all, like an alcoholic thirsting for his next drink, there's this craving, a desperate need to have that feeling again. That's what I'm thinking about when I stumble upon the bedroom. However, the very second I enter the room and catch sight of Jack by his mother's bedside, my addiction's forgotten.

The bedroom is as quiet as a deserted school. Unlike last time, a deathly hush hovers in the air.

The equipment Jack's mum was hooked up to is still there but it's disconnected, set back from the frail old woman who's propped up by several fat pillows on the bed. And there by her side is Jack.

"It won't be long now," he says, his soft words breaking the eerie silence.

"But…the machines and everything," I say, gesturing to the bed. "She isn't hooked up to them. Surely that means she's getting better?"

"I guess the medics think so, but they're wrong," he says, as he looks up from his mum's white face. "She'll die soon, I know she will. It's time." He pauses. Glances down at his mother and back to me. "She came for me, Minty."

Oh, God, I can see in his eyes that the poor old lady's almost done. Oh, Jack, how can you stand it? I would be gutted if that was my mum.

"I'm really sorry. This must be awful for you," I say, moving round the foot of the bed towards him.

He gives out a reflection of a smile, yet waves me away with the flap of a hand, so I go and stand at the window. Even though it's the middle of the night, the curtains are pulled back, so I look down onto the grounds of the estate, wondering how long it'll take.

Then what happens? I ponder. What will I see? I mean, what *does* actually happen when somebody dies? Will his mother be like I was and think she's still alive? Will she be stuck here, like Jack and me? Or will she move on, like you're supposed to? And what exactly does that mean? And if she does, how's Jack going to feel? Or will he go, too? Oh, God, what if he does?

At the sound of a vehicle crunching up the drive, Remus utters a low growl.

"Steady, Remus," I murmur, looking out of the window and catching the headlights of a dark-coloured four-by-four as they cut through the night.

The vehicle stops in front of the house, a door opens and a man hops out, banging the door behind him, He puts one foot on the steps leading to the front entrance, hesitates and goes back to the car and opens it again. Reaching inside, he pulls out a briefcase, then, with a soft slam and a beep, he locks the driver's door and climbs up the steps. Remus barks, his chin on the window ledge as he strains to see what's going on down there.

"Quiet, boy," I say, holding onto his lapel and urging him to come and sit beside me.

Poor Jack, this must be so hard for him, I think, as I sink onto the turquoise silk sofa in the window recess. Just then the bedroom door squeaks open and in shuffles an ancient, chubby woman I recognise as the housekeeper. Her carpet slippers scuffling across the thick carpet, she takes the jug of water she's carrying and puts it on the bedside table. Then she pours a trickle of water into a white plastic mug with a spout; it reminds me of a baby's feeding cup. Slowly lowering herself into the chair by the bed, she shuffles closer, leans over, supports Jack's mother's head and puts the mug to the dying woman's lips. But the sick old lady doesn't even sip a drop, instead there's this horrible rasping rattle as she struggles for breath.

Oh this is awful. Just dreadful. What must it be like to watch your mother die in front of you? Jack must be feeling like crap. Maybe I should go up there, hold his hand, or something.

All of a sudden, Jack bounds over with such an intense expression on his face it makes me gulp.

He sits beside me and when he talks it's like he's trying to force the words into my soul. "I want you to listen to me. You need to know the truth."

"The truth about what?"

He gazes out into the dark. "You're gonna hate me. You really are," he says, in a tone of voice that brings shivers to my spine. "I should've told you before but I didn't want to be alone again."

When he turns towards me his eyes are coal black. They bore into me with such ferocity that I shrink back in my seat.

"Jack, you're scaring me." I grind my teeth, dreading what's coming next. I have a feeling I'm not going to like this.

"You were right…when you called me a pig, a stinking rat. I am. I was wrong to withhold things from you." He jerks his head towards his mum. "She'll die very soon and I'll be free to go. But, you, Minty…" He peers at me through that floppy blond fringe. The expression in his eyes changes to something terrible, just terrible. A look that's beyond description. What's he trying to say? What?

I gasp.

My God, does he feel sorry for me?

Chapter Forty

His mother's rasping voice cries out to him. "Jack! Jack!"

I know he'll leave now but I can't let him. I have to know what he meant. "Tell me!" I demand.

He starts to get up. "I have to go to her."

"Tell me! What should you have told me?"

Glancing at the bed, Jack sits back down.

"I… The reason I was stuck…couldn't get to the next level was—" He sighs. "Look, I'll explain. I had all this." He throws a hand out. "I was happy. And then, when my old man died…" He groans. Rakes his fingers through his hair. "It was hard. As I said, my father and I were close." He nods to his mum. "She was shattered. We both were. And I…" He leaps onto his feet, paces up and down. "I went a bit crazy. A lot crazy. Started hanging out with guys who did drugs. LSD. Speed. Pot. That kinda gear. Tried to be this cool guy, someone who hadn't been hurt. Someone with no worries. I needed to do it. To forget." He frowns, glances at the bed. "She couldn't hack it. Was on my back, day after day." His expression softens. "She meant well but, well, I was confused, angry, couldn't take it anymore. Took an overdose. She tried to pretend it was an accident. But it wasn't. She knew it wasn't."

"You committed suicide?" I gasp.

Oh, Jack. No, you couldn't have. Not you.

He appeals to me with his eyes, his long lashes curling up like he'd a ton of brown mascara on. "I've never forgiven myself. That's why I'm stuck. The real reason. Not because she couldn't accept my death. But because I couldn't accept what I'd done to her."

"Oh, Jack. That's so sad." I go to touch his hand but he snatches it away. My face creases in sympathy.

He nods. "For years I hung around in this house, waiting, watching – a silent bystander to all the pain I'd created. Then it got too much, so I split. Came back occasionally. Then this year she became ill. So I started to come back more often. But it was tough. Seeing her like that. You remember what she was like that time you came with me?"

"The night after Iona's?"

He dips his head. "She looked so frail. Old. Sick. I knew then she hadn't long to live."

"And that's the real reason you taught me how to make contact? You knew you'd be going soon?"

"Hoped I would." He shrugs. Smiles. "Then tonight, when she came to me in the garden, I knew that the misery I'd caused her was almost over. That I'd done my penance. That we could move on together." The smile fizzles and dies. "But, Minty, I didn't teach you what I know just because of that." He rakes his unruly fringe with his fingertips. "I've been so unfair to you. I could've helped you way back when we first met. Shown you how to move on then. But I didn't. I kept you here for me. Shit, I even made you come here."

"You didn't make me, I wanted to come."

"I did. I coulda got here on my own." He taps his forehead. "The power of the mind. Remember? I could've concentrated on home and just appeared here. Instead, I trailed you through the night, miles along the road. Because I was chicken. Wanted to be here when she dies but was too scared to. I was stalling for time, I guess."

He stands up. Peers down at me. "Oh, Minty, you need to move on, too. You've done so much to help your sister but you have to let her go now. That's what she wants. But here's the key..."

"You kept so much stuff from me. How selfish can you get?"

He looks away. "I know I have, but I've been trying to put that right." He turns and looks me in the eye. "And yeah, OK, I've been a selfish prat but what about what you're doing to Jess, Minty? What about that, eh? To start with you wanted to help your sister, but what about now? Aren't you just helping yourself? Isn't that *you* being selfish?" He drops his voice to a whisper. "You think I don't know what you're doing? You don't even want to move on any more. But you must. For both your sakes." He looks at his mum and smiles.

Helping myself?

From the depths of my subconscious, I dredge up a picture of Jess in her room tonight. It flickers like an old newsreel, taunts me with images of her tear-stained face, of her hand dipping down into my urn – the way she lay so listless on the bed, her duvet wrapped around her legs.

And I told Jack she's happy? Now who's the selfish prat?

"Jack." His mother whispers his name and lets out a long, low sigh.

"*Obit anus, abit onus*: the old woman dies, the burden is lifted," Jack murmurs.

"Mrs Muir! Mrs Muir!" The housekeeper leans over Jack's mother and fumbles about for a pulse. Her stubby fingers settle at the side of the old woman's neck and, moments later, she hunches over the body in tears.

Right then, the murmur of voices ripples through her sobs. As they increase in volume, the housekeeper lifts her head, pulls back from Mrs Muir and puts a hand across to close each of her eyes. Instantly, a ghostly shape rises up from Jack's mother's dead body. It floats in the air above the bed and drifts down until it stands facing Jack and me.

The wispy figure shimmers and wavers, and slowly, oh so slowly, becomes more and more solid, until she is as life-like as we are.

"Jack," his mother says, "Jack, my boy, you came." Though the voice is hoarse and frail her smile is astoundingly bright, the eyes a blazing blue, like Jack's.

And then, an astonishing thing happens. Right before us, the old, sick-looking woman changes: the wrinkles round her mouth and eyes fade, her skin tightens, her shoulders lose their droop, until there in front of us is the same woman, only thirty or so years younger.

"She's… How did that happen?"

"I guess she's back to how she was when she was happiest," Jack says. He looks at me with an uncertain grin. "Gotta split now, Minty."

His mother extends a hand, her smile growing warmer and more youthful. "Jack," she says, the word ringing out clearly.

Jack steps forward, takes his mother's hand in his and turns back to me, his eyes shining.

And as they stand there, the sound of soft music appears. Note by note, it grows in volume until it surrounds us all: an orchestra of violins, harps, wind chimes – every instrument and more than I've ever heard.

"Dig that, man," he says, staring around him, his voice steeped in wonder.

My jaw drops. I gasp. "That music, it's amazing. What is it?"

"It's the Music of the Spheres. I heard it when Pete went – each time the other guys moved on. Got to thinking it'd never play for me." His eyes widen, his gaze softens. "Looks like it has. But it's nothing to how I feel. That thing that happened outside, when we touched, it's nothing compared to this."

He seems – God, he's almost angelic. And when he smiles it's with such contentment that it's almost unbearable to look at.

He looks to me, at his mother and with a little shrug he flashes me that grin of his. "Guess I've finally forgiven myself."

And know what, Jack? Despite your two-timing ways, I forgive you, too. Haven't you waited too long for this as it is?

"So, this is really it? You're leaving?" I whisper, moving towards him. "Should we shake hands goodbye, or something?"

We reach out to one another, laughing awkwardly, but when my fingers brush his the laughter dries in my throat, because I'm zapped by that feeling again, the one I had at the front door. But this time it's a thousand times more powerful: as if a million watts of energy is coursing through my veins, invading every atom of my body, sparking me back to life. It's as if I'm part of Jack and he of me.

"See ya, kid," Jack says.

He drops his hand and as he does so the sensation withers to nothing and I want to scream, shout, claw at him – anything to get it back again.

And then, a tremendous brightness falls on him and his mum, as if they're in some powerful spotlight. The bedroom fills with starry light, a light so warm and golden that I can't help feeling happy again, full of the purest, deepest joy I've ever known.

The radiance falling on them grows whiter, dazzlingly, almost blindingly whiter, and I see that they are standing at the end of a long, long shaft of brilliance that soars up and up, out of the window, cutting through the night sky to the heavens.

And, as I look, my friend and his mother melt into this shimmering mass and the golden light in the rest of the room is sucked, strand by strand, into the shaft, as if it's some great big celestial vacuum cleaner.

And then.

It's gone.

The music's gone.

His mother's gone.

Jack's gone.

And I'm all alone, all alone in this ghostly world of mine.

Chapter Forty-One

I stand there vaguely aware of the comings and goings in the room: the man with the briefcase – the Range Rover guy, who's a doctor as it turns out – examining the dead body; that smartly dressed woman I saw before, comforting Mrs Fuller; and it's as if I'm standing in a big, black hole. As if *I'm* the big, black hole. I never knew I could feel so empty.

I drag my gaze to the lifeless form of Jack's mother, lying on the bed covered in a crisply ironed cotton sheet and I think, that's only her shell, she isn't here. And *I* shouldn't be either. So, like the ghost I am, I slip away with Remus in my wake, out into the night, to go – who knows where? Where do I go now? What do I do?

The journey back to my home town is a slow one, for my feet don't seem to want to take me there. Why would they? What's there for me now? Just a big old heap of confusion.

As the morning sun filters through the clouds, I'm overwhelmed by a terrible emptiness that seeps into my being and I find myself parked on a metal bench inside a bus shelter in the centre of town. I don't know how long I'm there but, as I perch on the seat, my head resting on the glass panel to the side, a fair-haired girl in a baseball cap and a cool pair of khaki cargo pants comes in. Remus trots over to her, wags his tail. Gives her a paw.

Totally oblivious to us both, she puts down the bulging Co-op carrier bag she's carrying, shakes off her yellow cotton jacket, then rummages in the bag and pulls out a bottle of Irn Bru.

I used to love Irn Bru. I used to love drinking it from the bottle like that, letting the bubbles fizz over my tongue, letting the sugary, fruity taste wash over my throat. It's just another something to rub my nose in the fact that all these normal everyday things are lost to me. I don't want to feel sorry for myself but I can't help it.

I just want it back – my life.

No. That's not true. I want to be cocooned in that awesome light again. To feel that amazing joy. That incredible connection to Jack. To more than him, to the cosmos – whatever it is.

"God! I'm tired of all this," I say, taking a look around me. Remus nudges my leg. I reach down to pat his head. "You must be too, boy."

Just then another girl comes into the bus shelter. She smiles at the Irn Bru girl but the Irn Bru girl looks through her as if she's invisible. Then I have a thought – maybe she is! Maybe she's a ghost, just like me! Didn't Jack say they're out there? Dead folk?

"Hi," I say, watching to see if I get a reaction.

The girl swivels round to me. Her green eyes light up and she grins.

"Omigod! Omigod! You can see me?" I squeal, jumping up from the bench, a huge grin breaking out on my face. "I thought I'd never talk to anyone else again." I flick my hair away with the back of one hand. Hold out the other one. "The name's Minty. How long have you been dead?"

Out of the blue, there's a whooshing through my body and my mind fizzles into millions of tiny pieces.

"Becca! How you doing? Haven't seen you in ages," the green-eyed girl says to the teenager who's just walked through me.

"I'm good. What you been up to?"

No!

I don't hang around to hear the answer to that question. I should have known she was alive. How stupid could I be?

Stupid? Yeah, I'm stupid all right! Stupid! Stupid! Stupid! And selfish. I realise that now, thanks to Jack... And yet – oh yeah, I know I'm being selfish again, but... Oh Jack, where are you? I need you. I don't want to be on my own.

The streets are brimming with life: car horns honking, traffic lights bleeping, folk milling about – some strolling, some chatting, others whizzing by. Everywhere I look – life, life, life, going about its everyday business. But, as I wander through it all, all I can think of is Jack and that tunnel, that awesome, shining tunnel. And that incredible, golden light. And how happy I felt.

And I wish, I wish that it had taken me away, too.

Chapter Forty-Two

The thought of going back to my house filled me with dread. After seeing Jack and his mum so happy, I knew I couldn't hack seeing my sister sunk in misery again so I spent the rest of the night walking. Thinking. Wondering. With only my loyal pet for company. But those traitor feet of mine, they had other ideas. They led me here. Home. Whatever that means.

When I walk up the side path, into the back garden, Mum's there, chilling out with the Sunday papers. Though there's not much chilling going on as far as I can see because she's sitting at the wooden table, as stiff as a lump of Aberdeen granite, the newspapers spread out in front of her, and she's staring into the distance, past the birdbath in the middle of the lawn to the trees at the bottom of the garden.

Then, just as I approach her, she gathers up the papers and goes back indoors. With a sigh, I decide I may as well go too.

Time to man up, Minty. Go check on Jess.

And I'm not stalling for time – honest I'm not – but something stops me, draws me to the garage.

Walking over, I notice the double doors are only halfway rolled up. I think I hear scratching inside – perhaps it's a rat. No, it's a really strange noise: muffled, pained, like a sick creature or something. Even though I'm imagining a massive rodent, or worse, lurking in the back, I nip under the doors and there inside is my dad sitting on an upturned plastic crate with his hands across his face and he's – omigod, he's crying. I should be glad for him cos he's held in those tears for way too long. But…God, a girl shouldn't see her dad like this.

Rummaging around in the pockets of my jeans, I pull out a scrunched-up tissue and hold it out to him. "Here. It's clean – I think," I say, focussing on a roll of electric cable at my feet – anything to avoid looking at him.

Of course, he doesn't take my tissue.

It's not until he peels his hands away from his face that I notice his eyes – his dry, bloodshot eyes. That's not sobbing I've been hearing – it's something worse, something tortured. Animal almost. The raw keening of a broken man.

"Oh, Dad," I say moving towards him, arms outstretched. It's then I see his pupils, how they suddenly enlarge. Notice that he's looking right at… me!

Looking at you, Minty? Don't be dumb – he's just staring into space.

Isn't he?

I hesitate, inch closer, so close to him that even in the dim light I can see the open pores on his long nose, the thick black stubble from two days without shaving. So near that I notice the network of tiny red veins in the whites of his eyes.

His breathing is shallow now, rapid like Usain Bolt's must've been after the hundred metres Olympic final. It's horribly mesmerising, so when Dad's mobile goes off, my body jerks with fright.

Stepping back, I watch him pull his iPhone from his shirt pocket. His face darkens when he checks who's calling.

"Yes?" he says, real snippy-like.

As he listens to the person on the other end, his expression becomes thunderous.

"No, I can't. My daughter's not well."

I move closer, try to hear what the reply is. All I can make out is a jumble of indistinct words.

Meantime, Dad paces the floor, the mobile pressed to his ear, his fingers gripping it like a raptor's claw. "What part of no don't you understand?" he chimes in, through clenched teeth.

His shoulders grow tense at what the caller says next. "Call one of the others out, get them to look at it. I'm needed here."

Ah, it's his work on the phone! Oh shit.

I just manage to catch some of the garbled response before Dad yells down the phone, "There's a lot of it about? Jess doesn't have a summer cold, you moron, she's having a relapse. So forgive me if I don't jump to attention, dash out to fix your bloody problem. Because I'm putting my family first – if I'd done that long ago her sister would still be alive."

And with that, he cuts the call short and, like an athlete in the highland games throwing the hammer, hurls his iPhone into the corner of the garage.

It lands with a clatter. I expect it's smashed in a millions bits, not that he seems to care, he's—

Slam! Thump!

"Omigod! Dad, stop!" I say, as he begins to kick and kick at the bag of compost lying unopened on the floor, while simultaneously punching the surplus fencing panels propped up against the wall. With every hit, his groans and grunts grow more angry and desperate.

I make a grab for his hands just as Rommy bursts in and flings himself against him.

Dad goes rigid, except for his panting, heaving chest. His breathing reverberates around the place. He sinks to his knees, buries his face in Romulus's rough coat.

"Why did Minty have to die?" he says into Rommy's fur. "Why did she try to rescue Remus all by herself?"

"But I had to do it – don't you see?" I whisper. "Remus needed me. Was I supposed to just leave him to drown?"

And the irony of what I've just said strikes me like a thunderbolt from Jupiter.

"I thought I could save him," I whisper.

Then, as if on cue, Remus nuzzles my leg, lifts his golden head. Gazes up at me with that smiley expression that makes me think of a dolphin.

"I'm sorry, Dad," I say.

But I can't look at him any more. Like I said, a girl shouldn't see her dad this way. And a dad's entitled to privacy at a time like this.

So, patting Remus on the neck, I go to find my sister.

When I enter our bedroom, Octavius is on my bed. He greets me with this funny wee chirrup, plucks at the bedclothes and starts to purr.

I smile, but that quickly becomes a groan when I see Jess.

"Oh God, no Jess, no," I say, dropping onto the foot of her bed.

In spite of the fact that it's a blistering June day, Jess is bundled under the covers, with the duvet up to her armpits. But, what's worse, what's scarily, horribly worse, is that she's back wearing the repulsive woollen jumper that she's somehow rescued from the rubbish bin. I don't need to look at her face to see how she's feeling.

"Oh, Jess. Not this again. No. Please. Don't give up now. You were doing so well," I say, sitting beside her. Not that she notices I'm there: she doesn't give a flicker – as far as she's concerned there's just her and her grief. Cos even though I was hoping Dad was wrong about Jess having a relapse, I can see for myself that he's not. She's back to grieving… big-time.

"And you know what, Jess? I thought you were better than that. I didn't take you for a quitter," I say, and leap off the bed. I glance up at the *Gladiator* poster on the wall, the one of Maximus, standing there with his sword, so strong and determined. "Isn't that why you love that guy – cos he never gave up? He's not a quitter and neither are you." I kneel by her bed. "Go to sleep. We need to talk about this."

In my mind, I see Dad kicking the hell out of that fertiliser bag. Contrast it with the memory of Jess waving to him when he dropped her off outside the multiplex. Such a happy image, one full of hope. And it was down to me. *I* created that picture – made them happier. Surely I could do it again. Yeah?

With that lingering thought, I leap to my feet. "Oh what the heck! Why wait for dreamtime, Jess? I need to get you back on track right now."

So, I relax. Focus my thoughts, just as Jack taught me.

Seconds later, the unmistakable aroma of banana hangs in the air. I smile. I've got my powers back! Is that cos Jack's not here? Nah, that doesn't make sense. Whatever – I've got them back, and that's all that matters.

But maybe I haven't because Jess gives no sign of noticing, she just curls further up in her bed. Then I see what's tucked in the crook of her arms.

My urn, battered and scratched from when Jess lobbed it at the window.

"No! Enough!" I shout. "That's going!" With angry hands, I make a grab for it. "Damn!" Instead of snatching the urn, my fingers slice through the plastic, through the ashes inside.

Why can't I grasp it? Cos I'm nothing – a shade, a ghost, whatever I want to call it. I am a big fat zero.

I should be used to that by now – being in this world but not of it. The thought sickens me. This existence sickens me.

I drop my head into my palms. "Is this it? Is this what it's going to be like now, Jess? Me and you?"

No! This is no way to be! You have to buck up. And, in my head, I hear Jack's voice telling me to do something about it, so I spring onto my feet and stride to the stereo. Focus until I turn the radio on, only to hear Robbie Williams.

Omigod! *Angels*! The song they played at my funeral.

Jess slowly rolls round onto her side and pulls herself upright, listening. She's actually listening! So my powers *have* returned.

She stares at the stereo and tears tumble down her pale cheeks. When she wipes them away, my mind goes into shock as I notice those bruises, my bruises, back on her wrists again. Why? Why? What's going on? I wish I could help her – but there's nothing I can do. No wait! You can still contact her…

Omigod!

Is that why my powers have come back? Cos she's wretched again? But why is she? She knows I'm still with her. I don't understand.

Then, feeling that everything's spinning out of control, I watch as Jess crumples over onto the mattress with a shuddering sob, and howls. And her grief seems to waft off her. It hovers in the air, an invisible noxious mist that settles on me like a dose of flu.

And, like a flu victim, I begin to shiver, holding my hands to my stomach, asking myself what did I do to make her feel that way?

But all of a sudden, I don't want to be in this room anymore. So I leave.

I don't even dare to look back.

Chapter Forty-Three

I spend the night in the living room, watching telly with the sound turned off. Jack was right; it's really lonely on your own. So, in the morning on hearing my parents come downstairs into the kitchen, I head in there. They're both showered and dressed for work and back to wearing those same sad expressions. Neither of them speaks, they just get on with the usual Monday morning stuff – but this is no normal Monday. If it were, Dad would be teasing Mum about having too much make-up on, or her skirt being too short; and me and Jess would be having our usual moan about Mum making us eat muesli instead of letting us have Coco Pops.

Instead, Dad sits at the table, sifting through the newly delivered mail, while Mum bustles about preparing a breakfast tray for my twin. With Octavius rubbing up against her calves, she snips the end off a gerbera stalk and pops the bright orange flower into a slim glass vase. She places the vase on the wooden tray, adds a mug of coffee – made with one sugar and lots of hot semi-skimmed milk, just the way Jess likes it – plonks two slices of buttered wholemeal toast onto a pretty china plate and puts that on the tray as well.

"I'll take this up," she says.

Dad glances at Mum over the top of his reading glasses.

"She should have been up an hour ago. She'll be late for school," he mutters. "And you've no time to do all that. You have work, too. You shouldn't spoil her." He throws a dark look at the tray. "She's playing the sympathy card."

Mum purses her lips. Fastens her grip on the tray. "Where did my lovely husband go?" With a sigh, she puts the tray down on the table and studies Dad for a moment. "Why are you being so hard on her, Geoff? Where's your compassion? You know how close the two of them were. All right, Jess was doing fine there for a while but is it so surprising that she's slipped back a little? They were twins. She's lost her best friend and has to learn how to get by on her own now. It's hard for her."

He rips open what looks like another bill, glimpses at it and stuffs it back in its envelope. "Change the record, Mary," he says. Then his gritted jaw loosens. The letter drops from his hand and he sags back against his chair. "Sorry. I'm out of order. It's just..." He stares at her – peers, really. "How can you stand it? How do you cope? God knows, I can't."

"It's hardly been any time at all since Minty died. Jess's bound to have her bad days. Goodness knows, I do." Mum places her hands on his shoulders. "Give it time. Give *her* time."

"I... It's all too painful – seeing her suffering. I feel so useless."

"Oh, love, grief doesn't conform to a script, or a set of rules." She stops, sinks onto the kitchen chair next to him and lightly touches his hand. "Geoff, don't take this the wrong way, but you go off like a tinder box at times. It can't help Jess, you being like that."

He lets out a massive sigh. Brushes Mum's cheek. "You're right." His fingers kiss her hairline. "Look, I'll talk to her about that party she wants, try to get more involved." He pushes back a few wispy hairs. "I only hope she doesn't start obsessing again about Minty trying to get in touch with her. Because honestly, Mary, you might be able to handle that, I can't."

"Love," Mum says, placing a hand on his. "You know it's her way of dealing with things."

"By pretending to get messages from the other side?" Dad says, slipping his specs on the top of his head. "Minty's gone, Mary. Gone for good. None of us will ever see her again."

Mum flinches.

"And hard as it is, Jess has to accept that," he whispers.

Picking up the mail, he shoves back his chair and, with heavy steps, walks off.

Probably hoping he'll come back, Mum waits for a moment, re-arranging the gerbera in its vase, touching the side of Jess's mug to see if the coffee's still hot, straightening the way the toast is lying on the plate, then, letting out a loud hiss of air, she lifts the tray and takes it upstairs.

I stay behind in the quiet of the kitchen because I really don't want to look at my twin – not yet.

"I can't take it, not now Jack's gone," I whisper and shuffle to the window to look out across the lawn. "Look at it," I say to myself as I take in every detail of the garden. "It's all so familiar and yet" – I throw my hands up to my face – "I don't belong here anymore."

Now, more than at any time since I died, I wish I could collapse in tears, to curl up into a ball, just like Jess, and cry, cry, cry.

I open my eyes, and there's the sun streaming through the branches of the trees, flooding the garden with light and I wonder how I'm ever going to cope with this existence in the shadows, a reluctant bystander to my sister's misery.

If only she would be content to see me in her dreams like she was before.

"Geoff! Come quick!"

Mum's scream, and the sound of Dad's feet hammering up the stairs, stop my thoughts in their tracks. I dash from the kitchen and fly up to my room.

"She's gone," Mum says, sitting on Jess's neatly made-up bed, with a thin sheet of paper in one hand and an envelope in the other. She flaps the paper in the air. "There's a note."

She passes it to Dad who drops down beside her and, as he soaks in each word, his hands begin to shake.

"What does she mean…*I need to know what it was like*?" he whispers.

"You read what she said!" Mum says.

"*I have to go there. I need to be with Minty. I need to do it.* By God, Mary. What does that mean? Where is she? Where has she gone?"

Where *have* you gone, Jess? Where would you go to be with me? If only you'd believed in me enough, you'd have realised you didn't have to go anywhere. You've been with me every single day since…

I need to do it.

"Elie!" Where it happened. That's where she would go! "She's gone to Elie," I groan.

We're identical twins. We saw the same things. Felt the same things. Did the same things. Except for once.

And that can only mean one thing. One dreadful, horrible thing. Of course Jess would go to Elie.

Because Jess is going to do something stupid.

"Let me see that again," Mum says, taking the note out of Dad's hands.

"Are you crazy? Why're you wasting time reading that? Get in the car. Drive to Elie! Come on! Let's go!" I shout, stamping my feet in frustration.

Romulus and Remus glance up from where they are curled together in Romulus's basket. Octavius, draped over the back of my headboard, stops licking his front paws and stares at me.

"She's run away," Dad says, kneading his temples. He stares at Mum. "What have I done, Mary?" He looks at Jess's carefully written note all crumpled up in Mum's hand. "This is because of me. I forced her to it."

"It's not you. She's depressed," Mum says, laying the note on her lap and flattening it out again.

"If I'd been more understanding."

"No! Enough with the chatter." I run to Dad. Yell into his face. "Listen! I know where she is! If you wait, it'll be too late!"

Remus begins to whine. He comes over to me, rubs his head against my legs. "You know where she is, don't you boy?" I lift his chin so he looks at me. He whimpers and pulls away.

Turning back to my parents, I say, "Please! Dad! Mum! Go to Elie!"

I have to make them realise. I have to make them see. I peer at the sheet of lined white paper on Mum's lap and think...move! Move! I visualise it rising up. Fluttering in the air.

"What the...?" Dad says, his puzzled gaze following the note as it glides to the carpet. "How odd."

It worked!

And, all of a sudden, I realise I can do this: I can get Mum and Dad to go to Elie. I'll use the power – the power in my mind.

Hard to believe but you can...get into people's heads. Just by channelling your mind power.

That's what Jack said – use your mind. Crikey, it's what you did with Iona – how could you have forgotten that? So, come on, Minty, let your mind decide. Make decisions. So do it, dammit, just do it. Do it! You've done it before. You can do it now.

I peer at Dad. Focus on one word.

ELIE.

Picture it. Transferring…

ELIE.

From my head…

ELIE

To his…

"Elie!" Dad says. "That's it, Mary! Why didn't we think of it before! Oh my God!"

He springs off the bed and darts out of the bedroom.

"Where are you going?" Mum calls. "Geoff?"

"Elie. That's where she's gone," he hollers.

She rushes down the stairs after him. When she reaches the kitchen, Dad's already grabbed his car keys off the hook and thrown open the back door, the dogs yelping and whirling round in excitement. Poor things, they probably think they're getting taken for a walk.

If only.

Dad grasps the door frame. Exhales. "*I need to know what it was like.* What *what* was like?" He stiffens. "*I have to go there.*" He utters a terrible sob. Dashes to the car. Unlocks it. Bawls at Mum. "Mary, get in the car!"

"Geoff?" Mum whimpers, clambering into the front passenger seat and tugging at her seat belt. "Tell me this is not what I think it is."

Dad turns round, stares at her, face suddenly chalky, hands gripping the steering wheel. "Oh, Mary, I have a horrible feeling it is."

Chapter Forty-Four

Dad speeds the charcoal grey Renault down the narrow lane, whipping past the Fife countryside to the East Neuk village of Elie. For once, Mum doesn't tell him off for driving too fast, even when we enter the village.

We race along to the end of the main street and turn right to go down to Ruby Bay. As the car bumps over the rough road, it hits a pothole and swerves to one side, jerking the steering wheel from Dad's hands.

"Damn!" he yells, as the engine stalls.

He turns the key in the ignition again and again but the friggin' thing won't start.

"You'll flood the engine," Mum says.

"Hurry, Dad!" I say, clinging on to Remus.

"What do you want me to do?" Dad snaps.

"Leave the car. We'll go on foot." Mum opens the door and gets out, slamming it behind her.

Dad's still trying to restart the car.

"Come on, Dad!" I yell. "Or we'll be too late!"

It's not far to Lady's Tower but it'll still take too much time.

Minty.

Jess! I can hear Jess. Her voice is dreamy, like she's half asleep. As I tear down the road with Remus by my side, a great sadness washes through me.

Minty.

Suddenly, I am freezing cold. I'm so cold I start to quake.

I've got to get to Jess. Now! I begin to run as fast as I can. Pounding the uneven surface of the road, desperate to get to my sister. Why did that stupid car have to cut out like that? Why?

And…why am I so thick? Why has it taken me the whole dumb journey to remember what Jack told me?

I could have got here on my own… The power of the mind. Remember? I could've concentrated at home. And just appeared here.

Just appeared here? At his mother's place the night she died? So, if he could do that, what's to stop me just appearing where Jess is?

Think, Minty. Think of Jess.

Minty!

Be Jess.

My legs are heavy. My arms are heavy. My lungs… I can't breathe. A salty taste floods my mouth. Water gushes up my nose. I gasp with pain. Blood trickles from the scar above my top lip.

I'm tired – so, so tired.

Minty!

I start coughing. Seawater pours from between my teeth.

Minty!

Jess is calling to you. She needs you.

Think!

Block out the voice and concentrate on the person.

I stop running. Stand very still. Thinking of Jess.

All at once, my mind appears to burst into tiny pieces and I am on the rocks, looking out to the churning sea, and there, down in the water, is Jess, fully clothed and struggling to keep afloat.

"Minty! Help me!"

"Jess!" I scramble to the water's edge and throw myself in.

And it's like last time, except now I'm fighting for my sister's life and not my dog's. Inexplicably, all the physical sensations, the ones I'd begun to experience back on the road to the bay, take over. Omigod – the myth! That urban myth Jack told me about. I've got my body back. It *is* possible. Oh, Jack, it isn't a myth at all.

"Hold on, Jess! I'm coming!" I shout, gulping in so much water that I begin to choke.

The waves slam against my face, weigh down my limbs. I try to keep my head above water but the sea just wants to drag me down.

"Help!" Jess's cry is weaker than before, as if she's losing the fight.

Don't give up! Please, don't give up!

I strike out further into the sea, my shoulders aching with the effort. I see Jess's hair swirling round her like tendrils of brown seaweed. I swim on, pushing through the waves, trying to keep Jess in my sights.

Where is she?

She's gone! My heart skips a beat.

"Jess!"

I do a desperate doggie paddle to keep afloat, and look about me, anxiously searching for her.

There! There she is!

Her head bobs up through the surface of the sea, almost in front of me. She's alive! I throw out an arm. Hook it round her neck. Her lips are pale blue and her face is bloodied and scarred, but she's still breathing. Although she weighs so much that we both go under, sinking into the swirling sea.

We're drowning! *Jess* is drowning!

But – wait! Is that so bad? If she does drown we'll be together at last. If I just let go we'll never have to be separated again.

Then do it, Minty. You know you want to. You and J together forever, just the way it ought to be. What's she got to go back to? Nothing but misery. Let go and you can take it all away. She called for you, Minty. She needs your help.

So do it. Free her. Help her.

And so, as we break through the waves, I take one last look at her lovely face. And loosening my grip, I let her slip out of my arms.

"It doesn't hurt, J, not really, you'll see. It'll soon be over," I say through my tears, my emotions churning as her head sinks under the water. "And I'm waiting for you. It's going to be all right."

Then she vanishes beneath the waves.

No!

What am I saying? What am I doing? How twisted am I that I would let that happen to my sister? And what about Dad? Mum? No! I can't do this!

I dive down, fumbling for Jess, searching the murky, churning waters. Finally, with my lungs burning inside my chest, I detect a dark shape. It's her! I grab her limp body and kick out with such force that we break through to the air in seconds.

But is it too late? What has my warped thinking done to her?

Coughing and spluttering and crying at the same time, I struggle for the shore, dragging my twin to safety.

Shoulders, arms, muscles, every part of me aches. But we get nearer to the land.

I slice an exhausted arm through the water. My fingers make contact with something rough and hard and so jagged that it slashes through my skin.

We've made it! We've made it to the shore!

Hanging on desperately to Jess's sopping woolly jumper, I pull myself up onto a rock, trying to ignore the awful pain in my shoulders, the knife-like edges jagging into me.

Twisting round, with her half-in, half-out of the water, and slipping and fumbling, I finally manage to pull Jess free of the sea's clutches.

"Jess, are you OK?" I say, slapping her cheek. "Omigod, you're all cut." I put my thumb to her top lip. Watery blood runs over my fingers. "Jess, speak to me."

No response.

Don'tbedeaddon'tbedeaddon'tbedead—

My God, what've I done to her?

"Jess, speak to me!"

Bile gathers in my stomach and spurts into my throat.

I vomit onto the rocks.

And just then I hear her moan.

Not even bothering to wipe away the sick, I throw myself at her.

"Thank Jupiter!" I cry, drawing her to me.

Slowly, her eyes flicker open. She smiles. "Minty?"

The tears flowing from my eyes mix with the salt water streaming from my hair. "Oh Jess. I thought you—"

"Mary! I've spotted her! She's down there!"

I crane round and see Mum and Dad up by Lady's Tower.

"She's OK, Dad! I got her! She's OK!"

Dad slithers down the rocks. He shouts back to Mum. "Call an ambulance!"

"Minty. You saved me," Jess rasps. "Or am I dead already?"

"Shh. Don't try to speak. We'll talk later." I turn and see Dad, plunging down, trying to keep his footing as he hurries to get Jess.

"Minty. I knew you'd come," Jess mutters.

"Dad's here."

Whoosh! A scorching wind sweeps through me as Dad moves into where I'm crouching. I crawl to the side, let him see to Jess.

"Jess." He peers into her eyes. "Oh, Jess."

"Minty..." Jess's voice fades away as she slips into sleep.

At least I think it's sleep... Oh, God, what if she dies? If she does I'll have murdered her.

"Help her! Please!" I scream into Dad's ear.

He checks her pulse, puts his face and then a hand to her mouth.

"Is she all right?" Mum says, as she scrambles down beside us.

"No. Yes. I don't know. She's unconscious," Dad cries, checking Jess's pulse once more. "Oh God, Jess. Not you, too. Please God, no. Hang on. Don't leave us."

He inhales deeply, then carefully he puts an arm round the back of Jess's neck and another under her waist and, sliding and stumbling on the slippery rocks, with Mum helping, he lifts her to safety.

Panting with exhaustion, Dad lays Jess down at the foot of the steps leading up to the tower. Sobbing, Mum collapses onto her knees next to her.

"I...need..." Dad gasps, "to catch my breath." He swipes an arm over his forehead and, leaning his hands on his thighs, takes in great gulps of air.

But Jess is so still, so deathly still. Then her eyelids flutter and, slowly, they open and she looks up at me.

"Minty," she says.

She smiles and suddenly she's right beside me, hugging me and kissing me and crushing me to her. Then we draw back and stare at one another.

"You scared the shit out of me!" I say, and punch her on shoulder, forgetting for a moment the danger I put her in. "What d'ya have to do that for? You coulda drowned!"

But I know the answer to that, of course I do. And if my sick mind had its way she probably would've.

"I wanted to, Minty." Tears well up over her bottom eyelids. "But…it was so cold…and I couldn't…I didn't…"

I swipe a hand over my mouth, wishing I could swipe away the guilt I'm feeling as easily as I can wipe off the traces of vomit.

What got into me back there? What the Hell was I thinking?

Fighting back the tears I say, "Jess, you didn't really want to die, did you?"

"Yes. No." She sobs. "Oh, Minty, I only wanted to be with you again – properly. That's what all this is about. Seeing you in my dreams was so good… but…" She gulps. "It wasn't enough. And then, I thought…why not? Why not do it? Why not just drown myself?" She clutches my fingers. "But I was too scared to go through with it…"

"Jess," I say, and give her a huge hug. "We'll be together again. One day. But not like this."

"But we are together. You're back."

"But Jess, that's just it – I'm not back, not really," I say, holding her at arm's length to peer into her eyes, willing myself to say what comes next. "I'm still dead. I was just hanging around cos you've been so upset."

"No! No, you're not dead." She kicks me on the shin.

"Ow! That hurt!"

"See?" she says, grinning. "You're *not* dead. If you were, you wouldn't have felt that. Would you?"

"But..."

I'm about to tell her that I'm only here cos she can't accept that I'm dead – but something stops me. It itches at the corners of my mind, scratches away at my memory bank.

Something about acceptance...something to do with Jack.

That's it! Jack couldn't accept what he'd done... couldn't forgive himself. That's why he was still here. It was his own doing, not his mum's. He couldn't accept—

Oh no – wait... Is...is that what I'm doing? Is it *me* who can't accept being dead, having to part ways with Jess?

Omigod! That's what he was trying to tell me at the end – what he meant by the key to all this. I'm not stuck because Jess can't let *me* go. It's because I won't let *her* go!

I squeeze my eyes tight, overwhelmed by a multitude of memories that prove I've stumbled on the truth. And the accompanying soundtrack in my head replays what she told Kirsty and Iona about the Carista.

I'm sure that's what Minty wants, a proper goodbye.

How could I have ignored what she said? How much evidence did I need? The Carista, the words Jack saw in her notebook, the ones I refused to acknowledge– it was to let me go. She wanted that to happen…and…

I make myself look at her – at her battered face, at her sopping clothes. I listen to her rapid breathing. Watch her chest expand and deflate as her lungs refill with air. And in my head I hear the words she spoke in the bedroom that day: *Minty, I just want to tell you I'm OK.*

She told you that and you glossed over it.

Well, she's not OK now though, is she, Minty? She wasn't all right when she wrote that note for Mum and Dad.

I drop my gaze.

You made her unhappy enough to want to kill herself. Iona said to Jess that time – as long as you're happy, she's happy. And she was beginning to be – until you put a stop to it! Damn you and your interference!

Look at her, Minty, really look at her. If you love her, you'll let her go. You must do it.

"I…" I can't!

"Minty? Talk to me," she says.

Now! Tell her!

"I… I *am* dead Jess and…" How can I say this?

Just do it.

I swallow, cradle her chin in my hands, and push out the words. "You need to get on with your life. And then we can both move on."

"But...how can I live without you? You're part of me, Minty!"

Oh, Jess, don't make this any harder. Please.

"I know. And you're part of me. But I need to go. And you need to start living again. Don't you see that?" I grasp her shoulders, wanting to hold on to her but knowing I must let her go. Forcing a smile, I say, "*Carpe Diem,* yeah? Seize the day. I wish I was still alive, but I'm not. But you are, Jess. So don't stop living because of me."

"I don't—"

"Geoff! I think she's stopped breathing!"

Both of us spin round.

"Oh!" Jess gasps, because there on the ground is her body with Dad crouched over it, giving mouth-to-mouth. She looks back to me, a terrified, confused look on her face.

This is it, Minty. Step up to the plate.

"You need to go back, J," I say, letting my hands fall from her, thinking that my heart will break into a million painful pieces if she does as I ask. "Go back. Have a good life. For me. For us both."

Will she do it? Dare I let her?

She looks at me. I hold her gaze for a long moment, then gesture to her inert form on the ground. Nod my head in encouragement.

We smile.

Then she's gone. Snapped back into her body.

She lies there pale and motionless, and then she coughs, water streaming out of her mouth, and opens her eyes.

"Thank God!" Mum says, stroking the wet hair from Jess's face.

"Minty, don't leave me," Jess murmurs.

Don't say that, Jess, don't.

I back away. "Jess, I must. It's for the best. Please, let me go."

Jess looks at me. Whimpers. "I'll try."

I force myself to drag my eyes from her face and gaze out to the water that claimed me all those weeks ago. And as the waves crash and roll against the rocky headland, I whisper, "You do that, J. You do that."

But I don't voice the question that's uppermost in my mind: do I have the courage to do the same?

Chapter Forty-Five

As Robbie's beautiful song, *Angels,* comes to an end, the three girls gaze out over the Firth of Forth. In their long white tunicas, they look like angels themselves.

"Minty'll be an angel now," Iona says, breaking the silence, as she looks out to where it all happened.

"I wonder," whispers Kirsty, the late evening sun gleaming golden on her shoulder-length hair as she looks quizzically at Jess.

"Will you play your sax now, Jess?" Mum says, bending down to switch off the portable CD player.

Jess fiddles with the drop on her amethyst necklace for a second, then takes the saxophone from its box and puts the mouthpiece to her lips. Mum wipes away a tear and cuddles into Dad as Jess tries out a couple of notes then launches into a Tommy Smith classic.

I don't reckon that the dogs think much of the music – they're scampering up and down the stairs in and out of Lady's Tower having a great old time. It seems that, finally, Romulus realises that Remus is there.

But Mum, she's really crying now, and she's not the only one. The girls are too, and, by the time Jess has finished there's not a pair of dry eyes between the four of them. Yet Dad...he just stands there, his arm round Mum, jaw clenched, as rigid as a Roman centurion at attention, dry eyes focused somewhere over the Forth.

"That was wonderful, love," Mum says, kissing Jess on the cheek. "Minty would have adored it."

Jess nods. Puts a finger to the scar above her lips, the scar she got the day she nearly drowned. She strokes it thoughtfully. "This itches. Minty always used to moan about that. Said her scar gave her gyp when she played."

"Yes," Mum says, touching Jess's fingers. "A scar in the very same place. It makes you think."

Dad comes up behind them, a sturdy canvas eco-bag in each hand. He puts one down on the grass and places his free hand on Mum's shoulder. He gazes at Jess and frowns. Then he clears his throat. "Ready?" he asks in a husky voice.

Picking up the bag, he marches on ahead. Mum watches him go for a second, then, with a sigh, lifts up the portable CD player while Jess boxes up her saxophone. They join Iona and Kirsty. No one speaks as they follow Dad in single file along the coastal path, leaving Lady's Tower behind.

It's very peaceful here today, there's not a soul about apart from us. A wee bird twitters in the clear sky above, a bee sneaks a late dinner on a cluster of tiny flowers and there, always there in the background, is the gentle roar of the sea.

When we come to the beach, they bunch up, walking purposefully to the shoreline, leaving their footprints in the sand. Dad lays the bags on the ground and I smile as I catch sight of his flip-flops. They make me think of Jack and those tan leather open-toed sandals. Maybe Jack fancied himself as a gladiator – even had a Roman thing going, in secret. Who knows with that guy?

Suddenly, Dad about turns, sending a flurry of damp sand into the air. "I can't do this," he groans, and strides off up the beach.

"Geoff!" Mum cries and runs after him.

Iona and Kirsty exchange worried glances, but Jess just looks on, a calm expression on her face.

Catching him up, Mum stops him and they huddle together as she murmurs something in his ear. Then, looking back at Jess, Dad gives a quick nod and they walk back to the shore.

Dad's eyes are dark, almost hooded, his hands trembling as he straightens his shoulders and stares out over the sea. With a slight nudge from Mum, he stiffens, tilts his chin and, taking a step forward, begins the Parentalia, his words ringing out into the evening.

"In ancient Rome we would have performed this at your tomb…" His mouth quivers and he rubs a thumb against his brow. "But you don't have a tomb, Minty…not even a grave…so we've come here, to where…we lost you…" His lips contort, his Adam's apple bobs in his throat when he looks at Mum. She smiles, inclines her head. "And to this, your favourite beach."

By now Dad's voice has dropped to a whisper. Jess's eyes are brimming with tears. He looks at her, drags his gaze away and swallows. "Not that we have lost you, really. As long as we have Jess, we have you."

Kirsty lets out a sob.

Dad draws breath, swipes a shaky hand across his head, mussing up his neat parting. "Jess tells me you saved her life. Well, I don't know about that – all I know is…we have her back now and…" He sucks at the air. "For that, I'm grateful."

Then Mum steps forward. From one of the bags she pulls a bottle of red wine and a large wine glass. The bottle's one of those screw top kinds; she untwists it, pours some wine into the glass and passes it to Dad.

He looks at it for a moment then takes a mouthful of the ruby liquor. "To you, Minty," he says, so softly I can hardly hear him, and hands the glass to Mum.

"To Minty," Mum says and sips. She passes the glass to Jess.

"In memoriam!" Jess cries and drinks some wine, spluttering at the taste, which makes me laugh.

She holds the glass out to Iona and, after her and Kirsty have taken some, Dad takes the half-full glass back, throws the remaining wine into the water and, with an encouraging nod from Mum, shouts, "In memory of Minty."

Then Mum takes my urn out of the bag. She looks at it for a moment and hands it to Jess, then goes into the other bag and gives Iona and Kirsty a garland of colourful fresh flowers each.

Jess cradles the battered, scratched plastic in her arms and stares out to sea.

"Geoff?" Mum says, raising her eyes to Dad and giving him another barely noticeable nod.

"Just a minute," Dad says, taking Jess gently by the shoulder. "I've got something for you."

As Mum smiles at him he offers my sister a small brown suede drawstring pouch.

Jess puts down the urn, takes the pouch and looks at him.

"Open it," Mum says.

From the suede leather, Jess pulls out a delicate gold chain with a golden teardrop.

"It's a bulla. A Roman good luck charm. I know you're meant to get one when you're a child, and you're hardly that, but we..." He glances at Mum, back to Jess. "I – thought you might like it. To remind you of today. And to say sorry. For being so hard on you lately."

"Dad...it's beautiful," Jess says, surprise filtering through her voice.

Mum and Dad's eyes lock. He blinks and smiles at Jess. "I'm told that's what fathers are supposed to do at the Parentalia...the Carista? Pay special attention to their families."

Mum slips an arm round Jess's waist, watches as she dangles the necklace in front of her. "It was your dad's idea to get it."

Jess runs to him and throws her arms around his neck, but Dad just stands there, his arms by his side, his face as grim as it was on the day of my funeral.

Then slowly, he wraps his arms around her, drops a kiss on the tip of her nose. Swallows. And points to the urn. "Let's do this, shall we?"

And, as I watch, Jess opens up my urn, walks to the sea and shakes the ashes onto the water. Then, Kirsty and Iona go to the water's edge and throw their garlands on top. After a moment of silence, when everyone stands watching the current pull the ashes and flowers out to sea, they turn, gather up their stuff and walk up the beach, leaving me on my own with Remus at my feet.

And, as they climb up onto the footpath, I think, just one last chance, just one more chance to talk to her.

"Jess," I say, against the sound of the waves.

Her feet freeze. Slowly, she swings round, still holding on to the empty plastic urn, the little suede pouch. She cranes her neck, rubs her eyes and stares and stares and stares.

Mum turns and looks behind her, sees Jess standing there, frowns and halts. "Jess?"

"Jess!" I cry, running across the sand, my arms flung wide open, ready to catch my twin in my grasp.

"Minty!" Iona gasps, staring straight at me as she clutches Kirsty's arm. "I knew it! I knew she was here all along!"

Suddenly, the beach is ablaze with the most intense brightness; it fills my head, my body, swamping me with a totally amazing sense of peace. And, as the dazzling light surrounds me, I see Jess and Iona stumble down onto the beach, their faces shimmering in the golden glow.

"Jess! Iona!" Mum calls after them, watching as Romulus runs yelping excitedly after them. "What's going on?"

Iona turns around, her face bathed in wonder. "Can't you see her? She's there. Right there."

"Who?" Mum says, puzzled.

"Minty," Iona sighs, watching as I hold out my arms to Jess.

"Oh Iona, don't," Kirsty says, peering down the beach. She then glances anxiously at Dad. "Don't start all that again. There's nothing to see."

Dad flinches, the tension in his jaw unmistakable. He shakes his head with a sigh and says, "I'm going back to the car." And with a lingering look out to sea, he trudges off.

Jess moves a step forward but pauses, her head jerking skywards to listen to the beautiful, unearthly music that's suddenly appeared.

"The music?" she mutters.

"The Music of the Spheres," I say. Smile to myself. "Or so I was told by a boy I once knew."

All at once, my memory brings Jack into focus, looking just as he did the last time I saw him. I recall his shining eyes, his soft gaze and the wonderment in his voice as he was preparing to leave. How astonishingly happy he was. Then I quiver with joy as I remember that awesome connection we had when we hugged, that feeling of belonging. And it's then that I finally realise, that being without Jess doesn't mean being alone; there'll be someone – something – waiting for me. Somewhere. And I know that moving on is the right thing to do – for me and for Jess.

But then I look at that face, so much a reflection of my own and I wonder – can I do this. Have I got the guts to go it alone?

Yet when I look at her smile, at her cheeks flushed with blood, at the life behind her eyes, I know what I must do.

"I'm going now, Jess." I smile. "Remember – *carpe diem* – yeah?"

She gives me a watery smile and nods. "*Carpe diem.*"

But, though I've done what I should've done weeks ago, I hesitate, my gaze drawn to the headland and the lonely figure of Dad as he strides along the coastal path.

"Dad!" I holler, my cry ringing out into the clear evening.

He just keeps on walking. But as he does, I remember all that Jack taught me.

"Let me say goodbye," I whisper, willing my words, my image, to float into his mind.

Then his back arches as if he's been shot, and he stops.

"Please, Dad," I say, my voice no more than a murmur.

And at that – omigod! – he whirls around and peers down the beach, out across the Forth.

Is it possible? Is it happening? Did he hear my voice?

I hardly dare to believe it, but when he rips back along the path and tears down onto the sand with Mum and Kirsty racing after him, the glimmer of hope inside me burns more brightly.

"My God," he says, coming to a halt when he reaches Kirsty and Iona.

He looks past them to where I am and I know by his tone of voice and by the tears filling his eyes that he sees me.

"Jess was right all along," he says, his legs buckling. Iona steadies him. He shakes his head and staggers back on one foot.

I hold out a hand. "Dad."

He lurches towards me, sobbing and laughing, and then falls into my arms. "It's you, it's really you. My Minty," he whispers into my hair.

He leans back, tilts up my chin and stares. His clean-shaven face is wet with tears but he's wearing such an elated expression that his skin is luminous.

"How can this be?" he asks, twisting round to Mum who's now standing beside Kirsty.

They both look as if they think Dad's lost it. Oh, if only they could see what he sees! He turns back to me, his elation morphing into bewilderment.

"I don't know why you can see me, and Mum can't," I say. "Maybe it's because you need to."

All at once he smothers me with a hug, and I never want him to let me go. "We didn't get the chance to say goodbye," he whispers, his voice cracking with emotion.

"I know, Dad. But we've got it now," I say.

Woof!

Remus comes bounding up to me, leaving Romulus hanging back by Jess's side.

Dad gasps, looks at my dog in amazement, but at that instant, I find my gaze drawn out to sea, and notice that I am at the end of a long, narrow, shimmering river that sweeps up and into the clouds. And along that river comes a boat with a hooded figure all dressed in white, hunched over an oar. And behind that figure sits a boy, a white-clad boy with golden hair and a crooked smile. As the boat glides silently to the shore, the boy jumps out and clicks his fingers at me.

"Hey, kid," he says. "Wanna hitch a ride?" With a wicked grin, he offers me his hand.

"Jack!"

So, it's true! I am moving on. And he's come back for me.

He smiles at Remus, slaps his thigh to gain my dog's attention. "You too, little guy. Off to Rainbow Bridge."

Remus watches me, as if to say 'What do I do here?' but when I gesture to the boat, he wags his tail, barks once at Romulus, then leaps in and settles at Jack's feet. "Isn't Remus coming with me?"

"Yip, but then I guess he'll wait at the bridge," Jack looks at me, at Remus, nods to Romulus and Jess. "Until you're all back together. Don't worry, it won't seem long. To you. Then you'll have all of time."

The music soars and I am filled with a happiness I could never have imagined.

I turn to Jess, to Iona standing behind her.

"Thank you," I say to my friend. She parts her lips as if to speak, but instead acknowledges me with a smile.

Jess strokes Romulus's head, gestures to the boat. "Charon," she says, glancing at the ferryman. "To take you across the River Styx." She gazes out at the river beyond.

"Hate to break this up, but it's time to hit the road," Jack says.

No. Not yet. Give me just a few more seconds and then I'll go.

I hear Dad gasp, Jess and Iona, too. In the background stand Mum and Kirsty. And as I gaze at them all – those five people I love most in the world – and glance at Romulus, think of Octavius at home, I ask myself, what will I do without them?

All sound drops away, except for the rhythmic lapping of waves petering out on the shore, as I take in every detail, relive each scene from my life: this place, these people, my pets, I won't be without them, not really, I'll carry them with me…I glance down at my chest… In here. And it'll be the same for them.

I smile at Mum, my strong, caring, wonderful mum; smile in turn at everyone.

Jack's right – it's time.

"I need to go now," I say to Jess, Dad, them all. "Don't worry, though – everything's going to be OK."

Dad goes to speak but instead just nods, kisses my cheek, and gives me a lingering look until the pressure of his arms around mine slackens. Then, he walks over to Mum, folds his arms around her and watches as I walk to the boat.

There's a lump in my throat, a real physical sensation of sadness at the thought of leaving. Except it's not, it's not that at all: it's a coin and it's in my mouth, not my throat. Reaching inside, I fish it out and it nestles there in my outstretched hand.

"To pay the ferryman?" I say to Jess, holding it up to her. She answers in a tearful smile. "Thank you," I say, my voice a mere croak. I take Jack's outstretched hand as he helps me into the boat.

And the instant our fingers connect it's as if every good feeling I've ever had is packaged into one yet amplified a trillion, zillion times, so much that I can't stop grinning at the sheer bliss of it all.

Then, passing the coin to the ferryman, and with a backward glance at my family and friends, I join Jack and Remus as the boat sails off into eternity.

Acknowledgements

The idea for the book appeared early one summer morning, just as the sun came up. During the night I thought I had sensed my late father's presence, so, unable to get back to sleep, I sat in the sunroom contemplating what had actually happened. While doing this I heard my dog panting and put out my hand to stroke her. Until I remembered - she had died the month before. That's when Minty's story came to me. It was June 2006.

For the next two years I let the idea ferment. Then, a few months into 2008, I began to develop the story, researching and taking notes as I went along. I wrote the first draft quickly but it was a long time before the book was ready for publication. Without the support and guidance of the following people it may well be languishing still on my computer.

I bless the day I decided to pick up the phone and chat to Cornerstones Literary Consultancy about the possibility of having a report done on a previous book I had written. That conversation led me to a long working relationship with Cornerstones' Managing Editor, the brilliant Kathryn Price. Without her, Minty wouldn't be the book it is today. Thank you, Kathyrn.

Thanks, too, to Jennie Rawlings for stepping into my subconscious and designing the perfect book cover for Minty's story and to Vanessa of Cornerstones who gave me such helpful feedback on the first draft of the story.

A shout out, too, to all my friends and family for their support, especially Carole Bozkurt and fellow SCBWI members, Maureen Lynas and Claira Jo, who made such insightful comments on an early draft of the book.

I am also indebted to my rescue dogs, Bonnie and Clyde. Although these two rascals are now in that great kennel in the sky they are born again in Romulus and Remus, as is our ginger tom, Mr Bo (short for Mr Bojangles) who was the inspiration for Octavius. Thanks guys for all the years of fun and companionship. A thank you, too, to Pebbles and Jess my current rescue dogs and muses. The desk wouldn't be the same without you pair under my feet!

If it hadn't been for my lovely dad, Roy Heywood, I might have given up on my childhood dream to become a writer. His love and encouragement knew no bounds. He was also very astute. When he gave me a laptop for my birthday at a point at which I had began to lose faith in my writing abilities, he knew what he was doing. I wrote much of Minty on that computer. Thanks Dad.

And now to that awesome double act, Helen Corner and Yasmin Standen. There are not enough words to express my gratitude to these fantastic women. It was Helen who, whilst Kathryn was on maternity leave, had the task of reading the latest draft of the book. It was Helen whose quick response beginning with the word 'Wow!' sent my hopes of publication soaring through the roof. Without Helen I wouldn't have met the wonderful Yasmin Standen, agent extraordinaire. Thank you both for your faith in me, and your love for Minty. My book could never have had two more energetic and enthusiastic champions. Three Hares rock!

Lastly, but certainly not least, a thousand thanks to my amazing husband, Edward Banach, who read, commented on and discussed every draft of Minty, and who, when I told him that I wanted to resign from my day job to become a full-time writer, uttered those magic words 'Go for it!' That was eight years ago! It took a while to get published, Edward, but we got there in the end.